WANTED: PARENTS FOR A BABY!

BY

LAURA IDING

HIS PERFECT BRIDE?

BY

LOUISA HEATON

Laura Iding loved reading as a child, and when she ran out of books she readily made up her own, completing a little detective mini-series when she was twelve. But when her parents insisted she get a 'real' career she turned to nursing—another truly rewarding job. After thirty years of experience in trauma/critical care, she's thrilled to combine her career and her hobby into one—writing Medical Romances™ for Mills & Boon®. Laura lives in the northern part of the United States with her husband of nearly thirty years and spends her time reading, writing and biking.

Louisa Heaton first started writing romance at school and would take her stories in to show her friends, scrawled in a big red binder, with plenty of crossing out. She dreamt of romance herself, and after knowing her husband-to-be for only three weeks shocked her parents by accepting his marriage proposal. After four children—including a set of twins—and fifteen years of trying to get published, she finally received 'The Call'! Now she lives on Hayling Island, and when she's not busy as a First Responder she creates her stories wandering along the wonderful Hampshire coastline with her two dogs, muttering to herself and scaring the locals.

Visit Louisa on Twitter @louisaheaton, on Facebook www.facebook.com/Louisaheatonauthor or on her website: www.louisaheaton.com

WANTED: PARENTS
FOR A BABY!

BY
LAURA IDING

Published in Great Britain 2015
by Mills & Boon, an imprint of Harlequin (UK) Limited,
Eton House, 18-24 Paradise Road, Richmond, Surrey, TW9 1SR

© 2015 Laura Iding

ISBN: 978-0-263-24703-9

Dear Reader,

As many of you know, I am a nurse by background and still work full-time at our local hospital.

Recently I was involved in a 'Safe Haven' baby situation: a young woman who gave birth at our hospital decided she couldn't be a good mother and wanted to give her baby up for adoption. So far the State of Wisconsin has had eighty-four Safe Haven babies since the law was passed in 1994.

The situation I was involved in was very different from the one I describe in this story, *Wanted: Parents for a Baby!*, but the idea of writing my own Medical Romance about a Safe Haven baby kept popping into my head, nagging at me, until I simply had to sit down and put my ideas on paper. In some ways I think this book wrote itself!

I hope you enjoy Ryan and Cassie's story as much as I do, and please drop by to visit my website at www.lauraiding.com if you have a moment. I always enjoy hearing from my readers.

Happy reading!

Laura Iding

This book is dedicated to Michelle Lahey Reed, an
amazing woman who opened her heart and her home to
foster twin babies in need. You are truly an inspiration!

CHAPTER ONE

"CASSIE?" ALICE, THE neonatal intensive care unit clerk, called across the unit. "The ER is asking you to come down with the emergency warmer."

"Really?" Neonatal nurse Cassandra Jordan glanced up from her computer in surprise. This was an interesting way to start her shift, and it was only Thursday. The unusual stuff mostly happened on the weekends. "Is there a pregnant woman waiting?"

"Not sure, but they asked you to hurry."

Cassie nodded and quickly abandoned her charting, heading over to where they kept the portable warmer stocked with emergency equipment. "What about a physician?" she asked as she wheeled the warmer toward the door.

"Already paged him. Dr. Ryan should be there soon."

Cassie's stomach clenched with a mixture of dread and anticipation even as she tipped her head to indicate she understood. After wheeling the infant warmer into the hallway, she pushed the button for the elevator, relieved when the doors immediately opened.

Dr. Ryan Murphy was one of the best neonatal intensivists she'd ever worked with. Unfortunately, he was far too tall, dark and handsome for her peace of mind. Not to mention single. Widowed, to be exact. According to the gossip mill, he wasn't interested in dating, much to the dismay of the single nurses working throughout the hospital.

To be fair, she wasn't particularly interested in dating either—one deep betrayal and subsequent failed marriage had been enough to put her off men for a long time. But somehow in the six months that she'd been in Cedar Bluff, her body hadn't seemed to get the message. Every time Dr. Ryan's penetrating blue eyes met hers, her stomach did a series of backward flips and she blushed like a fool. She mentally cursed her fair skin for constantly betraying her.

The elevator doors dinged and opened on the ground level, so she wheeled the warmer out and quickly jogged down the hall to Cedar Bluff's ER. There was a crowd of people gathered around the triage desk and, of course, Dr. Ryan's dark head, clearly visible above the crowd, drew her gaze like a magnet. Even wearing blue scrubs and long white lab coat, he was distinctly noticeable.

He glanced over and caught sight of her, acknowledging her presence with a brief nod. He made a gesture with his hand. "Please, step back and make room for the equipment."

Like the parting of the Red Sea, the group of people split down the middle to give Cassie the access she needed. She focused on the infant car seat that was propped on the desktop and frowned as she registered the fact that the baby was letting out a terrible high-pitched cry. "What happened? Where's the mother?"

"She left," Dr. Ryan said shortly. "This little girl is only a day or two old and desperately needs medical care. We need to get her in the warmer so I can examine her."

"Her name is Emma," Gloria, the ER nurse at the

triage desk, supplied helpfully. "The mother said she was unfit and asked me to take care of Emma."

Pretty name, Cassie thought as she quickly plugged in the warmer and turned on the heat lamps. She cracked open the oxygen tank and connected the tubing while Dr. Ryan lifted the tiny infant from the car seat. He set her gently in the center of the warmer, and the baby's arms and legs flailed about in protest.

Emma's high-pitched cry wasn't easy to ignore, but Cassie focused on setting up the open end of the oxygen tubing so it would gently stream past her tiny nose and mouth. Dr. Ryan undressed the baby, who was wearing clean yet well-worn clothing, his fingers looking ridiculously large in contrast to the tiny baby. Using his stethoscope, he listened to Emma's heart and lungs. Cassie placed small EKG patches on the baby's bare chest and their fingers brushed as they both worked over the small torso.

Cassie ignored the tingling sensation that rippled up her arms at his touch and peered at the cardiac monitor, making note of the baby's heart rate, which was higher than normal.

"Her lungs are clear," Dr. Ryan said in a low tone. "But she has hyperactive bowel sounds."

Cassie gave a nod. "Yes, she's also tachy, in the one-eighties. Dehydrated, perhaps?"

"Maybe," he agreed. "But could indicate something more serious. We don't have any history on the mother, unless we're lucky enough that the baby was born here. Let's get her upstairs to the NNICU. She'll need an IV and labs drawn."

"Okay. I'll check the records when we get upstairs, but I don't think she was born here. I've been on the past three days and would have remembered." Cassie disconnected the electrical cord and switched the warmer to battery power. "Ready? Let's go."

Dr. Ryan walked along on the opposite side of the warmer. Cassie steered the warmer while he kept a keen eye on Emma's heart rate.

The elevator seemed to take longer this time, or maybe she was just acutely aware of Dr. Ryan standing next to her while listening to Emma's high-pitched crying. Her maternal instincts wanted her to pick the baby up and cradle her to her chest, but that wasn't possible just yet. When the elevator doors finally opened, she pushed the warmer inside with a sense of relief.

The doors closed and the elevator began rising to the third floor when Emma's high-pitched cries abruptly trailed off and stopped. Cassie stared in shock as the heart monitor began triple-beeping in alarm as the baby's heart rate shot up to two hundred beats per minute.

"She's not breathing," Cassie said, grabbing the emergency airway kit.

"Hand me the Ambu bag, I'll try to support her that way," he said.

She nodded, handing over the tiny Ambu bag and then connecting it to the oxygen tank. Her gaze darted between the heart monitor and Emma as he pressed the bag over Emma's nose and mouth, giving several breaths.

"It's working," she whispered. "Her heart rate is dropping back to the one-eighties."

"Good." Dr. Ryan's intense gaze met hers and for a moment she saw a flash of relief and camaraderie reflected there.

She tore her gaze away to glance down at the baby. "Poor thing doesn't have anyone to care about her," she murmured.

"She has us," Dr. Ryan said firmly. "We care about her. And we're going to do everything possible to help her."

She caught her breath at the emotion shimmering in Dr. Ryan's eyes but the moment vanished as the elevator door opened on the third floor. She pushed the warmer down the hall slowly enough to allow Dr. Ryan the ability to walk alongside while providing breathing support for the baby.

When they entered the NNICU, Cassie headed toward the critical-care end of the twenty-bed nursery, knowing that it was possible Emma would eventually require ventilator support for her breathing.

"Cassandra, I hear you're the best, so will you please start an IV?" Dr. Ryan asked as soon as they were situated.

"Of course." Getting IVs placed in babies wasn't easy, but it happened to be one of her best skills. The other nurses often asked her to start their IVs for them, so it shouldn't have surprised her that Dr. Ryan was aware of her talent. She could feel her cheeks getting warm and tried to keep her head down as she gathered supplies.

She managed to find a vein in Emma's left arm and quickly placed the catheter. Unfortunately, peripheral IVs generally didn't last long in babies, twenty-four hours at the most, so the poor thing would likely need a new catheter placed tomorrow.

"What rate do you want the fluids to run at?" she asked, as she protected the catheter site with a plastic medicine cup cut in half and taped over the baby's arm so Emma couldn't dislodge it by accident.

"You have the IV placed already?" Dr. Ryan asked

in surprise. "Good job. Let's start with five ccs per hour for now."

Cassie nodded and turned away to adjust the IV pump in an effort to hide her flaming cheeks. Ridiculous to respond like a high school cheerleader working with the star quarterback of the football team. It wasn't as if Dr. Ryan had given her a personal compliment.

In fact, the nurses all talked about how nice it was to work with him, despite the fact that he kept an invisible but impermeable wall between himself and the rest of the staff. She'd heard a few of the nurses had tried to ask him out, only to be gently but firmly rebuffed.

Her hormones needed to get a grip on reality.

"Let's see if she'll breathe on her own now," Dr. Ryan murmured, as he removed the Ambu bag and face mask from Emma.

Cassie leaned forward, watching the baby closely for a few minutes. She was just about to turn away when things changed abruptly, just like they had in the elevator. Emma's breathing became shallow and her pulse skyrocketed.

"Give her a tenth of a milligram of midazolam," Dr. Ryan ordered in a grim tone. "I need to intubate."

"I'll get the meds," her coworker, Diane, piped up.

Cassie pulled out the intubation equipment while Dr. Ryan continued to breathe for Emma using the Ambu bag. When Diane returned a few minutes later, she held up the syringe for Cassie to verify the dose of the medication before injecting it into Emma's IV.

"Midazolam is in," Diane announced.

Cassie handed Dr. Ryan the tiny endotracheal tube. She found herself holding her breath, his words from the elevator echoing in her mind.

She has us. We care about her.

Soon Dr. Ryan had deftly placed the breathing tube down Emma's airway, a task that sounded simple but wasn't at all, not when working on a newborn baby. His large and capable fingers were never clumsy.

The entire procedure didn't take more than a few minutes and Cassie quickly secured the tube in place while Dr. Ryan held it steady. Nancy Kramer, the respiratory therapist, was manning the ventilator. "What settings do you want?" she asked.

He rattled off the parameters he wanted then turned toward Cassie. "I need you to get a set of arterial blood gases and a full drug screen."

"A drug screen?" Cassie glanced at what she could see of Emma's tiny face, half-covered with the endotracheal tube holder. "You think her mother was a drug addict?"

"Yes, I hate to say it, but I have a strong suspicion. The mother dropped the baby off in the ER, saying she wasn't a fit mother for Emma, and then left. Under the safe-haven law, we can't go after the mother to obtain a medical history, so we have to figure out what's going on ourselves. That high-pitched crying and the way she stopped breathing is a classic sign of narcotic withdrawal. We'll also need to keep an eye out for seizures. Run the lab work and call me with the results."

Cassie nodded, feeling sick to her stomach. She had to admit Emma's high-pitched cry did sound similar to those of the two other babies she'd cared for early in her career who'd been going through withdrawal. And the timing was right, too. No doubt the baby's mother hadn't been able to stand the baby's constant crying, which had likely gotten worse over the hours since the baby's birth.

She'd asked Alice to go through the records to see if

Emma had been born at their hospital, but soon discovered she was right, there was no record that matched this baby. So where had Emma's mother given birth? At home? Was she a resident of Cedar Bluff?

Even though Cassie had only worked at Cedar Bluff Hospital for the past six months she knew a safe-haven baby was a rare occurrence. Obviously they did get them, but not often.

She was glad Emma's mother had been unselfish enough to give up her baby, rather than neglect her or, worse, hurt the child.

Still, it wasn't easy to see how some mothers would easily give their babies away, when others, like herself, had been unable to carry one to term.

A loss that still left an empty feeling inside her.

Ryan strode out of the NNICU, a dull roaring echoing in his ears.

He knew the baby's blood tests would turn out positive for opiates. Thankfully he hadn't cared for drug-addicted babies often, but the few times he had were seared into his memory.

But worst of all, Emma was a painful reminder of the fact that if his son had lived, he would have made that same, high-pitched cry. Would have been born addicted to narcotics and would have suffered the same symptoms of opiate withdrawal.

At least Emma had been given a chance to survive. And, hopefully, thrive.

A chance his son hadn't been given.

He pinched the bridge of his nose with his fingers, trying to freeze out the horrible memories and the deep stabbing guilt. Three years had passed, yet the image of Victoria's pale, cold, lifeless face still haunted him.

He should have known. Somehow he should have known his wife had been addicted to painkillers. How had he missed the signs? Had he really been that blind to what had been going on?

Why hadn't he figured out the truth before it was too late? Before he'd found his wife and unborn son dead in the front seat of her car?

His fault. His son's premature death was his fault.

The elevator doors opened, and he pulled himself together, trying to remember where he was going. Oh, yeah, back to the ER. He doubted anyone would remember more than what he'd already been told but he felt compelled to ask.

The triage nurse—what was her name, Gloria?—was still sitting where he'd left her. "What do you remember about the mother?" he asked bluntly.

Gloria didn't seem too surprised by his question. "She had stringy blond hair and was young, not a teenager, maybe early to midtwenties? Her skin was super pale, as if she never stepped outside into the sun. And she wore long sleeves. Her arms shaking as if the car seat was too heavy for her."

Definitely drugs, he thought with a sigh. "Did she look at all familiar?"

"Not to me or anyone else who caught a glimpse of her. But I bet once the word gets out someone will come forward. Everyone knows everyone else's business in this town."

He nodded, knowing she spoke the truth. "Have the police been notified?"

Gloria thought for a minute. "I don't think so, to be honest. All I could think of was to get the NNICU team down here as quickly as possible. The way the baby was crying scared me."

He couldn't fault Gloria's logic. "All right, I'll give them a call." Emma's mother couldn't get into trouble for dropping off her baby at the hospital, but he figured the police should know about the possible drug connection.

And they'd have to get social services involved to find placement for the baby, too.

He walked to his office, seeking privacy to make his calls. First he notified the social worker on duty, who readily agreed to begin working on a temporary guardian and foster placement for Emma once she was stable enough for discharge. When he finished with that he debated between calling the police now or waiting until he had the actual test results.

A glance at his watch confirmed it was too late to get the drug-test results today as it was already five-thirty in the evening and drug tests were specialized enough that they couldn't be run on a stat basis. They'd be available in the morning, but he didn't want to wait that long to call the police. The sooner they knew about the issue, the better.

He dialed the sheriff's department, knowing the number by heart, and requested to be put through to a detective.

"This is Detective Trammel. What seems to be the problem?"

Of course Trammel would be the one on duty. Trammel had been the detective assigned to investigate Victoria's death. Ryan tightened his grip on the phone and tried to keep his voice steady. "This is Dr. Murphy at Cedar Bluff Hospital. I need to report we have a safe-haven baby here," Ryan informed him. "She was dropped off a little over an hour ago by a young woman with blond hair, roughly in her midtwenties."

"Dr. Murphy?" Detective Trammel echoed. "Dr. Ryan Murphy?"

"Yes." He knew that he wasn't a suspect any longer, but that first month after Victoria's death he'd been at the top of Trammel's list. Logically he understood that the police had wanted to rule out foul play, but it hadn't been easy to hold his head up within their small, tight-knit community.

Even three years later, it wasn't easy. But he hadn't wanted to leave, not until he'd uncovered the truth about the source of Victoria's drugs. He'd almost given up hope. Until now.

"How are you doing?" Detective Trammel asked, as if they were old friends. But they weren't. Not by a long shot.

"Fine," he said in a clipped tone. "You should know that I've already contacted the social worker, who's getting Child Protective Services involved."

"Okay, thanks. Wow, a safe-haven baby. We haven't had one of those in almost four years."

Ryan battled a wave of annoyance. This wasn't exactly a social call. "You need to know that I suspect the baby is addicted to drugs," he said bluntly. "We're running tests now."

A heavy silence hung between them and he imagined Detective Trammel finally figuring out why Ryan had bothered to make the call personally. "Okay, thanks for letting me know," the detective said finally. "But it's tricky to go after the mother in these situations. The safe-haven law offers protection, although there is wiggle room in cases of abuse."

"I'm well aware of the law," he said in a terse tone. "And I don't want to go after the mother per se. But what if we find that the baby was addicted to prescription narcotics? Don't you think that's something to be concerned about? Shouldn't we look for her supplier?"

"Your drug tests can't give that level of detail," Trammel protested.

He reined in his temper with an effort. "No, but the state lab in Madison could."

Another long silence. "Dr. Murphy, I told you before that we investigated the prescription-drug angle after your wife's death. There's no evidence of a prescription drug ring operating here in Cedar Bluff. Trust me, I'd know if there were."

Ryan felt his shoulders sag in defeat. He didn't believe the detective, yet there was nothing he could say that would change his mind, either. Because he didn't have proof.

Just a gut-level certainty he was right.

"Listen, Dr. Murphy, it's been almost three years and I know it's difficult, but you need to move on with your life."

For an instant the image of Cassie's heart-shaped face, long chocolate-brown hair and warm brown eyes flashed in his mind. But he impatiently shoved it away.

"Let me know if the mother comes forward for some reason," he said to Detective Trammel, changing the subject. "Having some sort of medical history would be helpful."

"I will."

Ryan hung up the phone and sat back in his chair with a weary sigh. The detective was wrong—he *had* moved on with his life. He worked, and played softball in the summer and basketball in the winter with several other physicians on staff. So what if he avoided going out with women? He'd tried about a year or so ago, but the entire event had been a disaster. He'd wanted no-strings sex, but apparently that wasn't what Shana had wanted, despite the fact she'd assured him she did.

Even worse, the debacle had spread throughout Cedar Bluff Hospital. Staff whispering behind his back had only reminded him of that terrible time after Victoria's death.

No, getting tangled up with a woman wasn't part of his plan. No matter how tempted he might be, at least when it came to Cassie. And she was doubly off limits, since they worked together.

No, he had to remain focused on the issues at hand. He wished Detective Trammel had found some evidence of a prescription-drug ring in Cedar Bluff.

Because he wouldn't mind sharing a bit of the guilt that still weighed heavily on his shoulders over the deaths of his wife and unborn son.

CHAPTER TWO

CASSIE HOVERED OVER Emma's warmer, lightly stroking the tip of her finger down the baby's downy soft cheek, as much as she could around the breathing-tube holder.

Emma F. Safe Haven, the name they'd given her, was doing a great job of hanging in there. No sign of seizures yet, but Cassie was afraid that if she took her eye off the baby for an instant she'd miss the telltale jerky movements.

The good news so far was that Emma's blood gases had come back well within normal range. She'd placed a page in to Dr. Ryan to share the results. Maybe they could work on weaning the baby off the ventilator. They'd have to go slowly, because removing the tube, only to replace it a few hours later, would be traumatic and possibly cause damage to Emma's tiny airway. However, getting the baby off the vent was also better for Emma's lungs in the long run.

Finding the right balance was always tricky.

Cassie lingered a few minutes longer, wishing she could give Emma more of her attention, but then had to leave to care for the other baby assigned to her care. Thankfully Barton was stable. He'd been born four weeks too early, but was gaining weight and coming along nicely. He still had a couple instances of five

seconds or longer of apnea, a common problem in preemies, but so far he'd gone twelve hours without any
shallow breathing recorded on the monitor. If that trend
continued, in another day or two he'd be ready to move
up to the level-two nursery. And soon be discharged
home.

She quickly changed Barton's soiled diaper and
then disconnected him from the heart monitor for his
feeding. She sank into a rocker she'd pulled over near
Emma's warmer so she could keep an eye on Emma
while giving Barton his bottle. Normally they encouraged the parents to come in for the feedings, but Barton's mother had mentioned she might be later than
normal today because she had to wait for her husband
to get home from being out of town. She'd had an emergency C-section and hadn't been cleared to drive yet.

"Aren't you a good boy," she cooed, as Barton eagerly sucked at his bottle. "You're going to grow up to
be big and strong, just like your daddy."

She sensed someone's gaze on her and looked up to
find Dr. Ryan standing a few feet away, staring at her.
For a second she thought she saw a distinctive longing
reflected in his eyes, but in a flash the moment was
gone and the polite yet distant expression had returned
to his eyes.

"Emma's blood gases look great, and I've entered
new orders to drop her ventilator settings," he said
brusquely. "Should I ask the unit clerk to page the respiratory therapist?"

"I'd appreciate that, if you don't mind. I'll be here
for a while yet." More proof that Dr. Ryan was a great
doctor. He didn't think menial tasks were beneath him.
Or maybe he was simply anxious to get Emma's vent

settings changed. "So far I haven't seen any evidence of seizures."

"Good. You'll probably get a call from Child Protective Services, I put them on notice about Emma."

"Oh, okay." Cassie suppressed a flash of disappointment. Of course calling CPS was the right thing to do. "I guess, once she's stable, Emma will end up in foster care, then," she murmured, trying to hide the wistfulness in her tone. She had no right to be so emotionally attached to Emma. The baby wasn't hers to love and to care for. Except here, at work.

Dr. Ryan's lips tightened in a grim line. "I imagine so."

She couldn't say anything past the lump of regret lodged in her throat. Ridiculous to think she could become a foster parent for Emma. For one thing, there was a long process, including classes to take, along with other hoops to jump through, before she'd be granted that privilege. Even then, she knew that a married couple would have a better shot of getting custody of Emma than a single parent such as her.

Barton turned his face away from the bottle, reminding her it was time for a burp. She lifted him up, turned him and placed him against her shoulder, rubbing her hand in soothing circles over his back. She couldn't resist brushing a kiss against his downy temple, enjoying the scent of baby shampoo that clung to his skin. He squirmed a bit and made gurgling noises before letting out a loud belch.

"Good boy," she praised him with a wide smile. Gently she turned the baby round so she could try to give him the rest of his bottle. He was still pretty tiny, less than five pounds, so he usually only took a small portion of his bottle at each feeding.

"You're a natural," Dr. Ryan said in a low tone.

The longing to have a baby of her own stabbed deeply, but she pushed it away with an effort. Her cheeks warmed and she cursed herself for responding to every little thing Dr. Ryan said. He had no way of knowing that she'd miscarried twice before her marriage had shattered into irreparable pieces. "Thanks."

Abruptly he turned and walked toward the unit clerk's desk. She overheard him requesting the respiratory therapist on duty to be paged for vent setting changes.

Little Barton took another ounce before thrusting the nipple out of his mouth, indicating he wasn't interested in any more. She mentally calculated the total, pleased that he'd taken a half-ounce more at this feeding.

As she returned Barton to his bassinet and cranked on the mobile that hung over his head, she noticed Dr. Ryan was standing over Emma's warmer. She assumed that he was checking the baby's vital signs but as she approached she noticed that her little pink knit hat was off and he was softly stroking his thumb over Emma's downy head, murmuring softly.

"You're going to be fine, pretty girl. You'll see."

His words made tears prick her eyes and she subtly wiped them away. Dr. Ryan had called her a natural, but right now she was thinking the same about him. He was gazing down at Emma as if the baby was important on a personal level, rather than just another patient.

She hesitated, wondering if she was intruding, but he must have sensed her presence. He glanced at her and gently tugged the pink knit cap over Emma's head. "Do you need to get in here?" he asked.

"Yes, I need to check her vitals again," she said, trying to deal with her bizarre reaction to him. "But I can wait until you're finished."

"No, go ahead," he said, stepping back to give her plenty of room.

She avoided his gaze and tucked the buds of her stethoscope into her ears, taking her time to listen to Emma's heart, lungs and abdomen. When she straightened and pulled off the stethoscope, she caught Dr. Ryan's intense gaze resting on her once again.

She grappled for something intelligent to say. "Everything sounds good, but her bowel sounds are still hyperactive."

"I know. I'm reluctant to begin feeding her until we know for sure she won't start having seizures," he said, answering her unspoken question. "But if things continue to go well, I'll insert a feeding tube for bolus feedings."

"Sounds like a plan," she agreed. Since he was still logged on to the computer, she gestured toward it. "Do you need the computer?"

"Not at all." He leaned over to log off with quick keystrokes and she caught a whiff of his woodsy aftershave, the heady scent wreaking havoc with her senses. He stepped back, giving her room to sit, but he was still far too close for comfort.

Cassie tried to concentrate on documenting Emma's assessment, but it wasn't easy. She made several spelling mistakes, requiring her to backspace several times to fix them.

Why wouldn't he leave? Was he reading her charting, double-checking her work? Surely he had better things to do. Better places to be other than here.

Validating vital signs was easier, merely requiring a

point and click, and she was nearly finished when she heard him say her name in that deep, husky voice of his.

"Cassandra."

She couldn't seem to untie her tongue enough to tell him he could call her Cassie. After all, he insisted everyone call him by his first name, even though most continued to use his formal title, too. She glanced up, only to find his gaze glued to Emma.

Immediately, she rose to her feet. "What's wrong?"

"Get me point two milligrams of midazolam and a half milligram of phenobarbital. Emma is having a seizure."

Cassie's heart plunged to the pit of her stomach as she rushed over to the medication dispensing machine to get the medication.

She dashed back to Emma's warmer, holding each of the syringes up for him to see. "Point two milligrams of midazolam," she said. "And a half milligram of phenobarb."

"Yes, that's correct."

She gently injected the medications into Emma's IV then watched the baby's heart rate on the monitor.

She couldn't prevent an overwhelming sense of dread. Seizures were a bad sign. If they continued, there was a chance that Emma might suffer permanent brain damage.

The little girl could even die.

She has us. We care about her.

Cassie strengthened her resolve to do everything possible to make sure Emma had the best chance to survive.

Ryan shoved his hands in the pockets of his lab coat, hating every moment of feeling helpless.

This poor baby might not make it to her first birthday, all because her mother hadn't sought help for her addiction.

Anger was useless, so he did his best to breathe it away, keeping an eye on his patient instead. The medication worked and, thankfully, Emma's jerky movements stopped.

"I'm going to order the phenobarb to be given every six hours," he told Cassie. "And an EEG, too."

Cassie looked as upset as he felt, obviously already growing attached to their safe-haven baby. The same way he was. That moment in the elevator, when Cassie had mentioned the baby didn't have anyone to care about her, had tugged at his heart.

In the three years since losing Victoria and his son, he'd been able to keep a certain emotional distance from his tiny patients. Easy enough to do, as most of the time the babies got better and went home with their parents and families.

But knowing Emma was alone in the world made him feel differently towards her. He knew he was becoming emotionally involved with their safe-haven baby. And not just because she was sick enough to require his focused attention.

Because almost from the first moment he'd seen her, the little girl had found a way to break through the barriers surrounding what Shana had described as his stone-cold heart.

"Oh, Emma," Cassie murmured, stroking the baby's cheek. "You've got to fight this, sweetpea. We're going to help you fight this."

His heart squeezed at the tears shimmering in Cassie's eyes. From the first day she'd started working here—had it just been a few months ago?—he'd noticed her creamy skin, heart-shaped face, bright brown eyes and long dark hair that she always drew back in a ponytail at work, not to mention her curvy figure, mostly hidden beneath her baggy scrubs. What man wouldn't?

Look, but don't touch. That was his motto. Especially since the Shana debacle.

Yet for some reason, seeing Cassie cooing over the babies, especially Emma, hit him right in the center of his solar plexus.

He was irresistibly drawn to her. Had been from the moment they'd begun to work together. Resisting her was becoming more and more difficult. Maybe because she was the complete opposite in every way from Victoria. He'd never told anyone his deepest fear, that Victoria wouldn't have made a very good mother. Not the way Cassie would. She clearly loved her tiny patients.

Victoria had loved being a doctor's wife. Had loved entertaining guests and spending his money. He wasn't sure how she'd managed to keep herself busy every day, working out at the gym and then lunching with her friends.

When she'd blown out her Achilles tendon after a spin class, he'd supported her through surgery, impressed at how determined she'd been to get back to her normal routine. Even after she discovered she was pregnant, she didn't cut back on her exercise regimen. In fact, he suspected she'd doubled it in an effort to avoid gaining too much weight.

He'd gone back through his memories of that time often, trying to identify the signs he'd missed. But he'd been busy at work, taking everything Victoria had told him at face value.

Never suspecting, until far too late, that she'd become

addicted to the painkillers the orthopedic surgeon had initially prescribed.

He shook off the past and forced himself to focus on the present. Just because he was deeply attracted to Cassie, it didn't mean he had any intention of acting on it. She was young, full of life and could do better than a broken man like him. He didn't plan to ever have a family of his own. He didn't deserve a second chance.

Forcing himself to turn away, he went over to a different computer, far away from the one Cassie had been using, to enter the medication orders. When he'd finished, he sat down to scroll through his other patients' charts.

It took him a few minutes to realize he was stalling. Ridiculous to think about waiting around here until the end of Cassie's shift. Just because he was on call, it didn't mean he shouldn't take advantage of the downtime to get some rest.

But before he could leave, his pager went off, announcing a pending crash C-section.

Rest would have to wait. "We need an emergency warmer down in the OR," he said.

"I'm ready," Diane said, hurrying toward him with the equipment. He knew that Cassie was already tied up with Emma and Barton, so he wasn't surprised that Diana was the nurse up for the next admission.

He strode purposefully toward the door, managing to resist the urge to glance back once more at Cassie.

She and Emma would be fine.

A few minutes later he entered the OR, where a laboring mother was lying on the table, her eyes full of fear. "Save my baby," she pleaded as the anesthesiologist tried to cover her mouth and nose with an oxygen mask. "Save my baby!"

"She has a prolapsed umbilical cord," Dr. Eden Graves informed him. "We need to move fast."

"Understood," he agreed. "I'm ready as soon as you are."

Leaving Diane to prepare their equipment, he walked over to look at the fetal monitoring strip. There were several steep decelerations present, indicating severe fetal bradycardia. He noted that the sharp drop in the fetal pulse coincided with highest portion of the uterine contractions. Classic sign of a prolapsed umbilical cord.

"Tip her uterus so that the pressure isn't on her cervix," he instructed.

"I did, but you're right, we could use more blankets to prop beneath her bottom."

A couple of nurses came over to assist and soon the patient was ready. The anesthesiologist gave Eden the high sign and she quickly began the procedure.

The baby was removed from the uterus within five minutes, and the minute the cord was cut he quickly took the infant over to the warmer. The baby boy wasn't too limp and quickly pinked up as they worked on him.

When the baby let out a wail, there was a collective sigh of relief from everyone in the room.

"Let me know what the cord blood gases show," he said to the circulating nurse in the room. "Page me with the results."

"Okay."

He finished his assessment with Diane's help and then deemed the infant stable enough for transport up to the neonatal nursery. Even though the baby boy looked fine for the moment, he intended to watch the infant for a few hours upstairs.

It was a good feeling to save a baby's life. Even

though deep down he knew that no matter how many he saved, he'd always mourn the one that mattered most.

The son he'd lost.

Cassie was thankful Emma didn't show any more signs of seizures and the EEG tech seemed to think the test looked relatively normal. Of course, they needed the neurologist to read the test to know for sure, but she decided to remain optimistic.

Barton's parents were here, holding their son, so she decided this was a good time to take a quick break.

"Sally, would you mind keeping an eye on Emma for a few minutes? I'd like to run down to the cafeteria to grab something to eat."

"Sure, that's fine. But we're expecting that new baby to arrive within the next thirty minutes so make it quick, okay?"

"I will." She'd perfected the art of eating fast, to minimize disrupting patient care.

Leaving the unit, she took the stairs down to the cafeteria level. The grill line was too long, so she went over to the salad bar to make herself a quick grilled-chicken salad and fill a large cup with ice water. The hardest thing about working second shift was the inability to fall asleep once she got home, and the last thing she needed was the added impact of caffeine zipping through her system.

She sat down at a small table near the back of the cafeteria and quickly dug into her salad. A few nurses greeted her, but none of them lingered. Obviously the whole hospital was busy, not just her neonatal unit.

She kept an eye on her watch as she ate, knowing she needed to return to the unit before Dr. Ryan brought over his latest patient.

With any luck he'd be busy with the new admission for a while, giving her some badly needed breathing space. She really didn't understand what her problem was around him. There were plenty of other single guys around. James Green, one of the ER doctors, had asked her out just last month.

Too bad she hadn't felt one iota of interest in him. She'd politely declined James's offer, refusing to feel bad at the dejected expression in his eyes.

Her divorce had only been final for a little over a year. Six months ago she'd moved to Cedar Bluff to start afresh. It was too soon to enter the dating scene.

So why was she always so keenly aware of Dr. Ryan Murphy?

No clue. She shook her head, scraping the bottom of her salad bowl to get the last bit, before wiping her mouth with a napkin and rising to her feet.

Ten minutes. *Not bad*, she mused as she headed back toward the elevators. Walking up three flights of stairs seemed daunting after she'd practically inhaled her meal, so she took an elevator up.

She got off the elevator on the third floor and headed down the east hallway toward the neonatal unit.

Cassie frowned when she saw an older woman, probably in her midsixties, leaning heavily on a cane near the doorway. It looked as if the woman was trying to peer through the small window to see inside the unit.

"Good evening. Can I help you with something?" Cassie asked.

The woman started badly, spinning around so quickly she almost lost her balance. Cassie darted forward to slide a supportive arm around the woman's waist.

"Easy there, I don't want you to fall," Cassie said.

"Is there something you need? Are you waiting to go in to visit?"

"Oh, no. I'm not waiting to visit. I…um…" The woman seemed flustered and avoided her gaze. "I was visiting a friend and thought I'd come over to peek at the babies. I'm sorry, I didn't mean to break any rules."

Since the woman obviously felt bad, Cassie decided she wouldn't push it. "That's okay, but you can't go in there unless you're related to one of the babies. It's a locked unit to protect them from being taken."

"Oh, of course. I—I'm sorry. I have to go." The woman took a step and leaned on her cane, making her way back toward the elevators. Cassie waited a moment, watching her.

It wasn't until she was back at Emma's bedside that she realized the woman might have being trying to catch a glimpse of Emma. Surely the news of their safe-haven baby had already spread throughout the small town of Cedar Bluff.

She wished she'd asked the woman for her name. Had she been peeking into the unit out of pure curiosity?

Or because she knew Emma's mother?

CHAPTER THREE

RYAN KEPT A close eye on the newborn baby boy for the next hour, relieved when the umbilical-cord blood-gas results weren't as bad as he'd feared.

The infant seemed to be doing well, so he drifted over to where Cassie was working with Emma.

"How's Emma doing?" he asked.

"Good," she said with a tired smile. "I haven't seen any seizure activity since we started her on the medication."

"Glad to hear it." He forced himself to tear his gaze away from her to focus on the baby, although he was very much aware of Cassie's warm vanilla scent. "Isn't your shift ending soon?"

"In another hour," she agreed. "I was supposed to be off tomorrow, but one of the nurses called in sick, so I agreed to come back for the day shift. Gives me a good excuse to check up on Emma."

He wasn't surprised she'd agreed to come back in less than eight hours. Over the past few months he'd discovered Cassie was always jumping in to help cover shifts as needed.

Despite his attempts to keep his distance, he found himself curious about why she devoted so much time and energy to her work. He sensed she was using work as a distraction from not having a personal life, the same way he was.

He told himself the similarities between them didn't matter, since he wasn't interested in having a relationship.

"They should let you leave early," he said with a frown. "You deserve to get some rest."

"I'll be fine," she said with a wave of her hand. "I've doubled back before and it's not too bad."

He was hardly in a position to argue, since his job required him to be on call often. Too often, according to Victoria, who'd accused him of staying late at work on purpose. Had he? Looking back now, he had to admit there may have been a kernel of truth to Victoria's accusations.

He thrust the useless guilt aside. "I'm going to get some rest in the call room, but page me if you need anything."

"We will. But don't worry, I promise we won't bother you unless it's important."

For a moment he was taken aback by her statement. Was she actually trying to protect him? The concept was so foreign he could barely wrap his mind around it. "Call me anytime," he corrected, before turning away.

The attending physicians' call room was located just outside the neonatal intensive care unit, close enough for emergency situations but with enough soundproofing to be able to get some sleep.

Ryan kept his scrubs on as he stretched out on the narrow bed, so that he could rush out in a hurry for an emergency. He closed his eyes and took several deep breaths in an effort to relax.

Unfortunately, Cassie's face, etched with the deeply caring expression he'd seen while feeding Barton, bloomed in his mind. He cursed under his breath, knowing that if he didn't find a way to pry her out of his mind, he'd never get any sleep.

Too bad Cassie wasn't the type to go for a nice sweaty bout of no-strings sex. Because unfortunately, since he'd destroyed his chance to have a family, that's all he had left to offer.

Cassie groaned when her alarm went off at the ungodly hour of six o'clock in the morning. It felt as if she'd barely fallen asleep, as she'd tossed and turned until well past midnight, her thoughts darting from Dr. Ryan to Emma and back again. With a heavy sigh she dragged herself out of bed and stumbled toward the shower.

The hot water helped wake her up, although she wouldn't be human until she'd downed her first cup of coffee. Since blow-drying her hair would take too long, she pulled it back into a ponytail and applied enough makeup to cover the dark circles beneath her eyes.

Volunteering to help out had seemed like a good idea at the time, but in the bright light of morning she couldn't help wondering what in the world she'd been thinking.

Caring for Emma. That's what she'd been thinking.

Staring at the empty coffeepot, she realized grimly that she hadn't turned it on last night before crawling into bed. Feeling a bit desperate, she decided to stop at the local corner coffee shop before heading to the hospital.

The place was far more crowded than she'd have expected this early on a Friday morning. Although maybe the tourist crowd liked to get an early start. There wasn't any drive-through service, not since someone had knocked over the post holding the intercom and speaker, so she took her place in line, hoping things would move quickly.

Of course, they didn't. She glanced at her watch for the third time, thinking she should give up gourmet coffee for the icky stuff they brewed at work, when a second line opened up. "I can help the next person?" a woman called out.

The woman in front of Cassie darted over and she followed, figuring it would be quicker. Another person came up behind her and tapped her on the shoulder.

"Hey, Cass, how are you?"

Cassie glanced over her shoulder to see Gloria, her friend from the ER, standing behind her. "Good. How are you?"

"Fine. How's our safe-haven baby?" Gloria asked in a low tone.

"Critical but stable," she replied, knowing that the privacy laws prevented them from discussing patients. Although small towns like Cedar Bluff had a hard time with the concept of privacy. Everyone liked to meddle in everyone else's business.

"Oh, I heard about that," the woman in front of her said, turning around with her large coffee in hand. "Everyone's trying to figure out who the mother is."

Cassie shrugged and edged around the woman so she could place her order. "Large mocha coffee, please." She glanced back at the nosy woman. "The mother has the right to be anonymous, so I doubt we'll ever find out who she was. Besides, she did a good thing, giving her baby a chance at a better life."

"Cassie's right." Gloria spoke up, flashing Cassie an apologetic smile. "We should be thankful. I'm sure someone will step forward to adopt the baby."

"I guess you're right," the woman said, looking resigned at the fact she wasn't getting any good information.

Cassie turned back to accept her coffee, wishing once again that she'd gone through the process of becoming a foster parent back when she'd first investigated the option. At the time she'd convinced herself the notion was a knee-jerk reaction to losing her baby and discovering her ex-husband's betrayal. But if she had at least started the process, she'd be in a better position to adopt little Emma herself.

Was she crazy to even think of that as an option? Probably. But for some reason the idea wouldn't go away.

Cassie took a bracing sip of her coffee and headed back out to her car. The drive to the hospital didn't take long and she was still early enough to beat the worst of the traffic.

She stood by the elevator, sipping her coffee and thinking about the gossip that was already floating around about their safe-haven baby. If the mother was still around, she sincerely hoped the poor girl didn't overhear people talking about her.

Several of her coworkers joined her at the elevator, although it was too early for idle chitchat. When the elevator stopped on the third floor, Cassie waited for the nurses closest to the door to get out first, before following suit.

As she stepped out of the elevator she caught a glimpse of an older woman with a cane entering the adjacent elevator. Was it the same woman who had been peering through the window of the door last evening? She tried to dart around her coworkers, but the action proved difficult, like a salmon swimming upstream. By the time she cleared the group, the elevator doors had closed.

She hesitated, wondering if she should take the stairs down to the lobby to verify it was the same woman from yesterday. But a glance at her watch made her grimace. There wasn't enough time, she needed to punch in for her shift or she'd be late.

Besides, selfishly, she wanted to be sure Emma was assigned as her patient. So she hurried toward the door and swiped her ID badge over the electronic eye so she could get in.

Still carrying her coffee, she entered the staff lounge, where they generally congregated to make out the day's assignments. After glancing up at the whiteboard, she relaxed. The charge nurse on duty had already listed her name as the nurse for both Emma and Barton.

She sipped her coffee, waiting for the rest of the assignments to be made. Should she call security? And report what? A suspicious woman in her early sixties who used a cane?

Yeah, right. She was being ridiculous. For all she knew, the woman getting into the elevator wasn't the same one as the day before. And even if it was, so what? She'd mentioned she was here, visiting a patient. There were other units on the third floor besides the neonatal nursery.

Cassie pushed the thought of the cane lady out of her mind. Once the assignments were pretty much completed, she set her coffee aside, grabbed her stethoscope from her locker and headed over to Emma's warmer.

Her step faltered when she realized Dr. Ryan was sitting at the computer, reading through the baby's progress notes.

You are not a slave to your hormones, she told herself sternly. *You need to get over him already!*

She forced herself to continue walking, even as she swept her gaze over the area, looking for Debra, the night-shift nurse, who needed to give her the update on how Emma was doing.

"Good morning, Cassandra."

She blushed, giving him a nod. "Good morning, Dr. Ryan, and, please, call me Cassie."

There, she'd finally managed to sound casual, as if he were any other physician on staff.

"Only if you call me Ryan. And as you have such a beautiful name, it's a shame to shorten it." For a moment she felt her jaw drop in shock and did her best to close her mouth so she didn't look like a gaping fish. She was relieved when he changed the subject. "Emma's doing well this morning. I think we'll try to wean her a bit from the vent."

Okay, patient care she could handle. She took a deep breath. "That sounds like a good plan. What about nutrition?"

"She hasn't had any seizures since we started the medication, so it's probably okay to begin feeding her. As soon as I finish my morning rounds I'll come back to insert a feeding tube. Maybe you could get the pump set up so everything is ready to go."

"Of course." She avoided his direct gaze, not trusting her ability to stay cool, calm and collected.

Had he really called her beautiful? No, he'd called her name beautiful. And that was completely different.

Wasn't it?

Of course it was.

She pulled out her stethoscope and warmed the diaphragm in the palm of her hand before leaning over to listen to Emma's heart, lungs and abdomen. As she went through her basic assessment she swore she could feel Dr. Ryan's piercing gaze on the back of her neck.

Just as she finished her assessment Debra came rushing over. "Sorry I'm late, had to finish feeding Barton."

"We can start at his bassinet," Cassie said, hoping her need to escape Dr. Ryan's overwhelming presence wasn't too obvious. "I don't mind."

"Okay." Debra led the way over to where Barton's bassinet was located and quickly logged onto the computer to pull up his flow sheet. "He's up to two and a half ounces per feeding and he gained three ounces. His weight this morning is four pounds twelve ounces."

"Awesome news," Cassie said with a smile. "What about his breathing? Any periods of apnea noted on the monitor?"

"None. He's been clear for twenty hours now." Debra beamed as if she were the proud mama. Actually, they all tended to take great satisfaction from watching their tiny patients' progress. "If he lasts until tomorrow morning, Dr. Ryan is going to move him over to the level-two nursery."

"Wonderful," Cassie agreed. "His parents are going to be thrilled."

"They won't be here until later this afternoon, but I'm sure they will be." Debra clicked through the rest of the assessment, including the amount of time he needed to be placed under the bili lights, along with the medication list.

When they finished with Barton they went back over to Emma's warmer. Cassie was relieved yet oddly disappointed that Dr. Ryan had left. They quickly reviewed Emma's vitals, her vent settings and her medication list before Debra left to head home.

About an hour later Emma's IV pump began beeping. Fearing the worst, she hurried over to shut off the pump and check the IV site.

Emma's little vein had blown earlier than she'd expected. She removed the catheter, feeling bad about the bruise that marred Emma's pink skin.

"I'm so sorry, sweetpea," she murmured. "Unfortunately, I'm going to have to put this IV back in."

As much as she detesting having to poke the baby, she knew it was for Emma's own good. The poor thing needed to get her medication to prevent seizures. She was especially anxious to get some tube feedings into the little baby. Emma had lost the three ounces Barton had gained.

This time, she chose the opposite arm for the IV. Tiny beads of sweat rolled down from her temples as she concentrated on finding the vein. For some reason, putting an IV in Emma was much more stressful than when she placed them in other patients. Thankfully she managed to thread the tiny catheter in and breathed out a sigh of relief.

"Nice job," Dr. Ryan said from behind her.

Somehow she managed not to jerk the needle out of Emma's arm, in spite of the fact that he'd sneaked up on her. Again.

Completely her fault. After all, he had mentioned coming back after rounds to insert the feeding tube.

"Thanks. Just give me a minute here," she murmured, using the same contraption that she'd used yesterday to cover the IV site from being accidentally pulled out.

When she'd finished she stepped back and stripped off her gloves, trying not to imagine that most of her makeup had been sweated away. One thing about work-

ing over infants in warmers, you were never cold, even
in the winter. In the summer, like today, it was down-
right steamy.

Although worth the discomfort, since their tiny
babies needed every bit of the warmth.

"Has the social worker been by?" Ryan asked as he
set out the feeding-tube supplies.

"Yes. She informed me that someone from Child Protective Services would be here between nine and ten."

"That should give me enough time to get the feeding tube placed."

"The pump is here and the formula you've ordered
is ready to go."

A smile tugged at the corner of his mouth and she
stared, acutely aware of how his face softened, making
him look lighter. Younger. Not as detached.

"I should have known you'd be ready," he said.
"Okay, Emma, we're going to have to get this nasty tube
in," he said in a soft voice as he leaned over the baby.
He lightly ran his finger down the length of Emma's
arm and she was struck by the fact that this was the
second time he'd soothed Emma, something she hadn't
seen him do to any of the other babies in their care.
"But, trust me, you'll feel better with some food in
your tummy."

Just like the IV, a feeding tube was a necessity for
babies on ventilators. Even without the breathing support, Emma would likely need to be tube fed because
of the seizure medication.

She helped hold Emma's head and body steady as
Dr. Ryan inserted the feeding tube. Emma didn't like it
much. Her tiny arms and legs flailed a bit, but then the
tube was in her stomach and the worst of the discomfort
was over.

"I'm so glad she won't remember this," Cassie murmured. "I feel like we're torturing her."

"We're not," Dr. Ryan said softly. "She's strong, she'll pull through this."

"I know," she said huskily, trying not to give in to the urge to cry. No baby should have to suffer and it was hard not to pass judgment on the baby's mother for allowing this to happen.

She subtly swiped at her eyes and turned to the feeding pump to program in the proper rate. Ryan came up beside her and put his hand lightly on her arm.

"Are you all right?" he asked in a husky voice.

She wasn't, but partially because his skin was so warm and tingly, she couldn't think. "Um, sure. I'm fine. Emma's the one I'm worried about."

"Me, too. But I'm confident you'll take good care of her. You're an incredible nurse, Cassie," he murmured.

"I'm not," she protested. "I just happen to love babies."

"I can tell. As I said before, you're a natural."

She glanced up at him, mesmerized by his ocean-blue gaze. Awareness shimmered between them, and suddenly she couldn't seem to remember why she needed to keep her distance from him. He seemed to understand her so well.

Better than her husband ever had.

With an effort, she tore her gaze away to glance back down at Emma. She knew very well why she needed to stay away. She'd suffered two miscarriages and her doctor had told her not to get pregnant until she'd had surgery. And even then, he'd told her, there could be scarring, preventing her from ever having a baby of her own.

And deep down she was afraid to risk getting pregnant again. She might not survive the emotional distress of another miscarriage.

"Cassie?" Ryan's voice pulled her from her sad thoughts. But before he could say anything more, the social worker approached, accompanied by a woman in her midforties wearing a badly fitting suit.

"Hi, Cassie, Dr. Murphy. This is Judith from CPS."

Cassie stepped away from Ryan and nodded at Judith. "Good morning."

"Good morning. What can you tell me about Emma's condition?" Judith asked, getting right down to business. The way she barely glanced at the baby grated on Cassie's nerves.

"She's been a sick little girl, but she's stable at the moment. We're supporting her breathing and giving anti-seizure medication."

"I see. What's the cause of her illness?"

"Her lab tests just came back positive for opiates, although the level isn't as high as I expected," Ryan admitted.

"So the mother was a drug addict." Judith didn't look at all happy with the news. "We could go after the mother for child abuse."

"Please, don't." Cassie spoke up. "She gave up her child under the safe-haven law. If the word gets out that we're going after the mother, others may not risk doing the same."

Judith grimaced and nodded. "I know, but it still makes me angry. How long before the baby is able to be discharged?"

"I can't tell you for sure, but probably a week or two, maybe more. Depends on how well she responds to treatment."

"Do you have foster care lined up yet?" Cassie asked.

"No. Actually, the fact that she's likely going through withdrawal and will probably have ongoing medical issues makes placement more difficult." Judith scowled, as if Emma had done it on purpose.

"Why is that?" Cassie demanded. "What difference does it make if she has medical needs?"

Judith shrugged. "Many people aren't willing to take on that kind of commitment," she said.

"I will," Cassie blurted, without stopping to think. "I'll go through the process of becoming a foster parent and I'd be more than willing to take Emma home with me. No matter what her medical issues are."

Judith and Ryan stared at her as if she'd lost her mind, but now that she'd said it out loud, she knew she'd meant every word.

She couldn't help thinking that this was meant to be. That she was meant to be Emma's mother.

And she knew she'd love Emma as her own child, if given the chance.

CHAPTER FOUR

RYAN WAS STUNNED to hear Cassie blurt out how much she wanted to be a foster parent for Emma, although truthfully, he shouldn't have been. Her gaze was bright with compassion and from the way she cared for their tiny patients, he knew she'd make an excellent mother. In fact, he was surprised she hadn't already been snatched up by some lucky guy.

Just the mere idea of Cassie being with anyone else was repugnant, and he clenched his jaw, trying to hide his reaction. Certainly she wouldn't blush the way she did every time he spoke to her if she was seeing someone else.

Would she?

"Have you applied to be a foster parent?" Judith asked, staring at Cassie expectantly.

"No, but I'm happy to do that," Cassie said without hesitation. "I finish my shift today at three-thirty. I can be at city hall before four."

Judith's expression wasn't encouraging. "If you haven't started the process, then you likely won't be approved in time to take care of Emma."

Ryan felt compelled to butt in. "Is there anything Cassie could do to expedite the process? If placing Emma will be as difficult as you say, this would be a win-win situation for both of them."

Cassie's gaze met his, full of silent gratitude. "I'll do whatever you ask, provide whatever you need," she said to Judith. "I'll take days off work if I have to."

"There's no way I know of to get through the process any sooner, but you can certainly ask about that when you go to city hall." Judith obviously considered the matter closed as she turned back toward Ryan and the social worker. "I'll return to check on the baby early next week. If anything changes in the meantime, either for the better or for the worse, I'd appreciate a call."

"Of course," he agreed. Even though he didn't particularly like the case worker, he knew that they needed to try to stay on Judith's good side if at all possible. Especially if Cassie was really going to go through with the plan of becoming a foster parent, an idea he was still trying to wrap his mind around. "Is there anything else you need from us?"

"Not right now." Judith glanced at them and shrugged. "Have a good day."

"You, too," Cassie said, with a forced smile.

He waited until the social worker had escorted Judith out of the unit before turning toward Cassie. "Do you really think this is a good idea?" he asked.

"Yes, I do," she answered without hesitation. "I know it seems like a snap decision, but it's not."

Ryan wasn't sure why he kept pressing the issue. "I know you love babies, but don't you think that having a child as a single parent will be difficult? Not to mention putting a crimp in your social life?"

She squared her shoulders and lifted her chin stubbornly. "I don't have a social life. After my ex cheated on me, I'm not anxious to trust men enough to try the dating scene again. I know being a single mother won't be easy, but I'm determined to provide Emma with a loving home. And as a nurse I can help with any medical issues she might have. Maybe Judith is right and I'm too late, but I still plan to move forward, hoping for the best."

He wanted to tell her that her ex-husband was a jerk to sleep around on her, but hadn't he let Victoria down, too? Maybe he hadn't cheated on Victoria but he hadn't been there for her. Still, he deeply admired Cassie's willingness to put her needs on the back burner in order to provide a home for Emma. "I'll be willing to provide you a reference if needed," he offered.

"Really?" The way her entire face lit up with hope and happiness made his pulse jump erratically. She'd never looked more beautiful to him than she did in that moment. She literally took his breath away. "Thank you so much, Dr. Ryan! You have no idea how much that means to me."

He struggled to come up with a reasonable response when he could barely think straight. "No problem. And if you need help with the paperwork, let me know."

"Oh, I'm sure I'll figure it out," she assured him.

He hesitated, loath to leave, even though he knew his colleague, Matthew Marks, would be there soon to relieve him. Matt should have been there already, but had asked for a couple extra hours off.

"Is there anything else you need, Dr. Ryan?" she asked, when she noticed him still standing there.

Irrationally, he wished she'd call him by his first name, the way he'd asked her to. Ryan knew it was better to keep things on a professional level, but he still yearned for her to address him as more than a colleague. He shook off his ridiculous thought. "No, just make sure you document how well Emma tolerates her feedings. I'm leaving as soon as I sign off with Dr. Marks, but I'll check her chart later this afternoon."

"Okay. She's going to do great, I'm sure." She turned and stroked Emma's cheek, the way he'd seen her do many times before. "Hang in there, sweetpea. We're going to give you some food to help you grow big and strong. You're going to be just fine, you'll see."

The way Cassie soothed Emma made him wish desperately that things could be different. He'd been fighting the chemistry sizzling between them for a couple of months now, knowing he couldn't dare act on it. Not just because they worked together, although that certainly didn't help matters, but because she deserved someone better than him.

Finding Victoria and his unborn son dead from an accidental overdose had broken something deep inside him. A portion of his heart that he didn't have a clue how to fix.

As much as he adored children, he wasn't ready for a relationship. Not now.

Maybe not ever.

Cassie glanced over her shoulder, watching covertly as Ryan walked away. That had been the most personal conversation they'd ever had and she couldn't imagine why she'd told him about her ex. And then he'd shocked her further when he'd jumped to her defense with the case worker from Child Protective Services. Maybe he had reservations about her idea of applying to be a foster parent for Emma, but that hadn't stopped him from offering to give her a reference.

She knew she shouldn't read too much into his actions, although at the same time she was certain she hadn't imagined the spark of attraction that had sizzled between them.

The very idea that he might be as attracted to her as she was to him made her face go hot. And she couldn't deny a tiny sense of panic. How could she go out with someone as amazing as Ryan? Her ex had been a handsome pharmacist, with women throwing themselves at him, and she hadn't been enough to satisfy him. Plus, Ryan didn't know the truth about her miscarriages, either.

She took deep breaths to calm herself down. Most likely Ryan was just being nice. He obviously cared about Emma's fate. And she was exhausted from her restless night. Maybe she'd imagined the awareness between them. Imagined the husky way he'd said her full name.

Cassandra.

Her knees went weak and she dropped into the seat near Emma's computer. What was wrong with her? This wasn't the time or place to think about the attraction she felt for Ryan. She needed to keep her mind focused on important matters, like giving Emma her first tube feeding and placing eye protection on Barton prior to placing him beneath the bili lights.

But as she cared for little Barton, Ryan's voice lingered in her mind. When the baby's parents came in to give him his noon feeding, she was grateful to head over to spend more time with Emma.

The baby's seizure precautions were still in place, despite the fact that there hadn't been any documented seizure activity since the first one shortly after her admission. Still, Cassie knew they needed to be careful not to overstimulate Emma. Too much stimulation could actually cause the seizures to return. So after giving

Emma her second feeding Cassie settled behind the computer to look up information on being a foster parent.

The amount of paperwork was overwhelming, but she refused to let that stop her. She printed out the application and the instructions, tucking them in her purse so she could review the information on her break.

Her shift dragged by slowly, no doubt because she was anxious to get to city hall. The fact that Ryan had gone home, leaving Dr. Matthew as the neonatal intensivist in charge, had nothing to do with it.

At least, that's what she tried to tell herself. Not very convincingly either.

To keep Ryan from crowding her thoughts, she focused on getting all her work finished. By two forty-five, Cassie was ready to go. She went over one last time to Emma's warmer, realizing that as she was off on Saturday, she wouldn't get to see the baby until her shift started on Sunday at three o'clock in the afternoon.

"You're doing so well, sweetpea," Cassie murmured, stroking the baby's downy cheek. "I'm sorry I won't see you for a day and a half, but I'll be thinking of you."

She gently checked Emma's IV in her arm and stroked the tip of her finger down her forearm to her hand. The baby caught her off guard by grabbing hold of her index finger in a surprisingly tight grip.

"That's my girl," Cassie said, tears pricking her eyelids. "You're getting stronger already, aren't you?"

Emma clung to her finger for a long minute before letting go and Cassie found herself wishing Ryan were here to share the thrilling moment. With babies you had to measure success in small increments. Emma had kept down the two bolus feedings and had grasped her finger. Huge accomplishments for a three-day-old baby born addicted to narcotics.

Sheri, the second shift nurse, came over at ten minutes after three and Cassie quickly went through Emma's orders with her. They double-checked Emma's IV site and the pump settings together before crossing over to Barton's bassinet. Sheri was familiar with Barton's care as he'd been with them for a week already, so going through his orders didn't take long.

Since Sheri had everything under control with Emma and Barton, Cassie swiped out of work fifteen minutes early, anxious to head straight out to her car. She was so focused on her mission that she didn't hear her friend Gloria, who was leaving at the same time, call out to her.

"Cass? Wait up a minute," Gloria said in a loud voice, sounding a tad annoyed.

"I'm sorry, I didn't mean to be rude," Cassie apologized. "I'm just in a hurry." Cassie slowed down so Gloria could catch up. She tried not to glance at her watch, which would only broadcast her impatience.

"Ooh, does that mean you have a hot date?" Gloria teased.

Ryan's face involuntarily flashed in her mind, even as she let out a sigh. "Don't be silly, of course not."

"Listen, Cass, I know your ex was a jerk, betraying you in the worst way possible, but locking yourself away from all men isn't the answer. James was upset that you turned down his offer to take you out for dinner, but I'm sure he'd give you a second chance."

Oh, boy. She *so* did not want to have this conversation, especially now. Obviously Gloria was trying to help, but there was no way Cassie was going to confess feelings for Ryan that she didn't even understand herself. Dating anyone else was out of the question.

"Listen, Gloria, I'm not locking myself away from men. I can't help the fact I'm not the least bit attracted to James. Please, don't try to set me up with anyone else, either. I'll find someone on my own when the time is right for me. Besides, I'm really running late, so let's chat later, okay?" Without waiting for Gloria to respond, she quickened her step, using her key fob to unlock her car.

"Call me," Gloria shouted as she slid behind the wheel.

Cassie quickly started her car and opened the windows to let the stuffy air out. "I will," she called back, before putting the vehicle in Reverse and backing out of the parking space.

Cassie had to stop at her apartment to pick up a copy of her birth certificate and social security card. Since she was there, she decided to change out of her scrubs, donning a flowery skirt and short-sleeved top. Slipping her feet into comfy sandals, she headed back outside.

From her apartment, the drive to city hall didn't take long. Cedar Bluff was crowded with tourists in the summer, but even then there wasn't normally a rush-hour traffic problem.

She climbed out of her car and approached the building with all the paperwork clutched in her hand, struck by a feeling of trepidation. What if they immediately turned her down because she was single? What if they thought her apartment was too small to be an appropriate home for Emma? She planned on buying a small house, but needed to save some more money first.

"Cassandra, is something wrong?"

She jerked her head around at the sound of Ryan's

voice. For a moment she blinked, wondering if she was losing it. But, no, there he was, sexier than ever, wearing casual jeans and a well-worn ocean-blue T-shirt that brightened his already mesmerizing blue eyes. And she was suddenly relieved she'd changed out of her scrubs.

Had he really come there just for her?

"Um, no. Of course not." She smiled, shoving her irrational doubts away. "But I'm surprised to see you. Is there something you need? Did I forget to document something in Emma's chart?"

The corner of his mouth kicked up in a wry smile. "No, you didn't forget anything. I'm thrilled she's doing so well." He hesitated and then shrugged. "It's always better if I keep busy the day after I'm on call, otherwise I'm not able to sleep at night. I thought I'd meet you here in case you needed help."

She was humbled by the idea that Ryan had come there for nothing more than to offer his support. Was it possible that little Emma had captured his heart, the same way she'd captured hers? She'd assumed that he didn't date because he didn't want a family. But after seeing the way he'd been with Emma, she knew that couldn't be right. "That's so nice of you."

For a moment their gazes clung and the air sizzled with tension, but then he turned his head and gestured to the paperwork in her hand. "Do you need to finish up any of that paperwork before we go inside?"

It took her a minute for the synapses in her brain to fire on all cylinders. "Oh, no, I have it completed," she assured him, pushing aside the temptation to have him go through everything as a double check. "But thanks."

"No problem."

The low timbre of his voice sent shivers down her spine, causing her to blush. Again. Seriously, she really needed to stop feeling like a young teenager around him. She'd been married, for heavens' sake. And divorced.

The memory was sobering. Could she really trust another man not to hurt her the way Evan had? Her stomach clenched. A handsome, aloof doctor was not the best candidate.

But somehow Ryan didn't seem as aloof around her.

"Are you ready?" Ryan asked, interrupting her tumultuous thoughts by placing his hand beneath her elbow.

"Of course." She pulled herself together with an effort, taking the necessary steps to reach the front door of the building. Before she could open the door, Ryan was reaching around her to open it for her.

If anything, her blush deepened. "Thanks," she said, entering the building and hoping the blessedly cool air-conditioning would help make the redness fade from her skin.

There were a couple of people ahead of her, so she took her place in line to wait her turn. Ryan stood right beside her, making her more conscious of his intimidating height and the breadth of his shoulders. Did he work out in a gym in his spare time? Feeling insecure, she sucked in her stomach, making a mental note to go for a run later that evening.

When it was her turn, she walked up to the counter and spread out her application, along with the documents she'd brought from home, for the woman to review.

But she was disappointed when the clerk simply gathered them together into a pile, without reading a word. "Thanks. We'll get this processed and be in touch."

Crestfallen, Cassie turned away, but Ryan didn't.

"Good afternoon. I'm Dr. Ryan Murphy from Cedar

Bluff Hospital and Cassie needs to know if there is anything she can do to speed up the process of becoming a foster parent. There's a baby in my care that needs to be placed with her as soon as possible."

The woman's eyebrows shot up in surprise. "Um, I'm sorry, but I can't help you. I'm just a clerk. I take the paperwork and file it as instructed."

Cassie leaned forward, determined to stand up for herself, too. "Who is the person in charge, then? I need to talk to whoever that is."

"Mr. Davies is in charge of the Child Protective Services department, but I'm afraid you'll need an appointment."

"Fine. Will you please give me his contact information?" Cassie asked.

The flustered clerk took out a card and scribbled Mr. Davies's name and number on the back. "Here you go. He's probably already gone today, but I believe he'll be back in the office on Monday."

Cassie took the card and nodded. "Thank you." She turned and headed back outside, feeling foolish for having built her hopes up over nothing.

"Well, that was a bit anticlimactic," Cassie said with a wry smile. "But thanks for coming anyway, Dr.—er...Ryan."

Ryan's smile made her tummy flip-flop again. "Spending time with you is never anticlimactic," he assured her in his deep voice. "I want you to let me know if Mr. Davies doesn't get back to you. I'm willing to put on the heat if needed."

"Thanks, but I'll get through to him." Cassie was determined to get this accomplished on her own, even though it was nice to have Ryan cheering her on.

She was heading toward the parking lot when she caught a glimpse of the cane woman.

Her hand shot out to grasp Ryan's arm. "Do you see that woman with the gray hair, walking with a cane? The one wearing white slacks and a green blouse?"

"Yes, why?" Ryan asked with a frown.

"This is the third time I've seen her in the last two days," Cassie said, keeping her voice low so no one else could hear. "The first time I caught her peering in through the window of the neonatal unit."

"That's odd," Ryan agreed.

"It can't be a coincidence," Cassie murmured. "Although what is she doing here at city hall? She couldn't possibly have known I was coming. I only made that decision earlier today."

"I hope she's not following you," Ryan said with a scowl.

Cassie couldn't deny the thought of this woman following her was creepy. "Ryan, I think she knows something about Emma. I bet she knows Emma's mother. In fact, she might even be related to the baby in some way."

"There's only one way to find out," Ryan said. "We need to talk to her."

Cassie nodded. "I agree."

But when they skirted the parked cars to head over to the sidewalk, the woman wasn't anywhere in sight.

CHAPTER FIVE

RYAN COULDN'T BELIEVE the woman Cassie had pointed out to him had managed to disappear so quickly. "She must have gotten into a car and driven off," he muttered in disgust. "There's no way she could have walked that fast with a cane."

"You're right," Cassie agreed with a frown. "Too bad we didn't get a glimpse of the car, either."

"Do you think there's a chance she's faking the need for a cane?" he asked. "Maybe there's more sinister to this woman than we realize."

"No, I don't think so," Cassie argued. "I've seen her up close and she definitely isn't steady on her feet. In fact, she would have fallen down if I hadn't supported her. I'm sure she's harmless enough."

Ryan blew out a heavy breath. "Okay, then, there's nothing more we can do right now. We don't even know her name. Although I'd love to talk to her, especially if she really does know something about Emma. If we could validate the mother's medical history, we'd have a better chance of treating her."

"I know. Trust me, the next time I see her, I'll get her name," Cassie said. "She must be trying to find information about Emma, nothing else makes sense."

"Probably. Although I don't like the way she's latched onto you."

"I know," Cassie said with a grimace. "I mean, there are lots of neonatal intensive care nurses—why would she assume I'm the one who might know something about Emma?"

Ryan didn't like the idea of this woman following Cassie, even if she didn't pose a physical threat. He frowned, thinking back over the past two days. "Maybe she was in the ER when Emma's mother dropped her off," he theorized. "If she was there she would have seen us caring for Emma."

"Could be," she agreed. "Or if she was looking through the window of the neonatal unit for a while, she might have watched me taking care of Emma."

Cassie turned around to head back to her car, so Ryan fell into step beside her. The last thing he wanted to do was to go back to his empty house, which had actually never been a home. Too bad he hadn't figured that out until it had been too late.

He and Victoria had gotten married too young. Looking back, he knew he'd mistaken lust for love. But he'd tried to make their marriage work. Victoria's death proved he hadn't succeeded. More to feel guilty about. Had Victoria loved him in a way he hadn't been able to love her?

He shook his head to stop the endless round of useless questions. His steps slowed to a stop, and he knew he couldn't bear to spend the rest of the evening alone. And he hadn't been lying about his need to keep busy on his post-call day. Maybe Cassie was just the distraction he needed.

"Would you be willing to join me for dinner?" he asked.

She blinked, apparently caught off guard by his offer. "I don't know. From what I hear, you don't date nurses from the hospital."

He tried not to wince. "That's true. But this isn't a date, just two people sharing a friendly meal."

The way Cassie stared at him made him wonder if his nose was growing. Did she see right through his lie? And why was he breaking his cardinal rule now? After months of resisting her?

"I suppose sharing a friendly meal wouldn't hurt," she said, although the way she avoided his direct gaze made him realize he could have handled that better.

"Please," he added. "It's too nice to spend the evening indoors. And there's an outdoor café a few blocks from here." He wanted to rush her over there before she could change her mind.

Before he could change his mind.

He knew only too well the power of gossip. Once the citizens of Cedar Bluff saw them together, there would be no stopping the rumors. Just that thought alone should send him running in the opposite direction.

But he didn't move. For some reason, he didn't want to lose the tenuous connection he had with Cassie.

A connection that made him feel alive again.

"Do you think I can leave my car here?" She frowned, glancing around the mostly deserted parking lot. "Or will I get a ticket?"

"You can park here and I'll walk you back when we're finished," he promised. He rested his hand on the small of her back, guiding her toward the Sunshine Café, located just a couple of blocks down from city hall. He groaned inwardly when he noticed how crowded the place was, but fate seemed to be working in his favor because when they stepped up to the hostess stand, a couple vacated their seat on the patio.

"We'd like to sit outside, please," he said, gesturing to the now open table.

She smiled. "Of course. Follow me."

The hostess led them over to the empty table and he pulled out Cassie's chair for her, before taking the seat across from her.

"Maria, your server, will be with you shortly," the hostess said as she placed two menus on the table in front of them. "Enjoy your meal."

"This is nice," Cassie said, looking around in awe. "I haven't eaten here before."

"The food is excellent and they renovated this area last year to provide more patio seating."

"It's beautiful." She sat up, peering over his shoulder. "Ryan, look! We can see Lake Michigan from here."

He nodded, glancing over his shoulder and smiling at her enthusiasm. "Yes, the view is part of the charm. What would you like to drink?" he asked, when he noticed their server was headed in their direction. "Wine? Beer? Lemonade?"

"Oh, well, I'm not sure," she said, looking down at the menu. He loved the way she blushed, her pink cheeks making her even more adorable. "Actually, lemonade sounds great."

"Sounds good. We'll start off with two lemonades," he told the server.

"I'll get those for you right away," Maria assured them.

An awkward silence fell once they were left alone, and Ryan tried to think of something to say that wouldn't sound like they were on a date.

"So tell me, were you busy last night?" she asked.

He glanced up in surprise, not at all accustomed to talking about his job. Victoria hadn't wanted to know about the situations he'd faced on a daily basis, claiming she couldn't bear to hear about sick babies. At the time he hadn't blamed her, but now having Cassie's interest focused on him made him realize how much he'd missed sharing the important work he did. "There was a delivery about three in the morning that was touch and go for a while. Thankfully the baby survived."

Cassie's gaze softened. "I'm so glad. Daniel, right? His warmer is located next to Emma's. Poor little guy is on a ventilator, too."

"Yes, that's right. He was pretty pale at first, but his mother was healthy, so I'm sure he'll do fine." He relaxed in his seat, savoring the moment. When had the last time been that he'd simply enjoyed being with someone? He honestly couldn't remember. "I shouldn't complain. I managed to get about four hours of sleep before I was needed to head down to the delivery, so it could have been worse."

"That's not much sleep at all," Cassie protested. "But I understand now why you want to stay up today. I used to do the same thing when I worked the night shift. It's not easy to get back on a normal sleep schedule, is it?"

"No, it's not," he admitted wryly.

Maria returned with their lemonades. After going through their specials, she left them alone to peruse the menu.

"The grilled chicken and almond salad looks delicious," Cassie said, as she reviewed the selections.

"I'm having the Swiss mushroom burger," he said. He knew from experience that most women worried too much about what they ate.

"Yeah, you had to point that out, didn't you?" she

said with a groan. "The Swiss mushroom burger sounds delicious. To be honest, I'm really hungry. I skipped lunch so I could fill out the foster-care paperwork."

"You won't regret the burger," he promised, capturing her gaze with his. "And you shouldn't skip meals, it's not good for you."

She wrinkled her nose at him. "Trust me, I don't skip meals very often. Okay, you sold me on the Swiss mushroom burger." She closed her menu and set it aside.

Maria returned to take their order. He took a sip of his lemonade, liking the way Cassie looked, seated across from him.

"Tell me why you don't date nurses from the hospital," Cassie said, her tone deceptively casual.

He winced and set his glass down, surprised by the way she'd gotten straight to the point. "I tried that about a year ago, but things didn't work out."

"Hmm," she said, tipping her head to regard him thoughtfully. "I sense there's more to that story."

Ryan didn't want to admit that he'd been so callous as to want nothing more than sex. And since Cassie was new here, she might not know about his past.

A past that would haunt him forever.

But he couldn't bring himself to lie to her. "My wife died almost three years ago," he admitted, surprising himself with his willingness to talk about the past. "I wasn't ready for a serious relationship."

"Oh, Ryan." Cassie's expressive brown eyes filled with empathy and she reached across the table to take his hand in hers. "I'm so sorry for your loss."

He felt like a total fraud and could barely force air past his tight throat. "Thanks. The circumstances were…difficult." He cleared his throat, unable to say anything more. He couldn't bear the thought of Cassie knowing all the gory details. "Enough about me. I need you to know how much I admire you for wanting to be a foster mother to Emma. Being a parent is the most important job in the world."

Her gaze clung to his for a long moment, as if she knew he was changing the subject on purpose. But then she released his hand and sat back in her seat.

"Thanks. But I'm not doing this to impress anyone," she said softly. "I bonded with Emma right from the beginning. I know it sounds illogical, especially since I've only known her for twenty-four hours, but she's very special to me."

"To me, too," Ryan admitted. He gazed into Cassie's passionate eyes, struck by the sweeping desire to kiss her, right here, right now. He curled his fingers into a fist to prevent himself from reaching out to her. Thankfully their server chose that moment to return.

"Are you ready to order?" she asked cheerfully.

Ryan forced himself to nod. He took a big gulp of his cold lemonade, trying to get himself under control.

"I'd love to try your Swiss mushroom burger," Cassie announced.

"What would you like for a side? French fries, homemade chips or coleslaw?" Maria asked.

Cassie hesitated then shrugged. "Chips. I can't resist homemade chips," she confessed.

"I'll have the same," he managed. "And another refill on the lemonade when you have a minute."

"Sure thing," Maria promised, gathering their menus.

Ryan stared at his soft drink, wishing now that he had asked for something stronger. Maybe if he dumped the ice over his hot head, he'd cool off faster. Normally he didn't have trouble controlling his basic desires.

But he was beginning to think that there was nothing normal about his growing feelings for Cassie.

And he was damned if he knew what to do about that fact.

Cassie enjoyed every bite of the diabolically delicious Swiss mushroom burger, making a mental note to double the length of her planned run. The homemade chips were awesome, too, and she had to stop herself from eating them all, tossing her napkin over her plate to hide them from view, even though she knew Evan wasn't here to give her a hard time about what she ate.

Ironically, Ryan didn't seem to mind her hearty appetite. The way he kept staring at her with that intense gaze of his was a bit intimidating. She wasn't used to being the center of any man's attention. Especially a guy like Ryan.

Her heart ached for him. Losing his wife couldn't have been easy. No wonder he didn't date the nursing staff. She could easily imagine some nurse thinking she'd make the next Mrs. Ryan Murphy.

All the more reason to get any thoughts of being with him right out of her head. She had enough personal issues of her own to deal with, including becoming a foster mother to Emma.

Still, she couldn't help noticing just how different Ryan was from her ex-husband. Evan had never gazed at her so intently. In fact, he'd often stared at other women, even when she'd been sitting right there. Several times since the divorce, she'd wondered why she'd thought she'd loved Evan in the first place. It hurt to realize she may have been looking for the security of marriage rather than being truly in love. And she wished she'd figured that out sooner.

Before she'd lost her second baby.

She didn't want to ruin the moment by dwelling on the mistakes she'd made in the past, so she shook off the memories.

"You called it, that was amazing," she said, pushing her plate away and sitting back with a sigh. "I'll need to double my workouts if I keep eating like this."

He scowled and shook his head. "You look perfectly fine the way you are."

Fine wasn't exactly flattering, but that didn't stop her from blushing. "Thanks again for dinner," she said, trying to change the subject. "I should probably head back home."

"All right," he agreed, gesturing for Maria to bring their bill. "If you have time, it might be nice to take a walk up to the top of the bluff first. A short walk will help your food digest, making room for dessert."

She caught her breath, thinking that a walk to the top of the bluff and dessert sounded like something more intimate than a friendly meal. Or was she overreacting?

She needed to get a grip. His brain was probably foggy from sheer exhaustion and he just wanted to keep active so he wouldn't fall asleep.

She took a deep breath to calm her racing heart. "Sure. That sounds fun," she said lightly.

Ryan smiled and quickly signed off on the bill. Before he could say anything more, though, his cell phone rang. He stared at the screen for a moment, before lifting his gaze to hers. "It's the hospital," he said with obvious regret. "I'm sorry, I'll need to take this call."

"Oh, no, it's not Emma, is it?" she asked, leaning forward in concern.

"I'll find out," he promised, pushing the button on

his phone to connect to the caller. "This is Ryan Murphy," he said in a crisp, professional tone.

Cassie knew she shouldn't be listening to Ryan's side of the conversation—after all, there were rules about patient privacy. But she couldn't bear the thought of something happening to Emma. Or to any of their other tiny patients. Each baby in their care offered hope for the future.

"Discontinue her feedings immediately and get a chest X-ray, stat," Ryan said. "I'll be in to check on her and to write more orders shortly."

The way his eyes darkened with regret made her stomach clench. "What happened to Emma?" she demanded, fearing the worst.

"She aspirated some of her tube feeding while having a seizure," he admitted grimly. "I'm sorry, but I'll need to go in. I want to review her X-ray myself."

"I want to go with you," Cassie protested, rising to her feet. But then she let out a heavy breath. "But I can't. She doesn't belong to me yet."

"Give me your number," he urged, pulling out his phone. "I'll call you with an update."

"Really?" She readily gave him her number, watching with awe as he programmed her name into his phone. "Thank you, I really appreciate it."

Ryan slipped his phone back into his pocket. "Come on, I'll walk you back to your car."

"No, just go and take care of Emma," she said, putting her hand on his arm to stop him. For a moment his gaze dropped to her hand, before lifting up to look into her eyes, and she had to fight the urge to throw herself into his arms. "My car is only three blocks away. Emma needs you more than I do."

He hesitated, and then gave a brief nod. "All right.

Take care, Cassandra." He leaned over to brush her mouth with his in a kiss so brief she thought she imagined it. "I'll call you later."

Speechless, she watched him stride off toward his car, lightly pressing her fingertips to her tingling lips.

He'd kissed her. She had no idea why, but he'd kissed her!

And she knew, without a doubt, that he'd call her, too, the minute he had an update about Emma's condition.

She was definitely in over her head, because there was no denying she couldn't wait to talk to Ryan or to see him again.

Ryan forced himself to concentrate on driving, instead of reliving their brief but electric kiss. What had possessed him to kiss her like that? It was as if his hard-won control had abandoned him. He'd wanted desperately to kiss her, so he had. In a public place no less.

What if someone had seen them?

But even the thought of Shana-like rumors rippling through the hospital wasn't enough to make him regret his action. How could it?

Every cell in his body wanted to kiss Cassie again, a proper kiss, deep and intimate. The type of kiss that could lead to more.

But he couldn't turn his back on his patients either. Matthew was apparently stuck in a touchy delivery so Sheri had called him for help. He didn't mind, because waiting could prove deadly.

Well, he minded leaving Cassie, but his needs weren't important right now. If Emma ended up with aspiration pneumonia, she'd end up staying on the ventilator longer.

Not to mention that if the bacteria grew in her lungs

and transferred into her bloodstream, the overwhelming infection could kill her.

He tightened his grip on the steering wheel. No way was he about to let that happen.

Ryan made it to the hospital in ten minutes and as he strode into the neonatal intensive care unit the staff gaped at the fact that he was wearing casual clothes, but he ignored them, heading straight over to Emma's warmer.

"I'm sorry to call you back in, Dr. Ryan," Sheri said, looking flustered. "I pulled up her chest X-ray on the computer monitor, the way you asked me to."

"I don't mind," he assured her. He washed his hands at the sink and then turned toward the nurse. "Can I borrow your stethoscope?"

"Sure." Sheri handed it over and he took the time to listen to Emma's lungs before giving the stethoscope back and taking a seat at the computer.

"There's a small amount of atelectasis in the base of her right lung," he said, battling a wave of helplessness. "Her breath sounds are diminished in that area, too. I'm going to order respiratory therapy treatments for her as well as antibiotics. Roll her onto her left side a bit, so that her lung can expand."

"All right," Sheri agreed. "Anything else?"

He stared blindly at the computer screen for a long minute, wishing there was more he could do for Emma. But at this point there wasn't. All he and Cassie could do was to hope and pray the baby girl would continue to fight.

He'd failed to save his wife and son, but he was determined not to fail Emma.

No matter what.

CHAPTER SIX

WHEN HER PHONE RANG, Cassie tossed her mystery book aside and shot off the sofa. A whole hour had passed since Ryan had left her to go to the hospital and she was anxious to know what was going on. "Hello, Ryan?"

"Yes, it's me. I'm leaving the hospital shortly, but wanted you to know that Emma's condition has been stabilized for now. The next twenty-four hours will be critical for her, though."

She momentarily closed her eyes, letting out a sigh of relief. "I'm so glad you were able to go in to take care of her. She deserves the best."

"I'm glad you're not upset that I had to leave," he countered. "Not all women are as understanding."

"That's just stupid," she said, suspecting he was speaking from experience. From the nurse he'd dated last year? Or from his wife? Didn't matter, she told herself firmly. "What did Emma's chest X-ray show?"

"A small collapsed area in her right lower lung," he said. "I'm hoping that with the antibiotics and respiratory therapy treatments, we'll be able to prevent full-blown pneumonia. The worst part is that her feedings have to be stopped for a while."

"Oh, no," she said with a sigh. Poor Emma wouldn't gain much weight without being fed, but the risk was too high. "Thanks so much for calling me. Now go home and get some rest."

"I will, if you will," he said in that sexy, low, husky tone of his. "I'll give you a call in the morning."

"Okay. Goodnight, Ryan."

"Goodnight, Cassandra."

The way he said her full name in his husky voice made her want to stay on the phone with him forever. She disconnected from the call and then quickly added Ryan's name and number to her contact list. Why had he mentioned calling her in the morning? To give her an update on Emma's condition?

Or because he wanted to see her again?

She shook her head at her own foolishness. Ryan had made it clear he wasn't ready for a relationship. And she wasn't either. Her heart was still raw from the way Evan had trampled all over it. She really needed to stop microanalyzing Ryan's every move. Still, forgetting about him long enough to fall asleep wasn't easy.

And, of course, Ryan popped into her mind first thing in the morning. She needed to rein in her emotions. She and Ryan were friends, nothing more.

Besides, the last thing she needed was to be hurt by another man. Discovering Evan had cheated on her had been brutally painful. Not to mention the fact that she might not be able to have children of her own.

And Ryan clearly loved children. Hadn't he practically admitted that while they'd been in the elevator with Emma?

She has us. We care about her.

Cassie leaped out of bed, anxious to jump-start her day. She was worried about Emma, so she needed to keep busy. Since she'd promised herself she'd go for a run to work off the Swiss mushroom burger, she donned her running clothes and headed outside. Okay, so maybe she didn't exactly double her mileage but she ran a total of three miles and felt much better afterwards.

Saturday mornings were normally reserved for cleaning. She ate a quick breakfast of scrambled eggs and toast, and then decided there was no point in showering until she'd finished cleaning. She tossed a load of laundry into the machine and then began the tedious task of scrubbing her bathroom.

The sky outside had grown more cloudy, so she turned on the radio to listen for the weather report. Sure enough, there was a chance of thunderstorms rolling in, but not until later that afternoon. After finishing in her bathroom, she started on the tiny kitchen. She was singing along to a song on the radio when her phone rang. She tossed the sponge into the sink, dried her hands on the seat of her jeans and reached for the phone, her heart skipping when she saw Ryan's name on the screen.

"Hello?"

"Good morning, Cassie," Ryan greeted her. "Hope I'm not calling too early."

"Of course not," she said, glancing at the time. It was ten-thirty. She'd already gone for a run, cleaned her bathroom and finished two loads of laundry over the past two and a half hours. "I hope you were able to get a good night's sleep."

There was a brief pause and she wondered if that was too personal a question. Friends, remember? They were friends.

"I did, thanks," he finally said. "I don't have an update yet on Emma, but I'm sure I'll hear from Matthew soon."

"You read my mind," she teased. "I was going to ask how she was doing."

"I'll let you know as soon as I do," he promised. "Do you have any plans for your day off?"

No way was she going to confess that all she was doing was cleaning, which was nearly finished anyway. "Nothing special," she said slowly.

"I thought maybe we could head down to the park, see if we can find the woman we believe is connected to Emma. It's possible she might live close by."

Ridiculous to be disappointed that he had an ulterior motive for getting together. Friends, she reminded herself. They were friends. "Sure, why not? Although you have to know the chances of us just stumbling across her are slim to none."

"Maybe, but I bet we'll run into her sooner than later. How much time do you need?"

"Give me an hour," Cassie said, glancing at her kitchen. Surely finishing up in there wouldn't take long. "Where do you want to meet?"

"I'll pick you up," Ryan said.

It was on the tip of her tongue to argue, but she reminded herself that this wasn't a date. "Okay. I live in the apartments on Oakdale Drive. The third building. Apartment 302."

"All right, I'll see you in an hour."

Cassie set down her phone and rushed to finish cleaning her kitchen before jumping into the shower. She used the blow-dryer on her hair, even though she knew the humidity would eventually wreak havoc with it anyway.

Still, she wanted to look nice for Ryan, even if her long sleek hair would only last for an hour.

She pulled on a skirt, wincing a bit at her pale legs.

One would think that with her dark hair she'd tan eas-ily, but she didn't. A minute after she finished applying a light coat of makeup, the sound of her door buzzer echoed through the apartment.

Her heart stuttered and her stomach clenched with nerves, but she went over to the intercom to let him in.

He knocked at her door barely a minute later and she looped her purse over her shoulder before walking over to open the door. "Good morning," she greeted him. "I'm ready."

His blue eyes swept over her, glinting with approval. "You look amazing, Cassandra," he murmured.

She licked her suddenly dry lips. "Thanks," she mur-mured. "So do you." Oh, boy, what was wrong with her? She was acting like this was a date.

His gaze held hers for a long second, as if remember-ing their brief kiss. Or maybe that was just her memory working overtime. He stepped back, giving her room to leave her apartment. She released her pent-up breath and wondered if she was crazy to spend her day off with Ryan.

She already liked him too much already. And she couldn't bear the thought of giving him the power to hurt her. After all, his last relationship hadn't worked out, either.

No, she couldn't allow herself to become emotionally involved with Ryan. The nurses called him the Heart-breaker for a reason.

She wasn't sure she'd survive another emotional train wreck.

Ryan nearly swallowed his tongue when he saw Cassie standing there, looking breathtakingly beautiful.

He was playing with fire, but at the moment he couldn't seem to bring himself to care if he got burned.

"So, did Dr. Matthew call you back about Emma?"

He nodded. "Yes, she's doing pretty well. Her chest X-ray looks a little better, so I think the respiratory therapy treatments are working." He held the door open for her as they headed outside. "As I said before, the next twenty-four hours are critical. If she can turn the corner, she'll do great."

"I'm glad to hear that," Cassie said. Then her mouth gaped open when he crossed over to pull open the passenger-side door of his sporty cherry-red convertible. "You have a convertible?" she squeaked.

"Yes, I hope you don't mind," he said, glancing at her long hair. He remembered how Victoria hadn't liked the wind messing up her hair. "I can put the top up if you prefer."

"No way! I've always wanted to ride in a convertible." He watched in amusement as she rooted through her purse to find a hair tie. Pulling her hair back into a ponytail didn't take long. "This is going to be fun," she declared, sliding into the passenger seat.

Ryan smiled, closing the door behind her. Cassie was so different from Victoria, which made her dangerously attractive.

He hadn't been with a woman in a long time and forced himself to remember that Cassie wouldn't appreciate being used for sex. Truthfully, the idea didn't sit well with him, either. She deserved a man who would love and cherish her and little Emma.

Someone better than him. He didn't deserve a second chance. He hadn't loved Victoria the way he should have loved his wife, and his son had died because of it. Oh, he'd blamed Victoria, too, for becoming addicted to painkillers, but deep down he knew that he was the one at fault.

For not loving her enough.

For not noticing her addiction.

For not being home when she and his son had needed him.

He shook off the sobering thoughts with an effort. Ryan knew he'd need to find a way to keep his distance from Cassie. A task far easier said than done.

As he drove to the park, she lifted her face to the sky as if enjoying the wind against her skin. "This is fabulous!" she exclaimed. "You must love this car."

"It's just a car," he said mildly, enjoying the rapture on her face. "But I'm glad you're having fun."

He parked at the base of the walking path that would lead up the bluff, looking over Lake Michigan. "Come on, let's take a walk."

She climbed out of the car. "Okay, but I think we can safely assume that the woman we're trying to find wouldn't try to walk up this path with her cane."

He shrugged, refusing to admit that this part of the day was strictly for the two of them. "I know, but we can head into town to search for her after you see the view. It's amazing."

"Lead the way," she said with a smile.

Dark clouds swirled overhead and he hoped the rain would hold off, at least for a while. Cassie didn't say much as they climbed up the bluff, but he didn't find her silence awkward or strained.

She was an easy person to be with. Beautiful, compelling and nurturing, an intoxicating combination.

"Wow, you were right," she whispered once they reached the top. "This view is incredible."

He nodded, although his attention was focused more

on Cassie than the view. He didn't deserve her, but he wanted Cassie so much he ached. "I knew you'd like it. I'm surprised other people aren't up here, although maybe the rainclouds scared them away."

"Could be," she said, glancing up. "The weather report said the rain wouldn't come until two this afternoon, but those clouds look ominous."

"We'd better head back down," he murmured, hating to cut their time short. "Before the clouds let loose."

He caught her hand in his as they started their descent. Going down was faster than going up, and soon they were back in the convertible. "I'll put the top up," he said, reaching for the controls.

"Please, don't, it's not raining yet," she said, putting her hand on his arm.

Every nerve in his body went on alert at her touch. And at that moment he couldn't deny her anything. "All right, let's hope we don't get drenched. The car has to be in park before the mechanism will work to put the top up."

"We'll be fine," she assured him.

He fought with his chaotic emotions during the short ride back into town. A couple of sprinkles showered them as he parked. He closed up the car and slid out from behind the wheel. "Let's head over to Main Street."

"We'd better hurry." Cassie cast a glance up at the clouds just as a rumble of thunder echoed above them. "Run!"

This time Cassie grabbed his hand as they ran down the road toward Main Street. They reached the safety of the canopy over the window of the ice-cream parlor just as a heavy sheet of rain poured from the sky.

Cassie laughed, not at all upset about the raindrops

dampening her hair and skin. "We made it," she said breathlessly.

She was so beautiful, so warm and full of life that he couldn't help himself. He tugged her close, wrapped his arms around her and kissed her. A proper kiss. Delving deep into the sweet recesses of her mouth.

Kissing Cassie felt like nothing he'd experienced before. Like coming home.

And this time he didn't want to ever let her go.

Cassie gasped when Ryan pulled her in for a scorching kiss. She knew she should push him away, but her muscles melted against him, reveling in the desire that flared instantly between them.

This time he didn't settle for a chaste kiss, but angled his head and teased her lips until she opened for him, allowing him to deepen the intimacy.

His heady taste went straight to her brain, far more potent than whiskey or wine. He kissed her with a single-minded intensity that she'd never experienced before. Everything around them vanished. She was only aware of the smoldering heat of his mouth and the firmness and strength of his muscles beneath her exploring fingertips.

She wanted to stay in his arms, forever.

"Is that Dr. Ryan Murphy?" a woman nearby asked in a shocked voice. "Who is he kissing?"

It took a moment for the comment to register through the fiery heat, but once she realized people were talking about them, she pulled back, gulping in deep breaths of air. "We shouldn't be doing this," she whispered, resting her forehead on his broad chest. "People are watching."

The thundering beat of his heart gave her confidence that the impact of their kiss wasn't one-sided.

"I'm sorry," he murmured, smoothing his hand down her back, which only made her regret the fact that they were wearing clothes. "Not for kissing you, but for dragging you into the Cedar Bluff gossip mill."

Despite feeling embarrassed, she couldn't help but let out a chuckle. She lifted her head and stepped back, despite the way she longed for him to sweep her back into his arms. "Maybe I'm the one who dragged you into the gossip mill," she said wryly. "After all, I'm the new kid in town."

He cupped her cheek with his hand and she leaned into his caress. "You have no idea how much I wish I had more to offer you, Cassandra," he said, regret shimmering from his eyes. "But I don't."

Her heart twisted at the seriousness of his tone and she knew he was reminding her about how his last relationship hadn't worked out. Was he still grieving his dead wife? Probably.

"I know," she said simply. She forced herself to take another step back, immediately missing his warmth. "It's probably better this way," she added. "Especially since we work together."

Ryan looked as if he wanted to say something more, but she didn't want to hear any platitudes. Or, worse, find herself begging for anything he was willing to give.

Just remembering the devastation she'd gone through after suffering her second miscarriage and then listening as Evan had told his lover how glad he was that she'd lost the baby was enough to bring her to her senses. She hadn't been good enough for Evan, who was to say Ryan wouldn't get tired of her, too? Besides, Ryan didn't know about her inability to have children. Would he look at her differently once he knew the truth? The very thought was enough to convince her to put Ryan back into the friend category before things spiraled out of control.

Who was she kidding? They'd already spun out of control.

"How about we get some ice cream while we wait out the storm?" she suggested, hoping her desperation wasn't too obvious.

"Sure," he agreed.

They ducked out from beneath the awning over the window to head inside the ice-cream parlor. There were a few other customers inside and she could feel their curious gazes boring into her as they reviewed the ice-cream selections.

"I'll have double-chocolate fudge," she said, striving to sound normal. After that toe-curling kiss, and Ryan's emotional withdrawal, she was tempted to wallow in an entire vat of chocolate.

"Make that two," he told the woman behind the counter.

Once they had their dishes of ice cream, Cassie wanted nothing more than to leave. "I think the rain is lightening up," she said, gesturing toward the window. "Why don't we run over to the coffee shop next door?"

"Sounds good," Ryan agreed. She tried to ignore his closeness as they darted over to the coffee shop.

She noticed the cane woman seated in the booth farthest in the back right away. Grabbing the distraction with both hands, she headed straight toward her with steely determination.

"Hi, my name is Cassie Jordan. Do you remember meeting me outside the neonatal ICU?"

She looked shocked but recovered quickly. "Yes, of course."

"Do you mind telling me your name?" Cassie pressed,

sensing Ryan coming up to stand supportively beside her. "Do you know Emma's mother?"

"My name is Lydia and, no, I don't know anyone named Emma." The woman couldn't hold Cassie's gaze and she suspected the woman was lying. But why?

"Lydia, please know that I care about Emma, very much. And having some sort of medical history on Emma's mother would help us take better care of the baby. Do you understand? Emma's mother isn't in any trouble, we just want to ask her a few questions, that's all."

For a moment Cassie thought she'd gotten through to the woman, whose indecision was clearly reflected in her eyes, but Lydia abruptly shook her head and leaned hard on the table, pushing herself to her feet. She grabbed her cane. "I'm sorry, but I don't know anything. I can't help you."

Cassie glanced up at Ryan, feeling helpless. They were so close, but the woman wasn't talking.

"Ms. Lydia, please know that we are taking very good care of Emma. She's had a few setbacks, but I assure you I plan to do everything possible to help Emma get better."

Cassie thought she saw a flash of gratitude in Lydia's eyes before she moved past them to head for the door, obviously intending to leave, despite the rain.

And Cassie couldn't think of a way to stop her.

CHAPTER SEVEN

RYAN SCOWLED WITH frustration as Lydia left the coffee shop. He knew she was connected to Emma in some way, most likely by blood. He was convinced she was either Emma's grandmother or her great-aunt, despite her denials to the contrary.

But there wasn't much he could do, considering they were pushing Lydia for information she legally didn't have to give.

"She knows something," Cassie murmured, dropping down into a chair and staring morosely at her melting ice cream. "But for some reason she doesn't trust us."

He nodded, remaining on his feet because he didn't trust himself, not around Cassie. The memory of holding her in his arms and kissing her was still too fresh in his mind. The double-chocolate fudge ice cream was a poor substitute for her sweet taste.

"And she didn't give us her last name either," Cassie continued. "Which makes me think that she's related to Emma's mother closely enough that we might be able to figure out the connection if she'd told us."

"Good point," he agreed. Reluctantly, he took the seat across from Cassie, trying not to show his reaction to her nearness. His heart rate still hadn't returned to

normal after their kiss and her warm vanilla scent was
embedded in his mind.

He tried to think of something to say that would
make her feel better, but his brain cells were foggy
with desire.

Cassie only ate about half of her ice cream before
pushing her container aside. "Well, I guess our plan
didn't work out after all, although it was worth a try."
Her tone was offhand, but she didn't meet his gaze as
she stood. "I think I'll head home. Thanks for the ice
cream."

He shot to his feet, desperate to keep her with him.
"Wait, you can't walk in the rain, I'll drive you home."

"Actually, I'd rather walk," she said, finally meeting
his gaze, her eyes filled with steely determination. "It's
warm outside, I won't melt. And I'd like to be alone.
Take care, Ryan, see you around."

Panic hit hard and he reached out a hand to stop her
but she shook him off and hurried to the door. Helplessly, he watched her leave, wishing for the millionth
time that things could be different.

Sinking down in his seat, he sighed and dropped his
head into his hands. His body craved her warmth, but
his brain knew that letting Cassie go was the right thing
to do. She deserved the best.

Someone far better than him. He'd never told a single soul about how he'd planned to file for divorce from
Victoria. But then she'd announced she was pregnant
and he'd shoved aside the idea of divorcing her. For one
thing, he loved kids and had been thrilled at the thought
of having a child. Plus, he'd come from a broken home
and couldn't bear the idea of his child growing up under
the same circumstances. So he'd decided there had to be
a way to make things work out between them.

Five months later, he'd come home late one night to find Victoria sitting behind the wheel of the car, her skin cold and gray. The moment he'd touched the roundness of her abdomen he'd known she'd been dead for several hours.

Taking their son with her.

It wasn't until he'd found the empty prescription bottle in the cup holder next to her that he'd realized she'd still been taking oxycodone. Her surgery had been several months before she'd become pregnant, so finding them had been a terrible shock.

The police had right away assumed the worst, thinking that he'd either forced her to take the pills or had abused her to the point she'd needed to take them. The thought of suicide hit hard, but then he discovered the doctor's name on the pill bottle wasn't the same as her orthopedic surgeon's. The police had agreed to look into it. But the doctor's name was Oliver Stevenson and the address had turned out to be a vacant building.

Leaving no leads for Detective Trammel to follow.

He sighed and pulled himself together, taking the time to throw away their unfinished dishes of ice cream before heading outside. The rain had slowed to a steady drizzle, so logically he knew Cassie would be fine.

But he followed the path to her apartment building anyway, frowning when he didn't see her walking along the sidewalk.

Where had she gone? He reached for his phone and called her, but she didn't answer. He scowled and listened to her voice-mail greeting.

"Hi, you've reached Cassie. Leave a message and I'll call you back. Thanks!"

"Cassie, this is Ryan. Please call me back and let me know you've made it home safely. Thank you."

He scowled and shoved the phone back into his pocket, before making a U-turn and heading home.

When he pulled in the driveway, he stared at the large house Victoria had insisted they build, struck by the sudden urge to put the house up for sale. Yeah, the housing market sucked, but you couldn't sell what you didn't list. Besides, so what if he took a loss?

The place had never felt like home anyway.

With renewed determination he called a real estate agent and left a message about wanting to put his house up for sale. Then he called the hospital to check on Emma. She remained stable, thankfully showing no sign of running a fever.

Then he sat back and stared at his phone, willing Cassie to return his call.

But as the hours ticked by she didn't.

Cassie spent the rest of her Saturday with her friend Gloria, trying to forget about Ryan, at least for a little while. Gloria was happy to oblige. They ordered Chinese food and enjoyed a chick-flick marathon.

Her heart raced when she realized Ryan had called, but she couldn't bring herself to return his call. For one thing, why on earth would he think she hadn't made it home? This was Cedar Bluff, not the north side of Milwaukee. Sure, they had some crime, but nothing that would prevent her from getting home all right. He was simply being ridiculous and she feared that if she called him back she'd throw herself at him, begging for another kiss.

Not a good idea.

"This was great, Gloria. Thanks for picking me up and inviting me over," Cassie said, when the last movie finished. "I should head home, I have to work tomorrow."

"Poor thing," Gloria said with mock pity. "I'm off tomorrow for my brother's graduation party. You could come before work if you want, it starts at noon."

Cassie wrinkled her nose. "You'll be busy with your family. I'll just sleep in and then go to work."

"The invitation stands if you change your mind," Gloria assured her.

"Okay, I'll think about it," Cassie agreed. The last thing she needed was to wallow around her apartment all morning, thinking about Ryan. Maybe going to the graduation party would be a good way to keep from ruminating over things she couldn't change.

"Do you want me to drive you home?" Gloria asked, as she headed toward the door.

Cassie rolled her eyes. "Don't be silly, we live in the same apartment complex. I'm just two buildings down."

"Okay, maybe I'll see you tomorrow." Gloria gave her a quick hug and then closed and locked the door behind her.

Cassie had to force herself not to call Ryan as she trudged home. The urge to connect with him was strong so she mentally made a list of things to do once she was approved to be a foster parent.

The first thing on her list was to look for a two-bedroom apartment. She wasn't sure how many two-bedroom apartments were available at the moment and made a mental note to check with the manager as soon as possible. Plus, she had to convince the landlord to transfer her lease as it wasn't up until November. Once she had a second bedroom she could decorate for a new baby.

For Emma? God, she hoped so.

She knew she needed to be realistic. As much as she longed to have Emma, she had to be prepared for the fact that she might not get approved in time. At least she'd be ready for the next baby that needed her.

A baby that she wouldn't be able to have on her own.

That night, she shut her phone off so that she wouldn't be tempted to call Ryan. Or answer his call if he tried again.

She tossed and turned most of the night, leaving her feeling cranky and out of sorts when she switched her phone back on the next morning. She debated going over to Gloria's parents' place on the lake, but decided she wasn't really in the mood for company.

When her phone rang, she jumped, expecting the caller to be Ryan. But instead it was the hospital number. Even if it was Ryan calling from the hospital, he might have news about Emma, so she quickly picked it up. "Hello?"

"Cassie? This is Diane. One of our day-shift nurses started throwing up and needed to go home. Would you be willing to start your shift early? We could really use the help."

"Of course," Cassie agreed. "I can be there in fifteen minutes."

"Thanks so much," Diane said in a rush. "The nurse who left to go home sick was taking care of Emma and the newest baby from the other day, Daniel. So at least you'll be familiar with one of the patients."

Knowing that she would get to take care of Emma made all the difference in the world. Her mood brightened considerably. "Great. I'll be there soon." Cassie quickly disconnected from the call and hurried to change into her scrubs.

It wasn't until she was walking into the hospital, that she wondered if Ryan was working today, too.

Her cheerfulness dimmed a little as she realized how difficult it would be to work alongside him as if they hadn't shared that sizzling kiss. This was the reason it was better not to date your colleagues. When things fell apart, everything was affected, both your work life and home life.

All the more reason not to venture down the path of temptation again.

Cassie quickly swiped her badge to get into the unit and then went to punch in at the time clock. She hurried over to Emma's warmer, grateful to see that Daniel's warmer was immediately adjacent to Emma's. Both babies were on ventilators, but as she quickly reviewed the notes it was clear Daniel had been weaned down to the point he was ready to have the tube out.

"Thanks again for coming in," Diane said, hurrying over. "Do you have any questions? I've been keeping an eye on these two until you could get here."

"Looks like Daniel's ready to get rid of his ventilator. Who's the intensivist on call today?"

"Dr. Ryan was here earlier. He's in a delivery right now, but he should be back soon." Diane didn't seem to notice how Cassie had gone still at hearing Ryan's name. "Do you want me to double-check the drips with you?"

"Ah, sure, that would be great." Cassie forced her brain to go into work mode, even though she was secretly thrilled Ryan was working today.

Once she'd caught up with what had transpired over the past twenty-four to thirty-six hours, she hovered over Emma. "Hey, sweetpea, how are you? I'm going to be here with you for twelve hours today, isn't that great? And then tomorrow I'm going to enroll in foster-care classes. I'm fighting for you, sweetpea. All you need to do is to get better, okay?"

Of course Emma didn't respond, but Cassie didn't care. She stroked Emma's cheek, hoping to soothe the baby. She felt a bit disheartened to realize they'd had to raise the vent settings since Friday, but, of course, they couldn't risk the chance she might develop pneumonia.

She managed to keep busy for the next hour or so, between double-checking other nurse's medications and caring for her two babies. Every free moment she had she spent with Emma.

"Good afternoon, Cassandra, you're here early."

Ryan's deep voice made her shiver in awareness, despite the stern talking-to she'd given herself before her shift.

"Amy got sick, so they called me in to cover," she said, striving to keep her tone steady. "How does Emma's chest X-ray look? I thought her lungs sounded pretty good, but maybe I missed something."

"Her X-ray looks much better," Ryan said, glancing down at Emma with a smile. "Her lower lobe has expanded back to normal, and her breath sounds are definitely clearing up."

"Wonderful news," she said in relief. "I've been so worried about her."

"I know." Ryan stepped closer and dropped his voice. "I was worried about you, too. Why didn't you return my call?"

He was so close she found it hard to breathe normally. She took a hasty step back, knowing she didn't owe him any explanations, but feeling compelled to tell him anyway. "I spent time with my friend, Gloria. You remember her, she's the one who took care of Emma in the ER until we got down there."

"So she came and picked you up?" he asked.

"I actually ran into her and she offered to drive me home. We live in the same apartment complex but in different buildings." The alarm on Daniel's vent went off, indicating a high peak pressure, one of the signs that he was trying to overbreathe the vent. "Have you had a chance to examine Daniel? I think he's ready to be extubated."

"Let me double-check his weaning parameters." Ryan crossed over to Daniel's warmer. She followed, determined to keep things on a professional level between them.

No more mooning over him. And definitely no more kissing.

"You're right, these look good. Call the respiratory therapist to help me extubate him."

Grateful for something productive to do, Cassie did as Ryan asked. Jason was the respiratory therapist on duty today, and he promised to be right over.

Cassie concentrated on documenting in Daniel's chart, silently admitting it was an easy way to avoid Ryan.

"Hi, Cassie," Jason said as he approached. "I hear Daniel is about to get rid of that nasty tube."

"Absolutely," she agreed. "Dr. Ryan wants to extubate whenever you're ready."

The procedure of removing a breathing tube didn't take long and Daniel let out a loud cry as soon as the tube was gone. Ryan picked Daniel up and propped the baby against his shoulder. Ryan rubbed the boy's back as if he had a dozen children of his own.

"There, now, you're going to be much happier now that you can yell at us, aren't you?" he said with a wry smile. "Trust me, that crying is good for your lungs so don't hold back. Just let it all out. We can take it."

Cassie stared at him in shock, her heart melting like butter on a griddle as she watched Ryan caring for Daniel. Did he want children of his own? Or not? He should, because he'd make a great father.

Daniel quieted down, resting against Ryan's chest.

"You're a natural father," she murmured. "You must want children of your own."

The light in Ryan's eyes dimmed a bit, although he nodded. "Someday," he agreed.

Someday? What did that mean? Someday, as in once he was ready to risk having a relationship? Or someday, as in a long time from now?

Was he still grieving over his dead wife?

Her stomach clenched with worry. Ryan wanted children, babies she probably wasn't able to have. But did that desire extend to Emma? She had no idea.

Weary of her mental tug-of-war, she turned away. Staying away from Ryan was better for her in the long run.

When Emma's monitor alarm went off, she hurried over, relaxing a bit when she noticed that the baby had somehow dislodged one of the heart leads.

"False alarm," she said, when she saw Ryan had returned Daniel to his warmer and was crossing over to Emma. "One of her leads came loose."

He nodded, but didn't look in a hurry to leave. She took a breath, wishing he would just go away and leave her alone. She didn't want to feel all torn up inside like this. When the phone next to Emma's computer rang, she pounced on it. "This is Cassie in the NNICU, may I help you?"

"Cass? It's Gloria." Her friend's voice was thick with

tears. "My brother, Trey, is here in the ER. I think he overdosed on pain meds. The police are investigating."

"What? He overdosed on pain meds and the police are there?" Cassie said, her gaze clashing with Ryan's. "I don't understand. Where did he get pain meds?"

"I don't know, but his condition is pretty serious. I know you're working but if you have time to come down to the ER, I'd appreciate it."

"I'll come as soon as I can," Cassie promised.

"Who overdosed on pain meds?" Ryan demanded.

"Gloria Reynolds's brother, Trey," she admitted. Before she could say anything more Ryan spun on his heel and strode out of the unit, no doubt heading down to the ER.

She frowned at his retreating figure. Why was Ryan heading down to the ER? She couldn't come up with a single reason.

She turned back toward Emma, knowing that she couldn't leave her tiny patients, no matter how much she wanted to follow Ryan.

CHAPTER EIGHT

RYAN JOGGED DOWN the stairs to the ER, determined to talk to the police investigating Trey Reynolds's overdose. He desperately wanted to know where Gloria's brother had gotten his pain meds.

He knew the police wouldn't want to tell him anything, but he hoped that if Detective Trammel was there, he'd get something out of the detective. Ryan had a sick feeling in his gut that there was a connection between this young man's overdose and Victoria's death.

Surely Detective Trammel knew it, too?

No one questioned why he was there when he walked through the arena of the ER over to the trauma bay. He stopped short when he saw the ER team working with controlled chaos to save the young man's life. He was impressed at how quickly yet efficiently they performed live-saving measures. They'd already inserted a breathing tube and were in the process of giving medication into his stomach to prevent whatever pills he'd taken from being absorbed into his bloodstream.

In the corner of the room, Gloria, the ER nurse who'd been at the triage desk when Emma had been dropped off, stood with her hands over her mouth and tears trailing down her cheeks. He knew all about the helpless guilt of not being able to prevent the tragedy.

But before he could walk over there he caught a glimpse of Detective Trammel on the other side of the room.

Without hesitation, he headed over to where the detective and a uniformed officer were standing, giving the trauma team a wide berth to stay out of their way.

"Detective Trammel," he said with a nod. "I understand you have another pain med overdose?"

The detective scowled. "How did you hear about this case?"

"Through a friend," he acknowledged, refusing to feel guilty for eavesdropping on Cassie's conversation with Gloria. "Do you know what physician's name is listed on the prescription bottle?"

Trammel's expression darkened further. "Look, Dr. Murphy, I can't discuss the details of my investigation with you."

"Can't or won't?" Ryan challenged, refusing to give up. "I'm not asking for a full report on your investigation, I just want to validate the physician's name on the prescription bottle. Was it Oliver Stevenson?"

The uniformed cop standing beside Detective Trammel jerked his head around in surprise, giving away the truth. Ryan couldn't help feeling a surge of satisfaction when Trammel looked irritated for a moment, but then gave a brief nod.

"I knew it," Ryan muttered. Oliver Stevenson was the same physician who'd ordered the pain meds for Victoria. But her surgeon had been a different guy by the name of Dr. Geoff Avery. At the time, that knowledge had haunted him and he'd looked high and low for Stevenson.

Without finding a single trace of him.

"Before you get too excited at the connection,

remember that we weren't able to find this alleged doctor anywhere," Trammel said dryly. "If you recall, the address of his so-called doctor's office turned out to be nothing more than a vacant building at the end of a strip mall outside Madison. And there was no one listed in the state of Wisconsin by that name."

Ryan scowled. "Yeah, I remember. But at least you know this young man's prescription is fraudulent, too. There has to be some sort of group coordinating getting these scripts into the hands of people who are willing to pay for them."

"Maybe, but that doesn't mean we're going to have an easy time tracking down the source of the fraud," Trammel argued. "This could be a legit pain doctor who happened to move to a different office building or it could be someone who has stolen this physician's DEA number."

His brief satisfaction evaporated quickly, because Trammel was right. Ryan found himself leaning toward a stolen DEA number, but how on earth would they prove it? "I could help," he began to offer, but Trammel lifted up his hand to stop him.

"I understand your personal interest in this case, Dr. Murphy, but since I don't tell you how to take care of sick babies, I'd appreciate it if you wouldn't tell me how to run my investigation."

There wasn't a rational argument against his request, so Ryan forced himself to nod before turning away.

"Dr. Murphy?" Trammel called.

He turned to face the detective. "Yes?"

"I will let you know the outcome of our investigation," Trammel assured him, "once we have proof."

"Thanks," he murmured. Ryan knew he'd never be able to find closure related to Victoria's and his unborn son's deaths until he could help bring the perpetrators to justice.

But right now the best way to do that was to allow the detective to do his job. After all, he himself wasn't a cop. Ryan understood that Trammel had resources he didn't.

Ryan carefully made his way back around to the other side of the room to where Gloria was watching the resuscitative efforts being performed on her brother. The fact that she was here at all was unusual, but obviously being a nurse in the ER worked in her favor.

"Is there someone I can call for you?" he asked, his tone full of sympathy.

She slowly shook her head. "No, my parents are outside in the waiting room, but I can't talk to them yet. Not until I know more. Not until I know if Trey's going to be all right."

"What happened?"

Gloria sniffed and swiped at her tears. "He plays sports, football and baseball. I knew he hurt his shoulder late in the football season and was seeing one of the orthopedic surgeons, but he never had surgery, so I thought he was fine. But then one of his friends mentioned how he reinjured that same shoulder playing baseball last weekend. I think he must have been taking pain meds all along without any of us knowing."

Ryan's gut twisted. Trey's story was all too familiar. "Which surgeon?"

"Dr. Francowitz," she said.

Not the same orthopedic surgeon Victoria had used, which wasn't surprising, since orthopedic surgeons who worked on shoulders didn't normally also do Achilles tendons. He glanced back at the young man in the trauma bay, silently willing him to make it.

He couldn't bear the thought of losing another young life to an overdose of narcotic pain medication.

Cassie found a nurse to cover her two patients so she could dash briefly down to the ER to see Trey. When she arrived in the trauma bay it appeared the staff were finishing their resuscitation efforts. The rhythmic beat of Trey's heart on the monitor over his bed was reassuring. She swept her gaze over the room, finding Gloria standing well out of the way, with Ryan at her side.

"Gloria," she said, rushing over to give her friend a hug. "How is he doing?"

"They're getting ready to transfer him up to the ICU," Gloria said, returning her hug.

Cassie glanced up at Ryan with a questioning gaze. She wasn't sure why Ryan had come down here—did he have a previous relationship with Gloria? Was Gloria the nurse he'd been seeing when things hadn't worked out? She tried to squelch the flash of jealousy. "Then his condition has been stabilized, right?"

"Yes, from what I can tell," Ryan agreed.

"They intubated him and gave him charcoal to help get rid of the pills that might be still in his stomach," Gloria said in a low tone. "The biggest question is whether or not he'll wake up. It could be that he's suffered brain damage."

"He's young, Gloria." Cassie put a reassuring arm around her friend's shoulder. "I'm sure he'll be fine."

"I hope so," Gloria said in a strained voice. "He has his whole life ahead of him. He's supposed to attend college in the fall…" Her voice trailed off and her eyes filled with tears.

"I know," Cassie said, glancing up at Ryan helplessly. Ryan didn't offer Gloria physical comfort, which gave

Cassie a small measure of relief. Still, Ryan's reaction to the situation was odd.

They stood for a few minutes until the trauma team wheeled Trey out of the room.

"I guess I better go talk to my parents." Gloria's tone was grim.

Cassie nodded. "I'm sorry, Gloria, but I have to run back upstairs to my patients. I'll check on you again during my lunch hour. In the meantime, keep me updated on how he's doing, okay?"

Gloria sniffed and dabbed her eyes again. "Okay, thanks, Cass. You're a great friend."

Cassie gave her another quick hug before turning away.

"I'll head back upstairs with you," Ryan said, falling into step beside her.

Cassie waited until they were far enough away that Gloria couldn't overhear their conversation. "Do you really think her brother will be all right?"

Ryan hesitated and shrugged. "I honestly don't know. He has youth on his side, and he was given very good medical care. But the result will depend on how long his brain went without oxygen."

Cassie knew he was right. "Such a waste," she said under her breath. "I just don't understand how this kind of thing can happen."

Ryan's gaze was grim. "Me, either."

As they waited for the elevator, she glanced up at him curiously. "Ryan, why did you rush down here, like that?" she asked. "Did you go out with Gloria in the past? Do you know her younger brother?"

He shrugged but didn't meet her gaze. "No, I never dated Gloria and I don't know her brother, Trey. But I do have a special interest in narcotic-overdose cases," he finally said.

He did? Why? Cassie was ridiculously relieved to know he hadn't asked Gloria out, but she found she was more curious than ever. She wanted to ask more about why he cared so much about narcotic-overdose patients but two other staff members joined them, and when the elevator arrived the car was half-filled with people. They all rode together up to the third floor. She led the way into the NNICU, using her badge to get through the door, and then hurried over to Emma's warmer.

"How are Emma and Daniel doing?" she asked Christy, the nurse she'd asked to watch over them. "Any problems?"

"None at all," Christy assured her.

"Good, thanks for covering." Cassie glanced back at Ryan, wondering again why he had such a keen interest in narcotic-overdose patients. And even more strange, why he didn't seem willing to talk about it? Unless seeing Trey's young face had only reminded him of losing his wife?

It wasn't easy to focus on the issues at hand. Ryan's personal life wasn't any of her business. Hadn't she vowed to keep her distance? After all, he'd been the one who'd pulled away after their kiss.

So why was she still so drawn to him? The magnetic pull shimmering between them was so strong she doubted she'd be able to break the invisible bond.

And if she wasn't careful, he'd break her heart. Worse than Evan had.

"How is Daniel doing postextubation?" Ryan asked from behind her.

Once again, her pulse leapt at the husky sound of his voice. "He's doing great," she assured him. She moved away from him toward Daniel's warmer. "It's been about an hour since we pulled the tube. Do you want me to get a set of blood gases?"

"Yes, please." Ryan sat down at the computer and quickly entered the order.

Cassie busied herself with getting the supplies she'd need for the arterial blood gases. She didn't like having to poke the babies for lab work, but she knew the tests were needed to make the right medical decisions.

Thankfully she was able to get the arterial blood on the first try, although listening to Daniel's crying when she poked him wasn't easy. As soon as she'd finished holding pressure on the puncture site, she sent the blood off to the lab and then went over to lift him into her arms.

"There, there, big guy, you're fine. No more ouchies," she promised.

She could feel Ryan's penetrating gaze watching her with Daniel and it took every ounce of willpower she possessed not to turn around to face him, fearing her turbulent emotions would be reflected on her face.

Thankfully the arrival of Daniel's parents broke the tense moment. As Cassie handed over their baby, Ryan gave them a quick update on Daniel's medical status.

Cassie slipped over to Emma's warmer, focusing her attention on the baby girl.

Emma was all alone in the world, just like *she* was. Oh, she had friends, but no family. Her parents had died when she was young and her grandparents had raised her. They'd passed away when she'd been in college. Being alone and vulnerable, she had been easy prey for Evan's fake charm.

Staring down at Emma, she knew she didn't miss

Evan at all. But she missed the babies she hadn't been able to carry to term.

Emma F. Safe Haven was like a miracle dropped into her lap. A chance to have the family she'd always wanted. A chance to start over.

Maybe they weren't bonded by blood. But that didn't matter. The little girl was already the daughter of her heart.

Ryan tried to keep busy, but no matter what he was doing he found himself searching for Cassie. For a brief moment he'd considered telling her the truth about how he'd lost Victoria and his unborn son, but placing his burden on Cassie didn't seem fair. Especially as she was working.

Or maybe he was subconsciously avoiding the horror he might find in Cassie's eyes once she knew the truth.

He spent his downtime searching for Oliver Stevenson on the Wisconsin Department of Regulation and Licensing website, but of course there was no physician listed by that name. Just like there hadn't been three years ago.

Was this guy practicing without a license? Or was he practicing in another state? The DEA number had to be real or the pharmacy wouldn't have filled the script.

But what about out of state? Victoria's prescription had had a Madison address, so he hadn't broadened his search. But now he decided to check the bordering states of Minnesota, Michigan and Illinois. He found a couple of providers by that name, but none of them were pain specialists. Still, he wrote down their names and DEA numbers, determined to ask Trammel to verify if the number on both Trey's and Victoria's prescriptions was a match.

Cassie came over to stand beside him, and he quickly minimized the website. He noticed she glanced briefly at the names he'd written down, and shifted so that he partially blocked her view.

"How's Emma?" he asked, hoping to distract her.

She smiled. "Great. I was wondering if we couldn't start weaning her from the ventilator a bit?"

"I'm not sure that's a good idea," he said, true regret in his tone. "I want to see her come off that vent as much as you do, but I normally don't do much weaning after seven o'clock in the evening."

"I understand," Cassie murmured, her gaze full of obvious disappointment.

"If she's doing this well by tomorrow morning, I'll write the weaning orders," he promised. "That gives her another twenty-four hours of antibiotics."

She forced a smile and nodded. "Okay, that sounds like a good plan. The last thing I want is for her condition to take a turn for the worse."

When she turned away he reached out to grasp her arm, preventing her from leaving. "Have you figured out what your next steps are to becoming a foster parent?"

She glanced down at his hand, and then brought her gaze back up to meet his. "There are twelve classes I need to take once they approve my application."

"Twelve classes? That seems like a lot."

"I know. Too bad all parents don't have to take parenting classes, huh?" she said with a wry smile.

He nodded, thinking about the cases of child abuse they'd seen, thankfully not often.

"I can't sign up for the first class until tomorrow. The website won't accept sign-ups on the weekend," she added. "And I'm hoping that they'll approve my application fast."

"Can you sign up for all twelve classes right away?"

"I'm not sure, but even if I can, it might be too difficult anyway, since I have to work around my schedule or find a way to get off. Although that's not easy during the summer months when everyone else is off."

"Is there anything I can do to help?" he asked.

She shook her head and took a step back, severing the physical connection between them. He instantly missed her warmth. Her smile. Her laughter. "No. This is something I need to do myself."

He watched her walk back over to Emma's warmer, his heart aching with regret. He knew there was a tiny spot in his heart that had remained frozen ever since Victoria's and his son's deaths. He wasn't capable of loving Cassie the way she deserved.

So why did he long for her so desperately?

CHAPTER NINE

THE NEXT MORNING, Cassie woke up feeling energized, full of a new sense of purpose. Normally, she didn't look forward to Mondays—who did? But since it was a weekday, she was able to take the next steps in the process of becoming a foster parent. And even though there was a part of her that knew she was using the process as a way to forget about Ryan, she eagerly booted up her computer.

The sooner she signed up for the classes, the better her chances were of actually getting in.

When she'd read up on being a foster parent, she'd learned that safe-haven babies were able to go through the path from fostering to adopting much quicker than in other cases.

Of course there was always a six-month wait, in case the mother changed her mind.

Cassie couldn't deny that the thought of Emma's mother showing up and requesting custody was depressing. Especially since the baby had gone through narcotic withdrawal.

Still, anything was possible. For now, she needed to focus on the issues at hand, rather than worrying about the what-if scenarios.

As she ate breakfast, Cassie went to the Health and

Human Services website to find the classes she needed. She double-clicked on the first one and prayed that it wasn't already full.

It wasn't and she quickly entered the required fields on the website, letting out a squeal as she hit enter. The hourglass spun in the center of the screen for what seemed like forever, before a message finally popped up on the screen.

"Accepted! I'm accepted in the first class!" Cassie jumped up and danced around her postage-stamp-sized kitchen.

Music blared from her phone, and Cassie danced over, her enthusiasm dimming as she noted the caller was Gloria.

She did her best to hide her elation over being accepted in the first class as she answered. "Hi, Gloria, how are you doing?" By the time she'd left work last night, Trey still hadn't woken up, although the ICU team had put him on a hypothermia protocol to preserve his brain function, much like they did for cardiac-arrest patients.

Trey really was getting the best medical care possible.

"Better this morning. They're going to start bringing Trey's temperature back up," Gloria said. "Once his temperature is within normal range, they'll back off on the sedation and we'll know if he'll wake up or not."

"I know it's hard, but you have to be strong for him and your family, Gloria," Cassie said encouragingly.

"I know. I'm trying," Gloria admitted.

"What do the neurologists think?" she asked.

"They won't say much one way or the other, but based on how young he is, they're cautiously optimistic."

Of course the doctors wouldn't make promises they

couldn't keep, but at the same time they didn't want families to lose hope either. "Do you want me to come and sit with you in the ICU?" she offered.

"No, my parents are here, so there's no need for you to come. I just wanted to give you an update. It's good news they're bringing him out of the hypothermia protocol."

"I agree," she assured her friend. "Keep in touch, Gloria."

"I will."

Cassie disconnected from the call, set her phone aside, and then returned to sit at her kitchen table in front of the computer. Before she could log back in to the site, her phone sang again.

This time Ryan's name popped up on the screen and despite the way her pulse jumped, she hesitated for a moment, gathering her defenses, before answering. "Hello?"

"Good morning, Cassandra. How are you?"

She strove to keep her voice steady. "I'm fine, Ryan, how are you? I hope your night on call wasn't too bad."

"I managed to get a little over four hours of sleep, so I can't complain."

"That's good." Their conversation was awkward, stilted, and she wished he'd get to the point already. She couldn't believe he'd called just to ask how she was doing.

"We started weaning Emma this morning," he said, breaking the strained silence. "I don't know if she'll be extubated today or tomorrow, but hopefully soon."

"That's wonderful news," she said, thrilled beyond belief that the baby was improving. "That must mean her lungs still look good."

"Clear as a bell," he said, with a hint of humor in his

voice. He was so attractive when he smiled although really he didn't smile often enough. "We caught the aspiration quickly enough to prevent pneumonia."

"I'm so glad." Cassie imagined how great it would be once Emma's breathing tube was removed and she could finally hold the baby in her arms. Even though she was off today, she was tempted to go in just to hold Emma.

"Did you sign up for the foster-care classes?" he asked.

"Yes, the first class is Thursday and thankfully I'm off work, so that's good. I was about to sign up for the other classes, too, but Gloria called to let me know that they're warming Trey up today. They put him on the hypothermia protocol yesterday after he got up to the ICU to prevent his brain from swelling."

"I know. I checked on him late last night, too," Ryan admitted. "Once he's warmed up, they'll ease off on the sedation to see if he'll wake up."

She was tempted to ask him why he cared so much about Trey's overdose, but she doubted he'd tell her over the phone something he wouldn't tell her in person.

Besides, she wasn't going to dwell on the details regarding his personal life, right? Right.

"Will you let me know if Emma gets extubated?" she asked, changing the focus of the conversation back to the baby.

"Absolutely. Are you free for dinner?" he asked. "There's a great Italian place overlooking Lake Michigan. We won't see the sunset since the lake is obviously in the east, but it's still an amazing view."

She pulled her phone away from her ear and stared at it in confusion. Why was he asking her out? Especially after the way he'd pulled away after their kiss?

Despite how badly she wanted to say yes, she forced

herself to rein in her emotions. "I don't think so," she said. "You're the one who told me that you weren't ready for a relationship."

"I know, but I can't stop thinking about you, Cassandra," he admitted in a low, gravelly tone that sent shivers of awareness dancing down her spine. "For the first time since Victoria died, I feel alive. And I'm pretty sure it's because of you."

Her heart squeezed in her chest and she drew in a harsh breath. She knew she should refuse, if for no other reason than to protect her heart, but at the same time it was difficult to ignore his request. Did she dare believe that something more permanent might grow between them? Would her being a foster mother be enough for him someday? Or would he want children of his own?

"Cassie, please," he said, when she didn't answer. "Say you'll have dinner with me?"

Her heart spoke before her brain could overrule her snap decision. "Yes, Ryan," she said huskily. "I'd be happy to have dinner with you."

"Thanks," he murmured. "I'd like to bring the convertible since the weather is nice."

"I'd like that," she agreed, ignoring the tiny niggle of doubt that this was a good decision.

"Sounds good. I'll pick you up at seven o'clock."

"All right. See you then." Cassie disconnected and then buried her face in her hands.

What was she doing? Going out with Ryan again was not part of her plan. Hadn't she told herself not to risk getting emotionally involved with him?

Yes, but obviously she was too late.

She was already emotionally involved with Ryan, whether she wanted to be or not.

She cared about him, far too much.

* * *

Ryan knew he was grinning like a fool when he walked back into the NNICU to check on Emma's condition, but he didn't care if the staff stared at him.

Cassie was giving him another chance. Only this time he had to figure out a way not to blow it.

A feat easier said than done.

"She's tolerating the new vent settings very well," Claire said when he approached Emma's warmer. The speculation in the nurse's gaze made him wonder if the rumors had already started about him seeing Cassie.

Oddly enough, the idea didn't bring on a wave of desperate panic the way it had after the Shana fiasco.

"I'm glad to hear it," he said, glancing down at the arterial blood gas results Claire had given him. "Follow the weaning pattern for the rest of the day, but call me before you leave for the day."

"Okay," Claire agreed. "No big plans today?"

She was fishing for information, but instead of becoming annoyed he simply smiled. "Talk to you later."

He headed home, maintaining his good mood, happiness all but oozing from his pores. Knowing that he would see Cassie later that evening was enough to keep him motivated.

Because he hadn't lied to her about the effect she had on him. He felt alive, and couldn't help wondering if that small frozen part of his heart was beginning to thaw.

Because of her. And Emma, too.

He pulled into the driveway, glad to see the Realtor had already posted a For Sale sign in his front yard. He knew better than to get his hopes up that he'd manage to sell the albatross quickly, but his good mood refused to be dampened.

For months now he'd put off the job of packing up

the things he didn't need. Victoria's family had taken her things, along with the baby furniture, a long time ago, so only his belongings were left.

Way more things that one man needed, that was for sure.

Ryan forced himself to head to the gym before tackling the job of packing up the items he didn't need. The Realtor, Andrea, told him the less clutter in his house, the better it would look to prospective buyers.

He had no reason not to believe her.

A few hours later, after he'd packed four large boxes, his phone rang. He picked it up, recognizing Trammel's number.

"This is Ryan Murphy," he said by way of greeting.

"Dr. Murphy, did you leave a message asking me to call?" Trammel asked.

"Yes, I did," Ryan admitted. Holding the phone to his ear, he crossed the kitchen for the list he'd made earlier. "I did a search on physicians named Oliver Stevenson in neighboring states. It's possible one of their DEA numbers matches the one used to fill the prescriptions."

"Just the neighboring states?" Trammel asked dryly. "I'm surprised you didn't check all fifty."

"I will if you'd like," Ryan offered, even though he knew the detective was kidding. Trammel didn't understand how badly he wanted to find the identity of the person who was behind these fake scripts.

"I'll take this list for now," Trammel said, "but I have to be honest—it's possible the doctor could be from anywhere."

Trammel wasn't telling him anything he hadn't already considered himself. But they had to start somewhere and it made sense that the DEA number was from a physician close by, rather than on the other side of the country.

"I'll scan the list and email it to you," Ryan said. "Give me your email address."

Trammel rattled it off for him, while he scribbled the information on a scrap piece of paper.

"I'll let you know if anything pops from the list," Detective Trammel said.

Ryan knew that Trammel was making an effort to include him in as much of the investigation as possible and he was deeply grateful. "I appreciate that, Detective."

"Just remember to leave the investigating to me," Trammel added wryly.

He couldn't help but grin. "I'll try."

After disconnecting from the call, Ryan decided to go through his bedroom closet before ending his packing for the day. He grimaced when he saw the number of suits he had, along with all the golf pants and shirts.

He hadn't hit a single golf ball since Victoria's death. And, truthfully, he didn't miss it. Golf was part of the life he'd wanted nothing more to do with after losing his unborn son. So he started with those items first, putting them in a bag that he'd give to the Salvation Army.

As he worked, a small brown folder fell out from one of the pockets of his golf pants. He went still, realizing what the small envelope contained.

A copy of the sonogram photo of his unborn son.

His fingers shook a bit as he picked it up and opened the metal clasp. He pulled out the small square of radiology film and held it up to the light.

The tiny body of his son was easy to see.

His throat tightened and the old familiar guilt squeezed his heart. His marriage to Victoria hadn't been great, but he'd wanted this baby so badly. It had been difficult to accept that his son hadn't been given a fair chance to live.

His heart squeezed in his chest, but for the first time in years he wasn't consumed with anger at the unfairness of it all—mad at Victoria for being selfish and at himself for being blind and stupid.

Instead, he grew more determined than ever to make sure Emma was provided the chance to grow and thrive in a way his son hadn't been able to.

Cassie vacillated between looking forward to dinner with Ryan and wondering if she should cancel.

She'd spent the morning signing up for as many foster-care classes as she could with her current work schedule. When she was finished with that, she wrote down the dates and times of the other classes and headed to Cedar Bluff Hospital to talk to her boss.

There had to be a way to switch shifts with someone or to take vacation time. As a last resort, she could take a personal unpaid leave of absence, but even that would have to be approved by her boss and by Human Resources.

When she arrived, Michelle, the nurse manager for the neonatal ICU, was tied up in a meeting, so she headed down to the ICU to check on Gloria.

"How's Trey?" she asked.

"Oh, Cass, he's starting to wake up," Gloria said, hope shining from her eyes. "He's moving all his extremities but isn't quite following commands yet."

"Give him time, Gloria," she urged, giving her friend a hug. "I have a good feeling about this."

"Me, too," Gloria admitted. "Last night was the longest night of my life, but today things are looking up. If he begins to follow commands, I'll feel even better."

"He will." Cassie wouldn't allow her friend to worry about the worst-case scenario. "Do you mind if I sit here with you for a few minutes? I'm waiting for Michelle to come out of a meeting."

"No problem." Gloria dropped into the waiting room chair and Cassie sat down beside her. "Why do you need to talk to your boss?"

Cassie explained about how there were six foster-care classes that clashed with her schedule.

"I can't believe you're going to be a single mother," Gloria said, a tiny frown puckering her brow.

"You don't think it's a good idea," Cassie said, reading her body language. "But trust me, I know what I want."

"You'll be a great mother, Cass, it's just—don't you want to wait until you have a husband? Maybe give birth to a child of your own?"

Cassie took a deep breath. "I need surgery before I can even try to get pregnant again and even then there's a good chance I won't be able to carry a baby to term," she admitted, ignoring the way Ryan's face flashed into her mind at the thought of getting married again. "So, you see, this is the right thing to do. Emma needs me, Gloria, as much as I need her."

Gloria's expression softened. "I can tell you love her already, so if that's what you want to do, then any man who falls in love with you will just have to deal with it, right?"

An image of Ryan holding Daniel flashed in her mind. He obviously adored babies. Had admitted he wanted children of his own. But did that extend to fostering? She had no idea. Her phone vibrated. She'd turned off the ringer while in the hospital and recognized the hospital number. "Sorry, Gloria, I think this is Michelle."

"Go and meet with her. We'll chat later."

Cassie answered the phone. The unit clerk in the neonatal unit let her know that Michelle had returned. "Don't let her run off. I'll be right there."

She took the stairs up to the third floor, unwilling to wait for the elevator. Michelle was in her office and surprisingly supportive of the schedule changes Cassie needed.

Once she had everything set, Cassie hurried back home to sign up for the remaining classes. But this time, when she tried to register, the system spit back a message.

Your status as a potential foster parent has been temporarily suspended. Please make an appointment with our administrator as soon as possible.

Cassie stared at the message in horror. What was going on? She rummaged through her purse, looking for Mr. Davies's card for his number. She called and had to navigate through several auto voice-mail prompts before she was able to finally speak to a real person.

"My name is Cassandra Jordan and I've just been notified that my status as a potential foster parent has been temporarily suspended," she said with a hitch in her tone. She was trying very hard not to cry, hoping that this was just some horrible mistake.

"Oh, yes, I'm sorry, but that is correct," the woman said in a cheerful tone that made Cassie want to scream with frustration.

"Would you mind telling me why?" Cassie asked.

"Is there some form I forgot to fill out? Or some piece of information you need to clear this up?"

"Well, it appears that you listed a single-bedroom apartment as your current residence," the woman said. "I'm afraid we prefer that our foster children are given the opportunity to have their own rooms. However, we can make exceptions. You need approval from Mr. Davies."

"Two bedrooms," Cassie repeated, trying to absorb the implications. "Okay, I can understand that and actually I have a message in to my landlord to inquire if a two-bedroom apartment is available. Could I talk to Mr. Davies? I'd like an exception if possible so I can continue the process."

"I'm sorry, Mr. Davies is out of town for the rest of the week. He won't be back until next Monday. But I'll let him know that you called."

A week? But the classes started in three days! Cassie felt her phone slip from her fingers and crash to the table.

What if she lost the chance to be Emma's foster mother because of this delay? Especially since Emma was getting better.

Her dream of being Emma's mother cracked and then shattered. Tears burned her eyes and she buried her face in her hands, succumbing to an overwhelming wave of despair.

CHAPTER TEN

RYAN COULDN'T BELIEVE how nervous he was as he approached Cassie's apartment door. He'd managed to catch someone coming out, so he hadn't needed to buzz her apartment to get in.

He straightened his shoulders and took a deep breath. He knew he was overreacting, that they were just having dinner, but at the same time he didn't want to mess up.

He rapped lightly on Cassie's door, resisting the urge to double-check that his shirt was tucked in. He'd dressed casually in a black pair of dress pants and a blue polo shirt. Maybe he should have chosen a button-down shirt and a tie?

The seconds ticked by with no response, so he frowned and knocked again, louder. After several more seconds the door opened a crack.

"I'm sorry, Ryan, but I'm not going to be able to keep our date," Cassie said in a low voice.

His instincts went on red alert, and not just because she was wearing cut-off jeans and T-shirt. Her face was blotchy and her eyes were swollen. "What's wrong? Have you been crying?"

She shook her head and sniffled loudly. "It's nothing, really. I'm sorry about dinner. I'll take a rain-check, okay?"

She stepped back and started to shut the door, but he quickly slapped his hand against it, holding firm. "Cassie, please, talk to me. I don't care about dinner, but it's obvious you're upset. Please, tell me what's wrong."

With a listless shrug she stepped back farther and let go of the door. He pushed it open wider and then stepped inside, closing the door behind him.

Cassie stood with her arms crossed defensively over her chest. "I'm sorry, I should have called before you made the trip out here," she said, avoiding his gaze.

"I don't care about our plans, but I do wish you'd called me earlier, because then I could have been here for you."

She shrugged again and turned away.

He could barely stand to see her so torn up like this. This couldn't be about Emma's condition since he knew the baby was doing all right. Claire had called to let him know that Emma had tolerated her weaning fairly well, but looked as if she was getting tired, so he'd decided to let her rest overnight and then work on weaning her again in the morning.

So what had happened to make Cassie cry?

"Please, tell me what happened. Didn't you get into the foster-care classes? Or did your boss refuse to work with your schedule?"

She bit her lower lip and then turned to face him. "I don't think I can take the classes until I speak with the administrator and he's out of the office until next week," she said bluntly, her eyes filling with tears. "Which means, I may not be approved in time to be there for Emma."

He couldn't help it, he crossed over and drew her against him in a reassuring hug. She seemed to resist for a moment but then buried her face against his chest.

"I'm so sorry," he murmured, thinking it wasn't fair that her world was on hold until some administrator came back from his vacation.

"I know I'm being ridiculous but I wanted so badly to be Emma's mother," she said, her voice muffled against his shirt. "I should just be happy that Emma will go to a good home, but I'm selfish, Ryan. I wanted her to be with me."

"Shh, Cassie, you're not selfish," he said, resting his cheek against her hair and smoothing his hand down her back. Even though he was all too aware of her curves pressed against him, he kept his touch gentle, reassuring. "It's clear you two belong together. I wish there was something I could do to help."

"Thanks, Ryan, but there isn't anything we can do until next week. Which will probably be too late." She drew back a little to look up into his eyes. "But it's nice to know you care enough to try."

He did care, far more than he should. He wanted to give Cassie everything and it was frustrating to have this issue outside his control. "Don't give up," he urged in a low voice. "You're already signed up for the first class this week anyway, right?" When she gave a hesitant nod, he continued, "Then go and we'll get this cleared up next week. It will all be fine, you'll see. Besides, it's clear to anyone with eyes in their head that you and Emma belong together."

Her tremulous smile tugged at his heart. "Sure, why not?" Then she tipped her head to the side, her gaze quizzical. "Do you really think we belong together?"

"Yes, I do," he said with conviction. "Not everyone has the mothering instincts that you do, Cassie. Every time I see you holding Emma, you take my breath away."

"Oh, Ryan," she murmured. "I think that's the nicest thing anyone has ever said to me. Thank you."

His heart twisted in his chest and for a moment he wanted to smack that cheating ex-husband of hers for hurting her. He lowered his head to kiss her cheek, but she surprised him by coming up on tiptoe to press her mouth against his.

He tried to offer comfort, but Cassie's lips teased his until he opened his mouth and deepened their kiss. The way she melted into his arms, molding herself against him, made tiny stars explode behind his eyes.

Nothing had ever felt so right as having Cassie in his arms. His body was on fire and soon the flames were so stoked he wasn't capable of thinking at all.

Cassie knew that she'd broken her no-kissing rule in a big way but couldn't seem to find the energy to pull away. Ryan had been there for her emotionally when she'd needed him most, far different than Evan had ever been.

And when he deepened the kiss, exploring her mouth so intently, she wrapped her arms around his neck and hung on as her knees threatened to buckle.

Every nerve in her body hummed with sizzling awareness and she returned his kiss, letting all the passion she'd once buried deep inside burst free.

This was what she'd been missing from her life. For the life of her, she couldn't remember why she'd felt the need to stay away from him. Not when being in his arms felt so right.

Ryan lifted his head, his blue eyes glittering down at her with fierce intensity. "Cassandra, you're so beautiful," he murmured. He pressed his lips against the curve of her jaw, and then trailed a path down the side of her neck, making her shiver with anticipation.

"You make me feel beautiful," she whispered, and then gasped when he pulled her closer and she could feel the hard ridge of his erection.

Need zinged through her bloodstream and she found herself squirming against him, desperate to get closer still. His musky scent went straight to her head, more potent than a shot of liquor. What was Ryan doing to her? She'd never felt like this before.

"Cassandra," he murmured in a deep voice tinged with the same desperation she felt. "If you don't want to do this, tell me now."

By *this*, she knew he meant making love.

She hadn't been intimate with a man in well over a year and a half. In fact, she'd had no trouble staying celibate.

Until now.

"I do want this, Ryan," she said, drowning in his fierce blue eyes. "I want you."

A smile tugged at the corner of his mouth. "Thank God," he muttered, covering her mouth in another searing kiss. When he lifted his head to breathe, he added, "I'm glad to know I'm not in this alone."

The hint of vulnerability in his tone made her fall even more completely under his spell. She kissed the side of his neck, and then let out a squeal when he swept her legs out from under her.

He carried her into her bedroom before gently setting her on her feet. Before she could blink, he'd stripped off his shirt and then reached for the hem of her T-shirt.

She wished she'd dressed nicer for him, but as he peeled her shirt up and over her head, his gaze feasting on her breasts encased in a pink lacy bra, she realized it didn't matter. His fingers found the button on her ragged shorts and, with deft movements, he pushed them down to the floor so she could step out of them.

She fumbled with his belt and in a flash of impatience he whipped it off and took off his slacks. He wore black boxers that barely covered his arousal and for the first time since he'd kissed her she felt a sliver of unease.

Not for what they were about to do but whether or not she'd live up to his expectations.

Sex with her ex hadn't exactly been earth-shattering.

"Cassie, tell me what's going on in your head," Ryan urged, drawing her close. "Is something wrong? Have you changed your mind?"

She shoved away thoughts of her ex with an effort. "I haven't been with a man in a long time," she confessed. "I'm afraid of disappointing you."

"Trust me, there's no possible way in the world you could disappoint me. You're the warmth I desperately need," he murmured, his gaze serious. "And it's been a long time for me, too." He cupped her face in his hands and kissed her reverently and then with frank desire. He stripped away her bra and panties and gently drew her toward the bed.

She ran her hands over his taut muscles, reveling in the light dusting of hair sprinkled across his chest. He lowered his head to her breasts, lavishing his attention on one nipple and then the other, intensifying the ache between her legs to the point she wasn't sure she could stand the sensual torture much longer.

"Please," she begged, wrapping her legs around his waist. "Now. I want you inside me now!"

Ryan suckled her taut nipple even as he ran his hand down her abdomen, probing gently between her legs.

"Please," she said again, gasping as pleasure washed over her when he stroked his finger over her clit.

"You're so hot and ready for me," he murmured, drawing back to stare at her flushed body. She reached up for him, but he was busy tearing open a small foil packet.

She wanted to protest, even though she knew how foolish that would be. So she watched as he slid the condom on and then lifted her hips in a silent invitation.

He spread her legs wider and guided himself toward her moist entrance. She expected discomfort, but, surprisingly, there wasn't any pain as he thrust deep.

Ryan let out a low groan and began to move back and forth in gentle thrusts that soon became more and more urgent.

"Yes," she whispered, straining against him. "Oh, yes."

"Cassandra…" His voice broke on her name as he quickened his pace, gathering her even more tightly against him. "Come with me," he begged, before lowering his mouth to capture hers in a deep kiss.

A kaleidoscope of color burst behind her eyes as wave after wave of pleasure shuddered through her. His big body shook against hers, too, and she surrendered to him, reveling in the intensity of the moment, realizing that nothing had ever felt so right.

Ryan shifted onto his back, drawing Cassie over his chest and anchoring her with an arm across her waist, trying to drag badly needed oxygen into his lungs.

Incredible. Making love with Cassie had been absolutely incredible.

His heart thudded in his chest, slowly returning to a normal rhythm. Cassie's body lay sated and limp against him and he summoned the energy to trail his hand over her satiny-smooth skin. He couldn't help but smile, wishing they could stay like this forever.

"Wow," she murmured.

"Yeah, wow," he agreed.

She snuggled against him and amazingly he felt the stirring of desire. Apparently he hadn't had enough of Cassie.

Would he ever get enough of her?

A fissure of panic skated down his spine. He tried to ignore it, but it wasn't easy. Being with Cassie had been amazing.

Yet she deserved so much more than a quick release.

He told himself this wasn't anything like what he'd had with Shana, but the old self-doubts came marching back.

"Thanks for not being upset with me," she said, craning her neck to look up at him.

He frowned. "Upset? About this? No way."

She laughed and shook her head. "About falling apart and completely forgetting about our dinner date."

He wasn't at all angry with her about that. He knew how much being a foster parent for Emma meant to her.

"Cassie, it's going to be all right, you'll see." He kissed the top of her head, liking the way he could feel her smile against his chest. "And who knows, you might have children of your own someday."

There was a long pause and he sensed there was something he'd said wrong, but before he could try to backtrack his phone jangled, interrupting the moment.

He groaned inwardly, tempted to ignore it. But what if the call was from the hospital? Cassie must have had the same thought because she pulled away, wrapping the sheet around her as she moved to the side of the bed, giving him plenty of room to get up.

He didn't want to leave her, but the phone kept ringing so he rolled off the bed and knelt next to his discarded clothes, searching for the stupid thing.

When he saw Detective Trammel's number, his pulse jumped. "This is Ryan Murphy," he said.

"Dr. Murphy, I wanted to tell you we got a hit on one of the names you gave us," Trammel said, getting straight to the point. "The DEA number of Oliver Stevenson from Chicago, Illinois matches the one used on the prescription used by Trey Reynolds."

"It does?" Ryan sank down on the edge of Cassie's bed, uncaring that he was still stark naked. He'd been waiting so long for a clue related to Victoria's death.

And now they finally had one.

"Where's Stevenson's office?" Ryan demanded. "We need to get there before he closes up his pill shop and moves on."

"Whoa, there, not so fast," Trammel interrupted. "You aren't doing anything, understand? So help me, Murphy, if you interfere with my investigation, I'll cut you out of the information loop so fast your head will spin."

Ryan bit back a scathing retort, unwilling to make Trammel any angrier than he already was. He was fortunate that the detective even bothered to keep him abreast of the investigation at all, and he knew the older man wouldn't hesitate to follow through on his threat.

"I won't interfere with your investigation," Ryan said, forcing the words past his tight throat. He glanced over to find Cassie's intense gaze boring into his, unspoken questions reflected in her eyes, and his stomach dropped to the soles of his feet. He'd been so glad to hear from the detective that he'd forgotten about the fact that Cassie was listening to him. "Thanks for calling, Detective."

"You're welcome," Trammel said grudgingly.

Ryan disconnected from the call and tossed his phone on the bed.

"Detective? What was that about?" she asked, holding the sheet protectively against her chest. "Why would you interfere with a police investigation?"

Ryan grimaced, knowing it was well past time to tell her the truth. He pulled on his boxers, wishing he'd let Trammel's call go to his voice mail.

"Ryan?"

He let out a heavy breath. "Remember when I told you I had a personal interest in overdose cases?"

She nodded, taking a step backward as if needing to put more space between them. He wanted to cross over to her and pull her into his arms, but forced himself to stay where he was.

"I was interested in what happened to Gloria's brother Trey because my wife died of a narcotic overdose."

Cassie put her hand to her chest, her gaze full of compassion. "Accidental? Or on purpose?" she asked.

He raked his fingers through his hair, wishing he'd picked a better time to have this conversation. Talk about a buzzkill. "Accidental, according to the medical examiner. And I don't think Victoria would have taken her own life."

"Oh, Ryan, that must have been horrible for you." Her brown eyes were full of compassion, an emotion he didn't deserve.

"Don't," he said harshly, grabbing his pants and stepping into them. "You don't understand. It doesn't matter what the ME decided, because her death was completely my fault."

She stared at him for a long moment. "I don't understand," she whispered.

He shook his head, knowing he should tell her the rest but unable to get the words past his throat.

He never talked about Victoria or the loss of his unborn son. Especially not to other women. Even his buddy Simon only knew the watered-down version.

He couldn't do it.

"I have to go." Ryan knew that if he didn't leave now he'd tell her everything, only to see something worse than compassion in Cassie's eyes.

Condemnation. For the role he'd played in his son's death.

She stared at him without saying a word as he finished getting dressed. "Take care," he said, before walking out of the bedroom door.

He didn't hear a response, not that he blamed her. After all, he'd ruined their perfect evening.

And she didn't even know the worst about him yet.

Walking away wasn't easy. He cared about Cassie, too much. And as he left he realized that, despite everything, the small part of his heart that he'd thought frozen was aching painfully now.

CHAPTER ELEVEN

CASSIE SPENT A horribly restless night on her sofa, before dragging herself upright the moment the sun came up over the horizon.

So much had happened last night and she was still struggling to understand exactly why things had deteriorated so quickly after the most incredible lovemaking she'd ever experienced in her entire life. She'd felt so close to Ryan, had been about to confide about her miscarriages and her inability to have children—until his phone had rung. At first she'd thought it was the hospital, but had then realized he'd been talking to the detective who was investigating Trey's overdose.

She'd felt terrible for him, knowing that he'd lost his wife to a narcotic overdose. No wonder he'd gone flying down to the ER when he'd heard about Trey. His actions now made perfect sense.

He blamed himself, yet wouldn't tell her why.

Knowing he couldn't confide in her made her wonder if he was holding back because he knew the truth was something she might not be able to handle.

Nausea swirled in her belly. Maybe it was better that she hadn't confided her deepest secret. After watching him with Daniel and hearing him admit that he wanted kids someday, she knew that her medical issues would be a stumbling block. Oh, sure, he might convince himself that it didn't matter until at some point he'd keenly regret not being able to father his own child.

She never should have made love with him, even though that intimacy had only emphasized how deeply she cared about him. Clearly he had the power to hurt her far worse than Evan ever had.

The sick feeling in her stomach grew worse, but she did her best to ignore it. She forced herself to make a slice of toast, hoping the bit of food would help make her feel better.

She wasn't normally the type to skip meals, but she hadn't eaten anything for dinner last night and now could barely face breakfast. This was ridiculous; it wasn't as if anyone had died. Okay, maybe she'd jumped the gun by making love with Ryan when there was so much they obviously didn't know about each other, but at least Emma was getting better.

She needed to snap out of it, pull herself together.

She had plenty of things she could do to take her mind off her problems. It wasn't like her to wallow in self-pity so she forced herself to finish her toast, trying not to think about how much the bread tasted like cardboard. At least the nauseous feeling in her stomach subsided a bit.

After taking a shower, she felt a little more human, enough to face the day, anyway. She needed to do something productive to fill the hours between now and the start of her shift at three o'clock that afternoon.

She decided to call the apartment manager again and thankfully this time he answered. "Hey, Cassie, sorry I didn't get back to you yesterday."

"That's okay. Do you have a two-bedroom apartment available?"

"Not right now. I have several one bedrooms open, but for some reason the two-bedroom apartments go fast. I'll know more in a few months."

A few months? She tried not to succumb to a deep stab of disappointment. "Will you please let me know as soon as a two-bedroom unit becomes available?"

"Sure thing," he promised.

She set her phone aside, wishing there was more she could do to break down the obstacles standing between her and Emma. When her phone rang a short time later she thought for sure it was Ryan, calling to apologize. But her bubble of hope deflated, followed by a twinge of guilt, when she recognized Gloria's number on the screen.

"Hi, Gloria, how is Trey doing?" she said.

"Trey woke up this morning, Cass. He woke up!" Her friend's enthusiasm was contagious.

"Oh, Gloria, that's wonderful news! I'm so happy for you and your family."

"I'm ecstatic, too, believe me. I know Detective Trammel will want to talk to him about where he got the prescription, but that's the least of our worries now. No matter what happens, he'll be fine."

"I know what you mean," Cassie said with heartfelt sympathy. She decided not to mention Ryan's participation in Trey's prescription investigation. "Getting into a little trouble isn't anything compared with almost dying."

"Would you be willing to meet me for lunch?" Gloria asked. "I'm going to head home to shower and change. I'm too keyed up to sleep."

"Of course I'll have lunch with you," Cassie agreed. "Do you want me to come to your apartment? We can walk to the Sunshine Café, it's not too far. We can sit outside and enjoy the day."

"Perfect," Gloria said. "How about you head over here in about an hour?"

"Sure, see you then," she agreed. Since she had an hour to kill, she opened her notebook computer and began searching for houses in the Cedar Bluff area. Most of the homes were well beyond her price range, making her wince. Borrowing against her retirement fund wasn't going to help if she couldn't afford to make the monthly mortgage payments.

She regretted now that she'd refused the small settlement Evan had tried to give her during their divorce. Her lawyer tried to tell her to take the money, but she'd only taken enough to cover the legal fees and nothing more.

Thrusting the useless wish aside, she stumbled on a small townhouse that was for sale at a reasonable price. She stared at the property, her heart pounding with excitement. This could be the break she'd been waiting for.

She quickly jotted down the address, determined to swing by the place on her way to work. Then she scrolled down to the mortgage calculator, entering round numbers for an estimate of what she'd need to buy the place.

The projected mortgage plus property taxes was only about two hundred more than what she was paying in rent now.

She could do this. She really might be able to do this!

Cassie called the real estate agent listed on the website and left a message, stating she wanted to see the property as soon as possible. Then she clicked through the photos again, thinking that the townhouse was the perfect place for her and Emma.

And she had no doubt she'd be able to convince Mr. Davies to make an exception for her.

As she headed over to Gloria's building, she battled the need to call Ryan to share her good news.

But she didn't.

The excitement of being Emma's foster mother paled when she realized just how much she'd come to depend on Ryan's emotional support.

And how much she missed his support now that it was gone.

Ryan finished packing the last box in the back of his buddy's pickup truck, swiping a hand over his forehead in relief. Once this load had been hauled away, he'd be one step closer to getting rid of the albatross around his neck.

Simon came around the pickup to meet Ryan. "Is that everything?"

"Yes. Are you sure you don't mind taking it for me? I'd be happy to make the run over there myself."

"No problem." Simon waved away his offer. "Let me know if you need anything else."

"I don't, unless you know someone who wants to buy this place," he said wryly.

Simon made a face. "Sorry, man, but Holly's pregnant again and this place isn't exactly child-friendly."

Ryan couldn't blame his buddy considering they already had a three-year-old son who was constantly getting into everything. "Never mind. Thanks again."

"Okay, see you later."

Ryan watched as Simon jumped into the cab of the pickup truck, which slowly lumbered away.

Finishing up with the house had kept his mind busy, but now that he had the rest of the day stretching before him, thoughts of Cassie came flooding back. He'd come close to calling her at least a dozen times that morning, and the urge to do so again was strong.

He wanted to apologize for walking away, although at the same time he knew he'd wouldn't be able to live with himself until he'd told her the truth. The entire truth.

When had he become so dependent on Cassie to get through the day?

Since Emma. The safe-haven baby had been the catalyst to draw them together.

But his past was keeping them apart.

Trammel had called to let him know that they were still trying to track down the Oliver Stevenson from Illinois. Interestingly enough, the address listed on Trey's oxycodone prescription was also an abandoned office building in yet another strip mall just over the Wisconsin/Illinois border. Ryan was depressed that they'd hit another dead end.

Thankfully Trammel was like a dog with a bone, determined to get to the bottom of where exactly the prescription had come from.

Since Trammel didn't need his help, his thoughts swirled back to Cassie. The memory of their lovemaking kept looping over and over again in his mind, making him want nothing more than to have her again. He knew she'd been with him, too, begging for him to take her. Their lovemaking had been an experience that had pretty much blown him away.

Stop it, he told himself firmly. No matter how much he wanted Cassie, he'd been the one to walk away. He'd taken the easy way out, too cowardly to tell her the truth.

Would she give him a second chance? Even though he didn't deserve it?

And what if her feelings changed once she knew the real him?

Ryan's head pounded with indecision. He showered, shaved and changed his clothes, before reaching for his phone. They needed to be able to work together so he sucked in a deep breath and called Cassie. When she didn't answer, he decided against leaving a voice mail message.

Really, it would be better to talk to her in person. Without giving himself a chance to think too much, he headed out to the convertible.

With any luck, she'd be at her apartment.

But, of course, she didn't answer the door. Dejected, he turned away, wondering if she was avoiding him.

He didn't want to go back home, and since it was close to lunchtime he decided to stop and grab something to eat. Driving past the Sunshine Café, he did a double take when he saw Cassie standing next to Gloria as they waited for a table to be cleared. She looked happy, even laughing at something Gloria had said.

His stomach clenched painfully as he realized Cassie was doing fine without him. She wasn't upset about the way he'd left last night after all.

He forced himself to face the truth. That she might not be as emotionally involved in what had transpired between them.

Not the same way he'd been.

Cassie caught a glimpse of Ryan's red convertible, but before she could move, either toward him or away from him, he was gone.

There was no reason to be disappointed. He'd walked away last night and clearly didn't plan to apologize anytime soon.

And maybe putting distance between them was for the best.

While she and Gloria waited for their table to be cleared, she subtly checked her phone, hoping the real estate agent who had listed the townhouse had called her back.

Andrea Langley hadn't responded, but Cassie did find a missed call from Ryan.

She stared at the screen in shock. And despite her earlier vow to stay away from him, a warm glow spread through her at the fact that he'd tried to get in touch with her.

Maybe he did want to apologize after all. And if she was honest, she'd admit that Ryan wasn't the only one with secrets. Maybe they needed to clear the air between them once and for all.

"Hello, Cass, are you listening?" Gloria said in exasperation.

"What? Oh, sorry. What did you say?"

Gloria rolled her eyes. "I asked how our safe-haven baby was doing."

"She's had a rough couple of days, but she's doing better," Cassie said. She leaned forward and propped her elbows on the table. "Remember I told you how I'm trying to become a foster parent? Turns out I need a two-bedroom place or to get special approval from the administrator, first."

Gloria's jaw dropped open. "You're kidding."

"Nope, and, worse, the administrator is out of the office until next week. There aren't any two-bedroom apartments open at our place, so I've been scouring websites for potential houses. Right now, there isn't much out there that I can afford."

"Maybe you should hold off, Cass," Gloria said, her

eyes reflecting her concern. "Seems drastic to do all this when you don't know for sure you'll even have the chance to take care of Emma."

Cassie frowned, dejected by her friend's doom-and-gloom attitude. "Important things are never easy," she said, glancing down at her menu. Ironically, her appetite had returned with a vengeance. "Hmm, the grilled chicken sandwich looks awesome."

"It sure does. I should have a salad, but what the heck. Let's go for it." Gloria shoved her menu aside, as if just looking at it would change her mind.

"Okay. And I can vouch for the homemade chips, they're amazing."

"Really?" Gloria raised a brow. "I didn't realize you've eaten here before."

Cassie blushed, remembering the burger she'd had with Ryan. "Just once," she said. "Although I'm not sure why we haven't come here more often. This café is close enough to our apartment building."

Her phone rang and she pulled it out of her lap, her heart racing when she recognized the number of the Realtor. "Sorry, Gloria, I have to take this," she said hastily.

"Hello, this is Cassandra Jordan," she answered, rising to her feet and moving off to the side so she wouldn't bother anyone.

"Andrea Langley. I understand you're interested in seeing the townhouse on Lavender Drive?"

"Yes, I am," Cassie said firmly. "Can we set up a time to view it as soon as possible?"

"Yes. How about three o'clock this afternoon?"

Cassie's heart sank. "I start work at three. Could we meet at two instead?"

"Sure. I'll switch things around so I can meet you there at two o'clock."

"Great, thanks." Cassie disconnected from the call, tempted to do another little happy dance.

She managed to restrain herself, but as she turned back toward Gloria she caught a glimpse of Lydia, the cane lady.

It was starting to be uncanny the way she kept bumping into this woman, and Cassie headed over with steely determination.

"Hello, Ms. Lydia. How are you doing this afternoon?"

"Oh, I'm fine, just fine." Lydia looked flustered, although Cassie wasn't sure why. This woman seemed to be following her, not the other way around.

And suddenly Cassie was tired of playing games.

"Do you want an update on Emma's condition?" she asked bluntly. "Because I know you're related to that baby in some way."

Lydia opened her mouth and then closed it again without saying anything. She looked down at her cane and then dragged her gaze back up to meet Cassie's. "I have rheumatoid arthritis, and my doctor says that my physical condition is going to deteriorate rapidly over the next year or two."

Cassie wasn't sure why this poor woman was telling her this. "I'm sorry, that must have been very difficult to hear. Isn't there any treatment or medications available that might help?"

Lydia shrugged. "Steroids and anti-inflammatory medications, which I'm already taking. And physical therapy, which I attend three mornings a week."

"That's encouraging," Cassie said, sitting down

in the empty chair beside Lydia. "I've heard physical therapy can work wonders."

Lydia scowled down at her tea. "I haven't been impressed, considering I'm going to have to give up my cane for a walker soon. I've already fallen once. If I have another fall, I'm stuck with the stupid walker."

"I'm sorry," Cassie said helplessly. She truly did feel bad for this woman. She couldn't imagine what it must be like to know what physical limitations one was facing.

"None of that is the point," Lydia said in a feisty tone. Cassie had to give the woman credit for not letting her bleak prognosis get her down. "You asked me before if I knew Emma's mother, and I lied to you. I do know her. Emma's mother is my niece. My sister died several years ago and Avery—well, let's just say she's made a lot of bad decisions over the past few years."

Cassie didn't interrupt, silently encouraging the woman to talk.

"You see, Avery delivered in the hospital, but then left the very next day, without any support other than her boyfriend. And then she drove up here to ask for my help in raising the baby. But she also made it clear she wasn't going to stick around." Lydia's anguish was etched on her features. "It almost killed me, but as much as I wanted to take care of little Emma, I'm not physically able to. So I encouraged Avery to drop her off at the hospital. Giving Emma up as a safe-haven baby was the only option."

Cassie reached over and took Lydia's hand in hers. "You and Avery made the right decision," she said softly. "Emma is going to be fine. The doctor is hoping to take her breathing tube out soon, maybe even today. She's going to find a home with a lucky family one day soon, I promise."

"Thank you," Lydia said, tears welling in her eyes. "Thank you for taking such good care of my great-niece."

Cassie battled tears, too. "I'm taking good care of Emma. In fact, I'm hoping to become her foster mother, so I can take care of her, forever."

Saying the words out loud made them seem all the more real. But she didn't regret telling Lydia her dream.

She hoped the news would give the older woman some peace.

CHAPTER TWELVE

RYAN HEADED DOWN the highway that hugged the coast-line of Lake Michigan, trying to talk himself out of going back to the Sunshine Café, but it was no use. He couldn't find it in him to stay away.

He desperately wanted to talk to Cassie, to apologize for leaving. And to tell her the truth, so that she knew everything about him, once and for all.

He made a U-turn so he could head back to Cedar Bluff. Maybe Cassie had moved on. Maybe she didn't need him the way he needed her. Maybe he was only doing this for himself, but he knew he wouldn't be able to move forward until he'd apologized. He parked his car a couple of blocks down and walked along the café's outdoor seating area. When he caught sight of Cassie talking to Lydia, he quickened his pace.

"Take care, Ms. Lydia," Cassie said, rising to her feet. "Remember, you have my phone number now, so call if you need something."

"I will, dear, thank you."

He approached, glancing warily between them. It seemed as if their conversation was amicable, but what had changed? "Hi, Cassie. Is everything okay?"

Her smile didn't quite meet her eyes. "Absolutely.

Ms. Lydia, you remember Dr. Murphy? He's one of the doctors caring for Emma."

"Yes, of course. How are you, Dr. Murphy?" Lydia held out her hand to Ryan. "Forgive me for not standing up, but my old bones are a bit achy today."

"Please, sit and relax," Ryan said, raising a curious eyebrow toward Cassie. He couldn't imagine what had changed since the last time they'd tried to speak to the woman.

"Ms. Lydia was just telling me that she's Emma's great-aunt," Cassie said, answering his unspoken question. "Her niece, Avery, has had some trouble and it was Ms. Lydia who told her to bring Emma to the hospital as a safe-haven baby."

"I see," Ryan murmured, turning back toward Lydia. "That was a wonderful thing you and Avery did. Thank you so much for giving Emma a chance at a better life."

"I would have kept Emma myself if not for this stupid rheumatoid arthritis," Lydia said with real regret in her eyes. "But I'm glad to hear Emma is doing okay. I've been so worried about the baby."

Ryan suspected Lydia knew more about Avery's history and he took the seat next to the older woman, choosing his words carefully. "I believe your niece might have a prescription drug addiction," he said, keeping his tone gentle. "I know you don't want her to get into any trouble, but at the same time it's important that Avery gets help before something bad happens to her."

Lydia pursed her lips for a moment and then nodded. "Yes, I know. I'm doing my best, but she's been running wild since my sister passed away. Unfortunately, Avery was in the car crash that killed my sister and she's has been suffering terrible back pain ever since. You're right about the prescription drugs, that's the reason she didn't stay very long in the hospital. But I'm not sure how to get her off them. Especially when she refuses to stay here and live with me. Apparently, she'd rather shack up with that worthless boyfriend of hers."

Knowing his instincts were right didn't make him feel any better. Helping people with addictions wasn't easy. Would he have been able to help Victoria if he'd known the truth? He wasn't sure. "I know it's hard, but when you do see her, please keep encouraging her to get help."

The older woman flashed him a tremulous smile. "I will."

Ryan carefully shook her hand and then stood up and followed Cassie back to the table where Gloria was waiting rather impatiently.

"Sorry about that, Gloria," Cassie said, as she took her seat. "I didn't mean to leave you here alone."

Gloria shrugged and put her phone away. She glanced up at Ryan. "Hi, Dr. Ryan. Do you want to join us?" she offered.

He absolutely did, but he glanced at Cassie, trying to read the impassive expression on her face. He sensed she wasn't thrilled to have him there, but at the same time he didn't want to leave without talking to her.

Although he'd rather not bare his soul in front of Gloria.

"I don't want to intrude. I'll sit somewhere else, but I would like to talk to you, Cassie. Maybe we could talk after you've finished your lunch?"

Cassie hesitated. "I may not have time," she said slowly. "I have an appointment at two o'clock."

Gloria seemed impervious to the tension between

them. "It's silly of you to sit somewhere else. Cass, you don't mind if he joins us, do you?"

"No, of course not." Finally she met his gaze with a weak smile. "We've already placed our order so you may need to flag down the server."

Since she didn't seem too upset with him, he pulled out one of the empty chairs and sat down. He was hungry but was willing to forgo eating if it meant getting a chance to talk to Cassie. "Thank you," he murmured.

"Cass, what's your two o'clock appointment?" Gloria asked, taking a sip of her lemonade.

Cassie shrugged but he noticed that there was an excited glint in her eyes. "I found a townhouse for sale that happens to be close to my budget. I'm meeting the Realtor there this afternoon."

Ryan glanced at her in surprise. "Really?"

She nodded. "There aren't any two-bedroom units available so this is my best chance of getting Mr. Davies's approval to keep moving forward with the fostering process."

Was this why she'd looked so happy? Was it possible she didn't hate him for the way he left her so abruptly last night? "I'm glad to hear it. I could tag along if you like. I might be able to spot any problem areas."

She hesitated again, and he mentally kicked himself for pushing so hard. "I guess that would work." She surprised him by agreeing. "I don't know much about buying a house and need all the help I can get."

He was ridiculously pleased that she'd agreed to let him come along. "Thanks," he murmured.

Gloria cleared her throat loudly. "Do you two want me to leave?" she asked. "It seems like you have a lot to discuss."

"No, of course not," he said, wincing a little at the

fact that he'd made Gloria feel like a third wheel. "Let me know when you spot the server. I wouldn't mind having another one of their burgers. The last one I had was excellent."

Gloria snickered and raised an eyebrow toward Cassie, who blushed and stared down at her plate for a long moment.

He didn't understand the private joke but kept the conversation casual as the two women enjoyed their meal. Gloria updated him on her brother's progress and he was relieved to hear Trey had woken up and seemed to be doing okay. The server was so busy he didn't bother asking for a burger. Cassie insisted he share part of her lunch, so he helped himself to the smaller half of her sandwich and a handful of chips.

When the server returned with the bill, he quickly nabbed it and pulled out his wallet, ignoring Gloria and Cassie's loud protests.

"You had hardly anything to eat," Cassie said with exasperation. "Why should you pay?"

"Because I'm the one who interrupted your meal, forcing you to give up half your sandwich." He quickly stuffed cash into the plastic billfold and handed it back to the server. "Trust me, this is the least I can do."

Cassie sighed but didn't say anything more as she rose to her feet. He stood and followed her, longing for the easy camaraderie they'd once shared.

"I have a few errands to run," Gloria said. "I'll talk to you later, Cass, okay?"

"Sure. I'll check in on Trey during my dinner break," Cassie promised.

Ryan was grateful that Gloria had taken it upon herself to leave them alone. He felt a little guilty for interrupting their girl time, but thankfully Cassie didn't seem to mind.

"We have thirty minutes until we need to meet your Realtor," he said. "Would you like to take a drive in the convertible?"

She shook her head. "No, as much as I love your convertible, I need to stop by my apartment so I can pick up my scrubs and my stethoscope. I plan to head to work as soon as we're finished at the townhouse."

"No problem." He wondered if she regretted inviting him to go along. "I'll drive you over."

Stopping at Cassie's apartment didn't take long. When she came back out to his car with her bag over her shoulder, he wanted nothing more than to pull her close and kiss her.

But he forced himself to concentrate on telling her the truth first. "Cassie, I owe you an apology," he began, but she shook her head.

"Actually, there's no need for you to apologize. I have something I need to tell you," she said, cutting him off. "I think you should know why having Emma is so important to me."

He nodded, waiting for her to slide into the passenger seat of his convertible. "Okay."

She took a deep breath and let it out slowly. "I told you that my ex-husband cheated on me, but I didn't tell you everything."

He was surprised that she'd kept something back from him, too, although the tortured expression in her eyes didn't make him feel any better. "I'm listening," he encouraged.

"I suffered two miscarriages," she admitted. "Both at about twenty weeks' gestation."

His heart twisted in his chest. One was bad enough, but two? "I'm so sorry," he murmured.

"The worst part was that I had to be in the hospital after the second miscarriage because I wouldn't stop bleeding." Cassie turned in her seat to face him. "I heard my husband on the phone with his lover, telling her how glad he was that I'd lost the baby because now getting a divorce would be easier."

He curled his fingers into fists, wishing he could punch her ex right between the eyes. "I can't imagine how awful that must have been."

She dropped her gaze again. "I was getting ready to be taken into surgery for a D&C and told Evan to get out. I practically screamed at him that I wouldn't contest his stinking divorce."

Ryan wanted to pull her into his arms, and he must have reached toward her because she held up a hand.

"There's more. After surgery, the doctor told me that there was something wrong with my uterus, which was why I'd had the two miscarriages. There was some sort of tissue barrier making it smaller than normal. He told me that I needed to have another surgery before even trying to get pregnant again. And even then, the scar tissue might be too much to overcome."

"Cassie, I'm so sorry," he said tucking a strand of her dark hair behind her ear. "I wish there was something I could do to make you feel better."

Her attempt at a smile was pathetic. "Thanks, but there isn't anything you can do, although I appreciate your support. This is my burden to bear. I've always dreamed of having a family of my own, which is probably why I rushed into marriage with Evan."

"Just so you know, that loser is not worth a single tear," Ryan told her.

This time her smile looked real. "Thanks. I just wanted you to know that my chances of having a baby of my own are probably less than thirty percent. So now you know why I'm such an emotional wreck about being able to be a foster mother to Emma. And why this townhouse is so important to me."

"I do understand," he said slowly. "But, Cassie, you have to know that there are so many options available these days. The strides in reproductive medicine have been amazing. Even if you can't have children of your own, you can still have the family you've always dreamed of."

"Maybe," she admitted, although she looked far from convinced.

Ryan's desire to share the truth about losing his unborn son died on his tongue. Cassie was excited about seeing the townhouse and he didn't want to bring her down.

Besides, it suddenly hit him that he was more like her ex-husband than he wanted to admit.

Not because he hadn't wanted his son, because he had. Desperately.

But he hadn't wanted Victoria.

And in the midst of his anguish after her death he'd been unable to deny a small measure of relief to know that he wouldn't have to spend the rest of his life with her.

A fact that made him a terrible person. Not much better than Evan.

Certainly not good enough for Cassie.

Cassie felt better once she'd told Ryan the truth. And he'd been nothing but supportive.

She sensed that there were things he wanted to talk

about, too, and feared he'd go into detail again about what her options were as far as having a child of her own. For some reason, she couldn't help thinking that he'd been trying to convince himself that there were other opportunities to have a child. Maybe because deep down he knew how much he wanted to have children of his own.

Maybe it was for the best that there wasn't enough time for further discussion. "I'm sorry, Ryan, but can we head over to the townhouse now? I'd like to be there a few minutes early."

"Of course," he agreed. "Buckle up."

She pulled her hair back into a ponytail and then latched her seat belt. She pulled out her phone so she could give him directions.

"Take Main Street and then turn left on Lilac Road," she said.

"Lots of kids playing around here," he commented.

She nodded, loving the fact that this area seemed ideal for raising a family. "Turn left on Lavender, and the townhouse should be right there on the corner."

"I think I see the For Sale sign," he said as they approached.

"No, that's Rosewood," she said, glancing down at the paperwork she held in her hand. "Lavender is the next block."

He nodded and continued, although she found herself thinking that the moderate-sized Cape Cod with the For Sale sign in the front yard looked inviting, too.

Way beyond her price range, though.

"There it is," she said, craning her neck to see better. "They're side-by-side townhouses. And I love how close it is to the park."

"I see it," he said, pulling over to the curb.

"It only has two bedrooms," she said, feeling self-conscious about her choice. "But that's all Emma and I really need."

"It looks great," he said as he shut off the engine.

Cassie slid out of the passenger seat, thrilled to see the townhouse up close. Granted, it was small, but she refused to let that fact get her down. Besides, the price was already a stretch since she'd have to take out a loan against her retirement plan to afford her rent and the down payment.

"The roof looks to be in good shape," Ryan said, gesturing with his hand. "And the outside appears to be low maintenance."

"So far, so good," she agreed, glad he was there to give her some pointers. "I wonder who lives next door?"

"That's a good question, since you'll be sharing the building and the yard," he said. "Maybe the Realtor knows?"

"I wish she'd get here," Cassie muttered. "I'm dying to see the inside."

"That's probably her now."

Cassie shielded her eyes against the glare of the summer sun to check out the car that had turned onto the street. Sure enough, the driver was a woman who looked like the photograph of Andrea Langley she'd seen on the website. "I'm glad she came early, too."

Andrea parked the car in front of the townhouse and slid out from the driver's seat. Cassie met her halfway. "Thanks for coming on short notice," she said, holding out her hand to Andrea.

"My pleasure," Andrea said with a broad smile. She glanced over at Ryan. "Nice to see you, too, Dr. Murphy."

Cassie's eyebrows lifted in surprise. "I didn't realize you knew each other."

"I've listed my house with Andrea," Ryan said.

Really? Why on earth hadn't he mentioned that fact? But this wasn't the time or the place to ask. Especially as Andrea began talking about the property.

"The inside needs a little work," Andrea warned, as she unlocked the front door, "but a little paint and new carpeting will make it look as good as new."

Cassie's excitement faded to despair when she saw what Andrea meant. The walls must have been white once, but now had an icky brown tinge to them. The interior reeked of stale cigarette smoke, which made her gag. Maybe paint and pulling the old carpeting out might help, but what if that didn't work? She felt certain an entire can of air freshener wouldn't make a dent in the stench.

"It's worse than it looks on the website," Cassie said, breathing through her nose as she turned to Andrea. "I'm not sure if I'll have enough money to fix it up."

Andrea's smile slipped as she nodded. "I understand, but you could try a low offer, see if the sellers would be willing to move on the price."

"Maybe," Cassie agreed, glancing around the living room and kitchen area. Andrea threw open a few windows while she walked down the hall to the two bedrooms, which were small but serviceable.

"There's a half basement, too, where the washer and dryer are located," Andrea pointed out cheerfully, obviously trying to salvage her potential sale. "And the appliances are included."

"That helps," Cassie acknowledged, trying to battle a wave of depression. She couldn't imagine bringing Emma into this place as it was now.

"The foundation looks sound," Ryan pointed out, as they walked around the basement. "The basics are all here, so Andrea is right, it's just a matter of adding paint and carpeting."

"Absolutely," Andrea agreed, as they trooped back up to the main level. "What do you think, Cassie?"

Honestly, she wasn't sure what to think. Disappointment stabbed deep but she did her best to try and be optimistic. "It has potential, but the price would have to be at least twelve grand lower to make up for what I'd have to put into this to make it livable."

Andrea winced and then shrugged. "Well, it can't hurt to try," she said. "Maybe they'll counter and we can meet in the middle."

"I'm not sure I can afford much more," Cassie said frankly. "I have maybe a few thousand in wiggle room, but that's about all. If they'll accept a lower offer, then I can pay for the upgrades and the rent for the duration of my lease."

Andrea nodded, although her expression reflected her discouragement. "All right, I'll put the offer together before you have to go to work."

Cassie looked around the interior again, noting that the open windows didn't help the smell. Andrea was right, the place had potential, but the thought of doing all the work to make it worthwhile was a bit daunting.

"Do you know anything about the Cape Cod for sale on Rosewood?" Ryan asked. "That one has definite curb appeal."

Cassie glanced at him, wondering at his sudden decision to list his house. "Why are you interested in moving?"

He shrugged. "The place I have now is too big for me and isn't really to my taste."

She was surprised to hear that, mostly because the timing seemed off. After all, his wife had been dead for three years. Why the sudden desire to move now, after all this time?

Had investigating Trey's overdose caused his old feelings for his wife to resurface? Maybe, but he'd also said that her death had been his fault.

And she realized that even though they'd bonded over Emma and had made love, there was a chance that Ryan still wasn't ready for a more permanent type of relationship.

As kind and supportive as he'd been when she'd told him about her inability to have children, he hadn't mentioned that he didn't care.

In fact, he might secretly be disappointed in her inability to carry a child, but hadn't said anything out of kindness. Maybe, in his mind, she wasn't the right woman for him.

And she realized that it was entirely possible that she cared about him far more than he cared for her.

CHAPTER THIRTEEN

RYAN FELT TERRIBLE that Cassie's excitement over her townhouse had been crushed by the work that was needed inside. The place did have potential, but it would take a lot of elbow grease and money to make it a home.

And for some reason he couldn't get the Cape Cod house out of his mind.

But there was plenty of time to worry about that later. Right now he was more concerned about Cassie. As he drove her back to her apartment, her despair was evident on her face. "I can help you with the townhouse," he offered.

"Thanks, but first we have to find out if the sellers will drop the price," she said with a sad smile.

"Things will work out," he said encouragingly. Trying to keep his distance from her wasn't working too well. "You'll see."

"I hope so," she said wistfully, as she pushed open the passenger door. "Thanks again, Ryan."

Knowing she had to work, he forced himself to let her go. "Take care, Cassie."

He watched her walk toward her car, wishing he could make her feel better. But then his phone rang and he jumped on it, recognizing Detective Trammel's number. "This is Ryan Murphy."

"Dr. Murphy, I have good news. We've linked Oliver Stevenson to several other prescription drugs that have been filled here in Wisconsin. We're in the process of working with the Feds to bring him in."

"Really?" He tried to comprehend what Trammel was saying. "You think that he'll pay for his crimes?"

"I do. We found another strip-mall office of his and sent in an undercover cop with cash. The cop came out with a prescription for a month's supply of oxycodone. Unfortunately, the doc himself wasn't there, but it's just a matter of time. We're in the process of solidifying our case against him."

Relief was overwhelming. "Thank you for telling me," Ryan managed. "I'm glad he'll finally be brought to justice."

"Me, too," Trammel echoed. "And I'm sorry I didn't take your concerns more seriously back when your wife died."

That much was true, and he didn't want to think about how many deaths had occurred in the past three years as a result. But at least they could stop this guy moving forward. "It's okay, just make sure you get him into custody and soon."

"We will. Take care, Dr. Murphy."

Trammel disconnected from the call, leaving Ryan staring at his phone, still reeling from shock. It was over. So why didn't he feel better? Wasn't this the justice he'd sought?

Of course it was.

Yet he knew that arresting Oliver Stevenson wouldn't bring his son back.

And the guilt that had plagued him over the past three years hadn't lessened much at all.

He scrubbed his hands over his face. Maybe the first

step was to confide in Cassie. She was working, but he wasn't. Maybe he could meet her for dinner? Or wait to talk to her at the end of her shift?

Either way, the need to talk to Cassie couldn't be denied. Maybe she could give him the absolution he couldn't seem to give himself.

Cassie swiped in at work and immediately crossed over to Emma's warmer. Her mouth dropped open in surprise when she discovered Emma had been taken off the ventilator a few hours prior to the start of her shift. Even the feeding tube was gone.

"Oh, sweetpea, you look wonderful," she whispered. The baby appeared to be asleep, with only a reddened area on her cheek from where the feeding tube had been held in place remaining as a sign of what she'd been through.

Tears pricked her eyes at how wonderful Emma looked not being connected to a ventilator.

"Hey, are you ready for our bedside shift report?" Diane asked, crossing over to Emma's warmer.

"Absolutely," Cassie agreed. "Although I can already see how much progress little Emma has made."

"Yes, although we're still keeping a close eye on her for signs of apnea. And she'll need to be fed soon, so let's finish up. Are you taking care of Daniel, too?" When Cassie nodded, Diane smiled. "Great, then this won't take too long."

Cassie concentrated on listening to the detailed information Diane gave her, even though it wasn't easy. It was shocking to realize how much she wanted to call Ryan to share the good news about Emma.

Daniel was also doing much better and she finished her assessment just as he began to wake up. His par-

ents were coming in to feed him, but he was cranky
with having to wait, so she picked him up and walked
around the nursery, trying to soothe him.

When his parents arrived, his mother rushed over.
"Oh, thank you for waiting, although I feel terrible that
we didn't get here sooner."

She smiled as she handed Daniel over to his mother.
"It's been less than ten minutes, so don't worry, he's
fine."

Cassie made sure that Daniel's parents were settled
in to feed him before heading over to Emma's warmer.
The baby still looked peaceful, but she was starting to
squirm around a bit, indicating that she might wake
up soon.

And no doubt would be as hungry as Daniel had
been.

Diane had mentioned that Emma had taken her first
bottle feeding just two hours ago, but it wasn't uncom-
mon for babies to eat more frequently after being under
stress. Plus, the little girl had only taken two ounces,
so it wasn't surprising she needed more in her tummy.

Cassie quickly put a bottle together for Emma, sensing she was on borrowed time. When Emma let out
a plaintive wail, Cassie smiled, thinking that even
Emma's cry sounded good after days of silence while
she'd been supported on the ventilator.

"There, now, I'm here, sweetpea," she murmured as
she began changing Emma's diaper. When that task was
finished she quickly washed her hands and then picked
the baby up, nestling the little girl against her shoulder. Emma's crying grew louder and more insistent so
Cassie turned the baby so that Emma was propped in
the crook of her arm and sat down in the rocking chair
to feed her.

At that exact moment she looked up to find Ryan standing there, wearing casual nonwork clothes and staring at her, his deeply intent gaze making her shiver with awareness.

And just that quickly the memories of their lovemaking came rushing back, at the worst possible moment. She'd never experienced anything like making love with Ryan, and Cassie knew she needed to look away before everyone noticed the emotion shimmering in her eyes. But it wasn't easy. Only when Emma reached up to put her tiny hand on top of Cassie's hand holding the bottle did she find the strength to break the connection.

She tried to get her bearings, as Ryan came even closer. Telling herself to ignore him was impossible, but she did her best, gazing down at Emma, who sucked at the bottle like a pro.

"Isn't she beautiful?" she whispered, finding the nerve to glance up at him.

"Yes. And so are you," Ryan said in a low husky tone. Thankfully no one was standing right next to them.

Still, she felt her cheeks grow warm, knowing the other staff members were likely glancing at them curiously. "What are you doing here?" she asked in a whisper. "Did you come to see Emma?"

He slowly shook his head. "No, but I'm thrilled to see she's off the vent. I came to see you. I realize you're working but will you have dinner with me when you have time for a break?"

She wanted to refuse outright, but her tongue didn't seem to be working properly. "We have a woman who's in preterm labor," she finally managed. "I'm not sure I'll get a dinner break during my shift."

"I'll wait," he said, obviously unwilling to accept

any excuse. "And if you don't have time, then I'll wait until after your shift is over."

She stared at him helplessly. "Why?"

"Because I need to talk to you. Please? It's important."

The earnest expression in his eyes made it impossible for Cassie to refuse his request. "All right, but keep in mind that dinner isn't likely."

"That's okay. I'll swing by and if you're too busy I'll come back later." He stroked a hand over Emma's downy hair before turning to leave.

She watched him go, the urge to call him back nearly overwhelming. She focused her gaze on Emma instead. She knew that Ryan wanted to explain why he'd claimed that his wife's death had been his fault, and he deserved to be heard.

And with the way her pulse rate had tripled on seeing him again, she suspected that nothing he could say would change her feelings about him.

She cared about Ryan, more than she could ever articulate.

Was it possible he felt the same way? Or had their amazing night of passion been one-sided? Did he wish for someone different? Someone who could bear him the children he deserved?

Or was fostering children enough?

She gave herself a mental shake, knowing that she'd have her answers soon enough. Right now, Emma needed her attention.

After the baby finished one ounce, Cassie gently took the bottle away and held Emma against her shoulder, rubbing the baby's back to encourage a burp. The sound was little more than a hiccup, but did the trick.

It was so amazing to watch Emma drink from a

bottle, without having any tubes. The baby didn't even have the IV anymore, although the tiny bruises where the needles had been still lingered. No doubt Emma would soon be moved to the level-two nursery, which was one step closer to being discharged.

For a moment her heart squeezed in her breast. She was thrilled the baby was making progress, but at the same time, Emma's well-being was more proof that she might not be able to become a foster parent in time.

Fate might have other plans for Emma.

Plans that didn't include *her*.

For all she knew, there was a couple out there who would take Emma in and provide the baby with both a mother and a father. After all, Emma's medical needs were probably not nearly as bad as they'd initially feared.

A two-parent household would always take precedence over a single parent, like herself, even if she was given an exception for her one-bedroom apartment.

But she refused to let that selfish thought ruin her day. If Emma wasn't meant for her, then so be it. Having Emma move up to the level-two nursery was a huge accomplishment.

Normally Cassie cared for the sicker babies, but maybe her boss would make an exception. If not, she'd still rejoice in the news that Emma was getting better. Because Emma's health was all that mattered.

The baby's heath and finding a loving family to take care of her.

Ryan was disappointed when he learned that the neonatal unit was short-staffed over the dinner hour, thanks to a preemie delivery, so Cassie wasn't free to meet him.

He returned toward the end of her shift and she

looked surprised to see him waiting there. She smiled and crossed over. "You must be bored out of your mind with nothing to do during my entire shift."

"Not at all," he said, although the waiting had been pure torture. "Are you hungry? Did you get a chance to eat anything?"

"Yes, I'm hungry and, no, I didn't get a chance to eat dinner. It's been crazy. We had two preemies deliver right after each other."

He thought for a minute. "We can either eat in the cafeteria or at San Flippo's Pizzeria right across the street."

"Pizza sounds wonderful."

As they walked toward the elevator, he rested his hand in the small of her back, needing the brief physical connection. Watching her feed Emma had made him realize how much he cared about Cassie.

And emphasized just how important this conversation would be.

"Any news on the townhouse?" he asked, as they rode the elevator down to the lobby level.

She grimaced and shrugged. "They countered but only dropped the price three grand, so it's not looking good."

Once again, he thought about the Cape Cod located near the park. But he was getting way ahead of himself. First they needed to talk. A heavy conversation that might be better with food in their stomachs.

"I'm sorry, Cassie," he murmured.

"It's all right. Emma's doing so much better, anyway, that I'm sure other foster parents will step forward to claim her."

He wanted to reassure her, but unfortunately she

was right. Emma's medical needs might not be a barrier after all.

But deep down he knew that Emma and Cassie belonged together.

The walk across the street to San Flippo's didn't take long, and he had to smile when Cassie ordered a pizza with the works, just the way he liked it.

"Let's sit in the back," he said, choosing an isolated area of the eating space on purpose.

They took a seat as the server came over with their soft drinks. "The pizza will be ready soon."

"I hope so, because I'm starving," she muttered, half under her breath.

He couldn't help but grin. "Should I get an order of breadsticks to tide you over?"

She wrinkled her nose at him. "No, thanks. I'd rather eat the real deal."

He nodded. "Okay, we'll wait."

She played with her straw wrapper. "Ryan, why did you want to talk to me so badly that you couldn't wait until tomorrow?"

He cleared his throat, wondering where to start. "I heard from Detective Trammel after I dropped you off at your apartment. They've arrested Dr. Oliver Stevenson for running illegal drug clinics."

Cassie's eyes widened in shock. "Really? Trey got his prescription filled there?"

He nodded. "Yeah, and apparently this doc moved around a lot, slapping up clinics in strip malls and other cheap business rental places and then tearing them down to move again. But he won't hurt anyone else. He's done."

"Oh, Ryan, I'm so happy for you." Cassie reached

over to cover his hand in hers. "I'm sure this must be a huge relief."

"Thanks." He knew he had to tell her the rest, but at that moment their server showed up with their pizza.

"Yum, that looks delicious." Cassie helped herself to a generous slice, so he did the same.

They ate in silence for several minutes as he tried to figure out how to confess the rest of the story to Cassie.

As it turned out, she brought it up first.

"Ryan, if the police arrested the doctor who supplied your wife's pills, why do you feel responsible for her death?"

The pizza he'd eaten sat like a lump of dough in his gut. He gulped down some water before lifting his gaze to meet hers.

"I didn't love Victoria the way I should have," he finally said. "We were young, too young to realize what we were getting into. Victoria liked being a doctor's wife and was obsessed with her looks, to the point of weighing herself every single morning and freaking out if she gained a half a pound."

Cassie pushed her empty plate away, her gaze never wavering from his. "Go on," she encouraged.

He licked suddenly dry lips. "I was thinking about filing for divorce—in fact, I'd already met with a lawyer to begin the process. But that evening, when I came home, Victoria told me she was pregnant."

She gasped, so loudly that he was surprised the few patrons of the restaurant didn't turn around to see what was going on. "She was pregnant?" she whispered.

The pizza congealed in his gut. "Yeah. I was thrilled about the baby and decided to forget about the divorce. My parents divorced when I was young and I was shuffled between them for most of my early life. I didn't want that for my son." He let out a heavy sigh. "But I didn't know Victoria was still taking prescription pain-killers. She'd had surgery a year earlier, and it never occurred to me that she'd become addicted to them."

Cassie didn't say a word, her eyes wide with horror. He forced himself to finish it.

"Don't you see? I was clueless. I didn't know she was taking pills. And I can't help thinking that she used them as a crutch because I didn't love her enough."

He tossed his napkin over his plate with a wave of self-disgust. "When Victoria died of an accidental drug overdose, she took my son along with her. And as much as I missed him, there was a tiny part of me that was relieved she was gone."

Cassie stared at him for a long moment before she tore her gaze away. "I don't know what to say," she whispered. "I had no idea..."

Her voice trailed off and the way she wouldn't look at him only cemented the truth.

She was appalled by his actions. And obviously didn't want anything to do with him now that she knew.

And, worst of all, he couldn't blame her.

CHAPTER FOURTEEN

CASSIE PRESSED HER shaking hands together as she rose to her feet. "Excuse me," she said in a strangled tone before making her way to the woman's restroom. For long moments she stood, her hands braced on the countertop, trying to get a grip on her emotions.

Ryan had lost his son. A son he'd wanted desperately enough to try to make his loveless marriage work.

He'd lost his son!

Cassie took several deep breaths, trying to calm herself. After she'd told him about her two miscarriages and the need to have surgery, Ryan hadn't mentioned anything about losing his son.

To be fair, she hadn't given him a chance, since she'd been anxious to see the townhouse.

Still, it was clear that she might never be able to give Ryan the son he wanted. Sure, he'd been supportive of her quest to become a foster mother for Emma, and had claimed that there were many other options available to have children. But he'd want a son of his own.

She loved him. She loved him and he clearly deserved the chance to have his own child. No matter what he might say to the contrary.

Her instincts weren't reliable when it came to men.

"Cassandra? Are you all right?"

Hearing Ryan's voice on the other side of the door made tears spring to her eyes. She quickly splashed cold water on her face to hide the evidence and to bring some color back into her pale face.

She walked out of the restroom, surprised he'd come to see if she was all right. "I'm fine and I shouldn't have left you like that. I'm sorry, Ryan. So sorry for everything you've been through."

He stared at her, his gaze impassive. She couldn't figure out what he was thinking. "I've already paid the bill, so I'll drive you home."

She was surprised he wanted the evening to end so soon, especially after he'd waited her entire shift to talk to her. But then again, she'd left to pull herself together. "I'm sorry," she said again. "And my car is at the hospital."

"Then I'll take you to your car."

She followed him outside, still shaken by the news that he'd lost his son but feeling terrible that she'd reacted so badly. Why had she made it about her own loss, instead of supporting Ryan?

"Her death wasn't your fault," she murmured, as he drove back across the street to the hospital parking lot.

"Yeah, right." His sarcastic tone bit deep.

"Listen, Ryan, I'm not an expert, but I'm sure your wife tried to keep her addiction a secret."

"That isn't the point."

She wasn't sure what the point was, but he didn't say anything more as he pulled up alongside her car. She sat for a moment, trying to think of some way to ease his guilt.

"Goodnight, Cassie."

The finality of his tone couldn't be ignored. "Goodnight, Ryan," she murmured, her heart aching for him as she slid out of his car to climb into hers.

Ryan drove away without so much as a backward glance.

And she knew, with sick certainty, that he'd never love her the way she loved him. How could he? He wouldn't be able to love anyone until he learned to forgive himself.

Ryan kept seeing the horrified expression in Cassie's eyes over and over again. She'd tried to tell him that Victoria's death hadn't been his fault, but she hadn't mentioned anything about the way he'd been secretly relieved that he hadn't been stuck with Victoria for the rest of his life.

A statement that had sent her running to the bathroom so she could pull herself together in private.

He couldn't sleep and was glad to know that he wasn't scheduled to work the next day. Not that he'd mind keeping busy, but he wouldn't do his tiny patients any good coming in to work sleep deprived.

The thought of his infant patients reminded him of Emma. Beautiful Emma, who'd looked adorable in Cassie's arms.

He tried to slam the door on those images but they kept rolling through his mind like a movie that wouldn't end.

His heart squeezed painfully in his chest as he realized how much he loved Cassie.

He loved her.

But she would never return his feelings.

Somehow he must have dozed a bit because suddenly the early morning sunshine woke him up. He blinked and rolled out of bed with a low groan.

Maybe he should offer to work today. There were three neonatal intensivists and between them they covered the unit 24/7. Erica Ryerson was on today, and since she'd asked off for the past weekend he knew she'd insist on staying.

Which meant he had a long, endless day stretching ahead of him.

Ryan's phone rang and his pulse leaped as he grabbed his phone, but of course the caller wasn't Cassie. He answered it halfheartedly. "Hello?"

"Dr. Murphy? Andrea Langley here. First of all, I have a couple interested in looking at your house this afternoon. Isn't that fantastic?"

He rubbed the back of his neck, trying to garner some enthusiasm. "Yeah, that's great. What time?"

"Two o'clock. But I was also wondering if there were any properties you were interested in seeing? You might want to pick something out in case we get lucky and someone puts in an offer on your place."

The Cape Cod located next to the park flashed into his mind, although his previous excitement about the place had waned considerably.

"Sure, why not?" He mentioned the house he had in mind. At least seeing it would give him something to do. "I can meet you there in an hour or so, if that works?"

"Perfect. See you then."

He disconnected from the call, forcing himself to take a shower, change and grab something to eat before heading over to the house he'd glimpsed yesterday when he'd driven Cassie to the townhouse.

Seeing the Cape Cod up close only reinforced his belief that the place would be perfect for Cassie. For Cassie and Emma, or any other baby she decided to foster.

The thawed spot in his heart ached to the point he

pressed his hand to the center of his chest in a vain effort to ease the pain. This was why he'd held himself closed off from everyone since Victoria's death.

Because love hurt too damn much.

He hadn't loved Victoria enough, but he'd loved his son. And losing his baby boy had gutted him.

Now he felt the same way over losing Cassie.

Andrea babbled on and on about the house, but all he could see was Cassie everywhere he looked. Cassie in the kitchen, the bedroom. Holding Emma. Holding their child.

"Well? What do you think?" Andrea asked.

He nodded, wondering if he'd see Cassie in every house he viewed. "It's nice."

"Are you interested in putting in an offer?" she asked, not seeming to notice his lackluster attitude.

"Let me think about it a bit more," he hedged. "After all, this is the first house I've looked at."

Andrea looked disappointed, but she nodded. "Okay, do you have other places in mind?"

He didn't have a clue. And it was difficult to drum up the energy to care. "I'll make a list and get back to you," he promised.

Andrea wasn't thrilled, but he didn't care. He walked back out to his car, tempted to take a long drive along the coast of Lake Michigan.

But doing that only reminded him again of Cassie. The way she enjoyed riding in his convertible. The way she'd tipped her face up to the sun. The way she laughed.

As he drove home, he realized that he'd never be able to forget all the memories he'd shared with Cassie.

When he pulled into his driveway, there was a car

parked in front of his house. It took him a minute to realize the sedan belonged to Cassie.

A mixture of dread and pleasure filled his chest. He must be a glutton for punishment, because even knowing that all she wanted to do was to rehash everything from last night, he was still happy to see her.

"Hi," she greeted him awkwardly.

He tried, and failed, to summon a smile. "Cassie. What brings you here?"

"I didn't sleep very well last night," she said.

"Me, either," he admitted. "And don't worry, I understand."

Her brow knitted in confusion. "Understand what?"

"Why you ran off to the bathroom like that." He glanced around, thinking that standing in his driveway probably wasn't the best place to have this conversation. "Do you want to go inside?"

She hesitated. "Could we take a walk instead?"

"Sure." The fact that she didn't want to be inside Victoria's house wasn't too surprising. He fell into step beside her as they made their way down to the road.

"I shouldn't have run to the bathroom last night," she said. "I'm sorry. Hearing about how you lost a son similar to the way I lost two babies hit me harder than I expected."

He was surprised to hear that. "I figured you were upset about the fact that I was secretly glad to be free of Victoria." There, he'd said it again, in case she hadn't heard him the first time.

"Oh, Ryan, I know just how that feels. As much as I mourned the loss of my baby, I was also secretly glad to know that I found out about Evan, too. I wanted my child more than anything, but sharing that child with someone like him…" She shrugged. "It took me a long time to realize that maybe losing my baby was a mixed blessing."

He was flabbergasted by her admission. "You don't think I'm a terrible person?" he asked.

She frowned. "Of course not."

The relief that hit him was overwhelming. "You don't know how much hearing that means to me." He captured her hand in his and stopped so he could face her. "I'm glad you don't hate me."

Her eyes filled with compassion. "I don't hate you, Ryan. I can't hate you when I've fallen in love with you."

His mouth dropped open in surprise and the stabbing pain in his heart eased. "Cassandra, I love you, too."

He would have kissed her but she threw up her hand, planting it in the center of his chest. "I'm sorry, but I find that hard to believe," she said huskily. "How can you love me when you haven't forgiven yourself?"

He covered her hand on his chest with his. "Cassie, you have to understand that I've been trying to forgive myself since the day Victoria died."

Her smile was sad. "I know, and I suspect that finding that Dr. Stevenson, who'd supplied her pain meds, helped a bit."

"Yes, but that wasn't the biggest change that helped me," he said, gazing down into her wide brown eyes. He needed her to believe him. "It was you, Cassandra. All you. Your warmth, your laughter, your smile. After I lost my son, I refused to care that much about anyone. You healed the piece of my heart that I thought was lost forever."

"Oh, Ryan," she whispered. "I want so badly to believe you."

He understood that trust must be difficult, considering the way her ex had betrayed her. "What can I say to make you believe me? I love you so much. I love you and I want to be with you, forever."

Amazing how saying the words became easier and easier when they were right.

"You realize I probably can't give you children," she said, dropping her gaze. "I'll have the surgery, but there are no guarantees. And even though I probably won't get to foster Emma, I'd still like to complete the classes, just in case another baby comes along that needs a home."

"Of course you'll complete the classes," Ryan said. He gently tipped her chin up so that he could look into her eyes. "I love you, Cassandra. Babies, either foster-care babies or our own, will just be an added bonus. Don't you see? You're the most important person to me."

"How can you be so sure?" she asked.

He cupped her face in his hands. "Because you hold the tiny piece of my heart that I thought was frozen forever. Without you, I'm nothing but a shell of a man going through the motions of life. Emma may have brought us together initially, but you're the one who healed my heart. You healed my soul. I will always love you, so if you need time, I'll wait for as long as it takes. And I'll never hurt you. Because anything that upsets you hurts me worse."

Tears filled her eyes and he couldn't help himself.

He kissed her, trying to reinforce without words just how much she meant to him.

Cassie wrapped her arms around Ryan's neck, drowning in the sweetness of his kiss.

Was it possible that he really had forgiven himself? And if so, could she trust in his feelings for her? Trust him when he claimed that her ability to give him a child didn't matter?

A car horn honked, breaking them apart from their heated kiss.

"How about I drive us back to your place?" Ryan asked in a husky voice. "I need to be with you. Even if all we do is talk some more."

"I'd like that," she murmured. He'd promised to give her time, but right now she couldn't bear to be separated from him, either.

The expression of love in his eyes couldn't be faked. And if he loved her, then he surely accepted her the way she was, right? Faults and all.

The same way she loved him.

They walked back to his place and he insisted on leaving her car there so they could take the convertible. "We'll come back to get it later."

She nodded, thinking that right now she was feeling too emotional to drive anyway. Thankfully she still had the hair tie so she could pull her hair back in a ponytail.

"Um, Ryan? This isn't the way to my apartment," she said when he turned left instead of right.

"I know, but I have something I'd like to show you."

The smile on his face dazzled her. He looked so different from the aloof physician she'd first met when she'd moved here six months ago.

When he turned on Rosewood, she recognized the Cape Cod. "It's adorable," she said. "Are you thinking of buying it?"

He shrugged and glanced at her. "That depends on you."

"Me?" Her heart leaped into her throat.

"Yes, you. I'll give you all the time you need to believe how much I love you, but I refuse to buy a house you don't like. So whether or not I buy this house depends on you."

Cassie unbuckled her seat belt and threw herself into his arms. "Yes," she whispered. "Yes, I like this house. But I love you more."

This time their sizzling kiss wasn't easy to break off. "We need to get to your place," he muttered. "As soon as possible."

She couldn't help giggling as she buckled herself back in. Thankfully Cedar Bluff wasn't too big a town and they reached her apartment building in a few minutes.

And when Ryan tugged her toward the bedroom, she gladly followed him.

Cassie wanted nothing more than to spend the day in bed with Ryan, but when her phone rang for the third time, she decided she'd better answer it.

"Where are you going?" Ryan asked in a husky, sated tone, capturing her hand in his.

She smiled at him, still amazed at the fact that he loved her. And had gone to great lengths to prove it over the past two hours. "I need to get the phone, that's the third time it's gone off."

"I didn't hear it," he admitted, with a sexy smile. "I was too busy kissing every inch of your delectable body."

The urge to forget the stupid phone to crawl back next to him was strong, but she couldn't quite ignore the niggling worry. She dropped a quick kiss on his mouth. "I'll be right back," she promised.

"All right."

She felt self-conscious parading around naked, so she grabbed his T-shirt off the floor and pulled it over her head, grateful it was long enough to cover her bare bottom. She remembered leaving her phone on the kitchen counter and when she picked it up her heart leapt into her throat when she saw five missed calls from Lydia.

Five? She'd only heard it ring three times!

She quickly pushed the button to return the call, practically holding her breath. The older woman picked up on the second ring. "Hello?"

"Lydia, it's me, Cassie. I'm sorry I missed your calls. What's wrong? Are you okay? Did something happen to Emma?"

"Oh, Cassie, I'm so glad you returned my call. I wanted to tell you the news myself."

She frowned, trying to clear her sex-fogged mind. "What news?" Ryan appeared at her side wearing nothing but his boxers, looking so sexy, she momentarily forgot who she was talking to. Oh, yes, Lydia. She forced herself to peel her gaze away from Ryan and to focus on the call.

"I've talked to Avery and both she and her boyfriend are going to sign off on their parental rights to Emma."

Cassie knew that signing away parental rights meant that the adoption process would go faster, but obviously Lydia didn't know that she wasn't going to be able to foster Emma after all.

"That's great news, Lydia," she said, trying to inject enthusiasm in her tone. "I'm sure Emma's foster parents will be thrilled."

"What do you mean?" Lydia asked. "I thought you were fostering Emma?"

"I was, but—" She stopped, looking up at Ryan, who'd joined her. "I might not be able to get everything finished in time."

"Are you sure?" The disappointed note in Lydia's

voice stabbed deep. "I was feeling so much better know-ing that Emma was going to be living with you."

"And I want Emma, too. All I can promise is to do my best. But are you sure Avery and her boyfriend are really okay with this? After all, everyone deserves a second chance."

"Absolutely sure," Lydia assured her. "Avery knows that she has a long road ahead of her and is willing to go into rehab. Her boyfriend has agreed to go, too. And, honestly, she just wants the baby to go to a good home. And we'd like that to be with you."

"I'll try," Cassie said with a misty smile. "Good-bye, Lydia."

"We'll do more than try," Ryan said firmly, when she set her phone aside. "We'll do everything possible to get custody of Emma."

"Really?" Cassie's gaze was full of hope.

"Yes, really." Ryan's grin lit up his entire face and he picked her up so that her feet weren't even on the floor, twirling around until they were both dizzy, whispering into her ear how much he loved her.

"I love you, too," she managed.

"God, Cassie, just thinking of the possibility of adopting Emma is like a miracle," he said in awe. "Maybe together we can make this work."

"I know." She gazed up at Ryan, her heart melting at the moisture in the corners of his eyes. "Your love is my miracle, too, Ryan. I don't need extra time. I know how much I love you."

"And I love you, Cassandra." He cupped her face in his hands and gently kissed her. "Will you please marry me?"

"Yes, I'd love to marry you," she managed, before he kissed her again.

They ended up back in her bedroom, giggling and laughing as they made love. When they'd finished, she gathered the last remnants of energy to prop herself on her elbow, so she could gaze down at Ryan. "So, how about you take me over to see the inside of that house you picked out for us?"

A shadow crossed his features. "If you don't like it, we can choose something else."

"Don't be silly," she admonished him. "I already love the neighborhood, remember? And I really love the fact that it's located so close to the park. Besides, if you like the place, I'm sure I will, too. The house is just a structure, but it's the people inside that make it a home."

"I'm the luckiest man in the world. You've filled the void in my life, Cassie," he said huskily. "With love and with laughter."

"Always," she promised, knowing that he'd returned the favor tenfold. With Ryan and whatever children they were fortunate enough to have, she was thrilled to have the love of a good man and the family she'd always wanted.

EPILOGUE

Ten months later...

CASSIE WATCHED RYAN pushing Emma in the baby swing at the park, basking in the sound of the little girl's giggles. After Emma's initial struggles she had grown by leaps and bounds beneath their loving care. Emma was a little delayed at first, but she was coming along every day. And they were both happy that Aunt Lydia remained a part of the baby's life.

Emma was already calling Lydia "Nanna." And if all went well, their adoption of the little girl would be complete by the end of the month.

Cassie put a protective hand over her swollen belly, loving the feel of the baby moving around inside her. She and Ryan had been doubly blessed, first, having been able to adopt Emma and, second, when she'd successfully gone through the recommended surgery and had become pregnant.

"Are you all right?" Ryan asked in concern. He took Emma out of her swing and crossed over to her.

"I'm fine. Our baby is just a bit active today," she assured him, taking Emma into her arms. "Did you have fun with Daddy?" she asked.

"Dada," Emma agreed. The she nestled against Cassie. "Mama."

Hearing Emma speak was a huge blessing and she couldn't help tears gathering in her eyes. Then again, it could be the fact that her hormones were a bit out of control.

"I love you, too, sweetpea," she said, pressing a kiss to Emma's plump cheek.

"Maybe you should go home to rest," Ryan said, worry creasing his brow. Ever since she'd told him she was expecting, he'd become more protective than a papa bear.

Not that she blamed him. At first they'd both feared another miscarriage, but now that she was just past twenty weeks she was breathing easier. And she reveled in Ryan's love and attention.

Ryan held her close every single night that he wasn't working, reassuring her that, no matter what happened, he still loved her. And he often talked to her belly, telling the baby how much they loved him or her ,and how much they wanted him or her to grow healthy and strong.

"Are you sure you don't regret jumping into marriage and babies so fast?" Ryan asked, as he gently took Emma back into his arms so Cassie wouldn't have to carry the added weight as they turned toward home. She'd fallen in love with the Cape Cod and together they'd made it a home. "I feel like I rushed you into all this."

She leaned against him, reveling in his strength. "I don't regret one minute," she said with a contented sigh. Everyone in Cedar Bluff had thought they were crazy to get married so quickly but, oddly enough, they'd wanted to be married before welcoming Emma into their lives. "You, and Emma and this new baby are all I've ever wanted."

"Does that mean you've changed your mind about finding out the sex of the baby?" he asked with a teasing grin.

"No, I want the sex of the baby to be a surprise. For both of us."

"I'm holding out for a baby sister for Emma, a little girl who looks just like you," he said, just before he kissed her.

She kissed him back, not really caring one way or the other. A little boy like Ryan would be great, but a sister for Emma would be amazing, too. Either way, she was already blessed.

All that mattered was their love for each other.

And their new family.

* * * * *

HIS PERFECT BRIDE?

BY
LOUISA HEATON

Published in Great Britain 2015
by Mills & Boon, an imprint of Harlequin (UK) Limited,
Eton House, 18-24 Paradise Road, Richmond, Surrey, TW9 1SR

© 2015 Louisa Heaton

ISBN: 978-0-263-24703-9

Harlequin (UK) Limited's policy is to use papers that are natural,
renewable and recyclable products and made from wood grown in
sustainable forests. The logging and manufacturing processes conform
to the legal environmental regulations of the country of origin.

Printed and bound in Spain
by CPI, Barcelona

Dear Reader,

I have to admit to you that there are three pet rats in my house. Yes—three. Blaze, Finlay and Harper are three brothers that I rescued and one day, whilst they were out of their cage, playing on my shoulder, I wondered if there had ever been a Mills & Boon® heroine with pet rats who also needed rescuing herself?

That single question inspired this story! My heroine, Lula, came instantly—in all her glory—and Olly, my hero, quickly followed. I knew that these two, together, would create a love story that we all could fall in love with.

I absolutely adore their story and hope you do too.

Love

Louisa xx

Books by Louisa Heaton

The Baby That Changed Her Life

**Visit the author profile page
at millsandboon.co.uk for more titles**

For MJ and Honey x

CHAPTER ONE

DR OLIVER JAMES was just packing up for the day when his father, Patrick, put his head round the door.

'Got a minute?'

Olly looked up, his bright blue eyes curious. 'Yeah, sure. What's up?'

His father was the senior GP at their practice in the village of Atlee Wold, although not for long. He was taking early retirement, and he'd hired a locum to fill his space until a more permanent doctor could be found.

'That new locum I told you about. She's here. I thought I'd introduce you.'

Right. The new locum. It was a day he was dreading—his father stepping down and away from the practice—and the arrival of a locum brought that day another step closer.

And he was exhausted. It had been a long, cold day. With all the snow outside, it had taken a long time for his consulting room to warm up and he'd spent his time in between seeing patients sipping hot tea and leaning against the ancient radiators. What he really wanted, more than anything else, was to go home and take a long, hot shower and maybe not emerge until he could summon up the energy to get dry and fall into bed. Perhaps with a mug of cocoa?

But even a shower wasn't on the night's agenda, because it was his turn to be on call. Which meant a night trying to sleep fully dressed on his bed, ready to pull his shoes on if his pager sounded. Oh, and a coat, of course, with a scarf and a woolly hat and gloves. And hoping to hell that his old four-wheel drive started up.

'Is she here? I didn't know she was coming today?'

'Well, she's not *here*, exactly. She's at the village hall, running a class.'

Olly raised his eyebrows, impressed. 'She's not been here five minutes. How is she running a *class*?' What was she? Wonder Woman?

His father laughed. 'When she came for her interview she put up flyers. Haven't you seen them? Bellydancing classes at the village hall? All ages, both sexes welcome.'

Olly smirked. '*Belly dancing?* She'll be lucky if anyone turns up to *that*. The old dears round here consider knitting to be their only exercise, and the men their hanging baskets. Can't imagine any of them shaking their wobbly bits in the village hall. Besides, it's freezing.'

'Well, I said we'd pop in, show our support, and it will give you two the opportunity to meet. You'll be working together for a while—until I get a permanent replacement.'

There it was again. The harsh reminder that his father was *leaving*. That things were *changing*. That he had no say in it.

'She doesn't want to do it?'

He didn't quite understand locums. Why travel from one place to another, never really staying anywhere, never getting to know people? Why didn't they just put some roots down somewhere? He knew he'd hate it if it were him.

'She's not sure. But she wants to give the place a trial run.'

'Shouldn't *we* be the ones to offer *her* the trial run?'

Olly was quite territorial about their practice. It had been in the James family for some time. His own father, and Patrick's father, Dermot, had run it before him. The fact that his father had sought a *female* locum also annoyed him. His father was probably trying to match-make again. Find Olly a wife, who would then provide them all with the next line of doctors for the village of Atlee Wold.

'We can but see. She's a charming girl. I think you'll like her,' his father said, with a twinkle in his eyes that was obvious in its implication.

'Dad, you'd make an awful Cupid.'

His father frowned in wry amusement, his brow furrowing into long lines across his weathered forehead. 'Why?'

'Because the wings wouldn't suit you and I'm not sure I'd want to trust you with a bow and arrow.'

'Don't know what you mean. Besides, you've got no worries there, son. She won't match any of the criteria on your "perfect wife" list.'

Olly laughed. Everyone joked about his list. Even if he didn't. There was a serious point to it, after all. If a woman were to be his wife, then she'd need particular qualities. The wife of a country doctor had to have certain standards. Respectability, loyalty, charm, an inner beauty and a calm head on a solid pair of shoulders. Someone who could hold the fort and rear the children. Okay, it might make him seem a bit Victorian in his thinking, but what was wrong with wanting a dependable woman?

'Good. I'd hate to think you were Cupid in disguise. Like I said, with your eyesight the arrows could end up anywhere.'

Patrick helped his son pack up, switch off all the lights and then make sure his call bag was stocked with anything he might need for the night. Then, despite the snow, despite the cold, and despite his tiredness, Patrick and Olly got into Olly's four-wheel drive and set off for the village hall.

It really wasn't very far. Less than a mile. But the snow was thick and still falling. The towns and busy roads in the cities might have grit and salt, but here in Atlee Wold, a Hampshire backwater, they seemed to be lacking everything except table salt from the village shop, which the locals had put out. Some had even put out kitty litter to grit their pathways. Those that were able to shovelled the pathways of those that weren't.

Theirs was a strong community, where people helped each other out where they could. But Olly really hadn't expected that there would be nowhere for him to park in the village hall car park! Or that the pathway would be so well trampled by the many feet that had passed that he could actually see the pavement.

Or that there'd be the beat and throb of loud exotic music clearly heard from some distance away.

'Well, I'll be…'

He parked his four-wheel drive by a tall hedge and when he pushed open his car door to get out it sent down a spray of snow on top of him. Some of it went down the back of his neck and top and he shivered as the icy crystals tickled his spine.

'Ugh!'

Patrick laughed. 'Looks like a full house.'

'You don't have to be so delighted.'

The village hall was lit along its gutters with old Christmas lights that hadn't yet been taken down, and from the windows bright yellow light flared. There was the sound of Indian music, loud but muffled, emanating from the building itself, with an earthy beat.

Olly shook his head with disbelief. How had a complete stranger managed to rabble-rouse an entire village to do belly dancing? He might have expected the hall to be full if it was a gardening class or crochet, bingo or a knitting circle, but *belly dancing*?

Part of him just couldn't wait to meet this Wonder Woman. An image of her was building in his head. She was a GP, so she had to be somewhat sensible. Someone middle-aged and quite strait-laced who did belly dancing because it was just something different? Perhaps she had to fight for attention and this was her way… As his father said, *not* a woman to threaten his list of the attributes a 'perfect wife' ought to have.

Belly-dancing instructor was nowhere on the list at all!

Shaking the snow from his shoulders, he entered the village hall after his father. There was a small foyer that they went into first, with a tuck shop to one side. Then there were two large rooms in the village hall and one was in darkness. From the other the music blared.

'You ready?' His father had to raise his voice to be heard.

'Of course I am!' he called back, pulling open the door.

But he stopped in his tracks when he saw the woman leading the class. His dad even bumped into him from behind.

Olly gaped open-mouthed at the new locum GP.

This is not what I expected.

She was petite—elfin, almost—with a graceful, slim, but womanly figure which he couldn't help but notice due to her clothing. Or what there was of it. Her dark, almost black hair was cut short at the back, but at the front it was long and multicoloured—cyan blue, purple and pink streaks fell across her face. Her arms were layered with bangles and she had a red jewel in her belly button and she twirled and swirled and sashayed as she led the class in 'undulation one'.

'All right, Olly?' his dad asked, staring at his son in amusement.

How can this woman be a GP? She doesn't look like one.

But what was a GP *supposed* to look like? There was a shimmery wrap around her waist, tightly sheathing her perfectly curved bottom, and it tinkled and glimmered as she moved. Then, as she pointed her tiny feet, he noticed tattoos and nail polish and toe rings, before his eyes rose back up to her face to see large brown eyes, rosy cheeks and a cheeky smile.

Patrick leaned in closer to his son to whisper in his ear. 'Close your mouth. You look like a hungry hippo.'

Olly did as he was told and swallowed hard. This wasn't a GP. She looked like a pixie. An imp. Or a fairy. Yes, that was it—a fairy.

If she turns around I'll see she's got wings on her back.

But there were no wings. Just another tattoo. He couldn't make out what it was from this distance...

And the hall was full! Here were people and patients that he knew well. People who suffered from arthritis and hip problems and knee problems. And here they all were, shaking their booty with the best of them, smiles plastered across their faces.

They must be off their meds.

Or their heads.

One of his patients, Mrs Macabee, noticed him from her position midway down the class. 'Ooh, hello, Dr James! Fancy seeing you here! Are you joining us?'

He watched Mrs Macabee tilt her hip up and down, up and down. He blinked his head to clear the image, remembered what he was there for and then smiled politely. 'Sorry, Mrs M, I don't dance—and besides, I'm here on business.' He had to raise his voice to be heard.

'This is *business*?' She laughed as she followed their new GP in her instructions.

He simply couldn't believe it. Here was half the village, packing out the small hall—young and old, self-respect be damned, all kitted out with hip scarves and coin-edged skirts, shaking their backsides and waving their arms about.

The music was catchy, though, and he was unaware that his foot had been tapping to the beat until it suddenly stopped and everyone started clapping each other. Their new GP was thanking everyone for coming…patting herself down with a soft, pink towel.

There were lots of people fighting over each other to go to her and thank her for so much fun, the best time they'd had in ages, et cetera, et cetera.

Olly pursed his lips as he waited for everyone to file out after handing back their belly-dancing garb. He nodded hello at a lot of them.

His father looked bemused. 'Why are you smiling so much?' he asked his old man.

'It's the look on your face.'

'What's wrong with it?'

Patrick laughed. 'What's *right* with it? You look like you've been sucking lemons.'

'Don't be ridiculous.'

His father was being silly. Of course he didn't look that way. Why would he? That would imply that he was jealous of this woman or something, wouldn't it? And he had nothing to be jealous of! So she'd got the village out to an exercise class... So what?

The pixie came over, towelling her face dry. 'Hi!'

She was still full of energy, it seemed, and appeared quite happy with the way the class had gone.

His father stepped forward to make the introductions. 'Lula—this is my son, Oliver. Olly, this is Dr Lula Chance.'

He held out his hand to shake hers, aware of how much the bangles jingled as he did so. 'Lula? That's an odd name—where's that from?'

'It's short for Louise. I prefer Lula. Like hula.'

He looked at her bare slim waist and womanly curves. 'And do you?' he asked, dragging his eyes back up to her face.

'Do I what?'

He swallowed hard. 'Hula?'

She beamed a dazzling smile in his direction and it was like being smacked in the gut.

'I've been known to.'

She was patting her chest with the towel, attracting the attention of his gaze, and he had to fight *really hard* to keep his eyes on her face.

'So you're the guy with the list?'

Olly's cheeks coloured—and not from the cold. 'I am. Nothing's private here, it would seem. Welcome to village life.'

Patrick laughed and laid a hand on Lula's shoulder.

'Well done, Lula! Getting everyone out like that! Your class seemed a success!'

She nodded, her blue, purple and pink fringe quivering around her face. 'I hope so. The first class was free, to get people interested. The real test is in seeing if they come back and pay for it.'

'The real test is making sure none of them have a heart attack. Have you got oxygen on standby?' Olly asked.

Patrick laughed at his son. 'I'm sure they'll be fine. Now—to business. Have you moved in yet?'

'My boxes are in the car. You've got the key to the cottage?'

Olly looked up, his sulk gone. 'Which cottage?'

She frowned. 'Erm…Moonrose Cottage, I think it's called. Is that right, Patrick?'

Patrick? She's calling him Patrick? What happened to Dr James?

'Moonrose? You're moving into *Gran's* old cottage?'

His father looked at him sternly. 'Yes, she is—and you're going to help her.' He handed over the key.

His dad *knew* how he felt about Moonrose Cottage! It might be his gran's old place, but it was also where his own mother had grown up. The place had special memories. If they let it out to this pixie then God only knew what she'd fill it with. Parties, or raves, or something equally mad. Moonrose was a quiet, sedate house. Charming and conservative and quintessentially English.

'But I'm on call.'

'And Lula, here, has offered to be on call with you whilst you help her unpack.' He grinned. 'Isn't that kind of her?'

Olly looked at Lula and raised an eyebrow at those

large brown eyes twinkling madly at him and doing weird things to his stomach and other body parts.

'It is. Thank you, Lula. Though you must be tired— travelling, running a dance class, moving in, going on call?'

'I like to pack a lot into life.' She dabbed at her chest with the towel and again he had to concentrate really hard not to look.

'You don't say?'

Patrick stepped away. 'Well, I'll leave you two to it. Olly, I'll walk back home— it's not far. You go on with Lula and I'll see you both in the morning.'

He shook Lula's hand and then waved goodbye and stepped out, leaving Olly and Lula alone.

Olly felt uncomfortable. There were no women like Lula in Atlee Wold. Vivid and bright and crazy and...

And what?

'So, Moonrose Cottage, eh?' He stared at her hair. So many colours...like a rainbow.

'Yeah... Strange name, I thought.'

'It's after the Blue Moon roses my gran planted when she was a little girl. They're all around it and they won prizes in the village show. If you're still here in summer you'll see them in bloom. They're quite beautiful.'

She smiled. 'I'm sure they are.'

'So, shall I give you a hand to pack all this bling away?' He pointed at the box full of coin-edged skirts and multicoloured scarves she'd given to his patients.

Lula laughed. 'Thanks. It *is* a lot of bling. The hall warden said I could store it below the stage.'

'Okay.'

He helped her lift a large bag through the stage door opening. They were about to leave when Lula pointed out a couple of boxes covered by thick blankets.

'Could you help me take those out? They're mine. I couldn't leave them in the car.'

Olly nodded and hefted the two boxes one on top of the other, hearing metal clank inside. Then they left the village hall, pulling the door closed after switching off the lights.

Outside, the snow was lit by the fairy lights, so it blinked softly in reds and blues, yellows and greens. It was really quite pretty, and had the effect of making Lula look even more multicoloured than she had been before. Like a peacock.

Definitely a magical fairy.

'Are you okay?' she asked.

He blinked. 'Sorry?'

'You were staring. At me.' She grinned.

Olly licked his lips, thinking quickly. 'Ah, right... yes. Erm...I was just wondering where you'd parked your car? I don't see one.'

She pointed, her hand seeming to twinkle in the lights as they reflected off her rings and bangles. 'I parked down the road. I wanted the patients to be able to park close.'

'That's kind.'

She accepted the compliment. 'Thank you. I try to be. So...?'

'So...?'

'Will you drive in front? Show me where the cottage is?'

Of course! Idiot! Stupid!

'Sure. But let's make sure your car starts first.'

'Oh, she always does.'

'She?'

'Betsy.'

'Your car is called Betsy?'

'Betsy the Bug.' She stopped in front of a red car with large black polka dots on it, like a ladybird.

Once again Olly was left standing mute and blinking. After a moment he managed, 'Cute.'

'I think so. Here—why don't you put that large one in the front? This small one can go in the boot.'

Her engine rumbled into life straight away and he pointed out his four-wheel drive, further up the road. Lula said that she'd wait for him and he walked back up to his car, his boots crunching in the snow, muttering to himself.

Dad, I'm going to kill you... What on earth have you done?

As a choice of locum she was a tad...out there. Not the sort of locum he'd expected his father to hire. There had to have been plenty of other doctors he might have chosen from. Sensible, sedate people. The type to blend in with village life.

Not this firecracker...

His four-wheel drive started first time and he indicated to pull out, noticing her following him through the high street. He took a left and kept looking in his rearview mirror to make sure she was still there. Still following.

He thought of his 'perfect wife' list.

She didn't match any of the items on it.

But he felt mysteriously intrigued by her.

Bewitching. That's what she is.

Lula followed Olly through the village roads, realizing she'd made a big mistake. When she'd come for her interview with Patrick, she'd known she was getting involved with a father-and-son team and that had seemed fine. But Patrick was a silver-haired fox, with sparkling, kind eyes, and she should have just *known* that the son was going to be drop-dead gorgeous. However, she hadn't worried too much about it. She'd concentrated much more on her other reason for coming to Atlee Wold and assumed that Patrick's son would be just another person to work with.

But when he'd walked into that village hall... It had been as if a film star had walked in. She'd half expected to see paparazzi following him in. Gorgeous and sexy, yet a down-to-earth guy. She'd tried to ignore him so that she could carry on with her class. She'd even stumbled over her steps. But thankfully no one had seemed to notice.

And now she was following him. Through the snowy streets. In Betsy. Following his old jalopy.

Olly had pulled up outside a small thatched cottage surrounded by tall briar wood. It looked pretty, and she could only imagine how gorgeous it might look in the summertime, with its white walls and blue roses, butterflies and bees flitting about the place. There was an arched trellis over the front door, with what looked like an ancient Russian vine growing over it.

It really wasn't that far from the GP surgery, or the village hall, and she hoped that tomorrow she could try walking in to work. She had a pair of wellies somewhere in one of the boxes she already had in the car. A small removals lorry would drop off her other stuff tomorrow.

He stood back so she could make fresh tracks in the snow to the front door, and then he passed her a key.

Smiling, she took it and tried to reassure him. 'Don't worry—I'll look after the place.'

'I'm sure you will. Shall we get the lights on, the fire burning and then get your boxes in?'

Lula nodded. 'Sounds great.' Though it might be a bit awkward, the two of them alone before a roaring fire…

The key turned easily and she pushed open the door, wondering what to expect. Patrick had agreed to let the cottage out to her at a reduced rate and the price was very reasonable. She certainly wouldn't be able to get a place in London at the rate he'd given her—not even a bedsit! And here she was with the key to a beautiful, thatched, two-bedroom cottage.

Inside, she found the light switches and gasped in delight. The low roof created an immediate intimacy in the small rooms. The lounge furniture was covered in white sheets, but when she removed them she found old, chintzy chairs, with scatter cushions made from patchwork, and an old green leather sofa. The walls were whitewashed, with exposed dark beams, and there was a good-sized fireplace already stacked with logs.

'Shall I start the fire for you?' Olly said.

Lula smiled. 'That's okay. I can do it. Why don't you get me those boxes from Betsy?'

He nodded, but she could tell he would have been a lot happier playing with the fire.

Typical man.

She liked Olly already. He was charming and old-fashioned and very English. He had classic good looks, with dark blond hair and bright blue eyes like Chris Hemsworth. *Just my type.* But, despite the handsome looks and the knockout body, she hoped she didn't have to worry about there being an attraction between them whilst they worked. It wasn't the sort of thing she was looking for. Not here. There were other reasons for her being in Atlee Wold and romance wasn't one of them.

The firelighters worked quickly and Lula soon had a bright orange flame licking at the wood. There was a stack of old newspapers to one side, and she screwed up a few and inserted them into gaps in the wood to help it. Soon the crackling flames had taken hold and the fire began to build. She stood warming her hands as Olly came barging in, carrying the larger of her two blanketed boxes.

'What's *in* this thing?'

She took it from him, looked around and saw a table in the corner that looked suitable. Setting the box down, she freed the blanket and whipped it off. 'Say hello to Nefertiti and Cleo!'

She saw him take a step back, his mouth open in shock and horror. 'Are they…*rats*?'

Lula grinned and bit her lip as she stooped down to open the door of the cage and both rats—one dark brown and one pure white with pink eyes—climbed out onto her hands and ran up her arm to sit on her shoulder. 'Dumbo rats. Aren't they beautiful?'

He looked carefully at her, as if judging her sanity. 'They're *rats*.'

'They're very intelligent animals.'

'So are dolphins, but you don't have two of those, do you?' He watched the rats play around under the dark wisps of Lula's hair, their noses and whiskers twitching. Then he had a sudden dreadful thought. 'What's in the other box? The one in the boot of your car?'

Lula grinned. 'Anubis. You'd better get him—he's on a heat pad especially.'

Olly put his hands on his hips. '*What* is Anubis?'

She tilted her head to one side, amused by his reaction. 'I'll get him. Here.'

She reached up and took hold of the two rats from under her hair and planted them on his shoulder. She could see how he froze and winced and twitched at each of their movements as they gave him a good sniff. Their little pink noses and whiskers tickled his ears.

Olly stood frozen, as if rigor mortis had set in. 'Please hurry.'

Lula chuckled, threw her jacket on and rushed out into the snow. Pretty soon she came back with the smaller blanketed box and put it on the coffee table. There was a cable and plug for this one, and when she pressed the wall switch a small light came on inside the blanket.

Olly stood awkwardly with the two rats running about his shoulders. 'Could you take these?'

Lula laughed. He looked so funny standing there, with his shoulders all hunched up by his ears and two rats perched on his shoulder, trying to sniff the hair on his head. She scooped them up easily and placed them back in their cage.

Olly let out a big breath and then brushed off his shoulders. 'Thanks. So, Anubis...what is he?'

She looked at him slightly askance. 'He's my big challenge.'

'Challenge? Why?'

'Because I'm scared to death of him, and as I'm determined to beat all my fears I've borrowed him from a friend until I get over that fear.'

Olly gave a single nod. 'And that fear is called...?' Though he had a suspicion.

Lula removed the blanket. 'Arachnophobia.'

In the small tank, amongst some wood and soil, was a large, very dark, very hairy, red-kneed tarantula.

He peered closer. 'It's bigger than my hand.'

'Isn't he a beauty?'

'I thought you were scared?'

'I am. But I can still appreciate how gorgeous he is.'

'And it's your aim in life to pick this thing up?'

She nodded. 'One of my aims. Eventually.'

Olly shook his head. 'You're madder than a boxful of circus clowns.'

They both laughed, but then Lula shivered and headed over to the fire and stood with her back to it, hands stretched out behind her. 'Freezing!'

'Shall I get the rest of the boxes?'

'If you wouldn't mind?'

'It depends... Are there any more zoo creatures in Betsy?'

Lula smiled. 'Just woolly jumpers.'

'Safe enough. Though you might have warned me earlier that I was handling livestock.'

They'd unloaded all the boxes, and Lula had put her clothes away and freshened up, when Olly's phone rang. The out-of-hours doctor service informed him that one of his older patients in the area was suffering from chest pains. Could he go?

'It's Mr Maynard. He lives out on one of the farms. We'll take my car.'

Lula nodded. It would be best to start with, until she got to know her way around—where the best roads were, what shortcuts there were. And this was a good way to meet some of the patients who couldn't make it into the surgery for various reasons. She was particularly drawn to find all of those patients who tried to keep themselves hidden away and make sure she saw *everyone*.

As Olly drove he filled her in on Mr Maynard.

'He's eighty-two years old and lives alone. His farm was a dairy once, but he never married or had kids and during the nineties everything just fell to pieces. He had to sell his herd and now he lives in the farmhouse alone.'

Lula thought it sounded a very lonely existence. 'How does he get out and about?'

'He doesn't. His arthritis is bad, so he doesn't drive. Molly from the village shop goes up twice a week with his shopping and drops it into his kitchen. He generally looks after himself.'

'Any other health conditions I ought to know about?'

'He's got high blood pressure, but he's on medication for that.'

'Ramipril?'

Olly nodded. 'And a diuretic.'

The diuretic had been included to help reduce fluid in the body. The more fluid there was to be transported in thin arteries, the higher the blood pressure, so a diuretic helped to reduce fluid build-up.

Driving through the village at night was quite surreal. Everywhere was covered in snow, and yellow lamplight lit the way every thirty yards or so, until eventually they hit the outskirts of the village and the lamplight disappeared. They had to rely on the four-wheel drive's headlights, and with thick snow still falling it was very slow going.

Lula wondered how on earth Molly at the shop would even get to Mr Maynard's farm with the ground covered like this. Did she have a four-wheel drive?

A sign appeared—'Burner's Farm'—and Olly turned into its driveway. They were bumped and jostled along as he drove down the pitted road and eventually an old stone farmhouse appeared, surrounded by old barns and outbuildings in a crumbling state of decay. It was hard to see the property's true state at night, but Lula could see that there were sections of roof missing from the barn due to the snowfall, and that all the old machinery was decaying from lack of use.

Alighting from the car, Olly grabbed his bag and he and Lula trudged through the snow to the farmhouse door. Olly banged on it quite hard, before pushing it open and calling out. 'Mr Maynard? Donald? It's Dr James and Dr Chance.'

'In here,' a croaky voice called back.

The hallway was dark, but at the end of it was a brightly lit room from which warmth poured. Lula was glad he had a coal fire on the go, and was keeping warm at least. Their patient was sitting in a chair with blankets round him, and at his side were the remains of a hot dinner and a glass of red wine.

'Donald? This is Dr Chance—she's new at the surgery. How are you?'

Mr Maynard peered past Olly at her and beamed in a giant smile. 'Well, hello, dear, and what a pretty little thing you are!'

'Hello, Mr Maynard. How are you doing?' She sat down beside him, instantly taking in whatever information she could—the colour of his skin, whether or not he seemed clammy, his respiratory rate—but he looked good. He was a healthy colour, not out of breath and with no signs of sweating.

'I'm all right now. They just panic at the other end of the phone, don't they?'

She felt sure he was referring to the people who manned the out-of-hours doctor service. She herself didn't think they panicked, but they had to respond urgently if a patient mentioned chest pains. It could be life-threatening.

'What made you call in tonight?'

'Well, my chest was hurting, my dear, and when

you're all alone you convince yourself you're about to
kick the bucket at any moment so I rang up. But I had
a damned good belch and felt a lot better. Just indigestion, I think—all stuff and nonsense. No need for you
to have come out and checked on me.'

She shook her head, smiling, and patted the back of
his hand. 'There's every need to check on you. Now,
while we're here, let's check your blood pressure and
pulse—is that okay?'

He let them do their tests, and he seemed quite well.
His blood pressure was in the normal range for him and
his pulse rate was steady and strong. He had no pain,
and they could see that he'd eaten a particularly strong
curry, so perhaps he was right and it *was* just indigestion he'd experienced.

'You're on your own out here, Mr Maynard?' Lula
asked.

'Call me Donald, dear.'

'Donald.' She smiled.

'I am. Been this way for years—lost my Teddy eight
years back.'

'Teddy?'

'The dog,' Olly said. 'Gorgeous Border collie, he
was.'

'That he was,' said Donald.

'Don't you miss getting out and about, Donald? You
must get bored, being here in these four walls all the
time?'

'I do…but what am I going to do? I don't like bingo,
and I don't like going down the pub—it's not my thing.
I like a bit of culture, me, and there ain't no culture in
Atlee Wold.'

Lula nodded in understanding. 'You like wine?' She
pointed at his glass.

'Only the good stuff!' He chuckled.

'Well, you leave it with me, Donald. Let me see what I can arrange.'

When they got back in the car Olly looked at her questioningly. 'What are you planning?'

'I know someone who knows someone else. I think we can get Mr Maynard out and about and enjoying life again. Why should he be stuck at that farm with just memories? There's life in the old dog yet.'

He smiled. 'He seemed to like you.'

'He's a nice guy.'

'He *is* a nice guy. But I've been trying to get him involved with village life for years and he's never budged from that chair.'

She smiled mysteriously. 'Perhaps he needs something more than just this village? Never underestimate the power of a good woman.'

He looked at her askance. What was wrong with 'just' the village?

Perhaps she bewitches her patients, too.

The next morning Lula telephoned a colleague's friend in Petersfield, who ran coach holidays, and told him about Donald Maynard. After a quick discussion they found a trip for Donald that they thought would suit him down to the ground. It was a tour of wineries in the Loire region of France, over three days, stopping off at some lovely B & Bs along the way and all at a greatly reduced price.

Lula rang Mr Maynard and asked him if he could be ready in a week's time to catch a bus, if it collected him from the end of his driveway.

Donald was thrilled. 'Chuffed to mint balls' was his expression, and he couldn't thank Lula enough. She put the phone down at her end, feeling delighted that she'd been able to help a wonderful old man who deserved to enjoy life, despite his years.

She got herself ready for work. Determined to walk to the surgery, she rooted around for her wellies. With her woolly hat and scarf on, she was ready to go, and she opened her door, expecting to set straight off. She wanted to make a good impression on her very first day at the surgery.

But someone had left a cardboard box on her doorstep.

And inside something was crying.

CHAPTER TWO

LULA TOOK A sharp intake of breath in the cold morning air. There had been no more snow after their trip home from Mr Maynard's farm last night, and the top layer had frozen to a crisp. The cardboard box was from a biscuit manufacturer, and the top had all four corners folded into each other, with some air holes punched through by something like a ballpoint pen.

Lula almost couldn't believe her eyes.

This sort of thing didn't happen twice in a lifetime...

Kneeling down, she peeled back the corners and looked inside to see a newly born baby, swaddled in tight blankets and towels.

'Oh, my God!'

Lula scooped up the baby and stood up, holding it to her, undoing her coat buttons and scooting the baby inside her greatcoat. Beneath the baby there was a blue hot water bottle, and it was still quite warm, so Lula could only hope that the baby hadn't been left outside in the cold for too long. With her free hand she picked up the cardboard box and brought it inside, kicking the door closed, then she went back over to the fire to add more logs and get it really going again.

When that was done she picked up her phone and dialled the police. There was no police station in Atlee

Wold itself, but there was one in the next village over—
South Wold. She could only assume they'd send someone from there.

She wanted to examine the baby, but the need to keep
it warm and monitor its breathing overrode all other
instincts. Next she called the surgery, assuming one of
the receptionists would answer, but Olly did.

'Atlee Surgery.'

His voice was solid and reassuring to hear.

'Oliver?'

'Lula? What's up?'

'You need to come over.'

'I'm about to start morning surgery.'

'Can your father do it? I need you here. Now.'

He paused for a moment, but he must have been
swayed by the quiet desperation in her voice because
he said, 'I'll be right over.'

Lula paced the floor—back and forth, back and
forth—humming tunes, gently jigging the baby up
and down, trying to keep it monitored, checking on its
breathing. She had no idea if it was a boy or a girl, or
even if it had all its bits and pieces—there'd been no
time to check. When Olly got there maybe they could
check the baby together.

Suddenly she remembered she ought to have asked
him to bring his call-out bag, and hoped he'd have heard
from her tone that it might be needed.

Why didn't I tell him it was needed? So stupid!

Because the shock of finding the baby had been so
great. It wasn't what you expected to find when you
went out through the front door in the morning. At the
most you might expect a present from the cat, if you
kept one, or perhaps a friendly offering from a night-
time fox on your doorstep. But a baby…?

No.

She knew what would happen. The police would arrive, and they'd take everything. The baby, the blankets, the hot water bottle, the box. They'd try and trace its mother, but it would be difficult. There were never enough clues in this sort of situation, even if the mother left a note...

She rummaged in the box.

No note.

Where's the mother?

More importantly, *who* was the mother? She had to have been desperate to do this. To leave her baby in a cardboard box, in the middle of winter, on the doorstep of a stranger. She couldn't have known that the baby would be found early. Could she? What if Lula had been on a late shift? The baby would have frozen to death. It didn't bear thinking about.

It might be a teenage girl—someone afraid to tell her parents that she'd been pregnant. But how would you hide something like that? The baby looked a decent size—about seven pounds. It was obviously full term, so the pregnancy must have shown.

Perhaps it was an older woman who'd had an affair, and then her husband had come back from Afghanistan, or somewhere, and she'd had to get rid of it?

No, Lula, too far-fetched.

Or was it?

Finding a baby on her doorstep would probably have sounded too far-fetched yesterday.

There was a hammering on her front door and she rushed over to open it, letting Olly in. He stopped and stared at the baby and she saw the puzzlement on his face.

'It's not mine!'

'Where did it come from?' He closed the door behind him, pulling off his jacket.

She explained what had happened and they laid the baby on the rug in front of the roaring fire to examine it.

She was newborn. Barely hours old. The umbilical cord was tied off with navy blue string and still fresh. Vernix—the grease that covered a baby in the womb, to stop its skin getting waterlogged—was in the armpits and creases of the baby, indicating that maybe she was a little before term.

She was a little cold, but otherwise well.

She was extremely lucky.

'She can't have been outside long,' Olly said.

'Perhaps she'd only just been left by someone?'

'Did you see anyone when you went outside? When you opened the door?'

Lula tried to think. But the shock of finding an abandoned baby had overridden everything. She couldn't recall looking around the cottage or past the garden. She'd noticed the box, heard the crying and snuffling, and when she'd seen it was a baby had hurried back inside.

'I didn't look.'

'Lula...'

'I didn't *think*! I was in shock! I...you don't expect this, do you?' She wrapped the baby up again and scooped her up, holding her tight against her body.

Olly watched her pace back and forth. 'There must be a mother somewhere. She could be at risk if she doesn't get proper medical attention.'

She nodded. 'I know. I figure it has to be a teenager. Who do you know in the village that fits the bill?'

Olly sank onto the couch. 'There are a few teenagers in the village—about twenty or so, I think. Most of them catch the school bus to go to the comprehensive in South Wold. I don't see them very much—they don't tend to come and see the doctor.'

'Have any come to you about going on the pill? Any who you think could be sexually active?'

He shook his head. 'No. I honestly haven't seen any for a while. I think the last teenager I saw was the Blakes's daughter, and that was for an ear infection.'

He racked his brains, but Olly could think of no one he'd seen at the surgery lately. Nor had he seen any teenage girl about the village on his day-to-day travels who had aroused his suspicion.

Surely he would have noticed a pregnant teenager?

But, then again, the same could be said for the girl's parents. How did you *not* notice?

Olly made them both a drink, cringing at the sight of Anubis on the kitchen counter. All darkness and legs.

He'd just taken the tea through to the lounge when the police arrived.

There was a lot of questioning, a lot of hustle and bustle. Lula gave a statement, and then Olly told them the little he knew—that he couldn't think of anyone who might have been concealing a pregnancy.

Lula felt quite protective of the little mite, and almost didn't want to hand her over, but in the end she did, her heart sinking a little at the thought of what the future might hold for the little girl. Would she get lost in the system? Be passed from family to family?

She could only hope that they would find the baby's mother. Before it was too late.

After the police had gone, and the small lounge and kitchen had emptied of uniformed bodies, she sank down into the seat by the fire and stared at Olly, ignoring the way the firelight flickered in the reflection of his blue eyes.

'What a welcome to the village!'

He attempted a smile. 'We did what we could for her.'

'I worry that it's not enough. Poor thing.'

'We'll find the mum.'

'But what if we *don't*? That baby will enter the system and there's no guarantee of a happy ending for her, you know? Not all foster homes are great.'

He cocked his head to one side. 'Are you speaking from experience?'

She met his gaze, noticing how beautiful his dark blue eyes were, framed by thick dark lashes. Men could be so lucky with their eyelashes, it seemed.

Lula nodded, deciding to be open with him. 'I was like that little baby once. But I wasn't left in a cardboard box in the snow in the middle of winter. My mother left me in a Moses basket on a beach.'

'You were abandoned?' He sat forward.

She gave a wry smile. 'From what I know, I was found by a family who were packing up their beach hut. They'd been with their kids by the water's edge, paddling and stuff. When they came back they found me. My mother had left a note, saying how sorry she was, how much she regretted doing it, but that she couldn't keep me. With the note was this.' She reached into her neckline and pulled out a silver necklace with a heart charm on the end. 'She signed the note with the initials "EL".'

'"EL"? That's all you were left with?'

'And that she'd called me Louise.' Lula sipped her drink and smiled at him. 'You don't have to feel sorry for me, you know. I've lived my life to the full.'

'It's not over yet. You've got years left.'

'We never know, though, do we? I could get knocked down by a bus tomorrow.'

He frowned. 'Actually, you couldn't. There's no bus service tomorrow.'

She smiled, but then Olly was serious again. 'What happened to you?'

Lula shrugged. 'I went from home to home till I was about seven and then I got put with a family who decided they wanted to adopt me.'

'The Chances?'

'Yes. They were lovely—really sweet people—but I knew I didn't belong to them.'

'They'd chosen you. Out of all those children looking for a permanent home, they picked *you*. You should be pleased about that.'

'They had other adopted children and each of them had a problem, too. A health problem. Peter and Daisy Chance seemed to go after all the hard-luck cases—don't ask me why.'

'Perhaps they thought that children with issues needed the most love?'

She shrugged. 'Maybe.'

'But what was wrong with *you*? If you don't mind me asking?'

She smiled. 'I had leukaemia. Childhood leukaemia. They had no idea if I was going to live or die, and still the Chances wanted me. That was pretty brave of them, huh?'

He nodded, thoughtful.

'I got better—though the chemo did some horrible things.'

'But you got through it okay?'

'As okay as I could at that age.'

Olly smiled. 'You seem well now, though, and—as you say yourself—you pack everything into life. You work as a doctor, which is hard work and stressful, and you do other stuff, too.'

'I made the decision to be happy and enjoy life and take my medicine every day.' She smiled at him.

He looked at her strangely and she laughed at the curious frown on his face. 'Why are you laughing?'

'It was your face!' She chuckled.

'Thanks. A man likes to know his looks are amusing.'

'It's not your looks, Olly. There's nothing wrong with those. But it was the way you *looked* at me.'

'I was admiring you,' he protested. 'I mean, I was admiring your *attitude* to life. Not admiring *you*, per se. Not with that hair,' he added with a wry grin.

She pursed her lips with amusement and then stood up and looked in the mirror over the fireplace. 'There's nothing wrong with my hair.' She checked some of the strands, tweaking and rearranging her colours.

He stood up next to her and they both looked at each other in the mirror's reflection. 'No, of course not—it's very…conservative.'

'Hah! Now you're being a snob. I thought I might add another colour to it, actually.'

'Really?' He raised his eyebrows in question.

'What do you think to making the rest of it green?'

'You can't be serious?'

'I'm deadly serious.'

He opened his mouth to say something, but nothing came out. His open-mouthed flustering made her burst into more laughter and she punched him playfully on the arm. 'I'm just joshing with you. Of course I'm not going green.'

'Thank God for that!'

'I was thinking more like letter-box red.'

He didn't believe her this time. He picked up his jacket and threw it on. 'Well, though it has been fun, Dr Chance, deciding whether you want to look like your head has been in a collision with a paint factory, you and I need to put in an appearance at work. Otherwise the whole village may well fall foul of a deadly plague without our being in our chairs, ministering to the sick.'

'Hmm... I'm not one to turn down the chance of fighting an epidemic.'

'Ready to go, then?'

She put on her own coat and the incredibly long scarf that she'd been wearing earlier. 'As I'll ever be.'

'You don't need to feed the animals before we go?'

'Already done.'

'Any closer to picking up Anubis?' He meant the tarantula.

'No. But I gave him a damned good look this morning, and I got within two feet of the tank without shaking.'

'Progress!'

'Exactly!'

'Do you want to sit in with me this morning? We could do the clinic together and it would give me the opportunity to fill you in on some of our frequent flyers.'

He meant the regulars who always turned up to the surgery, no matter what the state of their health. Every surgery had them. They were the people you could depend upon to turn up, who had nothing wrong with them but had got themselves appointments because they were lonely, or they wanted to chat about their problems in life in general.

Then there were the hypochondriacs, who turned up over every little niggle—real or imagined. But you had to take them seriously each time, and check them out no matter what, or you'd get *The Boy Who Cried Wolf* syndrome. If one day you decided to ignore their call for help it would be the one time that they were actually ill and really needed you.

'Sure. I think that would be a good idea.'

'And if I introduce you they won't think that you're some sort of fairy.'

She was closing her front door and locking it. 'You think I look like a fairy?' She tried to sound offended, even though she wasn't.

'It was my first thought.'

Her head cocked to one side. 'And you, Dr James, look like a blond Clark Kent. Do I need to warn everyone that you don't actually wear your underpants over your trousers?'

Olly seemed to take the hint. And the reprimand. 'I'm sorry.'

She perked up and smiled. 'You're so *serious*! I was joking! I quite like the fact you think I look like a fairy. I'd hate to look boring and normal.'

'What's wrong with boring and normal?'

'It's *boring*. And normal. Be different. Stand out from the crowd. Have a list!' She laughed and he almost looked dismayed at her enjoyment.

'You think I'm wrong to have a list?'

'Not wrong, per se. Everyone has certain requirements for a partner.'

'Exactly.'

'They just don't usually write them down.'

He stopped her from trudging through the snow by grabbing hold of her arm. 'How do you know they're written down?'

She stopped to look at his hand, trying hard not to

think of how close it was to her smouldering skin. She met his gaze instead. 'Your father told me.'

'Dad did?'

She nodded and he let go.

They were crunching through the snow now, past Betsy and Olly's car and towards the surgery. It was picture-postcard perfect, with everything blanketed in white.

Lula turned to him. 'You know, Olly, a man like you shouldn't need a list.'

'A man like me? What does *that* mean?'

'A young man. Educated. Good-looking. An eligible bachelor. Though you could do with a different look.'

'What's wrong with my look?'

'Oh, come on, Olly. You think I don't already know that you're considered to be the "hottie" of the village? All the ladies last night at the belly dancing think you're a babe.'

He preened a little. 'Really?'

'Uh-huh.'

'And you?'

'And me what?'

'Do *you* think I'm a babe?'

'Well, as gorgeous as you are, I can tell your look hasn't changed for decades. Side parting...bit conservative. It would surprise me if you didn't have a pair of brown corduroy trousers in your wardrobe. You need to spice yourself up a bit.'

She stopped to look at him, at his dark hair, his bright blue eyes and solid jaw. He was narrow at the waist and broad at the shoulders. He might have been a male model. Olly was the epitome of male good looks, handsome and attractive, and if she was in the market for a man then he'd be the type that she would go for.

But I'm not. And I won't.

'You're okay, though.'

He laughed out loud, plumes of his warm breath freezing in the cold winter air. As she watched him chuckling to himself beside her, she felt a little twinge of regret that she'd sworn off men for good.

Olly wasn't sure what to make of Lula's assessment of his character. He was amused and offended at the same time. What was wrong with having a pair of brown corduroys? They were comfortable and warm and... Oh. Sensible.

Was he *very* sensible? Yes, he was, but he'd always thought of that as a strength. He was a loyal, dependable guy who enjoyed living a quiet life. Better than having to live in a big, noisy city, where no one talked to each other or looked out for their neighbours. Where there was no community spirit.

Lula seemed to think that his life was a little too staid. A little too quiet. Genteel. But when you enjoyed living in a small community it was what you got used to. Lula's arrival in the village, with her rainbow-splashed hair and joyful approach to life, was like dropping a lit firework into a dormant barrel of gunpowder.

She would set off sparks and there would be implications.

Some people might enjoy it. Some people might be glad of it—the village being woken up from its dreamy slumber.

Will I like it?

He liked *her.* He knew that already. She was bright and funny and clever, and he loved her attitude to life. But he couldn't help but wonder if she would leave him feeling a bit...*beige.* He was so used to a quiet life—

answering to no one but himself, really—and he'd resigned himself to the fact that the right woman hadn't come along... He'd always figured he'd end up running the practice when his dad retired. The business would be his. Everyone would expect him to carry on and he'd do it—easily, without complaint...

But what if he couldn't? What if Lula was exactly the sort of person he needed in his life before he lived the entire thing having never done anything challenging or exciting?

He didn't like to think she would make him feel his life was lacking in flavour.

He didn't like to think that she would disapprove of his life.

He wanted to prove her wrong.

It was nice and warm in the surgery. The receptionist made them cups of tea and Olly gave Lula a quick tour. He showed her where her consulting room was, and then they went to his and he instructed her in how to log on to the computer system.

Even though there'd been that morning's drama and they were a little behind, and the waiting room was full, Lula needed to see how to use the practice's system. It wasn't one of the newer ones she was familiar with, but it was quite an easy system.

The home screen for each patient gave a basic rundown of their personal details—name, address, date of birth, current age—and also their current medication, if any, details of their last few appointments and what they'd been diagnosed with. She could take a quick glance at the screen and get a pretty general idea about a patient before they came into the room to tell her their new problem.

Lula sat to one side of Olly and observed as he began to see patients.

First a mother brought her eight-year-old son in. He'd got a tummy ache, and his mother reported that he always got them before school. They had a little chat with the boy who told them that he didn't like school, or the other boys there, and so it was put down to stress and anxiety rather than any sort of bug or infection—or something more dramatic like appendicitis.

Next they saw another mother, much younger this time, with three-month-old twin girls. Basically, she wasn't coping. The twins fed erratically, she'd had to give up on breastfeeding and she felt a failure. They kept crying, and they wouldn't sleep, so neither could she. It was all getting a bit too much.

Olly gave her some information about a twins group over at South Wold, and a short prescription for antidepressants at a low dosage to see how she got on. He also told her that he would contact her local health visitor and ask her to call in and give her some advice on coping with the babies. She seemed happy with that and off she went, pushing her buggy with the two screaming babies in it. The surgery was much quieter after she left.

Then they saw a woman in her fifties called Eleanor Lomax. Lula sat up straighter when this woman came in, and studied her hard.

Eleanor was fifty-six. On her fiftieth birthday she had found a lump in her breast which had turned out to be cancer. She'd fought the disease and beaten it, but now she was having issues over her health again.

'Every night, Doctor, I lie in my bed and feel a twinge here or there, or a niggle somewhere else, and I keep thinking, *Is this it? Is it back?* I can't sleep for the worry that the cancer will return.'

Eleanor was sitting in her chair very upright, straight-backed and erect. Her hair was already silver, but beautifully cut and styled. She had large brown eyes, shaped like almonds, and a long, thin, aquiline nose in her perfectly made-up face. Her clothes were expensive and she looked like a woman who had refined tastes. Lula could only look at her and wonder...

Olly, meanwhile, was unaware of Lula's assessment and was doing his best to reassure his patient. 'It's perfectly natural to feel this way, Eleanor, after what you've been through. Have you tried talking to your cancer nurse about it?'

'She's so busy. I don't like to bother her.'

'You're not bothering her. It's what she's there for. Have you been to counselling since your recovery? A support group?'

She shook her head. 'That's not my thing.'

'What *is* your thing?' asked Lula.

Olly glanced at her sideways, surprised by her interruption.

Miss Lomax turned to Lula and shrugged. 'I've always taken care of things myself. Supported myself. I don't like to lean on others.'

Lula said nothing more as Olly put Miss Lomax in touch with a support group and gave her a few leaflets about counselling and cognitive behaviour therapy before she went on her way.

When Eleanor had left Olly turned in his chair. 'You okay?'

She nodded. 'Fine.' She didn't want to tell him that she was wondering if Eleanor Lomax was her mother. The mystery 'EL' she'd been searching for lately.

They saw an old man suffering with diarrhoea, a young man with a sore knee who'd played football with his work colleagues the day before, a baby with a cold, and a woman who'd come in to talk about her daughter.

'She's been very withdrawn lately.'

'And she's how old?'

'Thirteen. It could be puberty starting—I don't know. They get flooded with hormones at this age, don't they? But she's not herself and she hides away in her room all the time and doesn't eat.'

Olly was reluctant to diagnose anyone without actually seeing her. 'Perhaps you could get Ruby to come in? Do you think you could get her here? Then we could weigh her and allay any fears you may have about her eating.'

'I could try, but she's not very cooperative at the moment. Always arguing with us when we do see her.'

'Well, I can't do anything unless I examine her.'

'Could you come out to us?' she asked.

'I only really do home visits if it's impossible for my patients to get to me.'

Lula was surprised by this. She thought that it might be better if Olly *did* try to go and see Ruby at home and she suggested it. Especially after what had happened that morning with the baby. They were looking for a teenage girl. But Olly wasn't too happy about having his methods contradicted, although he tried his best not to show it.

For the rest of the day they saw a standard mix of patients—a lady who wanted a repeat prescription, another lady who had a chest infection and a man who'd come in to discuss his blood test results and was quite anaemic.

A typical day for a GP. Lula even saw some patients of her own.

When the clinic was over, and with only two house

visits left to do, they stopped for a cup of tea and a bite to eat.

'Mary might have brought in one of her delicious cakes for us to eat,' Olly said, and smiled.

Mary was the receptionist, and she had indeed brought in a coffee liqueur cake that was rich and moist and devilishly moreish.

'Mary, you *must* give me the recipe!' Lula said.

'I can't do that—it's a family secret!'

'What if I promise not to tell anyone?'

'We'll see, Dr Chance. Perhaps if you stay on then I might give it to you.'

Lula agreed that it was a deal, knowing she would never get the recipe. She had no plans to stay here in Atlee Wold. She was here to do two things. One was to work as a doctor, and the second... Well, Olly was about to find that out.

He sat down in the chair next to hers in the staff lounge. 'Well, how did you enjoy your first clinic here?'

'It was good. Interesting. There's a real community feel to a small village practice that you just don't get in a large city.'

'That's the truth. You can build relationships with people here that go on for years. Not that you can't do that in the city or in towns, but when you live amongst the people you treat, shop in their store, post your mail in their post office, you develop friendships, too.'

'Don't you find it sometimes restricts the amount of privacy you have?' Lula asked.

'Not at all. I don't mind that everyone knows I'm a doctor, and that my father was before me, and that I got the big scar on my leg from falling out of a tree in Mrs Macabee's orchard.'

'Ooh, let's see!'

Lula was always fascinated to see scars and hear the story behind them. She guessed it was part of being a doctor. She had a thing about noticing people's veins, too. Whether or not they had good juicy veins, ripe for a blood test. You developed an odd sense of humour, being a medical professional.

Olly put his tea down and rolled up his right trouser leg to reveal a slightly jagged scar running down the front of his shin. 'Broke my tib and fib. Open fracture.'

'Nasty.' She could imagine the bones sticking out through the skin. The pain, the blood. The panic. She ignored the fact that he had a beautifully muscular leg, covered in fine dark hair.

'Mrs Macabee got my dad and they took me to the A&E over at Petersfield. We were treated by people who were very kind and friendly, but I was just another casualty to come through the door. Here in Atlee Wold we really care about one another.'

'*All* doctors care about their patients, Olly.'

'I know, but you know what I'm trying to say. Don't you?'

She nodded. She did know. She was just playing devil's advocate.

'You say you know a lot about people here in Atlee Wold? Their histories? Does that include everybody in the village? Do you know absolutely *everyone*?'

'Pretty much. Why?'

'Eleanor Lomax. The lady who had breast cancer. What can you tell me about her past?'

'Eleanor? She's a lovely lady. Always lived on her own. Keeps herself to herself. Retired now, but she used to run a boutique, I think. Why?'

Lula shrugged. 'She just caught my attention. Mainly because… Well, to be perfectly honest with you, Olly,

I'm not just here to work.' She bit her lip and looked at him to gauge his reaction.

'Or to belly dance?'

She smiled. 'Or to belly dance. I'm here to find someone. Someone whose initials are EL.'

'EL…like your mother? You think Eleanor Lomax might be your *mother*?' He looked incredulous.

'Maybe. I don't know.'

'What makes you think your mother is in Atlee Wold? There must be hundreds, if not thousands of women in the UK with the initials EL.'

'Well, it's complicated…'

'When *isn't* it?'

'When I was abandoned there was obviously some press coverage.'

'Right.' He was listening intently, his brow furrowed.

'The papers asked for my mother to come forward, to let them know she was all right, to see if they could reunite us—that sort of thing. Well, the paper in Portsmouth—the *Portsmouth News*—was sent a letter by someone signing it "EL". The letter explained that she couldn't come forward. That her parents had made her give up the baby, there was no chance of us being together, and that she hoped they would leave her alone.'

'She sounded desperate?'

Lula nodded. 'There was a postmark from the Petersfield sorting office, and the handwriting was very distinctive. A journalist took it around the local post offices, to see if any of the staff could remember franking it, and one did. He also remembered the woman who'd posted it, because she'd been upset and had had red eyes from crying.'

'I can see why he'd remember a crying customer.'

'Anyway, they questioned this man and he said he'd seen her before. Getting off the bus from Atlee Wold.'

'*That's* what you're going on?' he asked incredulously. 'It's tenuous, at best.'

'It's all I have.'

'Did the journalist come here? Try and track her down?'

'He said there were a number of women with the initials EL in Atlee Wold and that none of them would talk to him.'

Olly looked at her. 'Oh, Lula... I wish I had something more constructive to say, but I think you're taking a long shot. It's all hearsay and secondhand, and relying on the memory of a guy who thinks he saw a woman get off a bus once. And EL—whoever she is—could have got off the bus from Atlee Wold to throw people off track.'

'It's better than having nothing at all, Olly. Imagine having that. No idea at all. You're close to your father. You know your family history. You have roots. Just think for a moment how you'd feel if you had none of that. Wouldn't you feel...adrift? A bit lost? Wouldn't a part of you want to know?'

He thought about it for a moment and then nodded. 'I guess so. My mother died when I was very young, so I don't remember her. I've always felt something's been missing.'

'So you understand that I have to try? Because if I didn't then I'd never forgive myself if it turned out my actual birth mother was living within a few miles of me and I never looked for her.'

'And if she *is* here? If you *do* find her?'

Lula smiled. 'Then I'll know where she is. And that will be enough. I'm not silly enough to expect that we'll suddenly fall into each other's arms and have a mother-daughter relationship.'

'And if she rejects you?'

'Then I can't hurt any more then I already do. She already did that once. Remember?'

Olly didn't often find himself not knowing what to say. He was usually the person people went to with their problems and he *always* had some sort of advice to give. But this…this was different. 'I think, Dr Lula Chance, that you are a very brave lady indeed.'

She looked up at him through her purple fringe and her eyes twinkled with appreciation. 'Thanks, Olly. I appreciate your help.'

'My pleasure. Not that I actually helped much.'

'You listened. And sometimes that's all someone needs.'

'For you, Lula, my ears are always open.'

He passed her another piece of cake and they sat there in companionable silence.

Before afternoon surgery began Olly spoke to his father over the phone.

'So she's looking for her mother? Here in the village?'

'Looks like it.'

'Well! Can't say I blame her…but I can't imagine who it might be.'

Olly nodded, doodling with his pen absentmindedly. 'Neither can I. But I want to help her if I can.'

'You like her, don't you?'

'Dad!' he warned. 'Don't start.'

'I'm not starting,' he replied innocently. 'Just encouraging you.'

'Let me get this straight. You'd *want* to see me with

a woman like Lula?' He almost couldn't believe his ears. His father was the most strait-laced man he knew!

'Why not?'

'Well, because she's…'

'She's what?'

Olly wasn't sure how to answer him. 'Out there!'

'She's just what you need. After all that business with Rachel.'

As if he needed reminding. That had been a really dark time. Rachel had barged into his life like a wrecking ball and left just as much devastation behind.

Would Lula do the same?

CHAPTER THREE

AFTER WORK, LULA TOOK herself over to the village library. It wasn't huge. In fact it was barely a library at all—just one small room, lined with books. Since the funding had been cut it was no longer staffed, and it relied on the goodwill of its customers to ensure it was looked after and that they signed out their own books.

It was a strange set-up, and for a while Lula felt odd, standing there alone, looking around the small room. One side was fiction, in alphabetical order, and the other side non-fiction, all in the Dewey decimal system. In the centre were racks of children's books and some old DVDs. In one corner, beneath a window, sat an ancient computer and a microfiche reader, alongside a filing cabinet. She headed over.

It didn't take her long to find the electoral roll for the area and, flicking through, she discovered that there were four families with a surname beginning with L in Atlee Wold—the Lomaxes, the Loves, the Lewises and the Louthams.

Any of those people might know something about leaving a baby on a Portsmouth beach. But they also might know nothing at all. The information she had about EL could be completely wrong. Who knew?

I won't find out unless I investigate.

She looked up and smiled at a little old lady who'd come in, holding her coat closed against her chest and wheeling a shopping basket behind her.

'Hello, dear.'

'Hi.'

'You're the new doctor, aren't you?'

Lula smiled and nodded. 'How did you know?'

The old lady let out a laboured breath, twinkled her eyes at her and smiled back. 'Can't be many young ladies with a rainbow in their hair. Phoebe Macabee lives next door to me and she told me about your belly-dancing class.'

'You ought to come. It's fun.'

'With my hips? I don't think so, dear.' She rubbed her left arm, absently.

Lula noticed the movement, but said nothing. It didn't have to mean anything, did it? She'd been wheeling her basket—perhaps it just ached? 'It doesn't have to be about the hips, you know. You could still come. Be with the group. Get some shimmying action with the arms?'

The old lady shook her head. 'My shimmying days are over, dear, but thank you for inviting me. You here for a book?'

'Research.'

She looked at the electoral roll in front of Lula. 'You need to know about the people round here?'

Lula shrugged. 'Maybe.'

'Well, I've lived here all my life, dear. I know pretty much everyone. My name's Yvonne, but everyone knows me as Bonnie.'

'Bonnie. That's a lovely name.'

'Thank you.' Bonnie settled into a chair next to her, her bones creaking as she did so, sighing the sigh of a woman who had finally found the time to sit down in the day. 'Now, what do you want to know?'

Lula was unsure of what to say. She appreciated Bonnie's offer, but did she want to tell the old lady *why* she needed knowledge?

Bonnie must have seen the look on her face because the old girl smiled and laid a hand on Lula's knee. 'I can keep a secret.'

'Secrets are the problem. The person I'm looking for has kept a secret for a long time, and I'm not sure I should be allowed to tell it.'

'Are you part of the secret?'

Lula nodded.

'I thought so. Figured you wouldn't be looking, otherwise. Well, my dear, to my way of thinking if you're part of the secret then you can tell whoever you want. I'm discreet, if that helps any, but I know you don't know me from Adam.'

'How about you just tell me what you know about certain people?'

'I can tell you general knowledge. But I can't go telling private stuff. Discreet, remember?'

Lula smiled back. 'Discreet. What do you know about Eleanor Lomax?'

A small radiator affixed to the wall beneath a cork board of notices ensured that the cold outside didn't permeate the small library and Lula and Bonnie sat pleasantly warm, discussing stories and people.

'Eleanor Lomax has had a hard time of it lately,' Bonnie began.

'I know about her health problems.'

Bonnie reached into her wheeled basket for a pile of heavy books and laid them on her lap with a sigh. 'Well, you would, being a doctor. The breast cancer? Yes, terrible it was. I went with her once to the hospital, to sit with her whilst she got her chemotherapy. I tried to stay bright for her, but it's an odd place, the cancer ward. All those people on hiatus, waiting for treatments, waiting for news, waiting to get back to their own lives.'

'It can be difficult.' Lula didn't need telling about that. She'd been there.

'Yes, it can. But she was strong—she fought it and she won. Physically, anyways.'

'What do you know about her before?'

Bonnie tilted her head to one side as she considered her answer. 'She's always lived alone. Never had a man about the place as far as I know.'

'Family?' So far Bonnie hadn't told her anything helpful.

'I think she mentioned a sister once, but there was a bit of a scandal so they don't talk to each other much.'

Lula perked up. A scandal? Like an unplanned pregnancy? That sort of thing could stop family members from getting along. Had Eleanor been forced to give up a baby? Or had she done it willingly and her family hated her for it? Or was it something else entirely and Eleanor Lomax was a woman who had nothing whatsoever to do with Lula at all?

'Does the sister live close by?'

'Over in the next village. She's much older than Eleanor, I think, and not well, last I heard.'

Lula nodded her head. Could be anything. But, as a doctor, she wondered whether she could somehow create a reason for visiting this sister. 'Do you know her name? Where she lives?'

Bonnie looked oddly at her. 'Something important is driving you, isn't it, Doctor? All these questions...'

'Something. Maybe. Do you know?'

Bonnie shook her head. 'No, sorry. But I think her name was Brenda, if that's any help?'

Brenda Lomax. Okay. I can check on that.

Bonnie rubbed at her chest.

'You okay?' There was a slight sheen of sweat on Bonnie's face.

'Touch of indigestion. Now…who else can I help you with?'

'This family…' Lula pointed at the electoral roll. 'The Love family. What do you know about them?'

'There's no "them". There's just Elizabeth.'

Elizabeth. Elizabeth Love. Another EL.

'Yes?'

'Keeps herself to herself. You don't see her much—though she takes in all manner of waifs and strays.'

'People?'

'Animals! Cats, dogs, mice, wildlife… She's got a real animal rescue thing going on up there.'

'Up where?'

'Burner's Road. It's on the very outer edge of Atlee Wold—leads to Burner's Farm. It's quite isolated, but she seems to like that. The vets round here bring her animals to care for and she takes them all in. Prefers them to people.'

Lula listened, thinking about how she'd driven to Burner's Farm just last night. Had she driven past her own mother's house and not known it? How likely a candidate might Elizabeth Love be? Apart from the initials, there weren't any clues.

'What about the Lewis family?'

'Big family. Lots of relatives. Well known around these parts…well liked. Phoebe Macabee used to be a Lewis, until she married her Ron.'

'Any of them have a name beginning with E?'

Bonnie pursed her lips, thinking. 'Let me see… Ron, Davey, Shaun, Marion, the kids… No, I don't think so. Who are you after?'

Lula smiled. 'And the Louthams?' She pointed at their name on the electoral roll. 'Any of *them* have the initial E?'

'Well, there's Edward Loutham…'

She rubbed at her chest again, and now Lula could see that Bonnie was looking a bit pale and clammy. But if she was ill surely she'd say something?

Since when has someone of Bonnie's generation ever been honest about the extent of their health? She said 'indigestion', but…

Bonnie tried to stand and lift her books to put them on the counter, but she gasped and leant against the unit.

'Bonnie?'

But Bonnie didn't answer. She groaned, clutching her arm, and then she slipped forward.

Lula tried to catch her, to break the old lady's fall, but Bonnie was heavier than she looked and she tumbled to the floor with a thud.

Lula rolled her over. 'Bonnie! Bonnie, can you hear me? Open your eyes!'

No response.

She grabbed Bonnie's shoulders and gave her a small shake. 'Bonnie!' Then she knelt over her, tilting Bonnie's head back and listening and watching for breaths.

She'd stopped breathing.

A million thoughts raced through Lula's head. She needed to start CPR, and she also needed help. She ran to the door of the library and yanked it open. Seeing an old man strolling along opposite, his rolled-up newspaper in his hands, she called out, 'I need help in here!' before dashing back to Bonnie to begin chest compressions.

She pressed down hard, keeping a continuous rhythm, trying to count the beats. She had done the first thirty compressions and was blowing air into Bonnie's lungs by the time the library door opened and the man she'd seen in the street appeared.

'Oh, my goodness!'

'I need you to call an ambulance! And fetch Dr James—see if he's got a defibrillator.'

She had no idea if they did or not. But some remote areas had them and she could only hope that Atlee Wold was one of them.

After breathing twice for Bonnie, Lula carried on with the compressions. 'Come on, Bonnie.' She pushed and pushed. Up. Down. Up. Down. A continuous rhythm she dared not break.

The library door closed behind her and time went slowly, yet also too fast. To Lula, it seemed as if she was doing compressions and CPR for ages, waiting for Dr James or an ambulance to turn up, when in reality only a few minutes had passed before Olly came rushing in. Thank goodness—he was carrying a small bag.

'Defibrillator?'

He nodded, unzipping the pack and grabbing the scissors to cut open Bonnie's clothes. 'I've called the ambulance.'

She heard him, but couldn't answer. Exhausted, she continued with compressions, her own breath labouring.

Olly looked at her. 'Let me take over.'

They switched places and Lula ripped open the packs that would allow her to attach pads to Bonnie's chest— one on the right side, up near her shoulder, and the second below her left breast. She switched on the machine and heard it give instructions to apply the pads, which she'd already done. She plugged in the cable for the pads and the machine began to assess Bonnie's heart rhythm.

If she was in asystole—essentially a flatline—then they wouldn't be able to shock her. Asystole was a rhythm that couldn't be changed through shocks, and the only thing they'd be able to do would be to continue with CPR until the ambulance arrived. But if she was in ventricular fibrillation—VF—they would be able to shock her and hopefully restart her heart in a normal rhythm.

'Stay clear of patient,' intoned the machine.

Olly stopped compressions and glanced up at Lula, who looked back at him uncertainly, sweating, her hair stuck to her forehead. She noticed tiny things then. Odd things. The snow stuck to Olly's shoes. A small butterfly pin stuck to Bonnie's shopping bag. The way one page of a book near to her, loose and unattached to the spine, stood out over and above all the others.

'Shocking.'

She's in VF!

'Stand clear,' Lula said, checking to make sure neither she nor Olly was touching Bonnie. It would be dangerous for them if they were in contact as she pressed the orange button with the picture of lightning on it.

She shocked Bonnie and waited for the machine's next instruction.

'Continue CPR.'

Olly began again and kept going.

It was hard to think that just moments ago she and Bonnie had been chatting with each other in this little library. Everything had been normal, day-to-day, and suddenly this... *She said she'd had indigestion. I should have paid more attention!*

But her focus had been on getting information about her mother.

Guilt filled her and she bit her lip hard as she watched Olly try to save Bonnie's life.

He stopped to listen for breaths. 'She's breathing!'

Lula let out a breath she hadn't known she'd been holding. *'Yes!'*

'There's oxygen in my car outside. I'll get it.'

Lula put Bonnie into the recovery position whilst she waited for the oxygen and then, when Olly returned, turned on the tank and attached the mask to Bonnie's face. She was breathing well, her breaths steaming up the small mask. They checked her pulse and respirations as they waited for the ambulance, which they could hear in the distance.

'That was quick. I thought they'd be a while.'

'There's a station in South Wold, and a small cottage hospital.'

'That's good.'

'What happened?'

She shrugged. 'We were just talking and she collapsed.'

He looked carefully at her. 'Are you okay?'

She nodded. 'I'm fine.'

The paramedics got Bonnie into the ambulance quickly, attaching her to their ECG machine and establishing a good trace. Lula jumped into the ambulance to go with her to the hospital and Olly said he'd follow later, once he'd finished clinic, to see how everything was and bring Lula home.

Olly and Lula were travelling back in Olly's car. He drove slowly through the snow, but couldn't help but glance at Lula to his left to try and gauge how she was doing. She seemed to be staring, unseeing, out of her window at the snow-covered fields and he wondered if he ought to try and talk. Try and break the silence. He wanted to know if she was all right.

'How are you?'

She turned to him and smiled. Her voice was perky and bright. 'I'm fine.'

His eyes twitched as he questioned her reply. 'Really?'

'Sure.'

'Because it's been a bit of a rollercoaster for you since you came to Atlee Wold.'

'You mean finding an abandoned baby and then having a patient have a heart attack in front of me?'

He glanced back at the road, ensuring he was driving carefully. 'Well, yeah. That'd be enough to freak anyone out.'

'I'm not *anyone*.'

He recalled his first sight of her, shaking her hips. 'I know that.'

'I'm made of stern stuff, Olly.'

He didn't doubt it. 'But finding that baby...having been abandoned yourself. It must have stirred up memories for you?'

'I don't recall the actual abandonment part. I was too young.'

'I know. And then having to do CPR—'

'I *am* a doctor. I haven't always been a GP. I once worked in A&E, and we had to do CPR a lot.'

Okay. A little prickly, maybe. This is one side of Lula I haven't seen yet. But I suppose it's normal, considering her past.

He decided to change the subject. 'So...did you find a good book?'

'I'm sorry?'

'At the library? Did you find a good book?'

'I wasn't after a book. I was looking at the electoral roll.'

He understood then. 'You were looking for your mother?'

'Four families whose surnames start with the letter L. Two of them have people whose names begin with E.'

'Right.'

'Bonnie was telling me about them.'

'Digging for clues, huh?'

'All good doctors dig for clues.'

'Bonnie wasn't in the role of patient at that point?' He steered to avoid a fallen tree branch. 'What did she tell you?'

'She told me about Eleanor Lomax and Elizabeth Love.'

'Elizabeth Love? I'm not sure I know her.'

'She's a recluse, Bonnie says. Runs an animal sanctuary, or something.'

He nodded. He recalled that someone did something like that on the edge of the village, but he hadn't known who. 'And you're going to talk to these ladies?'

'I am.'

'And say what, exactly? If they're not who you think they are don't you think they'll be a bit taken aback?'

'One of them will be taken aback if she *is* who I think she is.'

'You can't go barging in and asking if they're your long-lost mother.'

'Are you telling me what to do, Dr James?'

'I'm advising. And I'm also looking out for my patients.'

'They don't need protecting from me. I'm not scary.'

He smiled. No. She wasn't scary. *Quirky*, yes, but not scary. 'I know. But you know what I'm trying to say.'

'Don't worry, Olly. I won't upset anyone and I'll be very discreet.'

'You have I don't know how many colours in your hair, drive a spotty Beetle, keep rats and spiders, and you'll be *discreet*?' He laughed.

She smiled back at him. 'I *can* be discreet. Just you watch. And it's spider, singular. I don't keep spiders, plural.'

'I do beg your pardon. And you're not worried about people getting hold of some gossip about you?'

'They don't need to gossip about me. They've got you for that.'

'Me?'

'Of course *you*! You've got a list, remember? A list for the perfect wife?'

He felt his cheeks colour.

Ah, yes...that.

'It was a joke, and it was a long time ago.'

'And yet you still don't have a wife? Why *is* that, Olly? You're a professional man, good-looking, you work hard, you have good principles. Why no wife?'

'I don't need a wife to complete me. I'm happy as I am.' He stared straight ahead, his eyes on the road.

She looked at him. 'Even I can tell that's a forced response.'

'I am!'

She sat back in her chair. 'I don't believe you.'

He shrugged. 'That's fine. Though I must say you're the most unconventional person I've ever met, and yet you have such traditional views. Love and marriage? That's nice.'

'You don't believe in love and marriage?'

'I do. My parents had a very strong marriage.'

'So...?'

He quickly glanced at her. 'So what?'

'So why do you seem to go out of your way to avoid it?'

'Is that what I'm doing?'

'You made a list. Of the attributes your perfect wife must have. You're looking for perfection, and perfection is unattainable, so you *know* you're after something that doesn't exist—therefore you're not actually looking.'

'Well, thank you, Sherlock.' He could sense the twinkle in her eyes.

'Because perfection is not out there. *She's* not out there.'

Olly wasn't enjoying this line of questioning. His brow had become a field of ploughed lines and his eyes had darkened. 'I don't think there's anything wrong in having expectations of a future partner.' People needed to know where they stood in a relationship.

'Of course not—if that person has an outside chance of meeting those expectations.'

He glanced across at her. 'You think my list is unrealistic?'

'I do. I think any woman couldn't possibly hope to achieve your high standards.'

'Does that bother you?'

She paused. 'No. But *I'm* not trying to go out with you.'

'Why not?'

Lula laughed in delight. 'What?'

'Why aren't you trying to go out with me?'

She blushed. 'You're a colleague.'

'And you have rules for that sort of thing?'

'Yes.'

'But *I* can't have rules?' Now he was starting to enjoy the banter. Now *he* was on the offensive.

'Your list of the attributes a wife must have is not a list of rules. It's a different thing entirely.'

'So *you* can say you wouldn't date a colleague, but *I* can't say I wouldn't date a colleague?'

Lula bit her lip. Stuck in her own argument.

Olly indicated to turn left and began to head down a smaller lane, with thicker snow. 'You can't be allowed to have a standard, Lula, if I'm not allowed to have one.'

'I'm not saying that. What I mean is... Oh, I don't know what I mean. You've got me tied in knots.' She thought for a moment. 'Saying you'll only date a blonde is not the same as saying you wouldn't date a colleague.'

'Blonde? It's not a list of *physical* attributes. What kind of chauvinistic, shallow man do you take me for?' He was amused.

'So what *is* on your list?'

He let out a big sigh. 'Kindness, dedication, loyalty, a love of family, a desire to have children...'

'Ah, you can strike *me* off the list, then.'

'You don't want a family?' He was surprised. He could imagine Lula with children. She was just the sort to engage young children and he could imagine them being delighted by her, with her crazy hair and fairy-like features.

'I can't have a family, Olly. The chemo...it left me infertile.'

Her voice trailed away and he looked at her and saw her head droop. He'd never seen her look so low. It just wasn't Lula at all. Lula was bright and full of energy—not quiet or sad.

Her answer silenced him for a while. He couldn't imagine never having children. Or being told he couldn't. He hoped they were going to be a big part of his life. Technically, once he had had a child for a little while, even though it hadn't been born.

'I didn't know. I'm sorry.'

'You weren't to know. Besides…you're the first person I've ever told that to.'

He glanced at her quickly—these roads were full of S bends. 'I'm glad you felt you could. I'm really sorry, Lula.'

Olly had counselled people who'd come into his surgery because they couldn't have children, and he'd always had something to say to them. Why couldn't he find the exact right words for Lula? Was it different because she was a colleague?

It has to be. It's not because she's not my type.

'You don't have to apologize. It's not your fault.'

'Still…it's a big part of life that's being denied to you. You must have felt upset when you were told?' He knew how upset he'd been when Rachel had told him what she'd done…

'I was still a child when I found out. It didn't matter much to me then. It didn't seem a big deal.' She shrugged.

'And now?' He really wanted to know.

'And now I can't let it bother me. I fill my life with other things.'

He smiled. 'Rats and spiders?'

'Rats are very intelligent creatures.'

'And spiders?'

She laughed. 'Are more of a challenge.'

Olly turned into Lula's road and pulled up outside Moonrose Cottage. It looked mystical in the moonlight. An old, thatched cottage covered in snow like a frosting of thick icing sugar.

Lula couldn't wait to get inside, switch on the lights and draw up a fire. 'Are you coming in? I could make hot chocolate.'

He thought about it for a minute. He didn't want to impose—she'd barely been in the village five minutes and he felt he'd occupied more than enough of her time already. He was about to turn her down, but there was something about her that he couldn't resist.

'Sounds great—thanks.'

Lula was definitely not the type of woman he would normally go for. All his previous romantic interludes had been with fellow medics who were rather strait-laced and 'normal'. Nothing like Lula. His longest relationship had been with Rachel, and that had been years ago and an utter disaster.

Lula was so far out of 'normal' she was practically an alien from outer space! But he was fascinated by her. By her diminutive size, which made him want to put his arms around her and protect her, and the way the colours in her hair blended so beautifully it was like looking at a mystical rainbow. And those large brown eyes…like pools of chocolate he could dive into…

Calm yourself, Olly! Remember she's not your type!

Inside, he helped her light a fire and soon its crackling warmth filled the small room. They sat before it, enveloping their mugs of hot chocolate with their hands and staring at the leaping flames.

'Eventful day…' he said.

Lula nodded. 'Are all English villages this exciting, do you think?'

'No, I don't think so. It's just got this way since you've arrived. You know, I don't think I've had so many patients visit the surgery, just to see you. You've really brightened up their lives since they did that belly-dancing class of yours, and they can't wait for the next one.'

'I'm glad.' She smiled.

'You're a breath of fresh air.' He coloured as soon as he'd said it and sipped from his hot chocolate to cover his embarrassment.

Lula glanced at him, nodding at the compliment but wondering if it was the kind of fresh air that *Olly* needed? He needed *something*, the way he was, stuck in his ways.

'Thank you. I try to be.'

He glanced over at her. 'Why do you do it?'

She was confused by his question. 'Do what?'

'Belly dancing? I mean, you're good at it—don't get me wrong—but what made you choose to do it?'

'It was fun, it was different. I thought it suited me.'

Yes, she was definitely different—he had to give her that. For the first time that day he noticed that her delicate fingernails were all painted different colours. Red, pink, pale blue, peppermint-green and lilac. There was even a tiny tattoo on her ring finger of a bat.

A bat!

He smiled to himself and shook his head. She was unbelievable. Normally he would have said that he didn't like to see tattoos on women. He was quite traditional in that sense, and had always associated tattoos with men, but on Lula they were different. She managed to make them look amazing—tiny pieces of artwork, splashes of colour in intriguing places, making him want to know if there were any other tattoos on her body that he couldn't currently see.

Not that he would ask her, he thought, his face flushing again at the thought of slowly peeling away her clothes to reveal a veritable teasing trail of tattoos.

He stood up abruptly, clearing his throat. 'I ought to go. Leave you to your rats and spider.'

'Are you on call?'

'No, Dad's covering tonight.'

'I like your father. He seems a good man.' She looked up at him, her face glowing in the reflection from the warm fire.

Olly nodded. 'He is.' This was better. His father was a safer topic.

'What happened? With your mum? You don't mention her.'

What could he say? That he had no memories of her—only the stories that his father told about the amazing woman that Olly struggled to recall? How it hurt to admit that he didn't remember how it had felt to cuddle her, what she'd sounded like, what she'd smelt like?

He sank back down onto the edge of the sofa. 'She died when I was two.'

'I'm so sorry. I know what it's like not to have a mother. Your real mother, anyway.'

She looked it, too. Truly sorry.

'That's okay. It was a tragic accident. No one could have done anything about it.'

'Do you remember her *at all*?'

He shook his head. 'No. But my father tells me about her, and we've got lots of photos and some family videos. There's one of me and her lying on a picnic blanket, facing each other. She's laughing and smiling and beaming at me with such joy and pride on her face...' The memory of the picture, describing it to Lula, hurt. Olly cleared his throat. 'Dad loved her very much.'

'I'm glad. Though not that you lost her. In a way, I guess it means you had something missing from your childhood, too?'

Olly nodded. Definitely. He'd always been aware that there was a giant mother-shaped hole in his childhood. During his schooldays he'd hated the times when everyone but him had made cards or gifts for Mother's Day. Or when only his father turned up for assemblies or sports days or parents' evenings. When he was still small he'd used to imagine what it must be like to snuggle up to a mother at bedtime. Or to have one stroke his fevered brow when he was sick. To spoil him a bit.

His father had been good at dismissing a lot of his childhood illnesses: *'It's just a cold'* or *'It's just a tummy bug'*. He'd done his best, though, occasionally sitting on the edge of Olly's bed when he was poorly, but it had always been hard for him to switch from 'doctor mode' to 'father mode'.

'I guess so.'

Stuck for something to break the tension, he handed her his mug and thanked her for the hot chocolate.

She walked him to the front door, opened it. He walked out into the snow, his footsteps crunching on its crispy surface. He turned to say goodbye.

'Thank you for your help today, Olly.'

'It was nothing.' He smiled.

'No, I mean it. You've really been so kind about me taking your grandmother's cottage and putting my little zoo in it. I appreciate they must have been a shock.'

He looked deeply into her warm brown eyes. 'I'm learning to expect the unexpected with you, Lula. Don't worry.'

She smiled, then leaned forward to stand on tiptoe and peck him on the cheek.

As her lips brushed against his face he froze, his eyes closing in surprised delight at the feel of her soft, warm lips against his skin. Close up, he could smell her slight perfume, but couldn't identify it. Whatever it was, it was delightful. Summery and warm. A hint of jasmine...?

Quickly he regained control of himself, knowing he probably looked a bit idiotic with his eyes closed, inhaling her scent like a kid on a gravy advert. Flushing, he stepped back further into the snow and wished her goodnight, his heart sinking as she closed the door and he was no longer exposed to the warmth and light of the cottage.

Olly trudged back to his four-wheel drive, his thoughts as deep as the snow.

What was going on?

Am I developing feelings for Lula? I can't be... She's...what? Different? Quirky? No. She's beautiful— that's what she is. Inside and out.

Lula closed the cottage door and touched her lips with her fingers. They were still tingling from the kiss and she was shocked. It had only been meant as a goodnight kiss, a thank-you kiss. It hadn't been meant as anything else.

So why did it *feel* like something else?

I like Olly. He's lovely, yes. But...

She wasn't here to start a relationship.

He can be my friend, but that's got to be all.

It would be too complicated if she allowed a relationship to start up—and with Olly, of all people! He was her colleague. In a small village practice. It couldn't develop into anything. He'd already told her that he wanted to have children, and she couldn't have them, so... No. She couldn't pursue *anything* with Olly.

But he's so delicious!

No, Lula. Behave yourself...

She groaned and took the mugs into the kitchen.

She stared out of the window into the white expanse of the still garden. She put the mugs in the sink and saw Anubis in his tank. Sighing, she took a step closer and slowly lifted off the lid.

All I've got to do is put my hand in.

Just reach out.

That's not hard, is it?

But her hands stayed where they were. It was still too scary.

She closed the lid, shivering as Anubis stretched out one long hairy leg and began to move.

'Time for bed, I think.'

Lula switched off the lights and then spent many hours staring at the roof of her bedroom ceiling, lost in thought.

Olly sat at his kitchen table, holding a mug of cold tea and staring into space. Lula had only been here a short while and yet he felt she'd begun to turn his ordered life upside down and inside out.

He felt uncomfortable with it. The last time he'd been thrown upside down with his thoughts had been after Rachel had left. When he'd discovered what she'd done...

Lula isn't anything like Rachel.

Lula's attitude to life was so refreshing. She believed in challenging herself, facing her fears, stepping out of the ruts and taking risks. She followed her heart. But she wasn't whimsical or wishy-washy. She had a purpose, she had fun and she was extremely intelligent.

And he was attracted to her.

Simple as that, really, and that scared him. She was nothing like his perfect woman. Or the vision of a perfect woman he'd stupidly concocted in his infamous list.

He'd never expected to be intrigued by a woman with tattoos and multicoloured hair. He'd always thought he'd be the type to fall for a regular woman, with normal hair and her only body decoration being a sedate pair of earrings, perhaps a ring or two. A woman who wore suits to work, who drove a sensible car. A woman with class.

Lula has class.

Was it her differences that intrigued him? Was it the fact that she was so unique and so unlike anyone he'd ever met before that made him unable to help gravitating towards her?

No. It was more than that.

He felt *different* when he was with her. He couldn't explain it. It was as if he was seeing life differently. Through her eyes the world was a place of wonder and possibility again, rather than a world of...what?

Beige. That was what. Lula was right about him. Perhaps he had been stuck in his rut for too long? That thing with Rachel had forced him into it even more. Perhaps he did need his world to be shaken up?

Was Lula the woman to do it?

Did he want her to?

Olly got up and threw his tea down the sink, rinsed out his mug and left it on the drainer, staring into the snow through his kitchen window.

He *did* want her to. But he was worried about letting go of who he was. Would he lose himself? Would he lose the respect of others if he let go and went wild for a bit?

I'm a doctor. A GP. I'm meant to be sensible. People rely on that sensibility.

He'd always been strait-laced. Run of the mill. Down to earth. He'd always thought that was an attractive quality. That people liked to know where they were with him. That he wasn't unpredictable.

But hearing Lula's story—hearing how her life had been, all the challenges she'd faced—had made him look twice at himself.

What challenges had *he* had to face? Just two. The death of his mother and the loss of Rachel and the baby. The one she'd never told him about. And it hadn't been an accidental loss, either...

Even so, regarding his mum, he'd been too young to feel the grief of what the loss of her had actually meant. He'd never known her—not really. He only knew what his dad had told him about her. What a wonderful woman she'd been and how in love with her his dad had been.

And Rachel...? He'd blundered wholeheartedly into a relationship with her, expecting it to be exactly like his father's with his mother. He'd assumed Rachel would be the same type of woman as his mother. Someone perhaps looking for family the way he was? Dedicated to him.

Only it hadn't happened that way, had it?

Rachel had been so many things, but none of those that he'd expected. She'd not been as dedicated to him as he'd hoped, and she'd hated village life. Too rural for her. She'd been a city girl, through and through, and he should have seen that from the start.

And then I wrote that damned list! That stupid list!

He'd thought the list would protect him from getting his heart broken again. That if he only went out with women whose life goals and attitudes matched those on his list, then he would be safe from heartbreak and pain and loss.

And what was he doing now? Ignoring the list and

falling for the most outrageous, multicoloured, tattooed zookeeper he'd ever met!

Falling for her...

Was he? It felt like it. He knew he couldn't stop thinking about her. When he was with her he soaked up her vitality and presence like a sponge, and when she was absent his mind lingered on her, returning his thoughts to her every single time, like an obsessed teenager with a crush.

That kiss tonight... Goose pimples shivered over his skin in torment. The touch of her lips had been magical. He'd wanted more. Had craved more. And yet... he'd been afraid to seek it out. What if he pursued her and got it all wrong? He'd done that before. If he got involved with her, feeling as he was now, and it didn't work out... Well, he'd be devastated. Floored. And he didn't need that. He'd had heartbreak and he didn't want to experience it again.

He sought happiness and love and respect—the type of relationship his father had had with his mother.

Ideal.

Could he have that with Lula? She couldn't have children, but was that important?

The uncertainty that filled him made his steps heavy as he went up to bed.

CHAPTER FOUR

AFTER A SLEEPLESS NIGHT, Lula woke feeling exhausted.

She fed Anubis, dropping a couple of crickets into his tank, and then gave Nefertiti and Cleo fresh water. They were pleased to see her, holding onto her fingers with their little pink paws and licking her happily. She loved their ratty kisses and stroked them both before putting them back into their cage. She'd not had them out as often as she'd have liked since moving into the cottage. They were used to free ranging, and she knew she ought to organize some sort of safe play area for them so they could come out more.

However, she'd have to pick her place carefully. This cottage was a rental and she didn't expect to stay in Atlee Wold for long. She didn't want them damaging any of the old furniture in Moonrose Cottage, especially as she knew how much the place meant to Olly.

Olly...

She really liked him. She knew it deep in her soul. They'd just connected so easily, the pair of them. It was easy to be in his company, and it was strange to think that they'd only really known each other for a couple of days. Lula felt as if she'd known him for ages.

He was an old soul in the body of a young, fit, handsome man. But she liked that a lot.

Today Lula was going to be running her own surgery, rather than sitting in with him, and she was looking forward to it. But she was also looking forward to seeing Olly again and finding out if he'd heard anything about the abandoned baby yet. She hoped so. She was worried about the mother. Where was she? *Who* was she? Was she all right? She couldn't imagine what it must feel like to give birth and then abandon the baby somewhere…

Whoever had felt pushed into that situation had to be incredibly scared. Or brave. Or a bit of both of those. Selfless, too. Perhaps whoever it was had hoped that by doing so she would be giving the baby the best chance in life. She'd obviously cared about the baby or she wouldn't have wrapped it up so well, provided it with a hot water bottle to keep it warm in the snow.

Lula slipped her feet into her Union Jack wellingtons and put her pink shoes into her backpack. Wrapping up tightly against the cold, she set off to work.

As she tramped through the snow she waved hello to various villagers who were braving the drifts to get their morning paper and milk from the local store. When she entered the surgery she stamped her feet on the mat, glad to be in the warmth again.

Olly was already there, standing behind the reception desk. He was on the telephone and acknowledged her with a smile. She paused briefly to look at him, slowly taking off her scarf and gloves.

He was very tall and broad. Through his shirt she could see he had some nicely defined muscles, especially in his arms.

I wonder if he works out?

He had a sickeningly flat belly that she would have died for, and a trim waist. Boy, did he look good! Yummy—despite the sensible pale blue shirt and navy chinos. Flushing, she put her scarf and gloves in her backpack and pulled off her wellies to reveal stripy multicoloured socks with individual toes.

'Nice.' Olly pointed at her feet as he came off the phone.

'Thanks. They're cosy. Something urgent?' She was referring to the phone call.

'Just checking on Bonnie and the baby. Both are fine. Baby's taking milk well and Bonnie had a comfortable night.'

'That's great.' She slipped her pink boots on. 'No sign of the baby's mother yet?'

He shook his head, and she could see he was eyeing her boots.

'You ready to heal the sick?'

'As always.' She smiled. 'Though I might just grab a cup of tea first.'

'How's the zoo this morning?'

'They're all well.'

He walked with her into the small staff area, watching whilst she made a cup of tea.

'Want one?'

He nodded. 'Thanks.'

She was aware he was still watching her, and surprisingly she felt quite self-conscious. What had happened?

One tingly kiss and I turn into an awkward teenager again?

'Do you have sugar? I forget.'

'One, please.' He seemed amused by her forgetfulness, but took the drink from her with thanks, their fingers brushing and causing electrifying alertness. She eyed his strong hands wrapped around the mug and wondered what it might be like to be held by them...

Stop it, Lula! You're not here for Olly.

She made an excuse to disappear into her room, switching on the computer and booting up the patient file system. The room was bare of her personality, but it would do for the brief time she was there. Normally she would put her own things up—have her own knick-knacks on the desk to entertain smaller patients and her own artwork on the walls in bright colours to make the room more lively—but she wasn't there permanently. This was just a short-term locum position. She wasn't planning on staying.

Just as soon as she'd tracked down whether her mother was here or not she'd move on. If she did find her mother she wouldn't want to stay in the village and pressure her into anything. She'd keep her distance. And if she *wasn't* here then it didn't matter. She would move on and try...what? There were no other clues. She had to be *here*.

Somewhere.

Her first patient arrived—Arthur Cross. He'd developed a nasty cough, so she listened to his chest and it sounded quite crackly. Concerned about a possible infection, she wrote a prescription for some antibiotics and said goodbye. Next was a young mother with a baby, who wanted to know whether she could go back on the contraceptive pill. Her husband wanted more babies—she didn't. Lula suggested they have a discussion with each other, but wrote a script for it anyway and hoped it wouldn't cause a huge marital argument between the two of them.

She saw a steady influx of patients all morning and was busy. The work kept her mind off her mother, and most definitely off Olly. It was only when it got to about eleven o'clock that she noticed the time, because Olly brought her through another drink.

'Made you a tea.' He put it down on the desk and she took it gratefully.

'Oh, thanks. Busy morning, isn't it?'

'It is. I was wondering if you'd come out with me on a house call later?'

'Oh?'

'Can you remember yesterday we had Ruby's mum in? The teenage girl who was being a bit weird?'

Yes, she remembered.

'Well, the mum's more concerned and has asked us to come out and talk to the girl. If she *is* the mother of the baby left on your doorstep I think I'd quite like some female backup, if that's okay?'

She nodded. 'Sure. You really think it might be her?'

Olly shrugged. 'I don't know Ruby very well. I've only seen her for vaccinations when she was a baby herself. But she's the only possible I've got at the minute.'

'Okay. What time are we going?'

'About two? She's not at school. Refusing to speak or come out of her room for the last day or so.'

Oh, dear. Lula hoped it *was* her, so that they could get her urgent medical attention, but she also didn't want to think that a scared thirteen-year-old had had to go through labour and birth on her own—and then dispose of a baby...

'Get me when you're ready to go. And thanks for the tea.'

He winked as he left and she smiled, finding herself wishing he would come back and talk to her some more.

Oh, my goodness! What am I doing to myself?

Olly could only be a friend. There was no point in having those sorts of feelings or thoughts.

As two o'clock approached Lula hid in her room, eating her lunch and trying to stay out of Olly's way as much as she could. But when he came to collect her she could put it off no longer. She would have to be in the car with him and go on this house call.

But that's fine. It's just a ride out. It's work, not pleasure. There's nothing to be afraid of.

She got in his car, highly aware of how close his hand came to her thighs every time he had to change gear or adjust the heating, but thankfully it wasn't for long. Ruby's family didn't live too far from the surgery.

There was a deep drift of snow beside where Olly parked, so she had to climb out of his side. He held the door open for her as she clambered over the gearstick and proffered his hand for her to steady herself before getting out. Blushing, she took it, hoping he assumed her cheeks were going red from the cold and nothing else. And then they were both tramping through the snow to Ruby's front door.

Olly knocked and they waited.

When Ruby's mum answered the door she invited them in and they went inside, happy to be in the stifling warmth of the house. Lula and Olly removed their snow-caked boots in the hall and padded into the lounge in their socks. They sat down.

'Ruby's still in her room. I told her you were coming but she still won't speak or open the door.'

'Do you want me to go up to talk to her?' Lula offered.

'If you want…but mind the mess. I've not had a chance to tidy up.'

Lula smiled sympathetically, then left Olly to talk to Ruby's mum as she went upstairs. At the top of the stairs were three doors. One had a giant yellow *'Danger! Keep Out!'* sign on it, which she presumed was Ruby's, so she gently knocked and waited for a reply.

'Ruby?'

Silence, except for the gentle murmur of voices coming from downstairs.

'Ruby? It's Dr Chance. Can I come in for a chat?'

Still nothing. It seemed odd. She'd expected something. An outburst. A yell to go away—*something*.

Lula tapped on the door again. 'I'm going to come in.' She took hold of the handle, not sure if it would open or not, and gave the door a push.

It did open.

But Ruby wasn't there. The room was empty.

'Oh, no…'

Lula hurried back down the stairs and into the lounge. 'She's not there.'

Ruby's mum stood up, frowning. 'What do you mean, she's not there? She's got to be!'

'She isn't. The room's empty.'

Ruby's mum hurried upstairs to check for herself and then came back, looking completely bewildered. 'I don't know where she's gone!'

'Does she have any money? Are any clothes missing?' asked Olly. 'Her coat?'

She shook her head. 'I don't know. Let me check.'

She disappeared leaving Olly and Lula in the lounge, looking at each other.

'What do you think?'

'I think she may be our girl,' Lula admitted.

'It's looking like it. Perhaps she did a bunk because she knew doctors coming to the house would notice if she'd just given birth or not.'

Lula glanced over at Ruby's mother as she came back in. 'Her coat's gone, and her boots. She must have sneaked out when I was in the kitchen.'

'Call the police. Give them a description.'

Her mum frowned. 'Why? She's only been gone a few minutes. She's probably at a mate's house, or something.' She noticed the conspiring glances between the two medics. 'Is something going on?'

Lula sat her down. 'A baby was abandoned at my home yesterday morning and we've been trying to find the mother, who we believe may be a teenager.'

'You think Ruby…?' She looked horrified. 'But…I'd have noticed if she was pregnant. She's only thirteen!'

'I know, and it might not be her, but we have to take the possibility into consideration.'

She nodded slowly. 'Right. I'll phone the police, then.'

'Could we check her room? See if there are any signs in there?'

Ruby's mum nodded and picked up the phone. 'Go on up.'

Upstairs, Olly and Lula searched for clues as if they were a pair of detectives. Olly rummaged through Ruby's wardrobe whilst Lula was on her knees, pulling things out from under the bed.

She could see something at the back—a large bedsheet, or something like it—all screwed up into a ball… Grabbing it, she pulled it out and saw that it was covered in blood.

'I'd say this nails it, Olly.'

Olly turned around and his shoulders slumped. 'Poor Ruby. We need to tell the police she's our new mother and it's imperative they find her.'

'She can't have gone far, surely? Perhaps we could organise a search ourselves?'

Olly liked the idea. 'I can get Dad to cover the surgery. We could ask for volunteers to help us search.'

'We need to search the bins, too. See if we can find

the placenta—check if it's intact.' If a piece of the afterbirth—the placenta—had been left behind inside Ruby it might cause some very serious complications. Bleeding, haemorrhage or infection.

He nodded. 'I'll do that. Why don't you talk to the police?'

Lula headed downstairs to find Ruby's mother already on the phone with them. She asked to speak to them, too, and informed them of her and Olly's findings. The police responded that they'd send officers straight away.

'We're going to organise a search,' she told Ruby's mother. 'You stay here in case Ruby returns. This is my mobile number.' She handed over a card. 'Call me if she comes back.'

'I want to search, too.'

'We need you here.' She laid a reassuring hand on the woman's arm. 'I know you want to be doing something. But the best place you can be is here. We need to know where to find you if we find Ruby first.'

The solemnity of her words must have hit home, because Ruby's mother nodded quickly and sank onto the sofa.

Olly didn't find anything in the bins, and once the police had arrived at the house they set off to organise a search party.

The village hall was thrumming with locals. A quick ring round the village, asking people to spread the word, had prompted a large turnout.

Lula was touched by how many people from the village had come out of their lovely, warm and cosy homes to go searching in the cold, wet snow for someone who was nothing to do with them—except for belonging to their village.

Most of these people are sixty or over. It's an amazing community spirit...

When Lula had arrived in Atlee Wold she'd been the only person on a search for a mother. Now the majority of the village had turned out to do it.

Not for the same mother, obviously. They didn't know about Lula's circumstances and she wasn't about to share that information—even if it was tempting to ask people what they might know whilst they were all gathered in one place.

No. These people were all here for Ruby. Poor little Ruby, who was probably running scared, unaware that her life might be at risk.

Where is she? It's the middle of winter. It's freezing out here.

Lula couldn't imagine for one second how that poor girl must be feeling. Cold, for sure. Alone, definitely. But what else? What had run through Ruby's head to make her go through labour alone and give up her baby? Like Lula's mother. What was the situation that prompted someone to give up a baby?

It was such a massive thing to do. Once it was done there was no turning back. There would always be that knowledge in your head that you'd given up a baby. Even if the reasons for it had been honourable, even if you'd hoped the child would have a better life somewhere else, there would still be that pain, that hole in your heart, to tell you that something was missing.

Something loved...?

Did my mum love me when she abandoned me? Or didn't she care one way or the other? Has she ever regretted her decision? Does she think about me every day?

Ruby having gone missing was prompting this torment in Lula now. There'd always been some element of it inside her, but she'd always kept it in check before. It had been a fleeting thought, a passing wonder or consideration, soon flattened down by more pressing matters. But here, now, with another abandoned baby and another missing mother, Lula couldn't help but think about her own situation.

Olly stood up behind the table and called the meeting to order. The mass of voices in the room were suddenly silenced as everyone turned to hear what he was about to say.

Lula studied him as he spoke. Tall, straight backed, he'd turned his shirtsleeves back to the elbow and she could see his strong, muscular forearms. He really was an attractive man. Solid, dependable, down to earth. The sort of man you could settle down with.

If that was what you were looking for.

If I was the type to settle down, he'd be the type I'd go for...

She watched the faces of the people from the village. They were listening to Olly's every word, some of them even writing down the description of Ruby as he presented it.

He spoke easily, not afraid of addressing the whole room, and there was a command to his voice that she'd never noticed before. It was reassuring. Even though this was a difficult moment—an awful situation—his voice gave the sense that there was someone in charge who knew what to do. If they all just did as he suggested the matter would soon be settled.

She hoped so. She hoped Ruby would be found quickly.

A police officer then added his bit and Olly sat down, glancing at her with a quick smile.

Lula smiled back, her heart warming. He'd done a great job.

She could only hope that now the village would do a great job and find the poor missing girl.

The police presented a map of the village that they'd segregated into different zones, including the large woods that Olly and Lula had been assigned to. They were all given a whistle to blow if they found Ruby, or any sign of the young teen. With a wish for good luck, the villagers were ready to search, and they stood up with much scraping of chairs and mumbling as they wrapped up in their coats and scarves and headed out into the snow.

Outside, fresh snow was falling. It would almost have been pretty if the situation hadn't been so dire.

Lula got into Olly's car and he drove them to the woods. As he drove Lula glanced at him, seeing the strain on his face, the worry lines across his brow, his white knuckles gripping tight about the steering wheel. She asked him if he was all right?

He glanced at her. 'Yeah, I'm fine. This just reminds me of Mum, that's all.'

'What happened?'

He shook his head. 'Mum and Dad went hiking one year, when I was two. My grandma looked after me whilst they went backpacking in America.' He indicated quickly and took a turning that took them in the direction of the woods they were heading for. 'They were walking the Pacific Crest Trail, but they'd not planned it very well and had picked the wrong time of year. There was a lot of snowfall, but they thought that as they were together they'd be fine.'

'What happened?' she asked, with tenderness in her voice.

'Dad went to get water from a stream and Mum apparently headed out to find some firewood. When he came back to their campsite there was no sight of her, but he wasn't too worried. She was an accomplished walker—he figured she'd be back...not realising she'd slipped on some ice and cracked her head open on a rock.'

'How long did he leave it?'

'Long enough. Thirty minutes? He knew they had a long trek ahead of them that day and thought he'd better track her down. When he found her she was cold and hypothermic.'

'Alive, though?'

He nodded. 'But unconscious. They had no mobile phones then, so he had to go for help on foot. They were miles from civilisation, and by the time he got back...'

Lula swallowed hard, feeling his pain and tragedy. 'She'd died?'

Olly grimaced. 'Dad was inconsolable, apparently.'

'It doesn't mean the same thing will happen today. We could find Ruby quickly. There's lots of people out looking for her.'

'I know. It's just a part of my past that's always haunted me, that's all.'

She looked at him. Was this the reason he never stepped out of his comfort zone? Because he'd seen what could happen if you veered off track?

'It was bound to. If it didn't haunt you then I'd be concerned. It just shows you're human.'

She touched his sleeve in companionable solidarity, glad that she could be there to comfort him at this time. It was also nice to hear more about him. He knew quite a bit about her, but she'd not really had the time to ask lots of questions about him. Even though it was a dark story she was glad that he'd shared it with her, and it helped her understand him a bit more.

'You like helping people. It's part of being a doctor. It just gets frustrating when you can't help everybody.'

Olly smiled at her. 'Thanks. You're right. That's why I've always enjoyed being a GP. It's grass-roots medicine. Okay, you don't have the thrill of the operating theatre, or CPR, or the exciting stuff most times, but I value its basics and the opportunity it gives me to get to know my patients.'

'Have you ever considered any other type of medicine or did you always want to be a GP? Follow your father into the family practice?'

'I always wanted to be a doctor—I knew that. It was only natural that I became a GP. But did I want to do anything else? No. I don't think so. My heart has always been here.'

The parking area by the woods was empty, and Olly parked the car as close as he could to the stile that marked the entry point. Getting out of his car, Olly walked to the back and pulled out a flask and a thick blanket that he stuffed into a backpack and hoisted over his shoulders.

'Just in case.'

Lula pulled on her gloves and zipped up her coat. It really was cold, and the snowflakes that were falling were large and heavy-looking.

The wood looked mystical in its white carpet, with the icing of snow upon the black, skeletal trees and the crows calling out from the treetops in protest.

It didn't look like the sort of place that might be hiding a teenager. But they needed to look there. They needed to look everywhere.

She almost hesitated to ask. 'Shall we split up?'

'Let's stick together as much as we can.'

'I can't see the path—there's too much snow.'

'Even more reason to stick together. If we wander off track it could become hazardous. There's a stream somewhere in there, and lots of dips and hidden rabbit holes. There's even a badger sett.'

Lula nodded, hoping neither of them would get an injury searching through what might be hazardous terrain. They could easily drop through a snowdrift and twist an ankle in a rabbit hole or something.

'It's a pity we haven't got a sniffer dog.'

'If we don't find her that might be the next stage for the police.' He looked grim.

They put their whistles around their necks and clambered over the stile.

Their search for Ruby had begun.

CHAPTER FIVE

'RUBY? *RUBY!*' LULA called out loudly, but the vast emptiness of the woods and the thick layer of snow seemed to steal her voice away.

Everywhere was pure white, and it was hard work walking through the deep drifts, lifting their knees up high for each step. It was like a winter workout. A workout that had both of them huffing and puffing within minutes.

The ground underfoot seemed not only slippery but uneven, and full of unseen hazards. Occasionally Lula spotted a perky-looking robin, hopping here and there, searching for food, but mostly she just saw the crows up high and hoped they weren't an ominous omen.

There were a few animal tracks, but from what she wasn't sure. She scanned the ground, hoping to see a trail of footprints, but if there had been any they'd already been covered by the thick falling snow.

Olly's thick blond hair was covered in snowflakes and his cheeks were rosy. Looking at him, it was easy for her to imagine that they might have been on a pleasant winter walk, but the frown lines around his eyes and across his brow spoke deeply of his determination.

'Ruby?' he called.

There was no response.

They tramped on through the snow, hoping they were sticking to the path. At one point Lula stumbled, and she reached out automatically for him.

'Are you okay?' he asked, concern in his voice.

'I'm fine! Just a tree root or something...' She was anxious to reassure him, aware of how worried he might be.

But he pursed his lips and took her hand, slipping his fingers through her gloved ones. 'Let's take no chances.'

Lula's cheeks warmed at the contact and for a moment she didn't say anything. It felt strange to be walking through the woods holding Olly's hand. When had she last walked anywhere holding *anyone's* hand?

Years—that's how long. But this is nice...

His hand was strong and firm. His grip relentless. There was definitely no way he was going to let go of her and let her stumble again. Though he didn't seem affected by the contact the way she was.

Perhaps he's just much better at hiding things than I am? I've always worn my heart on my sleeve.

Or perhaps he was just keeping his mind on their task?

It might have amused her to know that his heart was actually racing. When she'd stumbled his stomach had flipped and his heart had almost literally gone into his mouth. He'd offered his hand without thinking. But now that he was holding her tightly he was intensely aware of the contact he had with her. He was doing his utmost to try and keep his mind on the task and definitely *off* the image in his head of pulling her into his arms and kissing her in the snow.

That would be kind of romantic. Kissing her whilst snowflakes fall gently onto our faces...

Lula felt him shiver and saw him mentally shake

himself. She wondered if he was reliving that story about his mother. Wanting to offer her support, she gave his fingers a little squeeze and noticed him glance at her.

'We'll find her.'

He nodded. 'Let's hope so.'

'She must be freezing if she's out in this.'

'Let's just hope she's conscious.'

Yes, Ruby would need enough medical attention already, having recently given birth, but if hypothermia had set in as well… A lot of people thought hypothermia simply meant you'd got a bit cold and needed some hot soup and a quilt wrapped round you, but it could be so much more life-threatening than that.

If you had hypothermia your body was unable to produce the range of protective reflex actions it would normally when you were cold. For example shivering—the activation of a mass amount of small muscle contractions—would be totally absent eventually, although at the onset of hypothermia shivering could be quite violent. People could become delirious, and also struggle to breathe or move about. They could suffer loss of judgement and reasoning and therefore end up in further dangerous situations.

What if Ruby had got herself into difficulties? What if she was already bleeding heavily and suffering hypothermia, too?

Lula trudged on, her head down, holding tightly onto Olly. She was glad she was out here with him. He seemed so dependable. So reliable. She knew he was the type of man you could trust.

The type of man you could love?

She glanced at him. Yes, he was. Easily. And that was why he needed to remain her friend and nothing more. She could imagine, in another situation, falling for Olly easily—but she wasn't here in Atlee Wold for that. She wasn't living her life to fall for anyone. There wasn't much point. There was so much else she had to do in her life—fitting in all the things she wanted to do.

Since the leukaemia and the diagnosis of her infertility Lula had made a vow to herself to live life for *her*. Experience everything. Do anything. She couldn't get bogged down in a relationship. She didn't want to have to ask anyone's permission to do anything. She wanted time and space to be her own person. Olly could still be a good friend. There was nothing wrong with that. But that was all she could offer him.

Friendship.

She knew that people were capable of having relationships even though they knew they couldn't have children, but Lula believed the need to procreate was strong in everyone. If you got into a relationship with someone the desire to have a child with them would be a natural progression. She didn't ever want to be the cause of heartache and pain to someone else.

She knew what that felt like already.

She'd tried it.

There'd been a boyfriend during medical school. Gavin. He'd been carefree and happy and fun, and they'd gone out with each other knowing that fun was all they could have together. She'd told him about being infertile and he'd said he was fine with it, that he didn't need to have children, that he had her and that was all that mattered.

Only it wasn't.

Gavin had eventually changed his mind. Said he wanted children in his future. It had caused many arguments and heartbreak, and when they'd split up Lula had vowed never to get into a serious relationship ever again.

And she hadn't.

And I can't now, either.

Olly wanted a 'perfect' wife. Someone kind, considerate and loving—and someone who wanted to have children. He'd said it himself that time, driving home from the hospital. As far as Lula was concerned Olly had a big red cross painted over him, marking him out as unavailable.

Olly wanted children in his future. His traditional future. He was a traditional guy, after all. And she could picture him at some rosy point in that future with a wife and little sandy-haired children running around.

Lula couldn't give that to him. Not in a million years.

Yes, there was adoption, and fostering, and all of that was great, but the need for your own biological child could still be a strong one. Knowing she could never provide a man with that was a big reason for her to stay away.

Because I don't want to get hurt, either.

What would be the point in investing all that time in a relationship? Of loving someone only to have to break your own heart when it all fell apart at the end? Because it always did in Lula's world. Children's homes... foster parents...Gavin. It all broke down when someone wanted something more than you could give them.

'Ruby?' she called out.

Her voice echoed out in the white emptiness. They needed to find the teenager—and quickly. Hopefully she was at a friend's house, or something as safe and un-terrifying as that. Hopefully this search wasn't actually necessary. Perhaps she'd hopped on a bus and gone into town? Did Ruby have a mobile phone? She'd not asked the mother. If she did, she presumed someone would have called it by now.

Lula had to assume Ruby didn't have a phone, or that she wasn't answering it. It would be nice to think that Ruby was tucked up somewhere, warm and safe...

'Ruby? Are you out here?' she called again.

Nothing.

Silence.

Just the crows up above.

How had it felt for Ruby to place her baby on Lula's doorstep and walk away? How had it felt for her own mother to place her on that beach and then leave? What did that do to a person? They had to be distraught. Heartbroken. Not thinking clearly.

They tramped on, Lula clutching Olly's hand, each hearing the other breathing hard, feeling the other stumble or slip occasionally, holding on tightly, not wanting to let go.

It had been a long time since Lula had truly felt a part of a team. She'd always kept herself on the sidelines. Involved, but not *part* of things.

But here in Atlee Wold, with Olly, she could feel just how easy it would be to accept the place and him into her heart. It felt so right. It felt so...

Tempting!

But I can't. It wouldn't be right. Olly wants so much more from a woman...

Strangely, she felt tears prick at her eyes and quickly blinked them away. Where had that emotion come from?

I can't cry!

Lula needed to keep this light-hearted. A fun, surface emotion—nothing too deep. When had she last cried?

I can't remember.

She had once believed that a woman was entitled to a good cry every month. But Lula hadn't cried for a long time. Why was that?

Perhaps not allowing myself to truly connect with people has done that?

With her spare hand she wiped the tears away with her glove and hoped Olly thought her eyes were watering from the cold. She could feel her nose turning red. Looking at Olly, she could see that his had turned a rosy colour, too, as they both huffed frozen breaths out into the air. She wanted to sniff—her nose was running...

Suddenly Lula slipped. Her left ankle went sideways, her foot caught some ice and she fell down, crashing onto her knees.

'Oof!'

The ground beneath was solid and icy and the snow soaked her trousers.

'Whoa! You all right?'

Olly knelt down beside her, his hands on her upper arms, care and concern in his bright blue eyes. The plumes of his frozen breath encircled her face and she tried hard not to stare into his eyes.

'Yes, I'm fine.' She thanked him and got to her feet, tenderly testing her ankle.

'I told you it was dangerous. Perhaps we've gone off the path a bit?'

Olly looked around them and thought that maybe they *had* veered off track. The natural track through the trees was off to the right.

'Come on—hold tight.' He grabbed her hand again and they continued to walk, though her ankle felt a little delicate. She knew she hadn't twisted or sprained it—the pain wasn't bad enough for that—but she'd certainly jarred it.

The ability to see the surface you were walking on was something everyone took for granted. But when that view was obscured—when you didn't know what you were walking on, or walking through—you couldn't have any idea of how dangerous it was. You had to trust to luck...or trust the person who walked alongside you.

I trust Olly. I know he's a man I can trust.

She knew she had to stop thinking of him in that way. But she couldn't help it. He was just so easy to like and depend upon, and those good looks of his didn't help any. He had a natural wholehearted appeal. He was a handsome, kind-hearted and generous man, who happened to be single, who happened to be holding her hand and trying to protect her. What was there not to like?

It would be so easy to kiss him and get carried away.

Even though her cheeks were already rosy from the cold and the exertion she flushed a deeper colour and felt her heart skip along a whole lot more merrily than it already had been! Thinking of Olly in such a way made her stomach do a tiny flip, too. It was like having a whole heap of cheerleaders in there, egging her on to find out how it would truly feel if she did give in to her desires and grab Olly and kiss him.

'Ruby?' she called again, trying to take her mind off her train of thought.

The track ahead curved off to the left, and then it looked as if there was a natural fork in the trail. She felt Olly slow, and when they got to the fork he stopped and frowned.

'The path splits. We need to check both ways, but I'm not happy about you going off on your own.'

'I'm sure I'll be fine. I'm a grown woman. I've looked after myself this long without getting hurt.' She smiled to take away some of the harshness of her words. She didn't want to offend him.

'But you've already slipped once, and you don't know these woods.'

'Do you?'

'A little—though I must admit I've never had the opportunity to enjoy them fully during the summer. Always too much work on.'

'Well, we need to check both paths if we're to search properly. Do the paths conjoin further on?'

'I think so. I'm sure I can remember Dad telling me they did. But it's been so long...'

'I'll be careful, Olly.' She pulled her hand free from his tight grip. 'You be careful, too.' She could see the uncertainty in his eyes.

'Blow your whistle if you see any sign of her or get into trouble.'

'I will.'

'Promise me?'

If someone could market the perfect picture of a face filled with concern, then Olly was it. It was nice that he was so worried about her. But Lula was used to looking out for herself.

'I promise.'

As she set off down her path she realised she could no longer feel her toes or her fingers. The socks she was wearing were normal socks, not hiking socks. They weren't fit for the purpose of trudging through deep snow for hours.

I wished I'd thought of that earlier.

She held on to the whistle around her neck as she hiked through the thicker snow. Looking over, she could see that Olly was now out of sight. Perhaps he'd gone down a dip, or the number of trees was blocking the view of him. It felt good to know that he was somewhat close, though.

'Ruby?' she called, hearing Olly call the same thing in the distance.

There were indentations in the snow, so it looked as if someone might have walked this path earlier. She had no idea if it had been Ruby. It might have just been a dog walker.

'Ruby? It's Dr Chance!'

No response still.

She trudged on, slipping slightly, feeling the ice beneath the surface snow. As she went to correct her balance, putting all her weight on her left foot, the snow gave way. She landed with a thump on her coccyx before sliding part way down a bank and into icy-cold water up to her bottom.

'Oh!'

When she struggled to a standing position the water was only ankle-deep, but her boots were going to be ruined and the back of her trousers was cold and soaked. The base of her spine hurt where she'd fallen directly on to it and she felt slightly winded. Turning, she noted the muddy track of her slide down into the water.

'Great. Just what I needed.'

There was no way to tell where the edge of the small stream was, so she lifted up her feet in her water-filled boots and tried to find the bank. A tree root stuck out slightly, so she reached to grab for that and pulled herself through the water and up onto firmer ground.

Her feet and legs were *freezing*!

Normally Lula loved snow. Loved the excitement of it and the fun of it. But having soaking wet, freezing cold feet in soggy socks and boots wasn't much fun. She wiped the mud off her bottom and clambered up. At the top of the bank she pulled off one boot and poured out the water. Then she did the same with the other foot. It felt awful to have to slide her feet back into them when all she could think of was warm, cosy slippers, or dry feet wriggling in front of a roaring open fire.

But she did it. She had to.

She continued on, cursing every step, feeling the ache in her bottom gradually fade away.

By the time she met up with Olly again a good twenty minutes had passed and her teeth were chattering.

'Any j-j-joy?'

Olly looked her up and down. 'You're soaked!'

'N-Not really. I'm more ice now than water.' She managed a smile.

'You can't go on like that. Come on—I'll take you home.'

'We need to look for Ruby.'

'And have my new doctor get hypothermia? I don't think so.'

'But the police think we're looking in this area. We can't leave.'

'I'll let them know what's happened and how far we searched. First rule of emergency support: make sure it's safe for yourself. I won't have you walking around in those boots and wet trousers.'

'What if I refuse?'

He looked hard at her, his steely blue eyes firm and sure. But then a hint of a twinkle filled them before he scooped her up into his arms suddenly, the way a groom might carry a new bride over the threshold. 'Then I'm forced to do this.' He looked into her eyes with amusement, daring her to say anything.

Lula blushed, but also laughed. Olly was strong. She could feel him holding her tightly and safely in his arms. 'Why, Dr James!'

He grinned and began walking the path back to the

car. 'Let's just hope I don't hit the ice or we'll both be doomed.'

Lula didn't think he'd continue to carry her all the way back to the car. It was so *far*! But somehow he did. Okay, he was huffing and puffing, and his cheeks were fiery red, and she'd sagged slightly in his arms by the time they got there, but he still held her. He only put her down when they reached the stile at the entry point to the woods.

'Thank you. You didn't have to carry me so far.'

'Yes, I did. I couldn't have your feet in the snow. Not wet like that.'

'Well, it was very chivalrous of you.'

He accepted her thanks with a grin and a nod of his head. 'I do try to be a gentleman.'

'You do it very well. This maiden is thankful.'

She smiled then, and kissed his cheek, but when she pulled away her smile faltered as she saw the way he was looking at her mouth. As if he was hungry for her. As if he was going to kiss her back and it wasn't going to be a friendly peck.

Hurriedly, suddenly afraid of what she might do if she let him, she turned away and clambered over the stile, her whistle clinking against the buttons on her coat. Lula waited on her side of the car, glad that she had the space of a car between them, but clambered in eagerly when he opened up her side and turned on the heater.

Hot air billowed into the car and gratefully she peeled off her boots and socks and perched her bare feet up on the console, near one of the heating vents.

'Oh...*bliss*!'

Her toes were very pale—almost white. She wriggled her toes to try and feel them, to try and get some life back into them, whilst Olly reversed out of the car park.

They passed some other searchers on the way back, identified by the whistles on their lanyards.

When they got back to Moonrose Cottage Olly insisted on carrying her to her front door.

'I can walk!'

'In bare feet?'

He scooped her out of her seat and once again carried her easily up to the front door. She had her keys ready and unlocked the door. She waited for him to set her down.

'I'll restart the fire.'

He nodded. 'I'll make you a hot drink.'

She watched him disappear into the kitchen. She scooped a pair of thick boot socks off the back of a chair and was just stacking some bigger logs onto the burgeoning flames when she heard him call out.

'Lula?'

'Yes?'

'Have you been in the garden shed?'

There was a garden shed?

'No, I haven't.'

'The door's hanging open. There's tracks.'

Lula padded into the kitchen, her brow lined in question.

But Olly had already unlocked the side door and set off into the garden. From the window, she watched him traverse the long length of the garden towards a ramshackle old shed that she'd not noticed earlier. Then she saw him dash in and heard him calling her name.

Lula rushed to the back door, unable to go out since she had nothing on her feet but clutching the door frame, hoping he'd found Ruby.

He had.

Moments later Olly emerged sideways from the shed with a pale young girl in his arms, wrapped in blankets. He carried her all the way up the garden.

Two maidens in one day.

'Be careful! It's slippery!' Lula warned. She didn't need him to fall over now and drop the young teenager in the snow.

He carried her into the house and Lula rushed to the front room to pull one of the chairs in front of the now roaring fire.

'I'll make her a hot drink.'

Normally Lula wouldn't give someone needing medical attention any drink or food, in case they needed an operation, but with Ruby it was essential she be warmed up slowly. As neither of them had any warm intravenous fluids handy to push into her veins, blankets, a fire and a hot drink would have to do.

When she hurried back into the front room, holding a steaming mug of sweet tea, Olly was just getting off the phone.

'I've called for an ambulance.'

'Notify the police, too. Call off the search.'

He nodded and flipped open his phone once again.

Lula knelt in front of the young girl, noting her pale features, the way she clutched the blankets. She was still shivering—which was good. It meant true hypothermia hadn't set in.

'Sip this. Slowly.' She held the mug to Ruby's lips and waited for her to take a sip. The solitary action seemed to exhaust the young girl. 'Oh, Ruby! Everyone's been looking for you. Your mother's been frantic.'

'E-E-Everyone?' she stammered.

Lula nodded slowly. 'A lot of the village came out in an organised search. And the police...Dr James and I.'

'I d-didn't know where else to go.'

Lula offered the tea again and Olly returned to kneel by her side. 'The police are on their way.'

Ruby looked frightened.

'It's okay, Ruby. They just want to make sure you're all right.'

'Am I in t-trouble?'

They both shook their heads, though truthfully neither of them knew exactly how Ruby's mother might react. Would she be angry that her daughter had disappeared and had a baby in secret? Or would she cry? Ask questions? Be sympathetic? Understanding?

'You had a baby, didn't you?' Lula asked.

Ruby met her gaze and tears welled up in her eyes. 'It hurt.'

Lula and Olly smiled. 'Of course it did. You were so brave to go through it on your own. Where did it happen?'

'In my bedroom. Mum was at work, so no one heard.'

'We searched the house. Didn't find any sign of the afterbirth or anything.'

'I used a plastic sheet. Mum p-painted the hall a few weeks ago, in time for Christmas, and bought plastic sheets to protect the carpet. I used one of those.'

'Where did you dispose of it?'

'The public litter bin by the church.' She sipped at the tea a bit more. 'That's good.' She paused briefly, her eyes welling once again, before she asked, 'How's my baby?'

Lula patted her knee. 'Good. Safe and warm in hospital. You did a good job, wrapping her up warm and placing that hot water bottle under her. It kept her safe.

Though you were lucky I found her. I'd only just moved in. Did you know that?'

Ruby nodded, pulling the blankets tighter around her. 'When I was smaller I used to play here in Mrs James's garden all the time. She used to let me play in the orchard at the bottom, and the shed was my Wendy house of sorts. She put an old chair in there, an oil heater, and some blankets for when the weather was cold and I didn't want to go home.'

'Why didn't you want to go home?'

'My mum and I didn't get along and Mrs James was always kind. Like a grandmother to me.'

'You knew my grandmother?' Olly asked.

'Very well.' Ruby smiled. 'She was lovely. When I'd left the baby on the doorstep I was so tired, and it hurt to walk, I knew I had to rest and I remembered the shed. I hoped the heater still had oil in it and it did.'

Lula looked incredulous. 'You were in there all that time?'

Ruby nodded.

'I never noticed. How did I not notice?'

'There weren't any lights. How would you know?'

She looked at the young girl. 'You could have frozen to death.'

'I was too tired to care.'

Lula glanced at Olly, trying her best not to cry at the young girl's revelation. He reached out and rubbed her shoulder in support.

She blinked away the tears. 'We were worried that you might have a retained placenta.'

'What's that?'

'It's where not all of the afterbirth comes away.'

'It seemed okay.'

'Are you in pain now?'

'A bit. But isn't that normal after giving birth?'

They all heard a siren in the distance, getting closer.

'I'm in so much trouble!' She began to cry.

Lula knelt forward and wrapped her arms around the young girl. She still felt so cold! And she was shuddering and shaking from crying so much.

It broke her heart to think of what this young girl had gone through. Had her own mother experienced the same thing? Had she been through labour and birth alone and then left Lula on the beach because she'd been too scared to tell anyone she'd had a baby?

As the ambulance stopped in front of the property and Olly let the paramedics in Lula vowed to stay by Ruby's side until the young girl's mother arrived.

Why should she be alone ever again?

Why should either of them?

Olly followed the ambulance to the hospital. Stuck in his own vehicle, he keenly felt his separation from Lula. She'd connected to Ruby—he could see that. She was obviously viewing her own past and abandonment in light of what had occurred with the young teenager.

He felt good that they'd found Ruby and that this story might end well. He hoped so. He could only hope that Lula would find her happy ending, too.

I'm going to help her find her mother.

It was the most important thing to her. How could he *not* help? And if Lula found her mother within Atlee Wold then perhaps she'd stay. There'd be no reason for her to leave, would there? And if she stayed, that meant…he could have a future with Lula in it.

Parking his vehicle in the car park, he strolled into A&E, waving at one of the receptionists he knew. Sally beckoned him over.

'Dr James! Good to see you. How long has it been?'

He was keen to get to Lula and Ruby, but he didn't want to be rude. 'Too long, Sally. How's Jack?' Jack was Sally's husband—a stroke nurse.

'Good, thanks. Getting all nervous about his parachute jump in May.'

Parachute jump? Was the whole world going mad and doing crazy things? 'Parachute jump?'

'It's for charity. They're raising money for brain tumour research. You could do it, too!'

Sally passed him a fundraising form and he took it, doubt in his head. But then he thought of Lula, and what she'd do and say if she knew he'd turned down an opportunity like this.

But did he want to throw himself out of an aeroplane to prove that he wasn't stuck in a rut? That he did occasionally challenge himself? Heights didn't bother him—but then he was normally inside tall buildings or planes, not about to throw himself out of one...

'I don't know...'

Sally smiled. 'It's a good cause. Think how you'll feel when your feet touch the ground.'

His feet *always* touched the ground. He liked them there. It was safe.

But wasn't that the issue?

Olly stared at the form.

Then at Sally.

He nodded.

CHAPTER SIX

IT WAS A LONG wait at the hospital. For the second time in two days, Lula sat by a patient's bedside, watching her sleep.

Ruby's mother had arrived—frantic, weeping, shaking with relief—and she and the young girl had had a tearful reunion. Ruby was physically all right, thankfully. No retained placenta, normal blood loss and she'd been slowly warmed up. Then the nurses had asked if Ruby had wanted to see her baby.

Ruby hadn't known how to answer, but her mother had answered for her. Yes, they wanted to see the baby—because Ruby's mother wanted to know if they could bring her grandchild home.

That had made Lula cry. It might have been a tragic story, Ruby and her baby. It might have had a disastrous ending. But it hadn't. The family was being reunited. As Lula had hoped all along. It hadn't happened in time for *her*. No one had found or tracked down EL from Atlee Wold for *her*. There'd been no desperate search in the snow for *her*.

Lula had remained alone. And then ill and alone. Until the Chance family had come along and offered her home comforts and love. She'd been grateful to them, but she had always known she didn't belong. That she wasn't one of them. That it wasn't her real family. And that yearning for actual roots, for actual blood relations, had burned her deep inside.

Olly hadn't had a mother, either. Was that why he was looking for perfection? Was that why he kept everything safe and normal? So that he didn't have to feel different from everyone else?

Because that was how not having a mother had felt to Lula.

Being on the outside, always looking in, had given her a tendency to keep away from people. When had she ever got involved with anyone? Deeply enough for it to hurt when it was over?

Just once.

But there was something different about being in Atlee Wold. The people, the community feeling... It was hard to describe, but Lula felt at home here. As if she was in the right place. She *knew* her mother was here. Maybe even her father? Who knew? And the urge to stay was strong, even though she knew the chances that her mother wouldn't welcome her with open arms could be strong. What if her mother wouldn't acknowledge her? Wanted nothing to do with her?

Well, that would hurt, but I'd cope with it.

Lula knew that if she was to stay strong then no matter how the search ended she'd have to walk away. Give her mother space. Give herself space and time to reflect. She'd have to put miles between them so as not to come on too strong and demand more from her mother than her mother was able to give. To build their relationship slowly if there was a chance of one.

Perhaps her mother had yearned for her over the years? It was possible, wasn't it?

I do hope so.

And the chance to learn about the choices her mother had made would give Lula some closure, too. Nobody wanted to feel not wanted. Not loved. Especially by their parents. It was meant to be an unbreakable bond, the bond between a mother and her child.

Just to know that she held me in her arms and loved me...

Lula wanted that feeling very much.

Olly drove Lula back from the hospital once again, glancing over at her, looking at her secretly, hoping she wasn't noticing how much he looked at her. It wasn't like her to be this quiet. In the short time he'd known her she'd always been so bubbly, always so full of something to say. It was strange to have her so quiet.

He knew the situation with Ruby must have hit home with her. He knew she was searching for her mother and he hoped she would find her. But he had no real idea of the anguish she was in.

He could only imagine it.

It must be terrible and he wanted to comfort her. Make her better. He decided to take the plunge and dive straight in.

'Guess what I'm going to do?'

He felt her turn to look at him. 'What?'

'You won't believe it.'

'Try me.'

He grinned, his stomach flipping over in shock as he finally admitted to it out loud. 'A sponsored parachute jump.'

Now she was *really* looking at him. '*What?*'

He could hear the delight in her voice, the surprise and the joy. It thrilled him immensely—much more than he'd expected it to. Pleasing her made him feel good. Made him acknowledge that he'd stepped out of Mediocre Land and was going to take a huge leap into Extraordinaryville.

'Really.'

'That's great, Olly! And so brave. I'm not sure I could do it—I'm afraid of heights.'

'I'm sure you'll think of something to challenge it.'

Back at Moonrose Cottage, she invited him in and he nodded his head, wanting to make sure she was okay before he left for the night. It was late. Almost eleven.

The fire had died out and there was a slight chill to the cottage, so he reset the fire whilst Lula sat on the sofa, holding an old quilt around her.

She looked so sad. It was an emotion he didn't associate with her and he so wanted to put it right. There was something about Lula that reached out to him and made him care. Something he'd never experienced before.

The flames took hold slowly, building into a strong red-orange heat. As the wood spat and crackled he sat back and took a seat beside her, taking her hand in his, squeezing her fingers.

'Will you be all right?'

She smiled and nodded at him. 'Sure. It's just been an eventful couple of days, that's all.'

'You can say that again.'

The flames were reflected in her eyes, dancing and leaping, and he suddenly found himself fighting the urge to reach out and stroke her face. Her skin looked so soft in the firelight. Instead he clenched his hands together, as if they were still cold, to stop himself from reaching out.

'I mean, this must have touched you…personally?'

Lula smiled again, and nodded, and he could see tears glazing her eyes. His stomach ached at the thought of her hurting, and as a solitary tear ran down her rosy cheek he couldn't stop himself. He had to reach out and wipe it away.

She looked at him as he did so, her eyes full of something he couldn't decipher. He was too busy trying to understand the feelings ripping through his own body with the force of a blizzard. Only it wasn't cold. It was intense heat. Heat he'd not felt for a long time.

'I can't help but think that...'

She didn't finish her sentence. She just looked at him, and he saw her gaze drop to his mouth, then move back up to his eyes again.

Should he kiss her?

She was his colleague. The new doctor. A locum. A drifter. She wasn't the type of woman he would normally go for. Lula was...*different*. And not just because she had the colours of the rainbow in her hair and a jewel in her belly button and tattoos on her toe-ringed feet. It was none of that. That was all window dressing.

It was Lula herself. So full of life! So full of spark! Always concerned for others, reaching out, doing that little extra. Never asking for anything herself even though she had her own troubles, her own concerns, her own needs.

She was funny and beautiful and kind and caring, and she made him feel he could achieve anything he wanted to. She made him feel as if...he wanted to kiss her.

Olly leaned in. Slowly.

What if she rejects me? What if...?

He never finished the thought because his lips touched hers and an explosion went off in his gut. His eyes closed as he sank into the kiss with Lula, enjoying the soft, sensual curve of her lips, the warmth of her mouth, the scent of her skin.

She didn't protest. She didn't push him away.

She welcomed him!

He took hold of her face and pulled her close, deepening the kiss.

She moaned a little and he couldn't help himself. He lost control at the sound. He pulled her to him, pressing her small, lithe body against his as his tongue delved into her mouth to claim her, taste her, enjoy her.

Lula was something else. He'd never, ever experienced this sort of passion with a woman before. Yes, there'd been heat—but it had been perfunctory and fleeting. A case of him just going through the motions.

But this... This was something else!

'Olly...' she breathed as his mouth left hers to cover her jawline and sink down her throat, nibbling her skin and kissing, biting and licking at her pulse points. She smelt delightful. It was as if she was some sort of life-giving nectar that he had to suckle from. He had to taste, lick, bite, kiss.

Inhale her.

He reached the waistline of her jumper and pulled it over her head, then removed the thermal tee shirt she had on underneath that. That was the problem with winter! Too many layers! He couldn't get to her skin quickly enough. He *had* to have her.

All sensible thought had left his head completely. That she was his new colleague. That she was his friend. That maybe there could be a risk in doing this with her and then having to work with her afterwards if it all went wrong.

Who says it's going to go wrong?

None of it mattered any more.

He unclipped her bra as she pulled off his top layers.
Their hands were all over each other, and his skin was
sizzling at her feathery touch. Cupping her breasts, he
lifted her delicate nipples into his mouth and squeezed
his eyes shut with ecstasy as she groaned above him,
clutching his head, her fingers raking through his hair.

Is there anything sweeter than this?

Pulling Lula to the soft rug in front of the fire, he
removed the rest of her clothes. When she'd pulled off
his straining trousers she agonisingly kissed his skin, all
the way down from his waist, and he thought he would
just implode there and then.

When her mouth came back up to his he claimed it
once again with his own, running his hands all over her.
Her soft, curvaceous body was lithe and delicate as he
pulled himself over her. And he'd been right. There *were*
tiny little tattoos all over her. A cute miniature mouse
on her hip, a heart in the dimple of her bottom, a trailing sparkle of stars at the top of her thigh...

Condom, Oliver!

'Damn, wait...' He looked for his jacket and saw
it over the back of a chair. Leaving her for just a moment, he grabbed his wallet, hoping and praying he had
a condom in there.

When had he last needed one?

A while at least...

He couldn't honestly remember if there was one in
there!

Oh, thank God!

A small silver packet, tucked behind an old credit
card that he never used any more but hadn't bothered
to dispose of yet.

Hoping it was in date, he tore at the wrapper with
his teeth.

'No. Let me,' she whispered, her breath tickling his chest.

He closed his eyes in agonised lust and tried to gather his control as she slowly and tantalisingly rolled the condom down the length of his penis, almost gasping at the feel of her fingers wrapped tightly around him.

'I want you...' he muttered, but the words didn't mean enough. Not enough to convey just how much he wanted her and needed her right then.

She lay back and smiled at him, reaching out with her hands to pull him down on top of her.

He tortured himself as he deliberately teased her entrance, dying to thrust himself inside her but hesitating, touching briefly, sliding between her folds. Then, unable to hold back any more in case he physically imploded, he entered her. She gasped and grabbed his back, sliding her hands down to his bottom to pull him tighter against her.

Holy mother of...

He didn't want to come straight away. It would have been so easy, but he managed to hold back, enjoying the rise and fall as he moved above her. He crushed her mouth against his as she moaned and groaned. Her fingertips bit into his skin with their nails and all the time his orgasm built up, rising and rising.

Lula writhed beneath him, gasping for air, pulling him towards her, pulling him in deeper, her eyes closed. Her breathing grew faster. Shorter. Then she was crying out, arcing up into his body as he rode her through it.

He moved faster. Harder. He ground himself into her and exploded into a satisfying molten puddle above her as she gasped beneath him. Collapsing, his lips against the skin of her neck, he kissed her one last time, holding on to her, feeling the rise and fall of her chest. Both of them were just breathing, soaking in the moment.

It would have been so easy just to lie there for a while longer. But now that his mind was working clearly again he thought only about getting her to bed. He scooped her up, smiling as she laughed, and made his way up the stairs, kicking open the main bedroom door, shivering slightly at the cold and hurrying them both into bed.

Laughing, they pulled the bedcovers over themselves and snuggled up close, warming each other with their body heat.

Olly held her body against him, kissing her nose, her face, her neck, inhaling her scent once again. It would be so easy for him to take her once again, but he knew there were no more condoms—and he ought to show at least a modicum of self-control.

He felt her remove the condom and groaned at her touch, knowing he could have no more. Lying in her arms, he fell asleep—only to wake in the early hours feeling guilty.

It was still dark. Olly blinked and turned to see the bedside clock, its digital numerals glowing red in the early hours.

Just gone two o'clock.

His head sank back onto the pillow and he looked at Lula, sleeping peacefully and contentedly beside him.

She was stretched out like a cat, the duvet covering one shoulder, the other bare almost to her breast. He eyed the gentle up-swell of her skin in the dark and re-membered how he'd taken her pink nipples in his mouth. Feeling guilty about what he'd done, he pulled the duvet over her shoulder to cover her.

I should never have slept with her. It's Lula, for good-ness' sake! My colleague! And she was feeling down.

I should never have taken advantage. What does that say about me? What if this changes things between us and makes it awkward?

He'd always thought of himself as an upstanding man. A man who would never take advantage of a woman for his own pleasure. But wasn't that what he'd done with Lula? This whole baby business, the search for her own mother, the Ruby episode—it had all affected her. Made her think about her own situation. It had hit home.

And what did I do?

No clear thinking, that was for sure.

Feeling gutted by his actions, Olly sat up, swinging his legs out of bed. The air was cooler outside of the duvet and all his clothes were still downstairs. Lula hadn't stirred, but he didn't feel he could stay in her bed—not feeling like this—so he got up and padded downstairs, slipping on his clothes as he found them and then building up the fire once again.

He could hear noises, and turned to see Nefertiti and Cleo looking at him through the bars of their cage, their noses twitching. 'I guess you saw all of that earlier?' he muttered quietly, wondering why on earth he was talking to two rats. 'I admit it—I'm not proud of myself. No matter how lovely your owner is.'

He stood by the cage in two minds. Should he stay? Or go? If he stayed there'd be that awkward morning-after conversation and he didn't think he could bear to go through that. Even if *she* didn't feel awkward, he certainly would. But if he left what would she think of him?

I could leave her a note.

He grabbed some paper and a pen from his grandmother's bureau and scribbled something quickly to imply that he'd got beeped on his pager and would see her later. It seemed the lesser of the two evils, and even though it was a lie he hoped that as it was a white lie it wouldn't hurt her and make her think that he'd abandoned her, too.

There was no way he wanted her to think that. He didn't want to hurt Lula. She was special. She meant something to him. But he thought it was important that they had a proper talk about what happened last night. And the immediate morning after—right before they both had to go to work—wouldn't be the right time.

Pulling on his jacket, he quietly slipped from the cottage, closing the door without making a sound. Standing in the snow outside, he looked up at the bedroom window, imagining himself back beneath the duvet with her.

I wouldn't be able to keep my hands off her!

He wanted her so much! But he also wanted the situation to be right. For her not to be grieving over her mother. For her not to be feeling lost because Ruby had her happy ending and she did not. He didn't want to take advantage of her again.

I hope she doesn't think I used her. I didn't. I wasn't.

Olly sloped away, his feet crunching through the top layer of snow that had begun to freeze overnight.

Lula woke to birdsong. For a long time she just lay there without opening her eyes, feeling content and enjoying the warmth of her bed, remembering the events of the night before. She blinked slowly, thinking she could turn to Olly and hold him before they both had to get up for work.

He wasn't there.

She sat up and looked about the room. No sign of him. But then she remembered they'd stripped each other of their clothes downstairs—perhaps he was down there, making breakfast? She couldn't smell any food. She couldn't hear any sounds.

Was he even there?

He has to be. He wouldn't just disappear in the night, would he?

She got out of her warm bed and slipped on her robe, tying it tightly at the waist before padding downstairs. 'Olly?'

There was no one in the lounge. And no answer to her call.

But there was a note with her name on, propped up on the mantelpiece. Her heart felt heavy as she went over to it, wondering what it might say. Flipping open the paper, she quickly scanned the words and sagged with relief. He'd been paged! Called away in the night to a patient!

She held the note to her chest and beamed. Last night had been amazing! Beautiful and passionate and just what she'd needed. And Olly had been perfect. He'd tasted tantalising. The feel of his strong, broad masculine form encircling her and entering her had made her nerve endings sing like choristers praising God on high with the most beautiful voices.

His very touch had been magical. She'd felt *everything*. Tingled at every caress, whether with his fingertips or his tongue. She'd almost wanted to consume him. She'd never have guessed it could have been that way with him. Dear Dr Oliver James.

Just thinking about him made her want him again!

But I have to be careful. I'm not meant to be starting something here. I'm here for my mother. That's all. What happened with Olly was fun, but that's all it can be.

She slipped the note into her pocket and went into the kitchen to start breakfast. Anubis sat in his cage, awaiting the sacrifice of some food. She opened the tank's top and dropped in some insects. She kept her hand there, thinking about touching him. Touching that large, plump, hairy body.

Her stomach squirmed, but she knew she had to force herself to try.

She reached down slowly, her breaths long and steady as her nerves shot into overdrive and her flight instinct kicked in. She would have to be gentle. Tarantulas could be damaged by rough handling.

Her fingers were about an inch away and she was just about to touch him…but he moved. Lightning fast she whipped her hand out of the tank, breathing heavily.

Close. So close!

But not yet. Maybe later she'd try again.

The clock in the kitchen told her she had twenty minutes before she needed to be at work. She headed upstairs for a shower.

Lula strode into the surgery, said good morning to the receptionists, and headed off into her room. She switched on the computer system and then went to the staff room to make a cup of coffee.

Whilst she was there Helen, the practice manager, came in, bearing packets of biscuits.

'Oh, they look nice.'

Helen smiled. 'Can't beat a chocolate digestive, I always say.'

'Absolutely. Do you know you can get some with pieces of stem ginger in, too?'

'Ginger's good for you, isn't it?' Helen smirked. 'Might have to get them, then.'

Lula nodded and laughed. 'For medical reasons, yes!' She stirred her tea. 'Do we know what the call-out was last night?'

Helen paused. 'I think it was Mr Levinson. He lives on Old School Road. Chest pains—but it turned out to be indigestion, I think, nothing major.'

She nodded, understanding. 'What time did Olly get called out to him? It must have been in the early hours?'

Helen frowned. 'Olly wasn't on call last night. It was Patrick who went out to the patient.'

'Oh.' Had she misunderstood? Had she read the note wrong? No. Surely not. Olly had been quite clear that he'd been called out to a patient. So why had he written that? Had he *lied*? Had he felt bad about last night and not been able to face her?

Why?

They were both adults. They both knew what they'd done. She knew he was a sensitive soul, but surely he hadn't had second thoughts and run out on her in the middle of the night?

Lula felt as if she'd been kicked in the guts. But not wanting to let her sadness and disappointment show, especially in front of Helen, she forced a smile and went back to her room.

If Olly didn't want to face her then she'd happily give him all the space he needed.

Olly sat in his room, writing up his notes for the last patient he'd seen, but his mind wasn't really on his task. Lula would be here by now. Just down the corridor from him. He could feel her presence, even separated as they were by a few unfeeling walls. She'd not come in to see him—not even to just pop her head round the door and say good morning.

What was going through her mind?

Was she angry with him? No, that couldn't be it. She thought he'd got called out to a patient—there was no reason for her to be angry with him. Perhaps she'd got up late and rushed in, not wanting to be late for work, and just hadn't had the time yet to say hello?

What if she'd not seen his note? That would be awful. She'd think he'd run out on her...

I could go and say hello.

I don't want her to think I'm hiding.

In fact it would be better if I did. Act normal.

He closed the patient's file and headed down the corridor, pausing outside her surgery room. Her name plate practically had an accusing stare and, swallowing down his guilt, he rapped on the door briefly and then opened it.

His beautiful Lula sat behind her desk, her rainbow hair hanging down over her face as she wrote a note, but she looked up at the sound of her door.

'Oh—hi, Olly.'

She didn't seem angry, or mad—or anything, to be honest. He smiled broadly and launched himself further into his lie from last night. 'Sorry I had to leave so quickly last night...'

'Right...that's okay. Sometimes it happens when you're on call.'

Good. She'd got his note. 'I didn't want you to think I'd just left.'

'I didn't.'

'I...er...had a great time last night and...erm...' He stood awkwardly in the doorway, not knowing the best way to finish his sentence. 'I want you to know that it meant a great deal to me, that...erm...that it wasn't just a—' He didn't want to say *one-night stand*. He didn't want to cheapen their experience by saying the words out loud.

'It's fine, Olly. Really. We both wanted it. We're both adults. But it was what it was. Just sex. Nothing more. It doesn't have to affect our work, does it?'

Just sex? *Just?* That hadn't been *just* sex.

'No. Course not. I just wanted to make sure you're okay, that's all. We work together. I don't want it to be awkward, or for there to be an atmosphere.'

Lula beamed him a smile that could have lit a thousand illuminations. 'Of course. Is there anything else?'

How could she be so *normal*? Other women he'd met and had slept with—not that there'd been a lot—had always wanted more commitment from him. Sex had equalled furthering their relationship. Being *in* a relationship, for one thing. Wanting to make sure that he wanted to see them again. That he would be hanging around. That they would continue to go out and be a 'couple'.

But not Lula. She seemed rather blasé about it and he was thrown.

However, he wasn't going to push it. If she wanted that distance between them then he would give it to her. After all, he was the one who had got up in the middle of the early hours of the morning. He was the one who had made up a lie because he'd felt guilty about what he'd done.

I put the surgery and my patients at risk by sleeping with Lula. What if it had caused problems? Where would we have been then? We'd have had to find another locum.

Olly knew he was lying to himself. This wasn't about the surgery. Or the patients. He felt *guilty*. He'd slept with Lula when she'd been feeling vulnerable and now that she was acting as if the sex didn't matter he was protecting himself by telling himself that *she* was the one acting strangely.

It's all my fault.

She was the most beautiful, strange, exotic creature he'd ever met! Last night had been amazing. The caress of her hands on his skin had been mind-blowing. The way her mouth had moved over his body, the way she'd kissed him... It had been like nothing he'd ever experienced before!

I'd love to feel that way again.

But Lula was indicating that it had been nothing more than perfunctory sex. No attachments. Nothing amazing for her. Otherwise she'd want more, wouldn't she?

Like I do?

Nonsense!

Olly slipped from her room and visibly sagged after he'd closed the door behind him. What did he actually want? Lula begging and pleading to see him again? Lula indicating that last night had meant more to her than she was revealing?

That *he* meant something to her?

The idea plagued him. Did he *want* to mean more to Lula?

He ambled back to his own room and sat down in front of the computer. He had patients to see. They were waiting. Sick people—people who needed his help and expertise. Coughing and moaning and staring at the hands on the clock in the waiting room.

That had always mattered to him. He liked to feel needed and valued. He liked the fact that his patients valued his comments and suggestions and came to him for advice.

But not Lula.

The one person I want to want me, doesn't.

He called his next patient through.

Lula sat back in her chair after Olly left and closed her eyes. A headache was beginning to form, tightly furled, like a fist ready to punch her with its might.

She had paracetamol in her handbag and she popped two capsules and swallowed them down with her cold cup of tea from earlier.

Why did I pretend everything was all right?

She didn't want Olly to think of her as a woman who just slept with a man casually, as if it meant nothing. Because she wasn't like that. Lula Chance did *not* just sleep with men for fun. The last time she'd slept with a man had been years ago. And that had been in a relationship— nothing casual about it at all.

Being with Olly last night *had* meant something. She'd welcomed his arms around her, his lips on hers, the feel of his broad, masculine body above hers, moving within her, bringing her to the release that she'd needed. There'd been a connection. It had meant something.

The last two days with Ruby and the baby had hit her hard. It had brought forward a lot of emotions she'd thought she'd stamped down. For some reason all those feelings she'd fought for so long had become powerful and raw. Maybe it was because she felt so close to finding her own mother. Or perhaps it was just being here in Atlee Wold with Olly and his wonderful father, seeing how close they were as a family. Her emotions were exposed to the elements and the winter freeze had crystallised them and made them difficult to deal with.

And Olly...lovely, lovely Olly. His twinkling eyes

and warm smile and the way he cared had somehow broken through her defences, making her crave things she'd always denied herself.

She'd never meant to get involved with anyone. Why *do* that? Get involved romantically when it could only end badly? Infertility was a big enough burden for her— why force it on to someone else? Why go through all that? Tests and hormones and needles—God, the needles! She'd seen enough of those in her life. Felt the stress, the humiliation of feeling *less* than other women.

Women had babies. It was their primary function, wasn't it? They were the only people who could carry a baby, so that was what they were meant to do.

What did you do with your life if you couldn't even do that?

Her life had already been blighted with cancer, and chemotherapy had made her infertile. She'd decided long ago that she wouldn't burden anyone else with those concerns. What kind of life would that give them? No, Lula did enough worrying for two as it was.

Her life was about adventure and travel and meeting new people—experiencing everything the world had to offer until the day came when she couldn't do it any more.

It was *not* about moving to a small, quaint English village and falling for the local GP!

Have I fallen for Olly?

No. Of course not. That was ridiculous! She hadn't known him very long, and one night of sex didn't create serious feelings.

So why do I feel so upset that he lied about last night?

Lula sat there, feeling the edges of the headache prowling around her. She couldn't even see the pen she was twiddling in her fingers—she was thinking too hard about Olly and how he made her feel.

I can't get attached. I have to keep my distance, I'm not staying here.

Perhaps she needed to plan her next step? Forget Olly, forget how he'd made her feel last night, and especially forget how she'd felt waking up this morning to find him gone. There was no point in dwelling on that. No point in thinking about how much she'd looked forward to coming downstairs and finding him sitting in her kitchen, waiting to kiss her good morning.

I've never had that anyway, so I won't miss it.

Sleeping with Olly had been a mistake, no matter how much she'd enjoyed it or how much she craved more of the same. Not just the sex, but the feeling of closeness. The bonding they'd shared just for a few hours...

Stop it!

She had to think of it as a mistake. If she didn't she'd go insane. She couldn't have Olly. He wanted a different future from the one she could provide.

I am not here for anything else but finding my mother.

That was what her coming to Atlee Wold was all about. Finding her mother at last. Learning the truth about her past and then moving on to experience the next thing. Maybe keeping in contact with her mother if she wished it.

Lula looked at the names on the piece of paper in front of her.

Eleanor Lomax.

Elizabeth Love.

Edward Loutham.

The Louthams had to be ruled out, didn't they?

Bonnie had said that there was only Edward Loutham with an 'E' name in that family, as far as she knew. And even she didn't think that her mother had changed sex and fathered some children!

So he's ruled out.

That left two names. Two women. One of whom she'd met in Olly's surgery.

Eleanor Lomax.

The woman who'd survived breast cancer. The woman with a sister called Brenda in the next village over.

Lula thought back to their meeting. Eleanor had been very elegant. Silver-haired already, so Lula had no idea if her original hair colour had been dark like her own. But their eyes were the same colour. Was that enough to go on? She'd said she took care of herself. Didn't like to lean on anyone else for help. Much like Lula. Was that enough?

Then there was the enigmatic Elizabeth Love. A woman Olly didn't know much about. A woman who apparently ran an animal sanctuary and kept herself to herself.

I know nothing else about her. I don't even know what she looks like. I'm really chasing my own tail here.

It was frustrating. To be so close and yet so far. And the other thing Lula had to consider was that *neither* of those women had anything to do with her! They might just be complete strangers. Random women with the same initials as a woman who'd once written something in a letter. Even those initials could have been fake. Something to throw people off the trail.

What if I'm chasing smoke? What if my mother never even came from here and in reality I'm miles away from finding out the truth?

Lula groaned and put the paper back in her pocket. Then she took it back out again. There really was nothing else for her to go on. If she didn't check out these two leads then she'd never forgive herself.

Lula found the women's addresses on the surgery's system and went online to look at a street map of Atlee Wold. Eleanor Lomax lived just down the road from the surgery on Church Drive. Elizabeth Love lived out on Burner's Road, just down from the farm. She'd need to drive to that one.

Eleanor first, then.

She picked up her phone, pressing nine for an outside line, and dialled Eleanor's number. It was answered quickly.

'Hello?'

'Miss Lomax?'

'Yes?'

'Hello, there. My name's Dr Chance. I'm calling from the local surgery. I sat in with you and Dr James during your consultation the other day.'

'Oh…yes…is something wrong?'

'No—no! I just…erm…well, I wondered whether I might pop round after lunch and see you?'

There was a pause. 'What about?'

Lula felt awkward. 'It's a private matter. I'd prefer to discuss it in person, if that's okay?'

There was a sound of irritation, and then, 'I suppose so. But I'm going out at two o'clock—you'll have to be quick.'

Lula had seen all her morning patients. 'Could I come round now?'

Eleanor agreed and Lula said goodbye and grabbed her coat. Church Drive wasn't far—she'd walk.

She let the practice manager know she was popping

out briefly. 'But I'll be back in about an hour if you want to prepare the home visit list.' It was Lula's turn to do the home visits on her own.

She was just about to escape the surgery when Olly's door opened and he instantly spotted her, dressed in her coat, hat and boots.

'Going somewhere?'

Lula didn't want to discuss the matter in front of the others, so she went over to him and whispered, 'I'm going to see Eleanor Lomax.'

He stared deep into her eyes and she felt guilty for trying to sneak away.

'I'll come with you.'

'You've got patients.'

'I've just finished. Let me grab my coat.'

She waited, feeling awkward and unsure. She'd wanted to do this alone, but he seemed determined to tag along. She couldn't fault him for trying to help her, but she'd really wanted to sneak away. Get some distance between her and Olly so she could make plans to finalise her departure from Atlee Wold.

Out in the snow, she buttoned up her coat, enjoying the bright morning sunshine on her face. As they walked past gardens she could actually see evidence of melting. Icicles dripped and more bushes and greenery could be seen than a few days ago.

'Spring's coming, don't you think?' Olly asked.

'There's definitely a thaw.'

Lula loved the snow, but hated slush, and she hoped that if it were all about to melt it would do so quickly. No point in making everywhere a mess.

They passed a red-breasted robin, perched on a stone wall, and then the church and graveyard, with the old stones sticking up from the ground like teeth.

Soon they were standing outside Eleanor's door, ringing the bell, their noses red from the cold.

Eleanor answered, looking cosy in a mohair jumper, skirt and thick tights, a string of pearls about her neck.

'Oh, I wasn't expecting both of you. Come in.'

She walked them through to her lounge and Lula looked about for clues. Pictures—anything that might indicate that this woman's past was connected to hers. But there was nothing. Eleanor's furniture was expensive, and beautifully chosen, but the only pictures about the place were works by artists: hunting scenes, a landscape, a kingfisher perched above a river.

'So—I'm intrigued. What's this all about? Is it my cancer?'

Lula shook her head. 'Nothing to do with your health. Not now. This is awkward, but I'd like you to bear with me.'

'Go on.' Eleanor sat opposite, her hands clasped neatly on her lap, her back as erect as it had been in the surgery.

'This is about *me*, really, Miss Lomax.'

'Call me Eleanor, dear.'

'Eleanor. I'm just a locum here, as you know, but I'm not only here in Atlee Wold to work. I'm here to… to search for my mother.'

Eleanor was listening, but her face showed nothing. No surprise, no awkwardness, no indication that long ago she'd had a secret child and abandoned her on a beach.

'I believe my mother is in this village. She left a letter, signing it with the initials EL, and I think she was from Atlee Wold. I'm trying to track her down.'

The older woman frowned for a moment, then her

eyebrows were raised. 'You think…? EL…? You think it might be me? Oh, dear! I can assure you it's not.'

Lula felt Olly look at her and could almost physically feel his sympathy radiating from across the room.

She must have visibly sagged in her seat, for Eleanor continued, 'I'm so sorry to disappoint you, Dr Chance, but I'm not the lady you're looking for.'

Lula bit her lip and cast her gaze down to the floor. 'Have you always lived here, Eleanor?'

'I was born in the back room—so, yes, I have.'

'Do you recall anyone getting pregnant and going away? Coming back without a baby?'

Eleanor shook her head and was silent for a moment. 'Many things have happened here in Atlee Wold in my lifetime. I can't be expected to remember everything. Maybe… I don't know…'

'If I asked you about…someone else…would you tell me what you know?'

'It depends on who it is, my dear. I might know nothing, and even if I did would it be my secret to tell? I'm not sure that would be right of me.'

Lula nodded. 'I appreciate that.'

'Who do you want to know about?'

'You might not know her. Apparently she keeps herself to herself. Even Dr James knows nothing about her. Elizabeth Love? On Burner's Road?'

Eleanor took in a deep breath. 'I know Lizzy. We used to go to school together.'

Lula sat up again on the edge of her seat. 'You did?'

'I haven't seen her for years, though. You're right about her hiding away. She prefers to talk to her animals and most people round here call her Dr Dolittle. I've seen her once or twice, picking up groceries in the village shop, but it's just an acknowledgement. We don't stand and talk.'

'Why not?'

Eleanor shrugged. 'I'm not sure. I left the village school aged fourteen to go to secretarial college and she dropped off my radar, to be honest. She was a good friend. A nice girl. Bit too trusting, but she was nice. You think she might be your mother?'

'I don't know. She's the only other EL in the village that I could find on the electoral roll. Unless you know of any others?'

Eleanor glanced at her watch. 'I don't. And I'm afraid I'm going to have to rush you away. I have an appointment.'

Lula nodded and stood up. So now Eleanor Lomax was crossed off the list. All she had left was Elizabeth Love as a possibility, and if that was wrong, too...

Where would she go from there? There was nowhere else *to* go. She could contact the Salvation Army, maybe, or see if Social Services had any records on her, but the chances of finding her mother would be slim.

Outside, Olly laid his hand on hers. 'I'm so sorry.'

She shrugged. 'It's not your fault, is it?'

'No. But I still wish I could make you feel better.'

Oh, he could. By taking her in his arms and kissing her, smothering her with his mouth and his body, pulling at her clothes and taking her madly, as he'd never taken anyone before... But that wasn't going to happen.

Lula looked up at his bright blue eyes. 'I need to find her, Olly.'

A gloved finger stroked her cheek. 'I know.'

She wanted to kiss him then. Wanted it more than she'd ever wanted to do anything in the whole wide world. But she couldn't. She needed to separate from him. Stop relying on him to make her feel better.

I'm a lone spirit. I take care of myself.

Back at the surgery, Lula made herself a fresh cup of tea and sat in the staffroom, mulling over the events of the last few days. She couldn't call Elizabeth. She didn't have a number listed in the surgery records. All she could do was turn up unannounced and hope for the best.

But I've had enough disappointment for today. Maybe I'll do it tomorrow. It might have thawed some more and it'll be easier to park Betsy.

Do I want to go alone?

For some reason Lula felt as if this was her last-ditch attempt at trying to track down her mother, and that she'd like some moral support. That would be okay, wouldn't it? Would Olly go with her? Or maybe his father? All she needed was a friend.

No. She wanted Olly with her. It felt right—especially after the closeness they'd shared.

She took her tea to his room to ask him, but he'd gone. Disappointed, needing to see his smiling face, she decided to pop round to his house and ask him personally if he'd go with her tomorrow. There was no harm in that, was there? It was the sort of favour you'd ask of a friend, and if Olly was anything to her he was most definitely a friend.

Because I can't have him any other way.

CHAPTER SEVEN

IT WAS THE first time she'd been to Olly's home. He lived in a quaint house made of grey stone that sat on the end of a long terrace.

She rang the doorbell and waited, ignoring the cold that was seeping through her boots and into her toes. It wasn't as bad as the other day, when she'd slipped into the icy water, but it was getting there.

The door opened and Olly stood there, a smile on his face. 'Lula! I wasn't expecting you. Something wrong with the home visit rota?'

'No, no…I just wondered if I might ask you a favour?'

He nodded, then stepped back, welcoming her in, and she entered the house, enjoying the rich warmth inside. As she passed the living room she saw a large open fire, already lit, crackling and spitting its way through the logs. Then she followed him into the kitchen.

It was in an old style, full of faded beech, and the walls were painted a soft green. Copper-bottomed pans hung from the ceiling above a central breakfast bar, where he appeared to have been chopping some vegetables.

'I'm sorry if I've interrupted your lunch.'

'These are for this evening's casserole. Would you like to join us?'

It was a nice offer, but she didn't want to intrude on him any more than she already had done. He'd made it clear by leaving her after their passionate encounter, and then lying about his reasons for doing so, that he didn't want to get too involved with her.

'No, no, I wouldn't dream of—'

'It's not a problem. There's plenty, and Dad would love to catch up with you.'

Patrick would like to catch up with her? Not Olly? Another sign...

'Well, thank you.'

'You're happy with lamb?'

She nodded. It was her favourite.

'Drink? Tea? Coffee?'

'No, thanks. I just popped round to ask you a quick question.'

He stopped his chopping to focus on her and she found herself feeling awkward beneath his soft blue gaze. 'You know I'm still looking for my mother?'

Olly nodded.

'I want to speak to Elizabeth Love. She's my only lead left and I'm kind of nervous about that.'

He nodded his head slowly. 'When are you going to speak to her?'

'Tomorrow. And that's what I'm here for. I'd really feel better about going if you were with me. For moral support. But if you don't want to I don't want you to feel forced to do it.'

'Why wouldn't I want to support you?' He sounded genuinely perplexed by her explanation.

She looked away from his steely gaze, shrugging. 'Just...you know...last night... And now I'm asking you to maybe come and find my mother with me... I wouldn't want you to think I was pushing you into getting more involved with my circumstances than you need to be.'

'Lula, I'd *love* to help you. This is a big thing. Last night was...' he looked uncomfortable '...was something we should never have done.'

Lula stood looking at him across the breakfast bar, shocked to hear him actually say it to her. She'd assumed he'd try to skirt the issue. 'Right...no...that's fine. I understand. I mean, me, too... I don't want to get romantically involved with anyone, you know...' Her sentence drifted off into nothing.

He stepped around the bar towards her. 'In fact I'd like to apologise. I should never have slept with you. Not that I didn't want to! I did, and you were amazing. But...you were vulnerable and upset. I should never have taken advantage.'

He was standing very close to her now and she could smell his scent. A masculine scent of musk and something like sandalwood. It was delicious.

'Advantage? No, Olly, you didn't. I wanted it just as much as you did.' She frowned. 'Is that why you pretended you got a call-out?'

His cheeks flushed and he took a step back. 'You know?'

Lula smiled and nodded. 'I found out this morning. I thought you'd had second thoughts, but I wasn't sure why. Not that it matters anyway. We're both consenting adults. We both enjoyed it.'

Just talking about it brought memories of their night rushing back into her head. The heat. The way he'd moved above her. The way he'd touched her, kissed her, his mouth nibbling and licking in all the right places...

Lula flushed with need but, unable to pursue it, looked down at the floor to try and gain some control over her feelings and thoughts. She would have given anything to enjoy those sensations again, but she wouldn't allow herself.

Olly looked as if he was struggling to speak. His mouth opened as if he was about to say something, then closed as his gaze roamed over her, his blue eyes sparkling with hunger for her.

'So...you'll come with me? Tomorrow?' She looked back at him, in control once more.

'Sure.'

'And I'll come for dinner tonight?'

He nodded. 'About seven?'

Lula smiled. Yes. That was fine.

'Dad goes out after dinner on a Thursday night.'

Of course—it was Thursday! She had another belly-dancing class at six! 'I might be a little late. My class runs till seven o'clock, and then I'll have to lock up.'

'It'll keep for when you get here.'

Their gazes locked and they stood there for some time. Neither of them moving forward. Neither of them moving away. Just looking at each other, lost in their own emotions and needs.

Eventually the sound of the kitchen clock ticking away made her return to the here and now. 'I'll get going, then.'

Olly followed her to the front door.

She wasn't sure whether to kiss him goodbye or not, but she couldn't resist. What harm could one goodbye kiss do? She stood on tiptoe, closing her eyes as she planted her lips on his cheek. For a moment she hovered there, her eyes still closed, inhaling the scent of him, debating whether she should kiss him properly—

especially when she felt him brush his lips over the side of her mouth.

How easy it would be to turn her head...so tempting!

Instead, she lowered herself off her tiptoes and stepped back, smiling. 'Well, I'll see you.'

'Right.' He looked disappointed. 'Have you got many house calls to make?'

'Three. I'm on my way now.'

'Want company?'

Yes, she did. Olly's company would be nice right now. But was it fair to ask him to go with her? It was only three house calls, and he'd done his fair share of them for some time whilst the practice had searched for a locum. She wanted to pull her own weight properly, but she didn't want to offend him by saying no.

'That's up to you. I don't mind. I'm happy to do them on my own.'

'I'll grab my coat.' He reached for his jacket and shrugged it over his shoulders, then stuck his feet into some tough-looking hiking boots and tied the laces. 'Ready when you are.'

She went outside to her car and heard his steps falter as they neared the spotted Betsy.

'Ah, I forgot about her.' He grinned ruefully.

Lula smiled at his amusement. 'How could you ever forget Betsy? There aren't that many cars painted like a ladybird, you know.' She slid in the driver's side and leant over to pop his door open. When he got in she had to fight the urge to lean over and kiss him. It was what she wanted to do. Wanted very much indeed. But she knew it wouldn't be right and she started the engine, determined not to think about the way he kissed. Or touched. Or made her feel.

How could he have disrupted her state of mind so

much? He was just an ordinary man, like any other. Wasn't he? And though it might be fun and sexy and irresistible with him right now, as time went by the situation most certainly would change. There would have to be commitment and, Olly being Olly, he would undoubtedly start to want children. He was traditional that way. And she couldn't give him that. Nor did she want to go through the pain of splitting up with him. She'd been there, done that, and it had been hard and disruptive.

Best to keep things light and fun. They could have fun, right? Without it becoming too serious?

'So, who's first?'

She passed him the list. 'Karen Harper. What do you know about her?'

'Karen? She's a lovely old lady. She was at your dance class the other week.'

'Which one was she?'

'A few rows back from the front? Black leotard with pink leggings?' He smiled at the memory.

Lula nodded. She remembered her. She'd been the only lady there in a leotard—all the others had turned up in tee shirts or tracksuits. And the bright pink leggings had revealed a very good pair of shapely legs for an elderly lady. Lula had liked her. She'd really embraced the class and laughed and had fun.

'Apparently she's taken a fall in the snow and thinks she's sprained her ankle. She doesn't want to go to hospital to have it checked and couldn't make it in to the surgery for us to check it. Shame. Probably means she won't be at my class tonight.'

'You know she once made a play for my father?'

Lula glanced at him as she drove through the slush. 'Really?'

'He let her down very gently. There's never been anyone else for him apart from my mother.'

'He loved your mum very much?'

'She was an amazing woman.'

'I thought you didn't remember her?'

'I don't, but my father has told me so much about her I feel as if I do.'

Lula nodded in understanding. 'No wonder you have a list of attributes for your ideal woman. You're looking for what your father had.'

She felt him looking at her and burned beneath his gaze. 'That's deep. I didn't know you had psychology training as well as training in general practice.'

Lula laughed gently. 'I took a side class.'

He was quiet for a moment, then spoke again, his voice low. 'Perhaps you're right. When my dad speaks of her he gets this faraway look in his eyes and he goes all wistful. And he talks of her so...lovingly. Like she was perfect, you know? I'm sure they must have had their moments when they couldn't even look at each other, but the way he tells it...she was everything.'

Lula said nothing. Neither of them had had a mother. It was something they shared in common, even if for different reasons. She knew how much it had hurt *her* not to have a mother. Or a father, for that matter. She'd felt lost and rootless and unwanted as a little girl—had often felt that she had no value whatsoever. And at senior school she'd been picked on because of it. Kids had called her 'Annie' after the most famous orphan of Broadway. Lula had hated it and had been angry at a mother she didn't have for putting her through it.

How had it been for Olly? He had a mother he couldn't remember. One who had died unexpectedly in a tragic accident before her time. He couldn't get his mother back, but she might find hers. There was still an opportunity for her to build bridges. Or at least she hoped so. What would it be like to lose her forever?

As she pulled up in front of Karen's house she got out of the car and looked at him across the roof of Betsy. 'There's someone out there. For you. Someone who's perfect.'

He frowned. 'So it's not you, then?'

Lula stopped in her tracks.

No! I can't let it be me!

'I'm not the marrying kind, and you're after someone who wants to take a short walk down a church aisle and into a maternity unit.'

She turned away before he could answer her. But he caught up with her before she was halfway up the pathway.

'Who's to say that's what I want?'

She looked at his hand gripping her arm. 'Of *course* it's what you want. You've been telling yourself that for years.'

He let go. 'It's different now.'

'Why?'

'Because I met you.'

The intensity in his eyes frightened her. She pushed past him and rang the doorbell, her heart thundering away in her chest and her stomach rolling and dipping like a ship on a stormy sea.

They headed into Karen's house. She was surprised to see two doctors turn up for her sprained ankle. They strapped her ankle and advised her to rest, then spent their next two visits keeping their conversation light and noncommittal.

It was getting awkward. Already.

Lula grimaced her way through the afternoon,

determined more than ever that she was right to keep her distance from Olly.

The casserole was simmering nicely, and rich, meaty smells filled the James household. Patrick had opened a bottle of red and prepared a selection of soft drinks for Lula, who was on call that evening.

She arrived about fifteen minutes late and drifted into Olly's kitchen wearing her belly-dancing paraphernalia. Once again he was treated to the sight of her trim waist, with her belly button jewel twinkling in the firelight. Her bangles clinked and jingled, giving off a musical noise every time she moved, and she wore the most amazing skirt, that appeared to be made of some sort of wafting fabric that floated about her body as she walked.

He tried not to stare, but it was difficult.

'You're going to be on call wearing *that*?'

He could just imagine the reactions of some of the elderly male patients when she turned up wearing a skirt with a huge split up the side. He remembered what it had felt like to slide his fingers up the length of her legs and had to swallow hard and pretend he was checking the roast potatoes in the oven.

Since last night he'd not been able to think straight. She was in his head no matter which way he turned. She was at work, she was in his home, but always just out of reach. And he was sensing she really wanted to keep him there. Out of reach. And here she was again, looking all petite and beautiful and alluring, and all he could think of was sweeping her up into his arms and whisking her away up the stairs. Leaving his dad to eat the casserole alone whilst he and Lula enjoyed each other once more.

And it wasn't just the sex, he kept telling himself. It was Lula herself. She had no idea how amazing she was—the type of person she was. Her quirky traits, her unique look. They were all things he would never have normally been attracted to, but with Lula it was different. He *was* attracted to her—there was no denying that. There were strong feelings—he couldn't help those, either—but she was keeping him at a distance and he wasn't sure why.

There were the obvious reasons, of course. They were work colleagues. They were in a small village where gossip ran rife, and neither of them needed to be the main topic on the Atlee Wold grapevine.

But he sensed there was something more and he couldn't quite grasp it.

Was she being the sensible one? Last night had been amazing, and even though he felt guilty about taking advantage it hadn't stopped him craving her touch once again. They'd shared a lingering kiss, but she'd been quick to say they were both adults, that she wasn't his type, that she would never marry, and that he was after some sort of traditional wife.

Why did she always bring it back to that? As if a woman being a wife and mother were the only things that mattered to him?

Because it wasn't just that. Maybe he'd once thought so, but Rachel had changed all that. Having an abortion without telling him she'd even been pregnant, and then walking out on him without giving him a chance to say goodbye or even discuss why they were breaking up.

It had caused him to rethink life. And, yes, he'd been playing it safe—because by doing that he'd thought he could control the outcome. If he went out with someone who was a safe option then he wouldn't get hurt.

That was the basics of it.

He didn't want the pain he'd experienced before. He didn't want the agony of that.

And Lula wasn't a safe option. She was her own person—bright, funny, a risk-taker, a challenger of the norms, someone who'd made no promises to stay.

But Lula also had a way of changing the world. Even his dad had said so.

She looked down at herself, removing the coin-edged skirt that had been moulding the soft curve of her bottom, letting loose the floaty fabric that caressed the length of her legs.

'No—sorry. Can I pop upstairs to get changed? I didn't get time at the hall.'

'Of course.'

Patrick led her upstairs to show her where to get changed and Olly watched them go, jealous of how his dad's hand rested so easily—unthinkingly—in the small of Lula's back.

Jealous? He blinked the feeling away and concentrated on preparing the gravy for the meal. Why was he jealous? That was his *father*, for crying out loud! Lula hadn't committed to Olly, had she? It was her quintessential spirit of being free and life-affirming that intrigued him. She had no roots. Well, not yet. She might find some tomorrow, if Elizabeth Love was the woman she was looking for.

And what then? Surely if Elizabeth *was* Lula's mother then Lula would stay in Atlee Wold? And if she stayed there'd be a chance for him to be with her?

But what if Elizabeth *wasn't* her mother? Would Lula stay?

He endeavoured to ask her at some point. Maybe when his father left later and they were alone together.

Lula came downstairs wearing gorgeous tight black jeans and an off-the-shoulder red top. He tried not to look at the delicate dip where her neck met her chest, or at the long, slow curve of her collarbone. She'd enjoyed him kissing her there...

He blinked and offered her a drink. She took an orange juice and sat at the table as he served up.

'So, were there many at your class this evening?' he asked.

She nodded. 'Yes, I'm pleased to say. Three more people than last time.'

'That's good,' Patrick interjected. 'You've really aroused the spirit of the older generation in this village, Lula. You're just what *some* people needed.' He glanced at his son across the table. 'A breath of fresh air.'

She smiled and thanked him for his compliment.

'It's true, my dear! Even my Oliver has perked up since your arrival. For a long time I thought the poor lad was going to end up just like me.'

Olly looked at his father. 'What's wrong with being like you?'

'Nothing—if having a limited world is what you want. If Atlee Wold is to be the centre of your universe. There's such a big world out there, son, and I've always wanted you to experience it.'

It was the first time he'd heard his father speak like this.

'I know you felt a great sense of pressure about coming into the practice. Because of me and your grandad before you. If you wanted to do that, that's fine. But I'd really like to think there's more out there for you.'

'Dad, I—'

'It's okay, son. You'll never disappoint me.'

Olly looked stuck for something to say. His father's comments had come out of the blue.

Patrick smiled, a twinkle in his eyes. 'Can't a father look out for his son? Well, *I* can. Especially when I can see what's good for you.' He turned to Lula. 'Although I, for one, hope that *you* consider staying on in Atlee Wold, Lula.'

Lula didn't appear to be blushing, but she did seem pleased at his father's words.

'I haven't made any definite plans yet, Patrick.'

Olly pulled the casserole pot from the oven and set it in the centre of the table, removing the lid, allowing a plume of steam to swirl up to the ceiling and mouth-watering aromas to set them all salivating.

They set to the meal readily, all of them hungry, and pretty soon there were three empty plates and three full bellies. Patrick went into the living room whilst Olly and Lula cleared away the dishes. She scraped and rinsed the plates, and he set them in the dishwasher.

'Thanks, but you're meant to be my guest—not helping me do domestic duties.'

'Oh, I'm not afraid to get my hands dirty.'

He agreed. She'd certainly not shirked any work since she'd been here. 'How are you feeling about tomorrow? Nervous?'

Lula nodded. 'A bit. Everything could change, couldn't it?'

'And if she *is* your mother? What then?'

Lula stood still, her hands dripping water, before drying them on a towel. 'I don't allow myself to think that far ahead.'

'But you must have imagined it? Finding her?'

'Yes, but I find if I try and imagine a conversation

it never goes the way I heard it in my mind and I don't want to be disappointed.'

No. He hated to think of her being upset. Devastated and crying. Just the idea of it set his stomach churning and had him fighting the urge to hold her. He wanted to wrap his arms around her and hold her close. Protect her from anything that could do her harm—emotionally or physically.

'What time shall we go over there?'

'Well, your dad has the morning surgery, so I thought about ten? We should be back for the afternoon surgery, then, with plenty of time.'

'I hope you get what you want, Lula. I hope you find her.'

Lula looked at him steadily. He could see that her eyes were glazed, almost as if she might be about to cry. How easy it would be to take a step past the open dishwasher and hold her!

'Thank you, Olly.'

They finished off in the kitchen and went into the living room to have coffee with Patrick. Then Patrick said goodnight to them both and went off to meet up with his friends down at the local pub.

When he was gone Lula sat next to Olly on the couch, staring into the open fire. There was something hypnotic about the flames. Something soothing. And somehow, without realising how it came to happen, he realised that he had his arm about her shoulders and she was leaning into his chest.

She was a comforting weight against him and he looked down at her, staring at her amazing hair and at how all the colours blended so beautifully into one another, and how the firelight flickered and played off them. He could inhale the scent of her shampoo...

I could take her face in my hand and turn her to kiss me...

She turned and looked at him, startling him with the intensity in her eyes. It was almost magical, as if she'd heard his thoughts and granted his wishes. They said no words. They didn't have to. He could read everything he needed to in her beautiful large brown eyes. Pools of molten chocolate he would happily swim in...

He couldn't help himself... His gaze dropped to her lips. Her beautiful lips. Full and sensuously curved. Bubblegum pink and innately kissable...

He lowered his face to hers and saw her eyes close as she welcomed his mouth on hers. Their kiss was of exquisite beauty. Her lips melted against his and he felt her fingers in his hair. He heard her soft sigh as she turned to press herself against him.

Heat fired instantly in his groin and he fought its desire for instant gratification. He told himself that this time he would take it slowly and enjoy each delicious moment they were together. He'd sensed her trying to put distance between them. Sensed her stepping away. Well, if this was the last time he'd get to be with her then he was going to treasure every moment...

His arms held her tightly against him and her breathing became heavy. Their kisses deepened and he found himself stroking her skin, allowing his hands to roam her body. Their clothes were in the way. He wanted to touch her skin.

He wanted *her*. Not just in a physical sense. It was more than just sex. It was almost about consuming her. Touching, tasting, feeling everything that she was. Absorbing her into his very being.

Lula leaned back and pulled off her top, then began to tackle his shirt buttons. His mouth dropped to the gentle swell of her breasts, to the pert, taut nipples peaking beneath the lace of her bra.

How easy it would be just to rip it away...

Olly restrained himself, however. His fingers found the clip at the back and released it. The bra hit the floor and his hands cupped her, brought her to his mouth. His tongue teased and licked and his teeth nibbled gently, causing pain and pleasure at the same time, and her groans were like music to his ears. He filled his mouth with her.

She pulled off his shirt and began tackling his trousers. He tried to undo her jeans, but they were so tight they both stopped to laugh as she helped him undo them, and then they, too, were off and discarded upon the floor.

Olly gazed at the beautiful length of her. At her sex obscured by a small piece of flimsy red lace. She was amazing. Gorgeous. If he had an artistic bone in his body he would want to draw her, paint her as she lay in repose. Each brushstroke an imagined caress. That way he could look at her like that for as long as he wanted.

But she held out her arms, drawing him to her, and he fell upon her like a rabid wolf, his mouth consuming her, ravishing her, tasting her flesh and her scent as he peeled away the wisp of lacy underwear.

And there she lay. His beautiful Lula. Naked in his living room before the open fire. His mouth met hers once again. Her groaning almost sent him over the edge. He wanted her so badly.

He felt her flesh slip and slide beneath his touch, her nipples hardening as she ground herself against him, and then she gasped, arching her back, clutching herself against him, and he just knew in his heart that he wanted to experience that with her again and again and again.

She'd got beneath his skin…there was no denying it.

She was his beautiful, amazing Lula Chance, and if he got to be with her every day and know that she was his every night then he would be a very happy man.

Was it love? He didn't know. Maybe. It had happened quickly, if it was. He'd only ever committed himself like that to someone once before, and that had been a long time ago. So he wasn't sure, but he thought that maybe it did feel that way.

The last time he'd fallen in love it had been a disaster. He'd convinced himself that Rachel was the woman for him—perfect in every way, the perfect partner for a country village GP—but she hadn't been. He'd imposed his own expectations on to her and thought she would be what he wanted her to be. But she'd had other ideas. She'd been a free spirit, very much a city girl who didn't want to be tied down, the way he'd expected.

And wasn't Lula the same? A free spirit who might leave him?

Dismissing the doubt, he slid into her all the way, feeling her heat along the length of him, the taste of her still on his tongue, her soft skin beneath his fingers. He moved gently. Slowly at first, then quicker and harder, until the breath was escaping from him in bursts. He came in a shattering gasp, collapsing on top of her, his breath at her neck—her delicious neck, with that gentle dip and the collarbone that had intrigued him so much earlier.

It had been every bit as amazing as before. If not better.

I can't let her go.

But he still wasn't sure if she was his to keep.

They lay in each other's arms, content. Neither saying what they truly needed to say. Both knowing that this might be the last time they were together.

Elizabeth Love's house sat centrally in a square plot, surrounded by sheds and aviaries and outdoor hutches, all filled with animals of various kinds. Loose chickens and ducks roamed the gardens.

The gate to the garden path hung limply and rusting, off to one side. As the snow had now melted somewhat the ground beneath was starting to be seen—thick mud, almost black, but by the front door a cornucopia of clay pots held flowering snowdrops and crocus.

Lula smiled at Olly nervously and then took a step forward and rapped on the door. Some old flaking paint fell off at her touch, revealing the ancient, grey wood beneath, whilst the free-ranging chickens scratched at her feet.

The sun was shining and there was warmth in its gaze. Finally, it seemed, the snow would soon be gone.

Lula waited, Olly standing a little behind her. There'd been no awkwardness since last night. After she and Olly had made love they'd cuddled before the fire for a while, until she'd realised she needed to go home before Patrick came back and found them naked in his lounge! She'd dressed quickly and kissed him goodbye.

It had been fun to share that time with him, but that was all it could be. At least that was what she kept telling herself. It had been hard to leave his warm, strong arms. Difficult to walk away from him. They'd grown so close over the last few days together.

But that was all it was. Two adults who were good friends and occasionally had sex. That was all. No strings, no demands from either side. Friends with benefits. If it ended tomorrow and they just stayed as friends after that there'd be no recriminations from either side. She hoped he felt the same way. She'd indicated nothing else, even if she hadn't said it out loud. And he knew she never stayed anywhere for longer than a few months. That she always moved on. That she always sought something new. He had to know that was how it was going to end.

She was pulled from her thoughts when the door was opened by a small woman. She had dark hair, slightly tinted with grey at the front, and large brown eyes. She wore a comfortable, hard-wearing flannel shirt with jeans, boots and no make-up.

Lula smiled a greeting, then faltered as the sunlight caught on the silver necklace that hung at the woman's throat. It was the same as the necklace that Lula wore. The one she'd been left with by her mother.

The woman blinked at the bright sun, looking at them both enquiringly. 'Yes?'

Lula's voice caught in her throat. 'Miss Love?'

'Yes?'

'I'm Dr Chance, and this is Dr James from the local surgery. May we come in for a moment and talk to you?'

'What about? I'm busy.' Elizabeth's harsh response was clipped and fast.

Lula looked at the hard lines on this woman's face and saw a lifetime of heartache. 'It's a private matter.'

'I'm sure I have nothing worth discussing…'

The woman went to shut the door and Lula just stood there, but Olly stepped forward, jutting his boot into the doorway, his broad, square hand pressed against the door.

'It's about your daughter, Miss Love.'

The woman flinched visibly, staring at them both, then her eyes flicked to Lula, assessing her. Her gaze softened.

Lula stood there, letting her look, wondering what she was thinking. Wondering whether she'd guessed yet who she was. Whether she saw the similarities. Elizabeth Love had the same eyes as her.

'You'd better come in.' She stepped away and disappeared down a dark hall that was overflowing with piles of stuff.

Lula had seen television programmes about hoarders before, and though this house wasn't as bad as some of them she could tell that this woman didn't like to let things go. It was cluttered, and it wasn't very clean, but there was organisation here—and a love for animals that was clear for anyone to see.

Elizabeth indicated for them to sit down on the cat-covered sofa opposite, then sat herself, fidgeting and twisting the tails of her shirt in her fingertips. 'Well?'

Lula swallowed hard. She'd found her. This *had* to be her mother! 'We're here to talk about a baby girl who was left abandoned on a beach many years ago.'

'I see.' She didn't meet their eyes, but kept her gaze cast down upon the floor.

'I was that baby, and I've been looking for my mother. I have reason to believe that…that you are her.'

Elizabeth glanced at her then, her cheeks flushed, her eyes glazed with tears. 'You're Louise?'

Lula nodded, a lump in her own throat.

'My baby?'

She couldn't help it. Tears began. 'I am.'

'Oh…!'

Elizabeth stood up and pulled Lula into her arms, squeezing her tight against her, but then, sensing that Lula felt uncomfortable, she let her go. She stared at her instead, taking her in. Every tiny inch. Then she turned and began to pace the room, sniffing and clearing her throat, then stopping to look at her and pace some more, before she sat down again, suddenly stilled.

'I've thought of you *every day*.'

'What happened?' Lula looked at her through tear-glazed eyes. 'What made you leave me on the beach?'

Elizabeth got up once again, but this time settled down on the couch next to Lula. Tentatively she reached out and took Lula's hand in her own, gulping as she did so.

'So many things…so many hurtful things… I've hoped for this day for so long!'

Lula squeezed her fingers back and glanced at Olly, who was smiling at the pair of them. He indicated that he would step outside and leave them alone.

She appreciated his gesture. She and Elizabeth had a lot to talk about.

As Olly stood in the cluttered kitchen, trying to hunt down some clean mugs to use for some tea, he couldn't help but stand for a moment and imagine how Lula must currently be feeling.

She had to be overjoyed. Didn't she? As well as sad that she'd found her mother but had lost so much time with her? That circumstances had split them apart?

Would circumstances split Lula and himself? She'd made no commitment to stay.

Despite his strong feelings for her, he couldn't help but compare her to Rachel. Not physically. They were nothing alike. Rachel had been the conservative-looking woman of his 'list', and he'd imposed his own expectations on her. She'd turned out to be nothing like the woman he'd expected her to be.

Lula was nothing like the woman on his list. She had some of those qualities he craved, but she was right. He wanted marriage in his future, and children at some point. Lula couldn't give him that. Nor would she commit to him. She'd said so.

But commitment was what he wanted. Love was what he needed. There didn't have to be children. Not right away. And there were things they could do these days…it might still be possible…

Olly sighed. Was he trying to persuade himself or Lula?

He slammed the kettle down and leaned against the kitchen counter, his head hanging low.

Why couldn't she be perfect?

Lula could be perfect. She'd come into his world and completely turned it upside down and he loved it! Loved *her*.

He looked up and through the dirty kitchen window, out into the garden beyond. There were large runs out there and he could see foxes inside. Wild animals within cages and runs. They shouldn't be there. They shouldn't be caged. They needed to be free.

Like Lula.

She was the biggest free spirit he'd ever met. He couldn't snare her with his demands for love and marriage and children. She couldn't give him any of that, and look what had happened when he'd tried it with Rachel.

It had all gone pear-shaped and Rachel had left him—hating him, never wanting to see him again.

He couldn't bear the idea of that happening to him and Lula. Just thinking about it almost ripped him in two.

The milk in the fridge smelt a bit dodgy, and he had

no idea if the old bag of sugar was in date. Elizabeth Love needed to look after herself a bit better. The animals she cared for lived in better conditions than she did.

But perhaps she'd left herself in limbo after she'd had to give Lula away?

He could only imagine how it might feel to give her up...

It turned out that Lula's mother had fallen in love with an older boy whom she'd idolised. This boy, however, sensing her naivety, had slept with her and then discarded her when he'd got what he wanted. He'd then made sure everyone knew how *easy* Elizabeth had been. A few months later she'd discovered she was pregnant—just as she'd started college.

Unable to tell her parents, she'd hidden the pregnancy and given birth alone, then taken a bus to the seaside. Seeing a family that looked kind and caring, she'd left Lula in their beach hut and got back on the bus with a broken heart.

Hurt and betrayed, she had retreated into her own shell. Learning that it was easier to deal with animals rather than people, she had taken a course in veterinary nursing and, as soon as she'd been able to afford it, had moved out of her parents' home and started the animal rescue centre.

For all her adult life she'd looked after recovering birds, or hedgehogs, or kittens, or whatever was brought to her door, dumped and abandoned, shunning people. She'd lived this way, adopting and caring for strays and injured wildlife. And every day she'd thought of the baby she'd left behind at a beach and hoped that one day she'd find her.

'Did she look for you?' Olly asked in the car on their drive back home.

'She said she tried, but the bureaucracy and red tape were suffocating and trying to track me down through the foster system was hard. Once I'd been adopted by the Chances she lost all trace.'

Olly laid his hand on hers as she drove. 'I'm glad you've found each other.'

She nodded quickly. 'Me, too.'

The snow was turning quickly to slush, and as she drove through the lanes they could hear it splashing to the side of the road into bramble-covered ditches, revealing bright blades of grass that had been covered for too long. The sunlight glinted off the wet road and they had to shield their eyes.

When she pulled up outside Moonrose Cottage Lula did so with a big sigh.

'So what happens now?' he asked.

'How do you mean?'

'Well, you've found your mum. You've got roots now. History. A family tree. The search is over.'

'Well, just because we've found each other it doesn't mean we're suddenly going to live in each other's pockets. We'll take it slowly. Life will continue.'

He took a deep breath. 'Does this change your plans about staying in Atlee Wold? You don't *have* to be a locum, you know—you could be a permanent member of staff.' He smiled, his eyes full of hope.

She didn't want to be blunt. Nor did she want to hurt him. So she sidestepped the question. 'We'll see.'

They both got out of the car and he wandered onto the path. 'I'm going to walk back. Get some exercise. I'll see you this afternoon?'

She nodded. 'Sure.'

He leaned in to kiss her then, but she closed her eyes resolutely. 'See you later.'

'Alligator...'

She smiled and watched him walk away. Then the smile slowly disappeared from her face until she was frowning.

It had been a morning of ups and downs. She was thrilled to have finally found her mother, but had Olly read more into their relationship? *Had* he?

Perhaps I need to be more clear with him about where this is going?

Inside the cottage, she flipped open her computer and began to look for locum posts. Away from Atlee Wold. Away from Olly. Before he got too attached.

CHAPTER EIGHT

FOR A FEW WEEKS they were busy at the surgery. The winter weather had set off a string of appointments and everyone, it seemed, had a chest infection.

Lula had begun working on her own and she enjoyed the freedom it gave her to get to know the patients herself, without Olly there. But they went out on house calls together, so that Lula could learn her way around and get to know some of those who couldn't make it into the surgery, either due to ill health or the fact that they had no transport and lived on the outskirts of the village.

Patrick and Olly invited her over for a meal occasionally, and they had a few enjoyable evenings together. One night Patrick had fallen asleep in his chair and she and Olly had spent a lovely hour talking quietly in front of the fire, playing cards and, yes, she had to admit it: they'd held hands and kissed.

The next morning she had reprimanded herself.

I shouldn't be encouraging him!

But it was hard. Olly was just so…*so right for her!* And that was hard to resist when you were a young single woman, despite what she kept telling herself.

Would it matter if I let this develop?

Yes, she told herself, *it would*. It was known in the village that Olly was in the market for a possible future wife. He'd look at all relationships for their long-term value.

That wasn't what Lula was there for. Whatever they had between them, it had to be short-term fun only—no strings, no obligations.

Which would hurt him. And she didn't want to do that.

Lula liked him much too much to want to hurt him.

She'd tried keeping her distance from Olly, but it was difficult. He'd become such a close friend to her, and it was hard to resist his charming smile and his loving arms. There were a few more nights that she spent in his bed, and each time she found herself craving more and more of him. She hated herself every time she tore away from his embrace to go back to Moonrose.

Olly made their relationship seem so easy. But on her own she was troubled by how involved she was becoming, knowing she would have to break his heart.

The one thing I said I wouldn't do!

Why did she keep returning to his bed? To his arms? Every time she did it she'd go back to Moonrose berating herself, telling herself that it was absolutely the last time she would do it!

But it never stayed that way. She couldn't keep her distance from him—it was too hard.

Each time she attempted to create distance Olly just closed the gap more and more. And as the date came nearer for his father's retirement from the practice she found herself locked away with Olly, planning Patrick's surprise retirement party. Planning that quickly turned into hand-holding, then kissing, and then, before she knew what was happening, passionate lovemaking.

She was like a little bumble bee, and Olly was her pollen. The golden dust that she needed to survive.

Each time she went home she took a little piece of him in her heart. Each time she sat alone in her cottage, rats on her shoulder and Anubis in the palm of her hand, she would tell herself not to do it any more. Not to care for Olly as deeply as she did.

Not to...love him?

Did she love him? She hoped not. She'd not come to Atlee Wold to fall in love. She'd not come to have her heart broken, or to break someone else's.

The tarantula breakthrough had happened after she'd met her mother. She'd gone home, drunk a large glass of wine and then braved it. Putting her whole hand into the tank. Lula had been scared, but the terror had gone. She'd gained strength from her meeting with Elizabeth. As Anubis had tentatively stepped onto the palm of her hand with his long, hairy, surprisingly solid legs, she'd almost stopped breathing. But then she'd taken a deep breath, acknowledged the heavy spider on her palm and then begun breathing again.

Olly had been so proud of her when she'd told him. After all, it had been one of her greatest fears and challenges to herself and she'd overcome it.

All she had to do now was tell Olly that she would be leaving in a month's time and then create another challenge for herself. Something to do with heights? They'd always scared her, hadn't they? And if dependable Olly could do it, with his parachute jump...

She'd found another locum post. In Portsmouth—the place of her abandonment. It had seemed the perfect place to go to. To come full circle and visit the beach she'd been found on. The post would start one week after she'd left Atlee Wold. That should give her enough time to return Anubis to his rightful owner, unpack her belongings and choose some new challenges for herself.

The new post was on the coast, close to where she'd originally been left as a baby, and she wondered about all the things she hadn't tried—windsurfing, kitesurfing, jet-skiing, scuba-diving. A whole host of challenges she could set herself. Maybe a bungee jump for charity?

The post wouldn't be too far away from her mother. She could still visit her—maybe once a month. Although at the moment she was visiting Elizabeth a couple of times a week.

They'd shared quite a bit, and Elizabeth had shown Lula all the newspaper cuttings about her case that she kept in an old scrapbook, faded with time.

Getting to know her mother had been something Lula had imagined often, but the real thing far surpassed her dreams. They were similar in many ways—in their character, and in the way they thought about life and politics, and in the television programmes they both watched. Their shared love for animals was amazing. As Elizabeth taught Lula about the ways of foxes, and how to keep a baby bird alive, Lula told her mother about Nefertiti and Cleo and the exotic Anubis.

Elizabeth had gained something from their reunion, too. Each time Lula returned another part of her house had been cleared out and cleaned. It was as though Elizabeth was finally reclaiming her life from the dirt and the dust and the random objects that held a connection to the past.

Elizabeth had been upset to hear about her daughter's fight against leukaemia, and had been in tears as Lula told her about her years of struggle. She'd learnt about other members of her family who were still alive. Elizabeth's parents were both dead, but Elizabeth had two brothers. They were all going to meet up at some point, and she'd spoken to them on the phone about Lula. One had even cried, and she'd been touched by the way she was being received by everyone.

Being received by her family would be easier than saying goodbye.

She'd already told Elizabeth—just not Olly. Or his father. And they'd want to know. They'd need to know that they had to find another doctor to take her place.

I have to tell him now.

Lula rapped on his door. The spring sunshine was shining brightly. All the snow had gone and daffodils were blooming, showing their golden trumpets throughout the village.

When Olly opened the door he caught her biting her lip. 'Why are you knocking? I told you before—come straight in.'

He stepped back so she could follow him inside. They went into the kitchen, where his father sat reading a newspaper at the table.

Patrick peered at her over his glasses. 'Lula! How lovely to see you. How is our favourite locum? Thinking of becoming a permanent partner, I hope?'

He beamed a smile at her and Lula wished the floor would swallow her up whole. It wasn't just going to be Olly who would be upset at her plans.

'Actually, that's why I'm here. I've come to a decision.'

'Brilliant,' Olly said, sitting down at the table and pulling out a chair for her to sit down, too. 'Dad and I have been discussing it for some time—about how well you fit in and how everyone loves you.'

I do hope you *don't love me, Olly.*

Though she knew the truth in her heart. It was obvious he had strong feelings for her—even though he knew she couldn't give him what he wanted. It was in

the way he was with her...the way she caught him looking at her when he thought she wouldn't notice. The way
he acted...the way he thought of her. The way he held
her in his arms. The way he made love to her.

All the things she'd tried to avoid.

'Thank you. I have loved it here, but... The time has
come for me to move on. To take up a new post.' She
hurried on, seeing the smiles drop from their faces.
'I've found a new post—a locum post like this one—
down in Portsmouth. I think it could be perfect for me.'

Olly stared at her, his eyes darkening with disappointment and anger. 'You're...leaving?'

She licked her lips. 'I'm sorry. Maybe I should have
told you earlier. But there's been so much stuff going
on with Elizabeth and myself that I let it slide. I apologise for that.'

'But...your *mother*'s here—and the *practice* is
here—and patients that adore you.'

'And I'll miss them, Olly, but it was never my intention to stay. Even if I did find my mother.'

'But—'

His father interrupted him, laying a firm hand on his
son's arm. 'It's Lula's choice, son. We can't force her.'
He turned to Lula. 'I can't say I'm not disappointed. I really think you're an amazing person, and I for one would
have loved it if you'd stayed permanently. Part of me
was hoping that you and Olly would run the practice as
partners.' He coloured. 'In more ways than one, if you
catch my meaning. I know you two have grown close.'

Tears began to sting her eyes. She liked Patrick a
lot. It hurt to know she was disappointing him, but she
had to stick to her plan and leave. If she stayed she and
Olly would no doubt become even closer and their relationship would deepen. Then he would want to have

children. She knew he would. He'd told her he wanted kids. He was traditional that way.

But she couldn't give him that. She was infertile. She would never be able to have children and that would tear them apart. She'd seen it happen to so many couples. She wasn't going to put herself through it. Nor him. She loved him too much for that.

'I'm so sorry, Patrick. I know it's not what you wanted to hear.' She stood up and went to leave, but Olly grabbed her wrist.

'Wait!'

She turned, determined not to let the tears fall. 'Yes, Olly?'

'I can't lose you.'

A brave smile made her face even sadder. 'Yes, you can. And it's best we do it now. Before it hurts us all too much.'

She pulled her hand free and hurried from his house, slamming the door shut behind her. She burst into tears as she ran down the pathway and into Betsy.

After all her efforts not to get hurt, here she was, crying over leaving him. Leaving Atlee Wold. Leaving Patrick. Leaving her beloved patients whom she'd got to know. Leaving her mother—though they'd still visit each other. Portsmouth wasn't that far away...

She stuck her key into the ignition, cleared her eyes and drove away.

Olly stared in disbelief at the closed door. Lula was leaving? But...she *couldn't*! She was...perfect. She was... They'd been getting so close he'd assumed she'd stay—especially now that she knew her mother was here!

He took a step forward, as if to go after her, but something stopped him. He turned, sadness making his heart feel heavy, and looked at his father. 'I can't believe she won't stay.'

'No, but we always knew this was a possibility.'

'I can't lose her, Dad.'

'You have to let her go. You can't force her to stay. Look at what happened with Rachel.'

'Rachel was different! Rachel was wrong for me! Right from the start. I was trying to force a square peg into a round hole. She was a city girl—a medical rep. A party girl. I knew she wasn't right for me, but I tried to make her fit in with my life. To force her to enjoy quiet village life. I might as well have asked her to arrange the church flowers as something to do!'

'And Lula? *She's* not your run-of-the-mill girl.'

'No, she isn't. She's amazing. Sweet and loving and... We fit, Dad. We *fit*!'

'But you have the same problem, son. You can't force her to stay.'

'It wouldn't be force. She loves it here—I know she does. She loves the people, the practice, the ladies in her dance class. She loves the serenity here.'

'Does she love *you*?'

Olly looked at his father. He thought she did.

He hoped she did.

Because it was the only way he could make her stay.

Mrs Broadstairs had just left Lula's room and she was about to call in her last patient when Olly came in, closing the door firmly behind him. She could see he had something to say as he paced about before her desk.

It was her last day at the surgery. One patient to go. The atmosphere between herself and Olly had been functional, not frosty, since her announcement. He'd made no effort to go out of his way to see her and she had done the same with him. It was easier that way—the less they saw of each other the better.

But now he was here, standing tall and defiantly masculine in her room, opposite her desk. His sheer presence made her realise how much she'd missed him. Missed his touch. His arms around her. His lips upon her skin. His gentle kisses all over her body...

'Yes?' She hoped her voice sounded solid and unaffected.

His jaw was clenching and unclenching; his hands were upon his hips. 'I had to come and see you.'

She didn't say anything.

'I can't say I agree with your choice, but I don't want you to think I don't care. I...er...I'm here to offer to help you pack. That way I can put my grandmother's things into storage at the same time. We're putting the cottage up for sale.'

Oh. She hadn't expected that. She'd thought Moonrose Cottage would always be a part of the James family.

'There's no need.'

'There's every need. I need to catalogue everything, and I might as well do it whilst helping you pack. Make sure you don't leave anything behind.'

Lula nodded. 'Right. Well, there's not much left to do, but okay. If you want to help I've a few boxes I need to fill.'

'When's the removal lorry coming?'

'Around ten o'clock. But it's just a small one. I haven't got much to take with me.'

Olly clenched his jaw some more and she could tell he was fighting the urge to say something else to her. She would have given anything to run her fingers along his jawline, to soften his anger and release his tension.

But that wouldn't be a good idea.

It was best not to touch him. To remind herself of what he felt like. Though she could recall it quite easily. He was imprinted in her memory for evermore.

'Have you found someone yet?' she asked.

Olly frowned, his face like thunder. 'What do you mean?'

'Another locum. Someone to take my place.'

He stared hard at her, his brow creased with lines she'd never seen before, his eyes like the depths of a dark ocean. 'I could never find someone to take your place.'

And he turned in an instant, slamming the door as he left.

Lula stared at the spot he'd stood in, her breathing laboured, realising how much her leaving was upsetting him.

Well, it would hurt you a lot more further down the road, Olly. It might not feel like it now, but I'm doing the best thing for us.

I am.

Olly stood outside her surgery door and let out a pent-up breath. He was trying to use reverse psychology. By offering to help her pack, by offering to make sure she packed properly, he hoped she'd realise all the things she'd miss if she went away. He wanted her last thoughts of the village to be filled with him and his presence, and he knew that by being with her he'd be able to talk to her some more, try and persuade her otherwise if there was a chance that she'd show him she loved him.

Because wasn't love all that really mattered?

Wasn't love the most important thing? The thing

that made the world turn? That made people find the strength to get up each day and face life?

He wasn't going to force Lula to do anything. She had to stay of her own volition, but he wanted a choice. Options. When Rachel had left he hadn't been given a choice in anything. She'd made all the decisions. She'd decided on an abortion. She decided to leave without telling him. He'd never been given the courtesy of choice.

Well, he'd like it now, thank you very much.

It was the morning of moving day. Lula was dressed in old jeans and a green-and-black-checked lumberjack shirt that she usually did painting in. Her hair was tied back with a blue bandana, except for the long fringe of pink and purple hair that fell over the left side of her face.

Packing was hard work. She really hadn't thought she had much, but she was finding her belongings all over the cottage.

Anubis was still plugged in to the wall, with electricity powering the small lamp in the top of his tank, but she was hoping to drop him off at her friend's place on her way to Portsmouth. The rats had a blanket over their cage and were also ready to go, though she could see they'd managed to pull some of the blanket through the bars and chew on it.

A feeling of hurt filled her when she stood at the kitchen window and looked out upon the long back garden. A garden that was beginning to fill with bloom and blossom. A garden whose roses she would never see in full bloom. A garden that had once housed a scared teenager in its shed. A teenager who was now back home and being a mother to her baby with the support of her family.

So much had happened since Lula had come to Atlee Wold, and she knew she'd remember every part of it: Patrick, Ruby and the baby, Mrs Macabee, Bonnie, her dance class, all her patients and their families. The surgery.

Olly.

Dr Oliver James.

Possibly the most handsome man she would ever know or have the misfortune to love. A man she should never have got close to.

Just thinking about leaving him was painful. But she knew she had to do it. It was the only way to stop them both from hurting even more further down the line, when Olly wanted to realise his dream of having children.

She heard a bump from upstairs and wondered what he was doing. He'd arrived about an hour ago. Grey and glum, with enormous bags under his eyes that spoke volumes about a sleepless night. She'd had one herself. Going over it all in her mind.

But she was doing it for him. For *them*.

She'd come back for visits. Her mother was in Atlee Wold—that would always be true for as long as Elizabeth was alive. Every month or so she'd return. It wasn't a proper goodbye, after which they'd never see each other again. It wasn't as if she was deserting him, was it?

Another thud, and this time she heard him swear before he came thundering down the stairs and rushing over to the sink, holding his thumb under the cold tap.

'Are you okay?'

'Caught my hand on a nail.'

There was plenty of blood, and Lula ripped open one of her boxes and pulled out a first-aid kit, rummaging for bandages and scissors and tape. 'Let me see.'

'I'm all right, Lula.'

'Let me see—'

'I said I'm all *right*!' he shouted at her, and she stood back from him, shocked. He'd never, ever raised his voice at her like that and she wasn't used to it.

The shock on her face must have been clear, because he sighed and then apologised. 'I'm sorry. I didn't mean to shout.'

'I'm just trying to help,' she said quietly.

'I know. I'm just…frustrated, that's all.'

'With me?' She stood at his side, a whole head shorter than him.

'Who else would drive me to distraction?'

He grimaced and pulled his thumb free of the water. But the blood still seeped out and he had to push it back under the flow again.

She opened a gauze pad and then grabbed his hand, pulling it towards her and wrapping the pad tightly around his thumb.

'This might need stitches.' She held it firmly, then indicated that he should do so as she wound a bandage around his thumb.

By the time she was done his hand looked comical with its big bandage and he couldn't help but smile. 'Thanks.'

'No problem. Get someone to take you to A&E. That needs stitches.'

'Dad'll do it.'

'You need the proper equipment.'

'We have it at the surgery. We used to perform minor

ops there—don't worry about it.' He got up and moved away from her.

Lula could still feel the way his cold hand had felt in hers. His hands were so large compared to her dainty ones, but they had fitted so well together. She had spent hours one bedtime, lying there, examining his hands and looking at the way they interlocked with hers...

There was the toot of a horn from outside. She got up to walk to the front of the cottage. 'The lorry's here.'

'Right. Marvellous.'

'It shouldn't take them more than an hour to pack up my stuff...maybe half that.'

'And then you'll go?'

She nodded. Had his voice cracked on that last word? 'I'm sorry this hurts you, Olly. I can't say it enough, but it's the right thing to do.'

He shook his head. 'For who?'

'For us. You know this, Olly. You *know* it! You're a traditional guy. You want the whole relationship, marriage and kids package—you know you do! I can't give you that!'

He stalked across the room and took her hands in his. 'But I *love* you, Lula! Surely that counts for something?'

How could he do this to her? Today? 'Of course it does...and I love you, too. Yes, I do. I know you think I don't, and that I'm heartless and just walking away, but I'm not! I'm protecting us. I'm protecting *you*!'

'From what? I'm a big boy, Lula, I can look after myself.'

'From *me*. Believe me, you don't want the hurt that I'll cause you some day, when it finally sinks in that I can't have the babies you want.'

'I want to be with *you*. Babies is something for the future—I'm not thinking about that right now.'

'Well I am. Because I have to!' She pulled free and began stacking her boxes by the front door, slamming them down on top of each other, determined not to let him see her crying.

'You never even gave us a chance.'

'How dare you? Of course I did. We had fun, didn't we? We had our time together? Was that not giving us a chance?'

'You always intended to walk away, but you never bothered to tell me that.'

'I didn't think I had to. I was a locum. The word itself implies being temporary. I thought my life was my own.'

'It is. But then you slept with me, and we got involved and started going out. Forgive me if I'm wrong, but I thought if you were in a relationship with someone then you told them your intentions!'

She slammed another box down on the floor, its contents rattling dangerously. 'Did you tell me yours?'

'What?' He looked puzzled.

'Did you ever tell me *your* intentions?'

'Well...no. But we were in a relationship together, I thought we were moving forward. I thought we were together...'

'You *thought*... You never asked me once what I might think. Did you?'

'Because I thought you were telling me everything already. By being with me. I thought you were declaring your intention to stay.'

'You assumed—and you know what assumptions make...' She yanked open the front door and indicated the stack of boxes to the two removal guys.

Olly followed her into the blossoming front garden. The Blue Moon roses the cottage was named for had not yet bloomed. 'Aren't *you* assuming? Assuming that I'll want kids?'

'Don't you?'

He ground his teeth. 'Yes. But there are ways around that—ways to fight infertility. You should know that better than anyone. You *are* a doctor.'

'Yes, I am! Don't you see that's the reason? Olly? Don't you *see*?' She began to cry. Nothing could stop the tears from flowing. Nothing could stop this dam from opening. For now he'd got to the root of the problem that had bothered her for years. 'Don't you know why I fill my life to the brim and constantly challenge myself?'

He shook his head.

'Because I'm the *same* as you. I *am*. I'm a traditionalist, too. I want marriage and, dammit, yes, *I want children*. And I want to have them with you most of all. But I know I can't. I'm leaving now to protect *myself*—not just you. I have to leave because I can't bear to be with you and not be able to give you the one thing that I want most for myself!'

She leaned back against the garden gate, her arms folded over her chest as she sobbed.

'The hair, the rats, the dancing—all the crazy things that make me *me* are crazy things that keep my mind off the one thing I want most in the world. I have to leave, Olly. It would be *torture* to stay and see your face when every month nothing happens.'

She turned her back on him and walked into the cottage.

Olly stood there, shell-shocked, digesting her words. Wasn't there *anything* he could do to change this? He stood in the garden unmoving, like a statue. The removal men walked back and forth past him, loading up

Lula's boxes. The urge to get them from the lorry and put them back in the cottage was stronger than anything he'd ever experienced before.

How could he make her change her mind? He'd told her he loved her and it was true. He'd fallen in love with Dr Lula Chance. Lula Love. Louise. Whatever name she chose to go by. He didn't care about the crazy things that made her who she was. He *loved* those crazy things! He loved *her*! Lula! All five foot three of her. And he couldn't imagine his life without her in it!

Olly darted back into the house to try and persuade her to stay, to give them both a chance, but she was standing there, holding her rat cage, her handbag over her shoulder. Anubis was already gone. Packed safely in the lorry. He had to let her know that she was more than just a breeding machine. That her inability to have kids wasn't what defined her.

It all looked so final now.

'Don't go. Please.'

'Olly, don't do this…'

'I'm begging you. I will get down on my knees if you want—but, Lula, you can't go.'

'I have to.'

'Lula—'

She pushed past him. '*No*, Olly!'

She hurried down the path towards Betsy, placing the rat cage carefully in the back, then moved round to the driver's door.

Olly ran to her side and held the car door, preventing her from shutting it. 'You can't leave like this! I *love* you—does that not count for anything?'

There were tears all down her face, and her eyes were reddened and swollen from crying. 'Oh, it counts.'

But she wouldn't be stopped. She was determined to go and she pulled the door shut and started the engine.

Olly stepped back, contemplating throwing himself onto the bonnet of her car. He didn't care who saw. All he could think was that the woman he loved was about to drive out of his life because she couldn't give him children.

He banged on the window. 'I don't need to have children. I just need *you*!'

She shook her head sadly and then turned away.

He heard her shift the car into first gear and then the Beetle called Betsy carried his beloved Lula away down the lane. He watched her go, hoping that the car would stop, that she'd turn around, get out, come running back—anything… But she didn't do any of those things.

Betsy and Lula disappeared.

Olly sank to his knees in the street, tears on his face, oblivious to all who were watching.

CHAPTER NINE

OLLY STARED AT his computer. There were a patient's details up on the screen: name, address, date of birth and medical history. The patient herself was even sitting in front of him, talking about something or other, but he wasn't really listening.

Lula had been gone for four weeks. Four interminably long weeks in which his father had decided against early retirement and had promised to stay on at the practice until they found a suitable long-term replacement.

No more locums, he'd said. Unless they got desperate.

Olly was past desperate. He was forlorn and lost. The first few days after she'd gone he'd kept himself optimistic with the thought that she'd come back. That she'd realise her mistake, discover she couldn't live without him and return.

He'd believed it so much he'd even kept the cottage clean and the fire ready in case she needed it. But as those first few days had turned into a week, and then two, he'd stopped going to the cottage and had accepted that she wasn't coming back. Lula was well and truly gone.

He'd lost her. The one woman he'd ever truly loved. He kept checking his phones, his landline and mobile, to see if there were any texts or messages, but both phones were stubbornly silent and devoid of anything from Lula. He wasn't eating properly and seemed to exist on tea. Once he'd even gone round to Elizabeth Love's house and sat and talked to her, but even though Lula had been in contact with her mother she hadn't mentioned Olly at all.

He knew she'd started her post in Portsmouth and had thought about writing to her, but each time he took up a pen and paper or clicked on his emails, the words wouldn't come.

What could he say that he hadn't already said?

His patient was still talking.

'…and then he said he wouldn't take in my papers or mail or feed the cat because he had a life of his own, and that I'd have to find someone else to do it. I mean, does that sound like a kindly neighbour to you?'

He registered the last part. Mrs Bates was always in, complaining about her neighbour Mr Brown. Olly somewhat suspected there might be something between them, or maybe there once had been, because they certainly seemed to bicker about each other a lot.

'I don't know what to say, Mrs Bates. Mr Brown does like to keep himself to himself.'

'But that's not normal, is it? Neighbours aren't like what they used to be.' She tutted in a haughty manner. 'People used to look out for each other in my day. Help one another. Like that lady doctor that used to be here…Dr Chance. She helped me out whenever I asked, and she even gave me extra tuition at her dancing class. And she wasn't a neighbour. Just a friend, really. But she helped out.' Mrs Bates settled her hands on her lap, clutching the strap of her handbag. 'She was a lovely doctor—it's a pity she didn't stay.'

Olly swallowed hard, but the lump in his throat wouldn't budge. 'She was.'

'Such a pretty thing, too. Single, she said. I thought you and she might become an item…'

Mrs Bates was fishing. She knew full well that he and Lula had been seeing each other—she just wanted confirmation from the horse's mouth.

He stared at a pile of paperwork. 'She had to move on.'

'But not before she found her family—isn't that right, Doctor? Lizzy Love confirmed it herself—told me that Dr Chance was her long-lost daughter!'

He nodded. 'I believe so.'

'You'd think she'd stay. You know…for family.'

But it had never just been about family. Had it? Lula had come to find her mother, yes, but had got involved with Olly, too. And even though she wanted children— badly, as it turned out—she'd walked away from trying to find out if she could have them with him.

He'd lied about possibly not wanting children. Of *course* he wanted kids. His own parents had been great. His dad had told him about his mum—about how wonderful she'd been and all those cute stories about her. He'd had a good childhood even with just his father to look after him. He wanted to be a father himself, it was true. He was a traditionalist.

But Lula's leukaemia had made her infertile. Or rather the chemo had. And she believed that he would hate her eventually for not being able to give him the children he so badly wanted.

I could never have hated her. We would have found a way. I'm sure of it!

Medical technology was moving on all the time. Miracles happened. And if they didn't for them then there were other options—surrogacy, adoption, fostering, IVF. Solutions that other people used but Lula was not willing to contemplate.

Perhaps the urge to have a child was stronger for her than he'd realised?

Mrs Bates realised she wasn't going to get anything out of him gossip-wise and stood and saw herself out. After she'd gone he let out a big sigh and leaned back in his chair, his head in his hands.

No more patients today. His afternoon was free.

If he went back to the house he'd just rattle around the rooms until bedtime, and it was difficult being at home. So many of the rooms contained memories of Lula. Especially his bedroom, where they'd shared themselves physically. He hated climbing into bed alone, without her. He hated waking up alone just to go through another day of tormenting himself.

I'll go and see Lula's mother again.

She might have heard more from Lula.

Elizabeth Love was out feeding her chickens, spreading seed across the grass as the brown fluffy birds pecked and scratched at the ground, their heads bobbing back and forth, cackling away.

Olly got out of his car and waved a hand in greeting.

'Oliver! I haven't seen you for a week—have you been all right?'

'Existing. Still breathing. Does that count?'

'I miss her, too. But I guess I've had years of experience, so I can cope with it better.'

He smiled. It had been her choice. To give up Lula. He couldn't forget that. Though he understood her reasons.

'It is hard…' He leaned against her broken gate, and

then pushed away from it forcefully. 'There just doesn't seem to be any point to anything now!'

Elizabeth blinked at him. The sun was in her eyes. 'Of course there's a point.'

'I can't see it if it's there. Life just seems so...*flat*... without her in it.'

She came over to him and laid a hand on his arm. 'Oliver...sometimes it's darkest before dawn.'

'Are you saying everything will be better in the morning? Because my dad's been saying that for nearly a month now, and let me tell you the mornings are the worst.'

'Why?'

'Because she's not *there*. Her head isn't on my pillow...her body isn't beside me. I can't hear her laughter or see her smile or...' he laughed wryly '...watch her dancing in her belly-dancing class.'

'I don't know what to say. She made a choice. I can't judge her. Not after what I did.' She picked up a watering can and began to water her flowerpots.

'It was the wrong choice.'

'Not for her. Have you gone after her? Tried to persuade her to come back?'

He shook his head and waved away an annoying fly. 'I don't have her address.'

'I do.' Elizabeth smiled.

He looked up. 'You do?' Hope began to build.

'It's in the house. She sent it to me yesterday and made me promise not to give it to you.'

He frowned. 'But you will, right? Otherwise you wouldn't have told me about it, and if you held it back now that would be outright mental cruelty.'

'I'll give it to you—but only because I can see how

much she means to you and I saw what you were like together. You were good. You were right. Wait here.'

She disappeared into her house and came out after a minute or so, clutching a piece of paper. She passed it to him.

'I never gave it to you. You sneaked a look whilst I was making some tea, all right?'

He opened the paper, read the address, and then beamed a smile at her before leaning forward and kissing her cheek. 'You're a star.'

He could go and find her!

She laughed. 'I'm a romantic. Go get her. *Tell* her. Make her *believe*.'

He nodded and raced back to his car, gunning the engine.

The drive to Portsmouth seemed to take forever. It should have been no more than an hour's drive, but he got stuck behind a tractor on his way out of Atlee Wold, and then in a traffic jam on the A3. There'd been an accident. He'd been torn between staying in his car and remaining patient, or gnawing at his wrists to take his mind off his frustration! Once he got past the accident—an empty horse box had overturned—it was a straight drive down to the Solent.

He passed through the Hindhead Tunnel and drove through the hills of Petersfield. When he saw the first sign for the coastal town of Portsmouth his stomach began to churn with nerves.

He had no idea what he was going to say to her. What could he say that he hadn't told her already? But she *had* to see—especially after his drive down to seek her out—just how much she meant to him.

His heart was racing with excitement at the idea of

seeing her again. There'd been a palpable ache in his chest for weeks, and now that he knew he might see her again that weight had lifted and he felt he could breathe again.

Olly knew he had to persuade her somehow. And it felt so good to know that he was going to see her again! Her smile...her face...the wonderful colours in her hair... Hear her laughter... He'd missed her so much!

As he drove ever closer to Portsmouth, where Lula's story had begun, he began to feel his nerves drumming in his tight stomach. He looked across the water and saw all the boats resting at anchor. He thought how peaceful it all looked. Then, before he knew it, he was driving into the city, passing the big white sails, listening to his satnav as it guided him through the housing areas of Southsea. In the distance he could see, rising above everything else, a pure white tower that stretched up into the blue sky. The Spinnaker Tower. He'd heard of it. There was something similar in Dubai.

He couldn't help but wonder what kind of life she'd made for herself here. He could see its attraction. Its charm. The Isle of Wight was across the water...there was its length of beach. There was even a funfair, like the kind he'd visited as a child.

He drove on, looking for Dickens Way, and suddenly there it was. He hit the brakes and made a right-hand turn into the street, looking for her house. It was a long street, narrow, and packed with terraced houses that all looked quite similar. The road was jam-packed with cars, bumper to bumper on either side.

Gritting his teeth, and muttering curses at there being nowhere to park, he had to drive further away to find a side road, squeeze into a space and then hurry back. He was sweating and anxious and fidgety. His mind was racing. What would she say when she saw him? Would she be pleased? He was assuming she would be. But what if she wasn't? What if she thought this was an embarrassing errand? What if he'd misread her feelings for him?

No. She told me she loved me!

He wiped his brow, straightening his crooked tie and tucking in his shirt.

He let out a deep breath, squared his shoulders and walked up the path. He was a bag of nerves. His legs were like wobbly blancmange, no strength to them at all, and his stomach was churning and tumbling as if he was on a fairground ride. He wished he'd brought some water. Or something stronger. Like beer. Or a straight shot of vodka.

Something.

He was just seconds away from meeting her...seeing her...

Olly rapped his knuckles on the red door. Then, just for good measure, he rang the doorbell, too, hearing a deep gong noise inside. He waited and he waited. Then he waited some more.

What was going on? Where was she?

Perhaps she was at work? He decided to have a look through the downstairs window, but couldn't see anything through the net curtains.

He blocked the sun with his hands to peer in, but it didn't help at all.

What was he to do?

The surgery. The doctors' surgery. They'd know, surely?

But he didn't know where that was. He quickly stepped over a low brick wall and rapped on the door of the house next to Lula's. He heard some shouting inside, and a child crying.

A woman answered the door. 'Yes?'

'Hi—could you tell me where the local doctors' surgery is, please?'

'Oh, I thought you were going to try and sell me something. Right—it's a couple of streets over, in St Thomas' Avenue.' She leaned out to point. 'Down this road, take a left, go about a hundred yards and then it's on your right.'

'St Thomas' Avenue? Thank you.'

The woman nodded and closed the door.

He didn't bother going back for his car. He figured it would be easier to walk. Besides, he had no idea if he'd be able to get a parking space anywhere near!

His churning stomach was now mixing nervous energy with frustration. This wasn't the way he'd planned it! He'd expected to find her at the house. With the house empty, he was beginning to feel a little irritated.

It wasn't going as he'd wanted. He'd expected to be kissing her by now! To have surprised her and swept her off her feet, told her once again how much he loved her and asked would she come back?

The surgery was in the centre of Portsmouth, and because of the lovely hot weather he enjoyed the short walk to it, even if his mouth was as dry as the bottom of a birdcage.

The building was split into two practices, and she could have been at either one. The receptionist at the first one couldn't tell him anything, and he had to get in a queue at the next. Olly waited impatiently, tapping his feet and trying to peer round the people in front of him, sighing heavily when they took ages with their turns. When he got to the receptionist he rested against the chest-high counter and stated his request.

'I'm looking for Dr Lula Chance. I believe she may be here as a locum?'

The receptionist nodded and smiled. 'Yes, she started here—but she's left already, I'm afraid.'

'Left?' How could she have left? 'Where has she gone?'

'I'm afraid I don't know. It was very sudden.'

'Sudden? She wasn't taken ill?'

The receptionist shook her head. 'I can't give out any private details, I'm afraid.'

'I'm a doctor.'

'I'm afraid I'm not at liberty to say.'

She smiled sympathetically and Olly knew realistically that her hands were tied. Unfortunately that didn't help him.

So she'd been a no-show at the house, she'd left her job already, and no one could tell him why. Where would she have gone?

'Do you have a forwarding address?'

'I'm sorry. I can't give you that information.'

He was not a violent man, but this wasn't going the way he'd hoped. 'Of course not. Thank you.'

He was about to step away when the receptionist perked up and said, 'But I *can* tell you she's doing a sponsored abseil today.'

Olly looked up. 'A *what*?'

'A sponsored abseil. She's raising money for childhood leukaemia.'

He gripped the reception desk. 'Where?'

The receptionist smiled. 'The Spinnaker Tower. She must be crazy, if you ask me—it's over five hundred feet high!'

The tower. He'd seen it driving in to the city. She was up *there*? Of course she was! He couldn't help but smile to himself. Of *course* she was up there! She'd be challenging herself, or something, wouldn't she? Doing one of her crazy stunts.

Well, that was one tower he was quite happy to rescue a maiden from!

If she'd let him...

Olly thanked the receptionist and raced back for his car. All he had to do now was find the way to get there.

At Gunwharf Quays he went running through the crowds, pushing past, apologising for knocking into people as he passed.

The Spinnaker Tower loomed above him—a pure white needle stretching upwards into the azure-blue sky. At the top were some viewing platforms, and just below them he could see a group of dark figures—like blackfly on a rose.

The abseilers!

On the ground there was another group of people, wearing helmets and abseiling gear, grinning madly or having their photos taken.

Olly rushed over.

'Lula? *Lula?*' He looked at each of them, hoping that she was already down, that she'd done it already, that he wouldn't have to watch her do this.

But how amazing it would be for her! He knew she didn't like heights. She'd said so when he'd mentioned the parachute jump. The one he'd not actually done because... Well, heights weren't his thing, either!

He looked up at the tower, fearing where he might have to go to get Lula back.

The group's leader laid a hand on his shoulder. 'Can I help you?'

'I'm looking for Dr Lula Chance?'

The leader nodded, then pointed. 'She's up there. Last one to come down. But she's nervous and won't budge.'

Olly looked up. Higher and higher, to the top of the tower. 'Can I get up there?'

'In the lift—but you can't abseil. Not unless you sign up and pay for it.'

Sign up? *Abseil?* From up *there?*

Gulping away the nausea that suddenly filled him, he rushed into the base of the tower and grabbed a handful of notes from his wallet to pay for his ascendance to the top. The lift filled with sightseers—people who wanted to go to the viewing platforms and gaze out across the naval city—and they all seemed to take an age to file in before the lift doors closed.

Not him, though.

Portsmouth was probably gorgeous, but the one thing he wanted to see was Lula. Nothing else.

Eventually the door closed, and he felt his stomach drop as the lift moved upwards. Impatiently he stood with the tourists, waiting for them to climb to the top of the tower, hoping that she wouldn't start her descent before he could get to her. Hoping that her nerves would make her wait until he got there.

Ping.

The door opened and he rushed out, heading over to the roped-off area where he'd seen the people assembled earlier. There was a young guy there, with a ring piercing his nose, wearing abseiling gear and a helmet.

'Lula Chance? Where is she? I need to talk to her!' He grabbed the man's arm to make him look at him.

The young lad pointed through a door. 'She's in there, mate. About to descend. But you can't go through.'

'I need to speak to her. It's urgent!'

'I can't let you go through. Abseilers only, I'm afraid. The outer doors are open, and without safety equipment—'

'Then kit me up! Look.' He pulled his wallet from his back pocket. 'I'll pay the registration fee.'

'I dunno, mate…'

'Do you want to raise money for leukaemia or not? I'll sign one of those waivers—whatever—but I need to go through!'

The nose-ring lad seemed to think about it for a moment, then nodded and pulled a piece of paper from the desk behind him. 'Here you go.'

'Thanks!' Olly scribbled his signature on the form and then jumped over the rope and pushed past him, yanking open the door.

'*Lula!*'

He found himself in a corridor, with narrow stairs leading down to an open door through which a strong gust of warm wind was blowing. Outside there was a narrow platform, with a couple of people on it. One on the platform and the other climbing over. He saw wisps of purple hair…

'Lula! Wait!'

There was real fear in her eyes, and she was gripping onto the arms of the guide for dear life, but she heard him call out and looked up.

'Olly?'

Her eyes met his and it was like a thousand lightning bolts smacking him in the guts. There she was. Looking as wonderful and as gorgeous as he'd ever seen her!

And she was standing on a really narrow ledge with a massive drop behind her...

The guide took one look at him and held up a hand. 'Stay back! You can't come out here!'

He held up his hands. 'I'm abseiling, too.'

'Not without kit, you're not!'

Olly looked about him and saw an organised puddle of belts and metal clips arranged on the floor. He'd seen people do this, so he stepped into one of the harnesses and pulled it up over his trousers, tightening it about his waist.

'Better?'

'Look...she's about to descend a hundred metres, mate. I think she needs to concentrate on what she's doing, don't you?'

'I need to speak to her.'

'You'll have to do it at the bottom.' He grabbed his walkie-talkie and spoke into it.

Olly gazed at Lula. 'Lula...I love you. I need you.'

She smiled, her eyes brimming with tears. Then she nodded. 'I love you, too.'

'We can be together!' he shouted, hoping she could hear in his voice how much he meant it.

She stared at him. 'Olly, I'm scared.'

'You? You're the bravest woman I know.'

'I don't feel brave right now.'

'You can do anything you put your mind to. I need to be with you, Lula. I'm not going away.'

She locked eyes with him, then nodded. 'Watch me. Will you do that? I'll be able to do this if you're watching me.'

He nodded. 'I'll watch every step.'

Unbelievably, he saw her let go and his heart froze. She was going to go! She was going to do it! He couldn't help but see the map of the city spread out beneath her, and all he could think about was the drop.

The guy who was guiding the ropes from above beckoned him over. 'Let me check you're fastened correctly.' He patted him down and tested the ropes and harness were all set up correctly. 'You signed the form?'

Olly nodded and gulped. Was he really going to do this? There was nothing *making* him do it. He could turn around. Go down in the lift. He'd still give the money to the charity—it wouldn't matter if he backed out. What was a few hundred metres between strangers?

The guide beckoned him forward. 'She's frozen.'

His heart stopped beating. She was stuck on the way down? *How?* It should be impossible to get stuck doing something like this. The only reason she wouldn't be moving would be if...

If she was scared stiff.

Lula had to be scared. Terrified. Frozen to the side of the tower. He knew he had to help her.

'Let me go down, too. I'll talk her through it.'

The guy shook his head. 'All right, mate. But you'll follow my exact instructions, yes?'

'Absolutely.'

He ran through the instructions and Olly fastened on his helmet and clipped himself onto the rope. The guide made sure he was securely tethered, and then allowed him to step over the safety barrier.

'Wish me luck?'

The guy shook his head. 'You won't need it.' He tapped him on the helmet and let go.

Olly plummeted. Or at least he felt he did. Gravity had never felt so strong. Or so reliable. He could feel the pull of the ground and made the mistake of looking down. The ground seemed to rise up to meet him and he lost all the breath in his lungs, but a quick gulp of air, a squeeze of his eyes and a muttered prayer made his limbs move.

Lula was about twenty feet below him, a bright splash of colour against the pure white of the tower. Holding the rope in his right hand, he allowed himself to rappel steadily down the side of the building until he came level with his beloved Lula.

'Hi.' He tried to sound casual—as if this was something he did every day.

Her large brown eyes looked out at him from beneath her fringe of many colours. 'Hi.'

'You need some help?'

'Are you offering?' She gave a nervous laugh and attempted to look down.

'Don't look down! Don't look down…just…look at me. I'm here.'

He reached out and rubbed her arm and she closed her eyes with gratitude.

'I think I tried to do too much. I always knew heights would be the death of me.'

He looked nervously around them. 'Well, let's hope not. Will you listen to me? Let me help you?'

She rested her forehead against the rope. 'You want to help me? After what I did?'

'Do we need to talk about this up here? Can this not wait until we reach terra firma?'

'I hurt you.'

Ah, so we are *talking about it up here.*

'Yes, but that's okay, because since you've been gone it's clarified everything for me.'

She glanced his way. 'You see my point of view?'

'No. Not at all. You think your only value to me is

that of procreation? What about love? What about being connected? About being soul mates?'

'You think we're soul mates?'

'Don't you?'

She grimaced. 'It's hard to think clearly up here.'

The wind blew them slightly and she gasped and gripped the rope tighter.

'Are you kidding? This is the clearest I've ever thought! Lula? Lula, you can do this. Listen to me. You need to feed the rope through your right hand, nice and slow. As you do that you need to walk your toes down the side of the building. Little bits... That's it. Keep doing that.'

They were moving again, but he could see she was still terrified. Her legs were trembling and kept losing contact with the tower. He kept pace with her, staying level, making reassuring comments as she kept the rope moving.

'There are thousands of successful marriages in this world, Lula, where couples don't have children. Our happiness together is not based on that being the only criteria.'

'Easy for you to say *now*.'

He could hear the shakiness in her voice. 'Easy for me to say because it's true. I *love* you, Lula! Would I have come all this way—would I be abseiling down this tower for you—if I didn't love you?'

She looked at him and met his gaze. 'No.'

'You're my everything. I've been lost without you in Atlee Wold. Everything seems darker without you there. You put *light* into my life.'

Lula stopped. 'Light?'

The ground was getting closer, but they were still very high.

He reached out and laid his hand upon hers. 'Beautiful, bright light. It doesn't matter to me if we don't have children because I'll always have *you*, and if we decide that we want to have them in some other way, then that's good, too! We could get cats or dogs—they can be our family in the meantime. And if cats and dogs are too tame for you then we'll get something crazy—like an alpaca or a snake!'

She smiled at him. 'I've always wanted a house rabbit.'

'There you go! Lula, tell me you'll come back with me. That you'll come back with me and marry me and be with me in Atlee Wold!'

Lula looked up at how far they'd come. She'd done some of it on her own, but she'd accomplished far more with Olly at her side.

'Olly? Will you wait for me at the bottom?'

He frowned. 'What do you mean?'

'I think I can do this now. It's not far. Let me finish this abseil on my own. I'll meet you at the bottom and we'll talk then.'

'Are you sure you can do it on your own?'

'Abseiling? Yes.'

Olly nodded and rappelled down the last few feet to the bottom. She heard people clapping and cheering as she got closer and risked a glance down. It wasn't far. There were people, and boats on the water. All those faces looking up—looking at *her*. It felt right to finish the abseil on her own. It had been *her* challenge and she was determined to complete it—as she had done all the others. It was just that on some occasions, such as this, it helped to have Olly at her side.

Did she always have to do stuff alone? The way she had her entire life?

No. She didn't.

She'd found her mother at last—was there any reason she couldn't have Olly, too? Apart from the one thing she feared...?

But if she lost him because she walked away now, wouldn't that hurt just as much? She'd already faced that fear and lived through the pain of losing Olly once. But he'd offered a lifeline. A second chance. And there was no reason not to take it because if it was true what he said—that he could be happy with just her—then wouldn't they *both* be happy for many years together? Wasn't that worth more than worrying about something that might never happen?

What was that saying? *'Tis better to have loved and lost than never to have loved at all...*

Her heart soared at the possibility of hope. Hope that she could consider being with Olly and going back to Atlee Wold and Patrick and her mother and all the other wonderful people she'd met there.

As her feet touched the ground she felt Olly's arms embrace her and he turned her round to shower her face with kisses. She could hardly breathe, but that didn't matter—because Olly was there and together they could face anything! Wrapping her arms around him, she pulled him tight before they had to separate and remove their harnesses and helmets.

The man at the bottom presented them both with a T-shirt. Written across it was *I took the scenic route.*

Lula looked at it and laughed.

She'd done it!

Sitting in a cafeteria overlooking the waterfront, Lula stirred her tea and stared at Olly. She couldn't get enough of just looking at him. At one time she'd thought that she would never see his face again, and today here he was—her knight in shining armour, who'd rescued her from a tower!

'Would you really consider having a pet snake?' she asked, smiling.

Olly reached out and took her fingers in his own. 'I would do anything for you. You know that.' He smiled, then had a thought. 'Just don't expect me to hold it.'

'I quite like boa constrictors...'

'If that's what it takes.' He squeezed her fingers and smiled.

'We could also have a dog, if you wanted something a bit more traditional. I am prepared to compromise.'

Olly lifted her fingers to his lips and kissed her. 'All great relationships are based on it.'

'Is that what you think we'll have? A great relationship?'

'I don't think it. I know it. I feel amazing when I'm with you. I feel alive—I feel the whole world has woken up and I can see everything so clearly. It's right that we're together.'

'And if I wanted to pursue...other things...would that affect us?'

'Other things? What? More crazy stunts?'

She looked at him. 'Children. Babies. I want them, Olly. I spent so many years telling myself that I didn't, but I was lying to myself. Maybe I am a traditionalist at heart? But fertility treatment can be hard. Difficult. It can break people. That's what I'm scared of. Right now I know I can't have kids, and I've accepted that, but if we go down other routes and I accept the hope that I might get pregnant somehow...but it all fails anyway...I'm not sure I could live with the disappointment.'

'Not us. I'll go through every step of it with you.

With every ounce of my being. If it doesn't work out then we'll be upset and saddened, but it won't end us. We're stronger than that—we're bigger than that.'

'But how do you *know*?'

'Because we'll be in it together. Because we'll have made the choice together. I know my own heart. Even if I can't have children with you I will still have *you*. And you are so precious to me...'

'And if we can? If something can be done?'

'Then that will be amazing.' He looked deep into her eyes. 'I was so proud of you today. Conquering your fear. Finishing by yourself. Even though you scared me half to death.'

'Scared you? How?'

'By telling me you wanted to finish it alone. I thought you'd tell that to me, too.'

She shook her head. 'I couldn't.'

'No?'

'No. When I left you in the village, as I drove away, my heart broke in two. I had to stop around the corner because I couldn't drive. I couldn't see. I was crying so much and I have never experienced pain like it. You have no idea what it took me to carry on driving. To carry on putting distance between me and you. I couldn't go through that again. I wouldn't survive it.'

Olly got up from his seat opposite and slid into the chair next to her, putting his arm around her shoulders. 'I wept like a child when you left. On my knees, in the road. I didn't care who saw me. Then I had weeks of patients coming in and telling me that *they* were sad you'd left, and I wanted to rage at each and every one of them—ask them, *What about me?*'

'What did you do?'

'I hoped you'd come back. I hoped that somehow

something would make you turn around and come back. And then I realised that maybe you thought you couldn't.'

'I *was* coming back.'

He smiled. 'You were?'

'I couldn't bear to be away from you.' She reached out and clasped his hand. 'My mother told you where I was, didn't she?'

He smiled. 'Accidentally. I think she was embarrassed by having me sobbing all over her kitchen floor and she did it to get rid of me,' he joked.

Lula smiled. 'I'm glad she told you. Because if she hadn't then I would have come back to you. I've given up my job at the surgery. I couldn't work, I couldn't concentrate—all I could think of was what I'd lost...'

They looked into each other's eyes and Olly leaned in to kiss her, his eyes closing softly as his lips met hers and the tender sweetness of their connection made his heart sing with joy.

When he opened his eyes again and saw her dark chocolate eyes staring into his he stroked her cheek. 'Never leave me.'

'I won't.'

'You're everything to me.'

'And you to me.'

He reached into his pocket and pulled out a small jewellery box in red velvet. Opening it, he revealed a gold ring, set with a sapphire and surrounded by diamonds that glinted and shone in the light. 'Will you marry me, Lula?'

She looked at the ring, then at him, at the hope in his eyes, at the love she saw burning bright from within him, and knew that she could spend the rest of her life with this man.

'Yes!'

Beaming with joy, he took the ring from its box and slid it onto her finger. It was a perfect fit and he kissed her once again. 'I found it when I was sorting out Moonrose Cottage. It belonged to my grandmother.'

'It's beautiful.'

'Like you.'

They sank into each other's embrace and kissed again.

EPILOGUE

THE MARRIAGE OF Dr Louisa Chance to Dr Oliver James took place in the village church of Atlee Wold. Lula asked Bonnie and Ruby to be her bridesmaids, and decked them out in gorgeous red satin dresses. Ruby's daughter, Adele, toddled up the aisle, throwing rose petals everywhere.

It was a beautiful day for a summer wedding, and the whole village turned out to see it.

It had been a delight for Lula to return to Atlee. Everyone had been thrilled to see her, but none more so than her own mother.

Elizabeth Love had become a changed woman. Her poor neglected house, in which the only welcome guests had once been animals, was now often filled with villagers. She and Lula would often hold tea parties to raise funds for the animals, or for children's charities.

Everyone knew the story of Lula and Elizabeth. And no one could miss the love story between Lula and Oliver. It became the talk of the village for many years, and three years after the wedding, when Lula became pregnant, after a lot of help from medical science, the whole village waited with bated breath for the outcome!

She'd gone through so much with the IVF. She'd shared all her trials and tribulations of tests and the injecting of hormones. She'd never complained when she'd blown up like a balloon from all the medication and her ovaries had gone into overdrive and yet still only given up three eggs for harvesting.

A single egg had developed and it had looked healthy.

All their hopes and dreams focused on one tiny cell...

Lula had been her usual unconventional self and opted to go for a home birth, in a pool, listening to rock music and stroking the family dog, Buddy. When their baby daughter had been born, eleven hours after contractions had started, they'd all let out a sigh of relief.

The villagers knew the story of Lula's childhood. They knew how much being a mother meant to her. And everyone had rejoiced at the safe arrival of baby Mabel.

Tears of joy had streamed down Lula's cheeks. She'd gone from being rootless and without family to gaining a mother, a husband and now a baby daughter of her own.

She'd got roots. She'd got family. The two things she'd thought impossible and yet had craved her whole life.

And, to celebrate, she added the colour green to her hair.

* * * * *